John Gardner is the author of over forty bestselling novels including such classic espionage novels as *The Nostradamus Traitor* and *The Garden of Weapons*. His most famous character, Big Herbie Kruger, has featured in many of his most successful books, including his *Secret Generations* trilogy and *Maestro*, which is also published by Corgi.

He is a member of the International Brotherhood of Magicians, and he holds the degree of Associate of the Inner Magic Circle in London's prestigious Magic Circle. He lives in the United States with his wife Margaret and is currently working on the sequel to *Confessor*.

Also by John Gardner

MAESTRO

and published by Corgi Books

CONFESSOR

John Gardner

CORGI BOOKS

CONFESSOR
A CORGI BOOK : 0 552 14472 X

Originally published in Great Britain by Bantam Press,
a division of Transworld Publishers Ltd

PRINTING HISTORY
Bantam Press edition published 1995
Corgi edition published 1996

Set in 10/11pt Linotron Plantin by Falcon Oast Graphic Art

Corgi Books are published by Transworld Publishers Ltd,
61–63 Uxbridge Road, London W5 5SA,
in Australia by Transworld Publishers (Australia) Pty Ltd,
15–25 Helles Avenue, Moorebank, NSW 2170,
and in New Zealand by Transworld Publishers (NZ) Ltd,
3 William Pickering Drive, Albany, Auckland.

Reproduced, printed and bound in Great Britain by
Cox & Wyman Ltd, Reading, Berks.

For my friend in all things magical
Jeff Busby

Confess yourself to heaven;
Repent what's past; avoid what is to come;

WILLIAM SHAKESPEARE
Hamlet Act III, Scene 4

I

The eight men and four women had been chosen from over one hundred unknowing candidates. Each had a special skill and all at one time or another had lived in the West: attending universities or technical training colleges. All spoke at least two languages other than their own. All had proved their loyalty. They were called *Intiqam* – Vengeance.

They had left their country singly over a period of fourteen days. They had already spent two months together, pledging to bring true revenge onto the heads of the Western powers. The *Intiqam* prayed and meditated; had regular visits from instructors who counselled them on the way in which they could pass clandestine messages to one another, learned how they could become invisible in the cities of the West and evade security and law enforcement agencies.

They memorized lists of names and mastered a plethora of detail concerning the cities in which they would operate. Above all else, they were taught the ingenious ways in which they could bring sudden death to individuals and groups of people. Two members of *Intiqam* were already conversant with the most difficult and dangerous final stroke of the plan that they called *Magic Lightning*.

The night before the first man left, they stood together and swore that the terror they would take to New York, Washington, Paris, Rome and London would, in the end, make the inhabitants of those cities, and the countries to which they belonged, beg on their knees for mercy.

Their varied, solitary journeys took a further month: each of them taking a completely different route, so that by late March they were together again – one cell in London, the other in New York. The cells each consisted of four men and two women who settled down to a period of waiting so that, after a year had passed, the cells had become integrated within their particular areas, the individuals were known by sight to shopkeepers, neighbours, newspaper sellers and the staff of several banks. They were model citizens. They had become invisible.

It was over a year before the two cells received the message to start the first phase of their campaign. It came on a Friday afternoon, which meant they were to begin at midnight. In English the activating word was *Illusion*.

Later, on that Saturday, it was calculated that Gus Keene's car left the road – less than three miles from his destination – at a little after three in the morning. He was almost certainly dead by the time the vehicle exploded in the kind of fireball you usually see only in the movies, or on the television news from some war-torn part of this unstable planet.

At the time of this horrible death many things were going on across the world. In New York, because of the five-hour time difference, Andrew Lloyd Webber's *Phantom of the Opera* was nearing the conclusion of that night's performance. In his lair, under the Paris Opera House, the Phantom himself suddenly disappeared from a tall ornate chair. There one minute and gone the next. The illusion had been prepared by Britain's foremost magician, Paul Daniels. Mr Daniels had never heard of Gus Keene, yet he had met him on a number of occasions.

Even further away – an eight-hour time difference – in Las Vegas, at the fabulous *Mirage*, Siegfried and Roy, billed as Masters of the Impossible, were preparing for their first show of the evening. It would be the usual glittering and amazing performance of unparalleled theatrical magic, during which their white Bengal tigers would appear and disappear, an elephant would vanish in front of the audience's eyes and a huge cast, gorgeously apparelled, would fill the stage and provide what had become the biggest, most glamorous magic show in the world.

Neither Siegfried nor Roy had ever heard of Gus Keene, yet they had met him on three different occasions.

On stage at the Kennedy Center, in Washington DC, the world's most famous illusionist, David Copperfield, was coming to the end of the final performance of a three-night appearance. At the age of thirty-seven, Copperfield, one of the legends of magic, and the tenth highest-earning performer in the world, stood downstage, in his familiar costume of Levi 501s and a chambray shirt, telling his audience of the first time he ever saw snow as a child. Then, with calculated choreography and music, he moved to a raised plinth, centre stage, while snow appeared to pour from his cupped hands. As this snowstorm began to whirl around him, Copperfield turned to face the audience and jumped further downstage, only to disappear and become himself as a child, the snow still pouring from his hands. The young boy Copperfield turned his back to the audience, finding himself staring up at the man Copperfield, as the entire auditorium became a raging snowstorm that brought the audience to their feet, their applause mingling with the snow, many of them with tears streaming down their faces, for Mr Copperfield has the power to stage his illusions in a manner that can produce great emotion.

David Copperfield had never heard of Gus Keene but he, also, had met him on many occasions.

At three on that Saturday morning, Detective Chief Inspector Olesker, of Scotland Yard's anti-terrorist squad, lay on a cot set close to a small window in London's Camberwell area.

The DCI, together with a Detective Inspector and a Sergeant, was engaged in watching a house some fifty yards away, across the road. The occupants of the target house had no idea that Olesker's people had spiked two of the rooms and the telephone with listening devices. The Detective Inspector, sitting at a table behind Olesker, had his eyes closed and his hands clamped over a pair of earphones as he listened intently to a conversation between a man and a woman in the second-floor bedroom across the road. The full text of that conversation was being taped in a small grey van parked a couple of hundred yards down the street.

'They've got a visitor, guv',' the Detective Sergeant muttered, and Olesker raised the ultraviolet night binoculars, watching the figure who had arrived quietly in a small Japanese car.

'It's him,' Olesker said quietly. 'It's Billy Boyle the Bomb Maker; well, how about that?'

They were watching an Active Service Unit of a truly vicious terrorist organization: a splinter group of the original Provisional IRA who called themselves Freedom Fighters of the Irish Republican Army – the FFIRA. These people had cut themselves off entirely from the Provisionals and Sinn Féin, the political wing, and operated by their own rules. They were almost one hundred members strong and appeared to have access to as many weapons and explosives as they needed.

The FFIRA had become a poisoned thorn in the side of all the British Anti-Terrorist agencies. For since the ceasefire between the British Security Forces and the IRA the only trouble in the North of Ireland came from unofficial groups such as the so-called FFIRA. These people were true hard-liners who believed that talking was a waste of time. Their cause was exactly the same as the Provisional IRA, but they held to the old ideals: the only good Brit was a dead Brit, and the only good Protestant was a dead Protestant. Members of the FFIRA had no conscience and, it seemed, no morality. However, they had a very good grasp on the organization and logistics of a guerrilla force.

Detective Chief Inspector Olesker had never heard

of Gus Keene, and certainly had never met him.

At three in the morning, a man who *had* known Gus Keene as friend and colleague for more years than he would like to admit, staggered around a pretty little cottage, a couple of miles outside Lyndhurst, on the edge of the New Forest.

It was only recently that drink had started to affect him. For years he had been able to take vodka for vodka, or whiskey for whiskey, with the best of them, and remain so cold and actively sober that many a suspect had slurred out indiscretions which had finally led to a terrible downfall. Now, the man who blundered around the cottage had himself become prey to an entire bottle of vodka, riding lost on a sea of liquor.

He was also prone to deep depressions, conscious that he was no longer connected to the only life he had ever really known. When the Americans had picked him up in long-ago Berlin – a teenager of the ruins – and put him to work, hunting Nazis in the camps for displaced persons, happiness and purpose had taken him over. Eventually, the Americans handed him on a plate to the British, who saw a future for this clumsy, ill-proportioned young man. It was then that he grasped hold of the first rung of a ladder in the shadowland of what became the Cold War.

That was over now, even though he had accepted early retirement of his own volition long before the collapse of the Berlin Wall, in order to embrace what ultimately became a loveless marriage. They had called him back for one last delicate job and, when that finished, he became a man of sorrow, anger and bitterness: emotions which ate at him like a cancer, and changed him from a hero of the Cold War to a person enmeshed in brooding, vacillating self-pity.

In spite of his bulk, clumsiness and the face of a peasant, he had been a passionate man who had loved – really loved – only twice. One of these loves had betrayed him, the other was gone, while his wife, who was a kind of stopgap, had left him to live with her sister in Germany. So, he had cut himself off from life, with the bottle for company, memories that scarred his soul, and a loneliness which seared his mind and altered his perception of the real world.

On that night, when Gus Keene died in the fireball which had been his car, Eberhardt Lukas Kruger finally fell into bed, fully dressed, just after three in the morning, his furred brain already asleep, battered into subservience by intoxication.

At six-thirty the same morning, he was clawed back to consciousness, still unsteady and not a little drunk, by a persistent knocking at his front door. Grumbling and staggering, he swayed down the stairs, unlocked the door and found himself looking into a very familiar face from his past.

'Lord, Herb, you look terrible.' Tony Worboys, once, years ago, Herbie Kruger's assistant, now elevated to one of the five Deputy Chiefs at the 'Office' – or the 'Firm' – as the Secret Intelligence Service refers to itself, had been told of his old mentor's disintegration, but still could not believe it. Kruger's weight had dropped by at least a third so that his clothes – never a strong point – hung from him, giving the impression that he had purchased them cheaply in a sale, hoping that he might eventually grow into them. The wide goofy smile was not apparent, the skin of his face flabbed and the usual half-mocking, always mischievous glint had left his eyes, leaving them dead, almost like the eyes of a large fish on a slab.

'What you want, Young Worboys?' There was no sign of pleasure in his slurred greeting, and certainly no welcome, even though Herbie called him *Young* Worboys still, just as he had done all those years ago.

'I need to talk.'

'If it's asking me to come back, forget it. For me the war is over.'

Perhaps, Worboys thought, the last remark had about it some of the old Kruger style, but even as the idea ran briefly through his head, it was snuffed out by Herbie.

'I don't want to see any of you again. This, I mean, Tony, and you know why. I'm finished with it. It's all over. Consummatum est. Okay?'

Worboys paused. It was both profoundly sad and depressing to see Kruger like this, a husk of his old self; a man of such former vigour dragged down, with all his energy gone, and his physique taking on the form of a wraith. He was reminded of his own father at the end, riddled with cancer, his body and features unrecognizable, redrawn by disease, the body corrupted by nature.

'Sorry, Herb. Still got to talk to you. It's bad news, I'm afraid.'

Big Herbie, now not looking big, or strong enough to swat a fly, opened his mouth to say something, then changed his mind, pulled back the door and motioned Worboys into the tiny hall of the cottage.

For a second, Worboys recalled his visit to this same place some years ago when Herb and his bride, Martha – née Adler – one of Kruger's old agents, were married. Herbie had run her in East Berlin where she had boldly secured, entrapped and even killed at his bidding. On that last occasion, Herb the bridegroom had seemed to fill the hallway so that he gave the impression that he had to crouch and breathe in simply to open the door. Now two of him would have fitted into the space.

Predictably, the living-room was untidy and smelled strongly of liquor. He wondered when Herb had last opened a window. 'Spot of coffee, Herb? I've come a long way.'

'You weren't invited,' Kruger snapped. Then, 'Coffee, okay,' his legs stuttering him off in the direction of the kitchen.

'So what's the bad news?' he asked on his return with two large mugs of black liquid.

'Gus.'

'What about Gus?'

'He's dead, Herb.'

'Gus Keene dead? How so? Saw him a couple of months ago. Retired, like everyone but you. Retired and writing his memoirs. Told me so himself.'

'We think it was a car bomb. He was driving back to Warminster last night – well, early this morning. Car left the road and blew up. About half a mile from Wylye. He was coming back from Salisbury—'

'Warminster? What the hell was he doing in Warminster? He'd quit. Retired. Why Warminster?'

'We gave him the old Dower House. Him and Carole. He had the Dower House as part of the golden handshake, don't you remember?'

Somewhere at the back of Herbie Kruger's mind he heard a fragment from one of Mahler's symphonies – the Adagietto from the Fifth, he thought. Beautiful, but drenched in sadness. A year ago, he could have recognized it immediately without even thinking, for Mahler's music had been his prop and pillar through all the years of his secret life. A reflection mirrored in the glass of life for him. The very idea of not now being able to place it in context made him suddenly frightened. What had he allowed himself to become?

'I remember,' he murmured. 'You gave him that crummy little cottage near where was once the main entrance. After all those years that Gus served, you give him a little cottage where he can look at the place he controlled for so long. Very big of you, Tony.'

'It wasn't me, Herbie. It was an executive decision. Anyway, he wanted to be there. It was Office property and he wanted to be somewhere he could have files officially while he was writing.'

'His memoirs, sure. It's the big thing now. You take the golden handshake and the okay to write about your years in secrecy. The coming thing. KGB does it as well, I hear.'

Worboys sipped the hot, strong coffee and wondered if this had been a wise move, coming to old Herb, laying the news on him and then suggesting what he had been told to suggest.

'What a good idea, giving him the Dower House,' Kruger continued. 'Got him under your thumb, right? Got him by the short hairs while he's writing his secret life story.'

'I told you, that's what he wanted. He argued that it would be more secure.'

Big Herbie Kruger said nothing. For a long time, Tony Worboys left him alone, for he offered not a word and seemed suddenly an old man, sitting with both hands around the mug of coffee, his eyes looking out on something that Worboys could never see.

Kruger was, in fact, thinking of Gus Keene and how impossible it was that this man should be dead. Unthinkable. People like Gus did not die. Not at his age. Herbie felt the life running silently from him to join Gus. Citizen Keene. Herbie had called him that when he last saw him. Aloud, he said, 'Best Confessor the Office ever had, eh?'

'Best in the world,' Worboys agreed, but did not intrude on Herbie's private thoughts.

A Confessor was the way some people talked about those specialists whose job it is to act as inquisitors. Interrogators, inquisitors, confessors – what's in a name? He had even heard them called the men with the thumb-screws, but Gus Keene was certainly the best: a Confessor of Confessors. More. For years he had also been the Officer in Charge of what the Office called Warminster – the big old house, set in acre upon acre of grounds some six or seven miles outside the garrison town that bore its name. Warminster was, as someone else once said, the place where the Office did everything but kill people. At the thought, Herbie choked, for people *had* been known to die at Warminster, though it was used for many different things: the training of young probationers; the inquisition of suspects – sometimes highly illegal inquisitions; courses where they topped you up.

He supposed they had been topping people up on Middle East targets these days, for he knew that, contrary to the modern perception, the Secret Intelligence Service had been reduced only by 120 officers – most of them near retirement anyway – and was pursuing its old role with a new fervour.

'What's in it for me, Tony?'

Worboys looked up, caught Herbie's eyes and saw what he had not seen before. The glint was just visible.

'What d'you mean, Herb?'

'I'm not a fool. Why should you – a Deputy Chief – come all the way down here at sparrow fart just to tell me that our old mutual friend, Gus, is dead?'

'Thought it was the decent thing. I knew you were close to him. Didn't want you to hear his name on some radio or TV news.'

'Ha!'

Worboys realized something else had been missing since he had arrived. Whatever the deal, Herbie Kruger loved to play with his English. He spoke better English than most of his old colleagues, but he had this way, this thing, with language. He loved malapropisms, deliberately using wrong words or mixing sentences. It gave him not only joy but also time. It was a behaviour pattern which Big Herb used to the point of ruthlessness. But not this morning. It had gone, flown, together with the weight and sharpness.

'Anyway, Young Worboys, you're all run by committees now. Everyone knows C's real name. Poor bugger had to move house because everyone knew. C, or one of you Deputies, has to go running to committees in the Foreign Office to get permission to break wind. That's how I heard it.'

'C still has overall control, but yes. Yes, things *are* different.'

'A committee tell you to come and see me?'

'In a way.'

'Gus? You said a car bomb? We talking terrorists? We talking Gus as a specific target?'

'Possibly. We don't know.'

'So who's handling it?'

'The local plod – well, the plod in Salisbury.'

'Sure. The cops. What about anti-terrorist cops?'

'They'll be in on it. Probably take over the investigation in a couple of days.'

'So, what's in it for me?'

Slowly, Worboys removed a laminated card from his pocket and placed it on the small table next to his mug of coffee.

Kruger picked it up, squinting at it as though he had trouble focusing. Then, with a sound of irritation he flicked the card away, so that it spun through the air, hitting a wall and finally landing in the middle of the room. 'I told you, Tony. I won't come back. Never again. Through. Finished.'

'We're not asking you to come back, Herb. If you look at the ID it says you're a consultant. There's no money attached, though you'll get all the support within reason. Peeps into the files, transport, minders even.'

'Why would I consult for you, and why *me*?'

'Because you're one of the very few left who were close to Gus. Lord, Herb, you knew the man probably better than anyone. You were even interrogated by him . . .'

'For a year, sure. For a year after my bit of trouble in what was East Germany, sure. A year in the country. A year with Gus at his cleverest.'

'But you *were* close. Knew him from other things.'

'Carole was closer. Why not use the wife?'

'Come on, man, how in hell can we use Carole?'

Kruger did not answer. Instead he went through to the kitchen and made himself another mug of coffee.

'You want me to liaise with the plod – anti-terrorist boys?'

'Of course. We also want you to put Gus's life under the microscope. Read the manuscript he was

19

riting, look at his research, go through his dossier, talk to friends outside the Office. Discover the answer to the big question.'

'Find out why someone blew him to bits? Yes, easy. There must be hundreds of people out there who had reason to turn Gus into a bonfire.' He raised his head and looked at his old colleague. 'You think I'm a fit person to do this? Now you've seen me again, you think I'm even trustworthy any more?'

'I can see you're not yourself, but give it a go, Herb. Could be it's the answer to a lot of your problems. You've been sitting down here brooding, building up a head of grief and anger.'

'Like an old rusty kettle, yes? Be honest, Tony. I know what life's become for me. If it were up to you, would *you* put me on to this?'

The pause went on for thirty seconds too long.

'Yes.' Kruger laughed for the first time – his old laugh, not a pale imitation. 'You wouldn't even send me out to clean floors in a safe house, right?'

'Right, Herb. Now that I've seen you for myself.'

'So, it's easy. You go back and tell them Herbie Kruger ain't big no more. Gone to seed. Not the man for the job.'

'I can't do that, Herb.'

'Your job at stake, Tony?'

'I've been instructed to deliver you.'

'Ha! Would you buy a used micro dot from this man? Seriously, would you?'

'Not in your present state, Herb. No. No, I wouldn't but I have to. It also appears that I have to get you off the sauce and back in trim. Go and get a shower and shave. You have to meet the local plod before eleven o'clock.'

Kruger dry-washed his face with both hands. 'Tony, I can't. I'm out of it. Haven't got the balls for it any more.'

'Herb, this isn't field work. All you have to do is

move backwards and forwards through Gus Keene's life and come up with a couple of suggestions. Piece of cake. Couple of weeks, that's all. You've got nothing better to do, have you?'

Kruger gave a great sigh, shook his head and said that he'd take a shower and think about it.

'Give me your door key.' Worboys flashed him a smile which betokened great affection. 'Got a bit of shopping to do.'

Herbie did not argue, handed him the key and went slowly up the stairs to his bathroom.

He stripped and caught sight of himself in the mirror, saw the folds of flesh hanging off his long bones and the ravage he had brought to his face. As he showered, Kruger suddenly felt the old tingle, the sensation he had known for all his adult life. As he stepped from the shower he muttered, 'Herbie's himself again.' Paused, then added, 'Well, almost.'

In Washington it was two forty-five in the morning. Walid and the girl they called Khami had flown in from the New York cell of *Intiqam* earlier that evening. Their intention was to hit one of the targets of opportunity which had been well researched for them by an intelligence group known to both *Intiqam* teams by one name, *Yussif*.

Walid, in his early forties, was probably the most distinctive man in either group: short and muscular, but with a face badly scarred from smallpox. It was a face he could not disguise, even with the moustache he grew, then shaved off, in six-month cycles.

Khami was more striking than beautiful. Like so many girls from the Middle East her hair was black, as were her large eyes. When she wished to make a point she would open them wide. Men often thought they could drown in the pools of her eyes. More than one had drowned in his own blood while held hypnotically by her gaze.

They booked into the Willard Hotel as man and wife because the latest information told them that the station chief of Italian foreign intelligence, who had diplomatic cover in DC, spent most weekends at the Willard in the company of his American girlfriend. It was well known among diplomats, and even the switchboard operators at the Italian Embassy in Fuller Street had a room number for him, with a code-word to establish bona fides should he be required to return to the Embassy.

About the same time as Herbie Kruger was showering in England, Khami called the Italian's room and gave the codeword, *Dividersi*. Then, in faultless Italian, she told him the Ambassador required him at the Embassy as quickly as possible.

As soon as Khami put down the telephone, Walid took the elevator to the sixth floor. The Italian was only two doors from the bank of elevators serving the street end of the guest rooms.

When the Italian emerged quietly, Walid shot him three times in the face with a Walther P4, which has a long noise suppressor permanently attached to the muzzle. Walid wore gloves and the weapon was untraceable, so he simply dropped it next to the body, stepped back into the elevator and, within three minutes, was back in the room with Khami.

Like the other three women, she knew that part of their work would be both seduction and sexually servicing the men of the network. She probably enjoyed this side of her duties more than any other and this was obvious to the police who interrogated everyone in the hotel following the discovery of the Italian's body. They crossed the pair off as even possible killers for their eyes and demeanour shone with physical lust. Another couple from New York in DC to see the sights and make the most of the nights, they thought.

Showered, shaved, for the first time in four days, and smelling slightly of a cologne he had not used in

22

weeks, Herbie Kruger came downstairs to the aroma of bacon and eggs. He had changed into a pair of slacks that, while still a shade loose around the waist, looked as though they almost fitted him. The shirt and jacket he had also put on did seem a trifle large. He had a lot of weight to reclaim, or a new wardrobe to buy.

Worboys had driven into Lyndhurst and bought bacon, eggs, sausages and a decent brand of coffee. He stood at the stove, spatula in one hand, frying pan in the other. 'Welcome to the best breakfast you've had in weeks,' he cheerily greeted Herbie as though the kitchen belonged to him alone.

Kruger swallowed hard, bile in his mouth for he had eaten little of late. The alcohol, in its strange way, had sustained him while it drained away energy. The first few mouthfuls were difficult, but at last his stomach settled, and by the time he had done away with three eggs, two sausages and four rashers of bacon, he even began to feel a little like his old self. So much so that he started to grieve for Gus Keene.

'So, give me my marching orders.' A touch of the old confidence.

Now Worboys spelled it out to him, just in case he had missed it the first time. Gus's car had gone off the road and exploded. Herb had to see the plod, take a look at the site, hear the story, then come to London and sit with the captains and the kings. Tell them the tale in his own words. Speak to them in tongues and let them hear how he saw it.

'Okay, I got to talk with the local plod. Which local plod?'

'Salisbury. A Detective Inspector name of Roach . . .'

'Bet they call him "Cock". Provincial plod is usually predictable, ja?'

'Probably, Herb, but listen. You'll have to drive to Salisbury. See the plod, see where Gus died, and then come back to the Office, Okay?'

'I should go and see Carole?' Herb asked. Gus's

widow haunted his mind. He thought he knew what a widow must feel, when this thing called death struck so unexpectedly.

'The Chief went down an hour ago, Herb. Went down with one of the girls. Stay away for a while. Let's see what we've got here: accident or malice aforethought.'

'Murder most foul.' Kruger had already made up his mind.

2

'Not much call for you fellows these days, I suppose?'
Detective Inspector Roach, a tall, thin man, all angles
and sharp features, was trying to make polite conversation as they drove to the accident site between Salisbury and the old garrison town of Warminster.

'So they say.' Herbie felt sick, troubled and non-
committal. His head still ached; what he had already
seen made him want to throw up. What was left of Gus
Keene's car had been towed into the big garage behind
the Salisbury police station and the picture of that would
remain in his mind for a long time. A pile of blackened,
twisted scrap metal from which no human could have
got out alive. Death at the snap of two fingers. There
one minute, gone the next in a tangle of flame and steel.
Forensics were going over it with their plastic bags, scrap-
ing here and there, examining and measuring, combing
through the wreckage like buzzards.

Herb had also read the two statements which DI
Roach placed before him, like an acolyte opening the
gospel for a priest.

The first was signed by William Dunne, a military
police sergeant, on attachment to one of the many
units stationed in the town of Warminster which, being
adjacent to Salisbury Plain, has known the presence of
soldiers for centuries.

Sergeant Dunne had been driving back to his barracks following an evening spent with a young lady in
Salisbury. About a mile from the small village of Wylye,
on the Warminster Road, he had seen a car half pulled
off on the grass verge. Being a man of instinctive powers
of observation he had identified the vehicle as a Rover

with the registration number ED439B. In plain language, Gus Keene's car. Two men stood talking near the front of the Rover, and both had turned their backs to his headlights as he passed. The time was four minutes to three in the morning.

The second statement told how a Mrs Doreen Hood, who lived in one of the cottages on the outskirts of Wylye, had been awakened by what she called 'a terrible bang' – a phrase that had caused much ribald comment among the police who knew Mrs Doreen Hood's mode of life, which involved many hours in bed with numerous local worthies. On looking from her window, Mrs Hood saw the car, later identified as Gus Keene's Rover, engulfed in flames, lying on its side a good five metres off the road. 'It was one of them explosions like you see at the pictures: in those Arnold Schwartzanagle's films. Like *Legal Weapon*.' It was Mrs Hood who telephoned for police and ambulance. They had logged the time as 03.04. It was midsummer. July. The date/time was on the tape, spoken by an electronic voice. Such is progress.

DI Roach drove with the immense care of a police officer out to teach by example. In truth Kruger interested him, for he was the first member of the SIS Charlie Roach had ever come across. 'You weren't born in England, were you?' he asked.

Kruger gave not a flicker of a smile. 'Thought I'd fooled you.'

'I detected an accent. I suppose during the Cold War you spent time abroad?' Abroad for DI Roach really meant package deals to Malta or Marbella, but he was aware of the dark freezing days when secret men and women plied their trade across the Berlin Wall. Like millions of others, he had read *The Spy Who Came in from the Cold*, so he knew it all. Now, he glanced at the big man with a drawn and haunted face. In the wink of an eye he saw Herbie in the shadows of ruined Berlin, or stepping from a doorway like Orson Welles in *The Third Man*. 'It must be an adventurous life,' he added.

'Sure. Dead adventurous. I still go abroad. More call than you'd think for people like me. Even now.'

'Really? I've always wondered what it was like. Spying and that.'

'Not what it's cracked up to be.' Herb stared straight ahead. They were approaching the place where Gus Keene's Rover had gone off the road. He knew this particular route as well as the lines on his own hand.

The grey stone of Wylye village lay ahead; and they were deep in the Wylye Valley, which is not as beautiful as it sounds. The river is more of a brook for most of the way, pollarded willows dotting its banks, which are indefinable for they stretch out into little pools of marshland. On some days the view could be downright depressing. Herb hardly ever passed this way without hearing words about a willow aslant a brook, and thinking of dead, drowned Ophelia.

In a couple of minutes he was standing in the open, looking at the deep dark scars in the grass where the Rover had ploughed in and blown up. DI Roach heard the choke in the back of the tall man's throat, and the look of grief spread like blood across his face.

'You knew the gentleman well?' Roach asked, as though he had to make conversation.

'Alas poor Gus. I knew him, Inspector. Where be your gibes now? Your gambols? Your songs?'

'Your what?'

'He'll be mourned by many.' Herb simplified it.

The drive to London was slow and infuriating. Herbie had the radio on and there was some panic. Two mainline railway stations had been bomb targets. The FFIRA had telephoned codewords two minutes before the devices blew, killing seven and injuring two dozen more.

In the centre of London's West End two other bombs had exploded in cars – one carrying an American official to the Embassy in Grosvenor Square, the other taking a senior diplomat to Heathrow airport. Both men and their drivers had been killed. The names would not be released until the families had been informed. The FFIRA had made a second statement declaring that they had nothing to do with the car bombs.

'So that's it,' Herbie said later to those assembled on the fifth floor. 'No skid marks. No sign old Gus had to throw out the anchors. Just a couple of long deep ruts in the grass, then a wet burned patch. More like the car was detonated. Looked like a mortar bomb hit, not a car accident.'

'It's what the local law are saying.' Worboys looked down at the typewritten pages already stacking up in their red card folder. 'Jesus, poor old Gus.'

'Also, they're saying identification's going to be difficult.' Herbie steepled his fingers.

Tony Worboys nodded and looked, as if for help, around the room. The Chief was still down at Warminster, comforting the bereaved, but he had called two other people in to listen to Herbie. They were in a kind of shock, for Herbie had been right about Gus being mourned by many. They all knew they had lost a part of themselves – something that often happens with an unexpected death.

Four of them, including Herb and Worboys. Martin Brook, portly, bespectacled, owlish, once Gus Keene's pupil, and a young man called Angus Crook from Registry. Crook held a thick buff-coloured folder which contained a print-out of Keene's record. Worboys' eyes settled on the latter. 'Identifying marks?' he asked, as though this was a real question.

'If he's been burned to a frazzle there's going to be no way.' Crook was an earnest young man; a computer wizard, which is the main required skill for people who work in Registry these days. Nowadays, you fed subjects into a computer which asked for codewords and clearances before it spat out documents, and the SIS Registry was safe as proverbial houses because it was cut off from the world of modems and easy access by computer hackers. It had also led to many redundancies, for Angus

28

ran the place with the aid of one other officer and three female Registry Clerks, who were also computer experts. Those in the know called them 'The Secret Five'.

'They're going to be hard put to.' Crook had a gruff Scottish accent which some said was an affectation. 'If Gus is now just burned bone, they're not going to make a positive on him. Bits of wrist watch. Maybe some coins.'

'Surely dental records . . . ?' Worboys began, but Crook smiled grimly and shook his head. 'That's for thrillers. Gus had perfect teeth. All his own. Never saw a dentist in his life as far as I can see.'

Martin Brook got up and walked to the window, looking down the River Thames from this perch above London. 'So, what's the drill, Tony?'

'The drill?' Worboys shrugged. 'The drill is that we really don't want the law scratching deeply into Gus's life. The Chief's insistent on that. He said I have to do a deal.'

'Call off the plod and use one of our own sleuths?' Brook queried.

'Call off the plod and use Herb.'

Kruger growled, 'Now I play Sherlock?'

'That's the way it goes. Our Lord and Master is talking to the Chief Constable of Wiltshire, e'en as we speak, but that won't keep everyone off our necks.' He looked hard at Kruger. 'So, give it to us, Herb. Words of one syllable, eh? Your immediate thoughts.'

'Alka-Seltzer and a long lie down.'

'Immediate thoughts about Gus.'

'Impressions?'

'Impressions, Herb.'

'I believe he's dead. I seen the car. I seen where he went off the road.'

'But you have reservations?'

'Many. Gus, or I presume Gus, was seen pulled off the road talking with someone a few minutes before it happened. No skid marks. Road as dry as dust. Deep ruts into the grass – not skids, but ruts. Heavy, like he drove straight off, then boom.'

29

'Boom?'

'Boom, as in, shit I'm on fire and the car's in little pieces. Shouldn't be surprised if Gus was also in little pieces. When we get the medical stuff? Autopsy?'

'Maybe later today. If we're lucky.'

'You think he was definitely pushed, then?'

''Course he was pushed. Old Gus wouldn't just drive off a road only ten minutes from home and detonate himself into oblivion. If Gus wanted out he'd make it stick like a real accident, if only for the insurance. For Carole.'

'Then who'd want to do away with old Gus?' Worboys said it quietly, as though he were not really asking.

'You really want a head count?' Herbie prised himself out of his chair. 'How many people did Gus put in the poky during his long and varied career? How many secrets he take to the grave, eh?'

Martin Brook turned back into the room. 'He was writing his memoirs, Tony. People still alive, gentlemen in England, now abed, would possibly get their names all over the Sunday Funny Papers. There's motive for you.'

'Sure.' Herb sounded as though he did not believe a word of it.

One of the six telephones on Worboys' desk began to chirp.

It was the Chief, calling from Warminster. Worboys covered the mouthpiece with his right hand and whispered, 'Wants to talk with you, Herb.'

'Yes, Chief.' There were no jokes and no tripping over his English. It was all business, a serious, sober Kruger. They all felt the charge, and heard the grave note in his voice.

At last Herbie put down the telephone and turned to look each of them in the eye. He blinked once before speaking. 'He called me Herb, and he's new to the beat.'

'He's a quick study.' Brook grinned.

'It seems that I am to be dear Gus Keene's vengeance.'

Even Worboys shuddered at the way Herbie spoke. Only a couple of times in his long dealings with Kruger had he heard the big man talk like this. On both occasions there was hell to pay.

'The Chief says I can have anyone and anything I want as long as I find out the why and the who. I tell you exactly what I want, Tony. Okay?'

'Okay, but you'll get an anti-terrorist copper in tow, sooner or later. Possibly sooner.'

'I'll have to live with that, then, won't I?'

Kruger spent the night at a safe house he had known for years. A tall, narrow four-storey place in a pretty little square behind Kensington High Street. It was there that, in his own way, he mourned the death of Gus Keene, and reflected on his own mortality.

Before going across the river to Kensington, he had spoken to the Chief when he called from Warminster. 'I'm not going to ask you to sign on again, Herbie,' the Chief said. 'Though we'll give you anything you want. I'm just concerned about finding the truth of this business. You think it was an accident?'

'No.' Herbie's replies were now mostly monosyllabic.

'Suicide?'

'No. Someone had Gus killed, sir.'

There was a non-committal grunt at the other end of the line, and the Chief repeated that he could have any backing he wanted. Facilities, men – within reason – places to work. 'Gus was just about the best interrogator we ever had. I want you to get to the bottom of it. Find the truth. Okay?'

Herb was tempted to say, 'No problem,' but he held his peace and handed the telephone back to Young Worboys who told the others that Herbie was in charge from now on.

All of them looked at the big man as though he were Merlin and would solve puzzles in a minute flat. He took Worboys to one side and asked if he could stay in London overnight. Worboys nodded and went off to arrange things, and Big Herbie turned to Angus Crook, saying that he wanted Gus Keene's jacket – jacket being the word they used for confidential dossier.

The Scot broadened his accent, saying, 'Gus Keene's jacket hasnee been oot the Registry in my time, Hairb. Ye ken what I mean?'

'Well, it's got to be about eight inches thick.'

'Near sexteen inches, Hairb.' Crook cackled. For a relatively young man his laugh was a strange croak, as though some older ghost inhabited his body.

When he brought the print-out back to the office it was only around an inch thick. 'It's just the outline of his life, Hairb,' Angus told him. 'The full thing'll take a bit longer.'

After that, he was driven to the safe house where he saw that nothing had changed since he had last been there. Same décor which reached back to the 1970s. The fridge had been filled, and it was here that Herbie mourned his old friend. He even thought he could see him: tall, leathery face, features of a gypsy, sucking at his pipe with an unruly piece of his black hair falling across his forehead. Gus was sixty-nine years old, with not a grey hair on his head.

Herbie felt the agony of loss, wondered how Carole was taking it, and almost wept, feeling that someone should sing a Requiem for the old confessor.

Instead, he sat in the main room of the house, toying with hard-boiled eggs and tomatoes, his great brow wrinkled as he tried to think it through. Why Gus? Why now at this point when he was out and writing his memoirs?

Softly and tunelessly, he sang a snatch of a song he had learned sometime over the years:

'And here we sit, like birds in the wilderness,
   Birds in the wilderness,
   Birds in the wilderness,

And here we sit, like birds in the wilderness,
Down in Demerara.'

Later, he looked at the part of Gus Keene's jacket
that Angus had passed on. It turned out to be a neat
précis of the stepping stones of Gus's life – educated at
a grammar school, several notches down from what the
Brits called a public school and the Americans referred
to as a private school. Service during the Second World
War with the Intelligence Corps, where he was awarded
a Military Cross, which meant he had done something
relatively spectacular.

After the war, they gave him a grant to read law
at Oxford. Herb remembered Gus speaking of Oxford
as 'The city of dreaming spires – or really the city of
drunken squires'. He heard Keene laugh somewhere
upstairs, and felt the hairs on the back of his neck
tingle.

Towards the end of the 1940s, Gus had given up law
and married a short, blonde, sexy girl called Angela who
turned out to be a very flirtatious lady. Someone had once
said that Angela Keene would claim she had committed
adultery only once – with the band of the Life Guards.
Herb remembered her vividly, for he had groped her, and
done more at a Christmas party. Angela put it about, as
they say. He saw her vividly now, and recalled she wore
a gold ring on a chain around her neck. Never took it
off.

In the end, Gus began leading his own life. He joined
the Metropolitan Police, and was quickly shunted into
what used to be called Special Branch, which was hand
in glove with the Security Service. Eventually the Office
headhunted him, and within a few years the great Gus
Keene became their leading interrogator. He also started
to spend a lot of time with one of his juniors, Carole
Coles. Inevitably, the lady Angela found out. There was
a quiet divorce and Gus married Carole. Marriage of a
lifetime, everyone said.

Lord, Herb thought, Carole had loved Gus as though he were her sun, moon and stars. In his mind he saw them together. Gus in his old tweed jacket, looking like a gypsy prince, with a smile that would draw even the hardest case into his confidence.

Aloud, and to nobody, Herb said, 'Was it the curse of the gypsies, Gus? That your downfall?'

He wanted to weep over what remained of Augustus Claudius Keene, whose father had been an expert on ancient Rome. Augustus Claudius Keene. Down in Demerara – whatever that meant.

In his head, Herbie Kruger was almost praying to Gus. 'Help me. Show me the way. Light the path and I'll examine all you've already written in your memoirs. I'll dig out every friend and every enemy, and put them to the question. That's what you used to call it, Gus. Putting people to the question. People said that you had an unhealthy interest in torture. I wonder, old friend, did it go too far?'

He hardly slept that night, with the shade of Gus Keene hovering on the edge of his mind.

As Herbie Kruger tried to clarify his thoughts and mourn his old friend's death, Detective Chief Inspector Olesker could not sleep. None of them could work out how the FFIRA Active Service Unit had vanished from a house they had under surveillance and planted a couple of damned great bombs at two of London's busiest railway stations. DCI Olesker would be lucky to get away with it after the inquiry.

In another part of the city, the members of *Intiqam*'s London cell quietly celebrated their first victories. They had been in touch with their leaders back home. They had asked if they should issue a statement and were firmly told not yet. Give it a few months with more successes in Europe, then, before the big day, you can issue as many statements as you like.

Hisham, the very tall and muscular member, was the

leader of the London cell, and the only one who had any reservations about what had occurred that morning. Four days previously he had travelled to Dublin and met, in the Gresham Hotel, with a short well-dressed young man from the North called Declan. Declan was the FFIRA's officer in charge of foreign operations – which basically meant that he chose targets and sent out active service units to mainland Britain which he referred to as 'Across the water'. He also had some access to arms, equipment and explosives.

Hisham dined with Declan and took a step which he knew might be dangerous. 'We both have the same aim,' he told Declan, who remained impassive, neither acknowledging the remark nor confirming it. 'I am telling you, as a courtesy, that we are about to hit two, maybe three targets in and around London.' Hisham kept his eyes on the Irishman, trying to read something in his face. For almost a full minute he remained silent. His eyes were deep and dark, and from within their very centre there was a wariness that moved slightly, like twin snakes just before they were ready to strike.

Then Hisham gave the Irishman the date they expected to carry out their attacks, saying that should the FFIRA be about to carry out similar actions, it would do both of them some good, from the point of view of publicity. At the time, Hisham thought his own masters would welcome some kind of Press Release. In the event, they had refused which had forced the FFIRA to make a separate statement denying the car bombs which were the work of *Intiqam*. Earlier that evening, Hisham had taken a telephone call from an FFIRA contact in London. This man suggested that his Council in Belfast expected that, in future, *Intiqam* would claim responsibility for all their actions. The FFIRA was expressing its displeasure, implying a vague threat against *Intiqam*.

One of the reasons Hisham had been chosen as the leader of the British *Intiqam* group was that he had spent time in Europe. Two years based in London but travelling around the continent – mainly to Paris and various parts of Switzerland: 1983 and 1984. His masters knew this though members of the group did not. Later, they were surprised at the ease with which he travelled about the city and the country.

Hisham, in an attempt to lay the ghost of the threat, took Dinah, the better-looking of the two girls, to bed. She was the tallest of the women who had come out with the teams to Britain and the USA. At almost six feet – more with Western dress and high-heeled shoes – she stood out as a beauty. Slender, a kiss as cool as a cucumber which could turn into the heat of red pepper, and legs which appeared to be those of a contortionist. She could be fast and accurate with a gun, just as she could be slow and painstaking when it came to pleasuring a man. She had no desire for the so-called liberation of the Western women – though she was already liberated, working for her country, but mainly in the West. For her, using a pistol with great accuracy was as pleasurable as using her female parts to subjugate a man and so, by subjugation, give him exquisite pleasure. After a while neither Hisham nor Dinah were bothered by the noisy jokes and laughter coming from the celebration in the adjoining room.

3

The call from Salisbury came through at around seven the next morning, and was immediately patched through to Herbie in the Kensington house. He had not slept well, floating just under the first layer of consciousness, the world only a bed sheet away, his mind preying on the various permutations surrounding Gus Keene's death.

Never assume anything, they always said, but Herb had already assumed that someone had put Gus away and blasted him into the permanence of death. The question was why would anyone do that? His half-conscious mind decided it was unlikely that it had connections to the past history of the Cold War. So what was left? Merely the old motives for murder and sudden death: revenge, money, women. The staples of foul play.

Had Gus stolen his child bride, Carole, from another? That all happened in the sizzling sixties, so why would a previous lover wait three decades to seek recompense? Money, he would have to look at closely; while revenge, in the non-sexual sense, was something else altogether. Maybe revenge *had* come out of the past and thumped Gus into oblivion.

Around six, he dropped deeper into sleep and dreamed, so that the telephone hauled him from a wild colourful fantasy in which he was cavorting with elephants dressed in tutus to the music of Berlioz's *Requiem*. It might have been a scene straight out of *Fantasia* but that did not mean a thing because Herb had never seen *Fantasia*.

The voice at the distant end identified himself as Hard Luck, and Herb volleyed back with Incinerator. Why they still had to play tradecraft games was beyond him, but that was what the Chief had laid down, so who was he to argue? He reflected that Doris Day, many years ago, had defined the current status quo – 'Our secret's not a secret any more.'

Hard Luck was one of their bomb specialists. A person of macabre and bizarre humour, he was a gallows man who had risked death a hundred times in dealing with the terrorist bombs of the past three decades; a fellow of infinite jest where the minutiae of explosives and their triggering mechanisms, not to mention shattered corpses, were concerned. He had been sent down to Salisbury, with another of his ilk, during the previous afternoon when the Chief was busy issuing orders from Warminster.

'So?' Herb asked.

'So, I think you'd better come down. Gus was puffed, providing it *was* Gus in the car.'

'I don't think there're any doubting Thomases on that score.'

'Can't get an ID. No way.'

'A rag, a bone and a hank of hair? Kipling,' Herb provided.

'Strictly speaking that's a woman, sir. But no, there's no rags or hair. Charred bone, a bit of metal that could be from a spectacle case, something that was once a watch, and a couple of other odds and ends. There were three separate explosions which went off as one.'

'How?'

'Well, it's not the ubiquitous Semtex, and the handwriting isn't that of the boyos from our friends the FFIRA. Whoever did this used good old-fashioned industrial dynamite. A few sticks of the stuff here, another four there, and at least four right under the driver's seat – literally inside the car. There was also a lot of petrol in the boot as well as the tank. Come and take a look. I think you should.'

'Sure. Sure, I'll check it out.'

38

'We'll be here for a couple of days. Nice town, Salisbury.'

'Do a good line in cathedrals, ja?'

'And in dispatch. Death in fragments; death by fire.'

Herb called the Office, but nobody of importance was in yet. He showered, shaved and did the other thing. Then dressed and drank coffee, nibbling on a piece of toast as he again dialled the Office. This time Worboys was in.

'You have everyone's blessing,' said Worboys a shade too perkily. 'The Chief's dashed off to high-powered meetings in Europe. Told us you were in charge and that you could talk to Carole, but not a full inquisition. He's left Bitsy with her.'

'Bitsy Williams who does Guest Relations?'

'The one with the legs up to her armpits. GR and safe houses – which is not a full-time occupation these days.'

'Never met her, but I'm told she's good. Well over forty, but good.'

'I know people who claim she's better than good. Anyway, she's to keep Carole company until after the obsequies.'

'After the which?'

'Funeral, Herb.'

'Never heard that – obsequies. Is good. Nice long word. But these obsequies have to come after the ID, and I am told there's little to ID.'

'Your problem, Herb. You're the man in charge.'

Herbie gave a deep sigh, reminiscent of an old steam appliance. 'Get me a car and a good driver. Pick me up here, half an hour, okay?'

While he waited, Herbie called Registry and found Angus at his desk. The conversation was difficult and lengthy, with Kruger attempting to translate Angus's accent, and Angus allowing his brogue to get thicker all the time: possibly an act of malice. Heads of Registry are, in a way, similar to librarians. Their charges are like children and they are not happy to see anything go out of the house beyond their control.

Herb was after the methods used by Gus to research his memoirs and, between the 'Ayes' and 'Ochs' and 'Didnas' and 'Kens', he gathered that Gus had taken only a minimal number of print-outs from the building. It seemed that, for the most part, he had come in, read the stuff, and made notes.

'How far had he got?' Herbie asked, enunciating carefully.

'Around nineteen sixty-nine. He wasnee a fast laddie when it came to the resairch, ye ken.'

Herb kenned and put the telephone down, reflecting on a comment made some time ago by Young Worboys – 'Old Angus is a Scot of the Music Hall variety. You expect him to break into "I love a lassie, a bonnie Heeland lassie," any minute.'

It was all very confusing to Herbie who had perfected his own version of fractured English which he often used to great effect. In Angus he had almost met his match.

The driver was Ginger Bread. Anthony James Bread. The Office could be as predictable as provincial police forces when it came to nicknames. Ginger was a hood, no doubt about that; a bantamweight, with a streak of violence written clearly over his smooth face. Herbie knew him from way back and had seen him do things to people that would make a world-class kick-boxer wince with envy.

'Nice to be working with you again, Mr Kruger.'

'Nice to see you, Ginger. You dislocated any good joints lately?'

'Always looking for the excuse, sir. Salisbury, is it?'

'Salisbury. Then Warminster, I guess.'

As they pulled out of the little square in which the Kensington house stood, Ginger said something about a rumour that Warminster was on the chopping block.

'Shouldn't be surprised. We're being stripped to the bone, Ginger. Today Warminster, tomorrow the safe houses. People like yourself'll be moonlighting to make ends meet. See if I'm not wrong.' He amazed himself, for he was talking as though they had taken him back full time.

They travelled in a long, contemplative silence which lasted – with the odd punctuation of comment on other people's driving habits – all the way to the Salisbury nick.

Herb thought of his old friend Gus Keene. The man and the legend – only he knew some of the legends were true. Gus did it all by guile and stealth. Possibly a little psychology as well, yet he had an abiding interest in the more esoteric ways of torture and his library spoke clearly of that.

In the interrogation room at Warminster – the one he used for hard cases, not the luxury suites underground away from the house – there was a chair. The chair was high-backed, buttoned leather, with hard arms. The kind of chair that did not leave you alone. A chair that intruded and made you aware of posture. Gus called it his *lacrimae rerum* chair. There was also the famous picture. It was rumoured that he owned several copies, but Herbie had seen only one: a churchyard by moonlight, in which you could glimpse a tiny corner of the church. The canvas bulged with gravestones, some new, most very old, cracked and leaning askew, the whole lit by a gibbous moon; stark, bare trees in the winter background. It was an eerie thing, and after being in that room for more than ten minutes the eye was drawn to the large painting, and the mind became uneasy.

Clever bugger, Herbie had said to himself when he first saw it.

So, Gus had this dark side: a fascination with the old ways of interrogation, and a special knowledge and practice of more modern, less violent methods. Anybody like Gus would inspire myth, and his success rate with the villains of secret history had stood at around 93 per cent at the time of his retirement.

41

Gus the man was totally different. Meeting him for the first time you would think him less dangerous than a country farmer. He could have been anything from a bank manager to the man who wrote the country column in provincial weekly newspapers. Herb recalled someone telling Gus that to his face, and the inquisitor smiling and nodding. 'Yes, I would write a column called "Off The Beaten Track".' Then the smile again, infectious, wicked, with a hint of mockery.

Hard Luck's real name was Peter Gurney. Nobody knew if Peter was his real name, or a nickname taken from one of the legendary men who, in the old Devonshire song, had ridden on Tom Pierce's grey mare with Dan'l Widden, Harry Hawk, Peter Davie and Uncle Tom Cobley and all. Gurney had been a Sergeant Major of Marines at one time, trading in the spit and polish, *Per Mare Per Terram*, for spotless overalls and a more dangerous existence, when you came to think of it.

He had dismantled bombs in the streets of Belfast, on the dangerous border between Northern and Southern Ireland, and in London. He was at his best when examining the burned-out skeletons of vehicles, seeking out the truth of the way in which they had erupted in explosive flame. He knew the trademarks of terrorist bomb-makers from the back streets of Belfast to the alleys of Beirut. Many said that he only had to look at a scorch mark to name the culprit. Peter Gurney was, in fact and reality, *the* bomb man, and was owned by the Office who used him as a trump card. Like a star actor under the old Hollywood studio system, he was loaned out to police forces and military units as the ultimate man.

The desk sergeant at Salisbury nick showed an obviously unusual subservience when Herbie mentioned Peter Gurney, and flashed his little plastic ID card. They were led around to the big open garage at the back of the building, where Gurney appeared to be giving an impromptu lecture to an assorted bevy of cops – uniformed and plainclothed – who hung on his every word, knowing they listened to a legend.

'With cars,' he was saying, 'you must have a good knowledge of the wiring. If any of you are thinking about going into this line of work, start now: memorize the wiring of every car on the road and keep updated. I'm talking *all* vehicles, not just the most common wheels you see around your particular patch. The point is that, with car bombs, you *must* be able to sort out infiltrated wire from the stuff that's already there. I know it's difficult with more and more computerization coming in, but it *is* essential, as in this case. The first thing we found were the four strands of burned wire you see lying on the table here. That wire has no place in a Rover of this type – or any Rover come to that.'

What was left of Gus's car seemed to have been further dismantled, and a plain long folding table had been set up next to the burned and twisted thing that had been a Rover. Sections of it had been sliced away and now lay on a table together with smaller items: tiny pieces of metal, and the strands of wire to which Gurney was pointing.

He looked up, saw Herb, smiled and told his audience that his Guv'nor had arrived so they would have to call it a day.

'The wire?' Herbie asked him. 'That for real, or your usual line of bullshit?'

'Unhappily, it's for real.' Gurney traced a finger along the strands of charred wire, some of it almost crumbling to dust. 'There's no black magic, Mr Kruger. We were lucky. First thing we found. Someone had taken a lot of pains with this. It isn't your quick device with magnets plonked on the underside and blown at your leisure. It took time and trouble. I told you that there was a cluster of dynamite sticks inside, under the driver's seat.' He gestured to what had been the driver's seat which now looked like a piece of modern metal sculpture – the kind that Art Galleries paid thousands to own and exhibit. 'Another close to the petrol tank, and a third right under the boot.'

'Any takers?' Herb asked quietly.

'If I had to make a substantial bet, I'd say Middle East. It has Arab handwriting all over it. Also, they rarely work bombs over here so they'd probably go in for some petty pilfering. Some quarries and specialist firms aren't too careful with their dynamite.'

'You prove it?'

'Have to get analysis on the dynamite first. Find out if it's from one source or several but we know how the deed was done.'

'Show me.'

'There *was* a magnet.' The expert picked up a small, bent circle of metal, with varied attachments. 'Mercury switch,' he said. 'Mercury switch attached to a magnet and so to the underside of the chassis. You're conversant with mercury switches, sir?'

'Sure, but tell me just the same.'

'Glass vial containing mercury. Usually tilted so that the mercury lies at one end. When it slides down the vial it provides the necessary to make contact with wires and batteries so that a small amount of electricity takes a swipe at the detonator, or, in this case, detonators. Then bang!'

He turned the charred remnant in his fingers. A pair of AA batteries were visible, and some fragments of wire. 'This one', Gurney continued, 'was fairly highbrow. Mercury switch with a little flap to stop it running down to complete the circuit and boom. It had a solenoid here,' pointing, 'and the solenoid was probably operated by something as simple as a remote from one of those toy aircraft or cars. Press the button and Puff the Magic Dragon sends a bloody great firework straight up your arse – if you'll excuse the expression, sir – and two others which ignited the petrol.'

'Sure. You can prove all this in a court? In front of the beak?'

'Not at the moment, but we *will* be able to once we've got all this stuff into the lab, back in the Smoke.' For the uninitiated, the Smoke was London. Herb was initiated.

'So *where* they put the dynamite?'

'Under the driver's seat, as I've said. Another lot near the petrol tank, and the final handful under the boot, which had three four-gallon petrol containers inside. The explosive didn't even have to rupture the metal to set the Rover ablaze – though it did with the boot. When it pops, the stuff generates enough heat to cause spontaneous combustion – if it's set near some combustible material. The driver would be dead before the flames got near him. In fact they have what's left of him down at the hospital. The doc says it's like doing a jigsaw, and the local law's out combing the ground for more spare parts. Poor old Mr Keene's been rendered down to kit form, as it were.'

'Mmmmm.' Herb frowned. 'And nobody's going to be able to ID him, because there's no nice, convenient, dental records.'

'They'll be able to size him up, and we do have one or two small items. The forensic boys and the Coroner's Office will take an age to release what's left. His wife won't be able to bury him for a while.' Peter Gurney turned towards the table again. 'Oh, and it *was* his Rover. Engine serial number fits.'

'So what else you got?'

What was left of Augustus Claudius Keene's personal possessions was assembled in several small plastic bags. 'Bits of metal,' Gurney pointed. 'Looks like the remains of his watch, here. This is probably the metal lining of a spectacle case. A Zippo lighter, almost certainly. Then there's this little doo-dah.'

This little doo-dah was a tiny, twisted metal disc, the size of a small button. On the underside there was an almost inch-long pin. How *that* had escaped the fire was a mystery.

'What you reckon?' Herb asked.

'Lapel pin probably. Can't really tell. You taking charge of this stuff?'

Herbie nodded slowly. 'I have to get him ID'd. Bugger of a job. Ask his wife if he had a Zippo – which I am pretty sure he did. Find out what this dah-doo is.'

'Doo-dah,' Gurney corrected, for he was not cognizant with the English language according to Kruger.

'Sure.' Herb nodded. 'You done a lot in a short time, Pete. What else?'

'No idea.'

'I mean what's your general feelings about this?'

Peter Gurney could not meet his eye. He had known Gus *en passant* and realized that Big Herb had been a friend. 'It's a very pro job. Whoever did it knows all the tricks, and I'd say that the victim *had* to be dead or unconscious before someone did this to him. Mr Keene, I gather, was astute.'

'A what?' Herb was running on autopilot and did things like this instinctively.

'Astute, as in shrewd.'

'Ja. Yeah. Yeah he was. Shrewd, Gus was.'

'Wise to the ways of the badlands?'

'Very. Now is the taming of the shrewd, ja?'

Gurney frowned. 'I'd say the car was not rigged when he drove from Salisbury, or wherever he'd been. Or, put it another way, it was not completely ready. He'd have felt uncomfortable with those sticks of bang under the seat. If he was good in the ways of tradecraft, he'd have felt something fishy.'

'So, he was stopped on the road – which he was, Peter. You think they gave him a bounce on the melon, rigged the car, then set him off to his final destination?'

'Probably. A lot more work needs to be done.'

'How long it take, Pete? Rigging the car?'

'Ten, maybe seven, minutes. They'd have to have the clumps of dyno already rigged, put them in place,

46

push in the detonators, run the wires, screw them into the switch, then plug in the batteries. Really good boys would cut the time down to six or seven minutes, and I've no doubt these were really good boys.'

'Go do your stuff at the lab. I'll take the geegaws.' Kruger pointed to the neat plastic bags.

'You have the authority to take these?'

'Trust me.' Herb gathered the evidence bags into his huge paw, said he would be in touch, and lumbered away, Ginger in his wake like a tugboat.

'Warminster next?' the driver asked.

'Warminster, but stop off at a telephone booth on the way. There's one near the turn at Knook Camp.'

'Anything you say, sir.'

Big Herbie Kruger slumped himself into the passenger seat. He was in despair and heavy with emotion. Carole Keene, who had loved Gus with deep passion, waited at the end of this particular leg of the trip, and Herb was not looking forward to *that* meeting.

Knook Camp lies about two miles from Wylye and three from Warminster itself. It is an old, decrepit military complex, and to reach the Office's facility known as Warminster, you take a right at Knook Camp and go on for a couple of miles until you reach the high red-brick wall which is studded with electronic eyes and sensors. There is a lonely British Telecom telephone booth half a mile from the main entrance. From this booth, Herbie called the Office and spoke to Young Worboys.

'Touching boose with you, Tony.'

'Base, Herb.' Then he heard the chuckle at the distant end. 'So, what's the problem?'

'No problem. I seen Peter Gurney and they figured some of it. It's all nasty and I'll have to be doing lots of gumshoeing around. Whoever did Gus was good. Probably Middle East.'

'Yes, I've talked to Pete. It adds another dimension.'

'Several. Pete says it's got Arab handwriting. Anyway,

I'm pretty unhappy, Young Worboys. Just about to go talk with Carole and that's not going to be a barrel of laughs.'

'Yes. I've spoken to the Old Man. He has some rather good ideas. Want to hear them?'

'Shoot, old sheep.'

'You should have someone with you . . .'

'I got Ginger.'

'He's muscle, Herb, and you just might need muscle. Pete tells me whoever did the thing is a pro; but you know that already.'

'Sure. Okay, Ginger's muscle.'

'Any ideas about who you'd like with you to run interference?'

'You, old sport, like in the old days when you were my junior.'

'Be sensible, Herb. The Chief says Bitsy. She's already down there and she knows enough. I think he wants to keep her, in this time of dwindling resources and people taking golden handshakes. Wants to give her experience.'

'She looking after Carole?'

'Not for much longer. I've already got a pair of nurses on their way down.'

Herbie grunted. For nurses read minders and mind readers. 'Why?'

'It has been suggested that Carole should be moved into the luxury apartments . . .'

'Leave her home?' Slightly shocked.

'She'll be near enough. For her own safety, Herb. You'll have to tell her.'

'Great. I show her the bits of metal that, apart from a model kit that's his bones, is all that's left of her husband, then I tell her she has to get out of her home.'

'That's about it. You will stay there – in the Dower House – with Ginger doing the minding and Bitsy running the errands. You'll have peace and quiet, plus all Gus's documents, including what he's done on his memoir. Go through it like—'

'Grease through a duck, sure, I know.'

'It's handy, Herb.'

'Sure, it's also insulting to Carole.'

'Herb, for all we know, the dark and lovely Carole could be our first suspect. Isn't that the old rule? Wife is the first one you turn over.'

Big Herbie, cramped in the phone booth, gave another of his big sighs. 'His wife is former member of the Office as well. But okay, I call you from the Dower House. Is the line clear or have we got a dodgy bit of electronics there?'

'Safe as the Bank of England.'

'Oh, Christ.'

'Do it, Herb.'

'OK. You'll have to pick up the pieces.'

'Of course, Herb. You know the Office'll stand by you.' Pause for twenty seconds, ten seconds longer than necessary. 'We'll also stand by you when the anti-terrorist plod comes calling.'

'When'll that be?'

'Three, maybe four days. They're clearing a DCI from other work.'

'Keep him at bay, Tony. Get him to check out those two car bombs FFIRA say they didn't do, eh?'

'We'll try, but we're right behind you, old friend. Watch your back.'

Like hell, Kruger thought, easing himself from the booth. 'Let's go,' he said without looking at Ginger. 'Warminster. The place they call the Dower House. Where the old main entrance used to be.'

'Know it well, guv. Residence of the late Mr Keene, right?'

'And the lovely widow Keene, yes.' Herbie reflected that he truly did not know how he would do this.

4

The facility known as Warminster is very much alive and well in spite of the rumours; the reorganization; the shortage of government funds for the Office – apart from the much-criticized 200 million sterling for the new headquarters – now the Soviets have shouted *Pax*. In fact, in the past few years some of the security has been beefed up against the possible threat of terrorism. In reality nobody is about to close the place down or sell it off.

Since the demise of the old Evil Empire the world has become a more dangerous place, and some of those dangers were being addressed right here in the complex called Warminster.

The huge, rambling old house and its estate had originally been known as Fenley Hall. Indeed, that is still the correct Post Office address, and it is shown as such on ordnance survey maps. The Fenleys' reign as part of England's aristocracy had been relatively short. The baronetcy was created in Georgian times, and the first baronet, Sir Charles Fenley, had built the big house where he lived in grand style, and rode roughshod over his local tenant farmers.

Only two generations later the Fenley line died out, but during that period certain additions were made to the property. These included the building of the Dower House by the last Fenley, Sir William – or 'Billy Tuppence' as he was known – as a place to farm off his mother while he attempted to impregnate his wife, and several other ladies, in the big house, other houses, fields and, in one case, the stable of a coaching inn on the Brighton Road.

All this was to no avail. So perished the Fenley line of succession. The entire estate was sold off in the 1920s and acquired by the Office in the late 1930s, just in time to be used in the training of heroes who fought secretly for King, Country and Empire in the dark days between 1940 and 1944. At Warminster, and many other places, men and women were trained, then sent off to work inside Fortress Europe, as Hitler and *his* Evil Empire called the bulk of the imprisoned continent. Many did not return to Warminster. A large number were blown, but escaped back to England, home and, in some cases, beauty. The majority were not so lucky.

The Dower House, while of Victorian origin, had been built in Georgian style – and very successfully at that. Next to the big house it was a cottage, but put it out into the world and the Dower House would have comfortably served a family of eight, with room left over.

It stood close to where the original gates to Fenley Hall had welcomed callers into the long drive, which twisted and turned through high greenery, at last rounding a spectacular bend to reveal the main house in all its splendour. Those gates had long gone, replaced by red brick to match the remainder of the high, and effective, wall which surrounded the estate. The main entrance now lay a quarter of a mile back down the road towards Knook Camp, and while the gates looked original wrought iron they were, in fact, steel – which could be electrified when necessary. They were also, since 1991, the *only* way you could get into the grounds.

This was a trick in itself, for the main gates were monitored by security staff, hand-picked these days and mostly from former military backgrounds. When a car arrived at the main gates the vehicle was scrutinized via closed-circuit TV and the gates were opened from a secure room within the main house. You could never arrive unexpectedly at Warminster for there was a codeword, changed daily, and the authorization for a visit had to come in directly from the Office HQ in London.

Big Herbie Kruger had bad memories of the Dower House. As they approached it on that July afternoon he even experienced old dreads. On visits to Warminster over the past few years he had made certain never to go near the place. The memories still had claws and teeth.

In the days before the luxury 'guest suites' had been built as an underground complex away from the main house, the Dower House had been a kind of detention barracks, used almost exclusively for the interrogation of defectors and those who had possibly strayed.

Herbie's only true sin against the Office had been that time when, through folly and risk-taking, he had been trapped for too long behind the then sinister and flourishing Berlin Wall. On his return he had spent over a year as a guest of the Office in the Dower House, undergoing a long, weary and unsettling interrogation conducted mainly by his friend Gus Keene and the young Carole Coles – as she was then. Even Herb, wise to the ways of fleshly lusts, had not suspected that Gus was two-timing his wife, Angela, with the delightful and very young Ms Coles.

Eventually Kruger had been exonerated, but his time in the Dower House still haunted his dreams. Frankly, at this moment, he was more on edge because of the enforced visit to the place than talking to the grieving widow Keene. Yet, he considered, Gus's own study in the place would be alive with memories.

Some of his fear subsided as the car swept around the wall of rhododendron bushes and azaleas to reveal the glowing red-brick house with its large sash windows flanking an oak front door, the five windows above that, plus the two dormers in the roof. The Dower House had not just been spruced up with a paint job and work on the bricks and slates. Now, a small garden had been built to surround it, the border marked by what appeared to be genuine old iron railings behind which the lupin vied with the rose and delphinium. It was a far cry from the colourless, stark exterior Herb had known in his day.

Ginger was three paces behind him as he walked to the door, and his finger was still poised over the bellpush when the door swung open and Carole Keene almost catapulted out, her fists bunched and swinging.

'Who, Herbie? What bastards did this to him? They said you'd find out. Bloody Worboys and the Fat Boy say you might already know, and C's convinced you're close to the truth. So, who, Herb? Who'd do this to my lovely Gus?' It all came tumbling out, eyes red with anger, not tears, small fists pummelling against Herbie's barrel of a chest. C is how members of the SIS refer to the Chief, and it is said the initial comes from the first Chief of what was then the foreign section of the Secret Service Bureau, whose lengthy string of names was usually abbreviated to Cumming. That his real name was Mansfield George Smith is neither here nor there.

'Who, Herb? What idiots? Gus was the only man I ever looked at twice and they've pulped him. For Christ's sake, Herb, who?'

Herbie had never seen Carole in hysterics before. Serious, yes; moved to tears on two or three occasions; but never this uncontrolled fury of anger, loosed on him. He caught her wrists and barked sharply, 'Carole! Hold it! Calm down!' But Carole swept her arms down in classic hold break, pressuring his thumbs and banging him in the chest.

'Not another bloody airy-fairy-Lillian!' She all but screamed, turning on her heel and marching back into the cool hallway of the house. 'If you can't tell me now, don't bother me with platitudes, Herb. Not *me*,' thumping her own chest. 'Not *me*, not Carole Cool, mistress of this place and beloved widow of darling Gus. Out, Herbie! Out and find the sods!' She slammed across the hallway and through a door before Herbie could catch her again. He ended up in the tiled hall, looking at the slender figure of Bitsy Williams who moved in front of the door through which Carole had disappeared, as though barring his entrance.

'She's been like this since it happened.' Bitsy had an almost breathless voice, throaty, low. Like a cello, Herb thought, but then reflected that he often thought women had voices like cellos, only to find that, on closer listening, they were flutes. 'Not a tear,' Bitsy continued. 'No real grief. Just this terrible anger against everyone and everything. She used "language" at C on the telephone. Told him that he should be able to protect his f—ing stars, even if they were retired. Never seen anything like it. I'm Bitsy, by the way. Bitsy Williams.'

'Ja! Yes. Yes, I know.' Herb stared at her, considering the chauvinist pig gossip from inside the Office was true. Bitsy was just on the wrong side of forty, he thought. Not quite yet desperate, but fairly close to the border. Her legs did, indeed, seem to reach up to her armpits. As she moved, so her skirt floated over her thighs which appeared to be very high. In motion she was like a beautiful racehorse, though there was certainly nothing horsey about her face.

'And you're Mr Kruger.' She came close to him. For a second, long fingers untroubled by rings touched his sleeve. 'I was Pucky's friend. I was so sorry when . . .'

That was like a blade of ice piercing the big man's heart. Pucky Curtiss had been the second great female event in his life, an event which finally toppled into grief. He knew that emotion showed in his eyes, but he blinked it away, and from behind the door came music. Falla: *El amor brujo* – Love, the Magician – the *Ritual Fire Dance*.

'She's played that a hundred times since I arrived,' Bitsy told him.

Herb nodded. 'Could have been *their* song.' He tried a little smile in an attempt to lighten the load. 'The anger has to turn to the weeping. It'll come. I know what she's going through.' Then, as though breaking from some enchantment of his own making, he asked if Bitsy knew what was to happen.

'No?' Tentative, even a little frightened. 'No, what's to happen?'

'I'm here to evict her . . .'

'Oh, Jesus . . .'

'For her own good, and for *our* good also in finding whoever did this. She could be in danger. We could all be in danger. It has the distinct scent of Middle East terrorism, Ms Williams . . .'

'Bitsy. Please, Bitsy.'

He nodded his big head. 'Sure. They're sending down a pair of nurses and she's to be moved into the guest quarters. You, Ms Bitsy, are to be my gofer, and Ginger here is to lie across the door and make sure we don't get spooked. Okay?'

'If those are the orders, yes. Yes, of course it's okay. I'll do whatever you ask. It's an honour to . . .'

'Don' say it, Bitsy. Honour, schmonour. I'm just a burned-out case who wants to find out the whys and whos. In many ways I loved old Gus. Unnerstand? I'll talk to Carole now, okay?'

She stepped aside and he softly opened the door.

'Hey, Carole. It's me. Herbie. Remember.' Softly not to alarm her, quietly closing the door behind him.

Her back was to him as she sat on a settee covered in a rich, blue silk-like material. She said nothing, and did not move. Around them the luscious strings and throbbing rhythms of Manuel de Falla's dazzling ballet score worked their own magic ritual.

Herbie took a step forward. He felt like a child stalking a small bird, afraid it would up and fly away before he got close enough to touch it, and a thousand images passed through his mind.

When he was first brought to England, having proved his skills as a young teenager in post-war Berlin, someone had recommended that he should read poetry to help him with his English. Poetry and English history, he recalled, and he had found great solace in both. Not as great a comfort as he later discovered in music, but enough, so that he continued to read poems almost indiscriminately. The first time he had set eyes on Carole he thought of her as a schoolgirl. She had that fresh lithe kind of compact body which would keep her looking young until probably early middle age, and her complexion was that of a girl: clear, pink, peaches and cream, skin without a blemish. She was short and slim, and she moved with the unconscious charm of a fifteen- or sixteen-year-old.

That first time, he remembered a poem by John Betjeman – Poet Laureate, now gone – about a young girl called Myfanwy. After that he thought of Myfanwy whenever he saw Carole, even after she and Gus came out of the closet, went through the wormwood and gall of Gus's divorce, and the sweetness of their marriage. He heard it now.

> Were you a prefect and head of your
>   dormit'ry?
> Were you a hockey girl, tennis or gym?
> Who was your favourite? Who had a crush on you?
> Which were the baths where they taught you to
>   swim?

'Carole. Come on. Is Herb, come to talk. Let's talk this horror through, Carole. I loved him as well.'

Another step forward.

> Then what sardines in the half-lighted passages!
> Locking of fingers in long hide and seek.
> You will protect me, my silken Myfanwy,
> Ringleader, tom-boy, and chum to the weak.

'Carole. I'm your friend. No need to explain to me. Let's talk, yes?'

Her shoulders moved first. A little rising and falling, then her arm went up and a hand felt in the air behind her, as though trying to cling to something. Herb took another pace, grasped the hand, heard her choke and,

56

with the daintiness given only to big men, swung around the side of the settee and held her sobbing body in his arms.

Old Herb; Herb the comforter; Herb, always there when you needed him; Herb the hero, blubbing away with her. Friend and wife, weeping together over the death of friend and husband, appalled at the knowledge that life was not fair. He enfolded her small body in his bear-like arms, and waited for the storm of tears to pass.

He did not know how long it lasted, but it felt like an hour before Carole was all wept out, with her body just twitching occasionally, like the corpse of an animal in spasm long after death.

'Carole, I'll find them. You know that. My job now. Find the buggers who did it to him.'

She slowly disentangled herself from him and looked up, her face a wreck with tears and the horror of it all; the disbelief still there deep in her eyes.

'Why, Herb?'

'Why not, my dear? Is how I always tried to reconcile these things. Why me? Why not? Is the answer to all life's riddles.'

'Gus was . . .' she began, then took the handkerchief he offered, plunging her face into it as though it were a towel. Then: 'Gus was everything. You know that, Herb? For me, everything. Gus was my father, my brother, friend, lover, the whole thing rolled into one. God knows I'm liberated enough. Fought for women's bloody rights like a tiger. You know that, but this is something I can't deny to myself or anyone else. Gus was a reason for me. He was safety. Peace.'

'I know, like I know what this is like. I had my share.'

'But who, in hell, Herb? Who'd want . . . ?'

'Possibly terrorists, love. Gus had his moments with terrorists, yes?'

She nodded. Silent. Not really believing it.

'That's the Office line, and there's truth in it.' He sought, almost frantically, for words. 'Look, Carole, I

got to ask you a couple of things, and time . . . time
. . . well, is important.'

'Yes.' Not looking at him. The sound dead on her lips.

'Gus,' he said. 'Gus, did he use a Zippo?'

'A Zippo?'

'A Zippo. Lighter for his cigarettes or pipe.'

'He only smoked a pipe, and he always said you
should light a pipe with matches. Pipes and cigars, he
said. Matches always. Used those Swan Vesta things.'

'Ah. Then did he carry a Zippo?'

She looked up at him, sly. 'Yes. A joke. I gave it to
him a couple of Christmases ago. In his stocking. Zippo
with the KGB crest on it.'

'And he carried that?'

'Said it was his lucky Zippo.' Her voice cracked.

Herb swung in before she could start crying again.
'And a little pin, like a badge? Did he wear a little
badge in his lapel? I never saw him wear one.'

'Yes, sometimes. Yes, he wore a little badge.'

'What was it?'

The pause was a shade too long and the answer a
mite too fast. 'British Legion, I think. I never looked
properly.'

He did not believe it, and, for a fraction, wondered
if Carole was simply a very good actress. He dismissed
the idea, nodding and repeating, 'British Legion. Okay.'

'Why?'

'You know why, Carole.'

Again the silent nod.

'I got news for you,' he started again. 'We're all
in some danger. Could be anyway, if it *was* terrorists.
Particularly Middle East.'

'Danger?' she repeated, still flat, the voice dead like
her eyes.

'The Office says you got to move out. Go down the
Guest Quarters. Stay there for a while. They're sending
people to keep you company.'

'I have to leave here?'

'You'll only be a ten-minute walk away. It's just for the time being. They'll let you come back and stay.'

'I have to leave my . . . It has everything here. All of Gus is . . . Oh, yes, sorry, Herb. They want you to go through the place. Toss it? Isn't that the word they use?'

'I'll only be going through the notes and manuscript. His book. Not going to toss the place. But you need to be out. There *is* serious danger, Carole.'

'Truth. Cross your heart and hope to . . .'

His hand clamped around her wrist. Just a squeeze of comfort again and she began to cry once more, burying her head in his shoulder. Christ, Herbie thought, I need time, a lot of time, with this one. I need a couple of days minimum. Maybe more.

Presently, she said that she really did understand. Saw the wisdom of it. 'Can I get some things together? Is there time for that?'

'Sure. Also I'd like to see where Gus was working. Where he kept his manuscript and research notes. This is *very* important, the manuscript.'

She nodded. 'He wanted to call it *Ask No Questions and You'll Get No Lies*, but the publishers didn't like it. Then he tried *A Question of Fact*. They didn't like that either.' She rose, and he had to steady her with his hand, but she pushed him away.

'Bitsy'll help you get your things together.'

'I'll show you where Gus worked.' She started towards the door.

'Oh, one small thing, Carole.'

She turned, eyebrows raised in query.

'Why was he in Salisbury that night?'

'Gus?'

'Of course Gus.'

She gave a little shake of the head. 'Had a meeting. I don't know who it was. Except for the times we worked together on interrogations, I never asked details. He still behaved as though he were working for the Office. You know? He took all the right precautions. Said he had to see someone in Salisbury, so I didn't ask.'

'What did you suspect?'

'I . . .' she began, then stopped short. Jamming on the brakes, Herbie thought. 'I had a feeling that it was an old client.' She completed the sentence as if it had just come into her head.

'An old client?'

'Someone who had been through his personal wringer, yes.'

'Like me? I been through both your personal wringers.'

'No, not like you, Herb. It was just an impression. You know how it is when you live with someone a long time. You get a kind of ESP. I thought he was meeting someone he caught out along the road.'

'What gave you that idea?'

'Just the way he was so casual about going to Salisbury. I didn't think it was altogether kosher.'

'Could've been another woman?'

'No.' Firm and uncompromising. 'There were never any other women. I promise you that.'

Bitsy awaited them in the hall. She stood by the front door, well back from the room in which they had talked. Above them they could hear Ginger roaming around, getting the geography, which was his job.

The hall was large, with doors to left and right and a passage which ran along the right side of the staircase to a very big room which occupied almost the whole of the rear of the house. Short passages lay to left and right of this rather bare room. On the left the kitchen; on the right Gus's study.

She left him at the door. 'Please tell Bitsy which are the best rooms for us to sleep in,' he asked her. 'We're not here to pry, Carole.'

'I know.' A wan, sad smile and a 'Thanks Herb,' and she was off to pack a case and go underground, where the defectors used to live in the days that are now history.

About an hour later, two heavies from the Office arrived – Kenny Boyden and Mickey Crichton – together with a nurse whose name he could not put to the face. Pru something, he thought. Carole was going to be well looked after.

In New York, the cell had made themselves very comfortable. They had two apartments, next door to each other in a service building about two grades down from Trump Tower. This building was on Park Avenue, near the one on the corner of Park and 48th which has the Eternal Commuter statue just outside its atrium. This is the bronze guy who waits holding out one arm to hail a cab in all weathers, day and night. The Eternal Commuter made the girls laugh, but the apartments made them very happy. They were luxurious affairs full of comfortable furniture, kitchen appliances, Jacuzzis and the latest stereo equipment. No-one would have blamed the New York cell for sitting back and doing very little.

They split the team in two, two men and one girl in each apartment – Walid, Samih and Khami in one; Awdah, Kayid and Jamilla in the other. Walid did not like sharing Khami with Samih, but had no other option for Samih was the cell's leader, a very mature thirty-eight, with long hair and a taste for beautiful clothes, Armani suits and silk shirts. A man of the world and a carrier of death. It was said that he had originally been trained in one of the famous Libyan camps. Certainly he could put together a bomb that would not fail. Awdah and Kayid were, Walid thought, mere boys, in their early twenties. But they were boys who knew the discipline of the field. Both of them had become section leaders during the Time of the Wars. More, when they had trained for this very operation they had become devoted to Samih and would die for him as quickly as they would face death from the Leader of their country.

As for Khami and Jamilla, they were not simply women to be used like whores; having already proved themselves to be tenacious fighters. They feared nothing, so they were treated with respect. Because the girls both knew exactly what was expected of them, neither ever turned down the sexual advances of the males.

They were both attractive, particularly succulent in Western clothes: Khami had dark hair which she had cut short into a bubble of curls; she was also not as tall as Jamilla who was blessed with long raven hair which hung, shining, to her shoulders. Both were dark-eyed and – like the men – had paler skin than was normal to their countrymen. To be truthful there was a spirit of competition between the two, and this was fanned by the fact that Jamilla had obtained most of the documents which allowed all of them to live in peace, and without fear of the Immigration and Naturalization Service.

During her three years at Duke University, Jamilla had posed as the daughter of a wealthy, Jewish doctor and had pulled the whole thing off magnificently. She had assistance, of course, from her country's intelligence people. The doctor was completely fictitious, though his name and address showed up on the Federal computers. He even paid his Federal and State taxes, and, on one occasion, a member of her back-up group had come to the university posing as her father.

Jamilla had seduced a high-ranking official of the INS and her back-up team had sprung the honeytrap so that it looked as though the man – who was married to money – was in equal danger to Jamilla. The team had extorted various visa and passport stamps which were eventually used by *Intiqam*.

When the entire job had been completed, the INS man had been involved in a road accident which left his wife a widow. They knew things were completely safe when the widow married again within a year.

On the evening that Big Herbie Kruger had arrived

at Warminster, Samih called a meeting of the cell in the apartment he occupied with Walid and Khami. They sat around on pillows and spoke English as usual. Part of their briefing had stressed that they should never lapse into their native tongue.

Samih began by telling them how lucky they were to have been appointed to the United States. 'I prefer doing the work here than in Europe,' he began, going on to explain that Europe was attuned to freedom fighters or revenge squads. 'Their security agencies are more active, and their police are constantly aware. They can read the signs of our kind of activity as a blind man reads Braille. We must pray for our brothers and sisters who work in that hostile environment.'

He talked for some time about the way in which the people in the United States were of the opinion that what they called terrorist activities could never happen on a large scale. He told them that during the Time of the Wars their beefed-up security measures lasted only a minimum amount of time. 'For instance, they suspended curbside check-in of airline baggage during the time they called Desert Storm and Desert Sword, but lifted this ordinance almost before the war was over.' He spoke about the strict checks made on people who flew out of the United States – particularly on British Airways and El Al – yet the folly that surrounded other measures.

'There was panic for a few days after that bungled bombing attempt at the World Trade Center in New York in February of '93. But when no other attempts took place, the man in the street shrugged and took no real precautions. It would have been very different in Europe,' he nodded. 'Also, the media here is less sophisticated than in other countries which have been subject to righteous attacks by freedom fighters. After the World Trade Center bomb, the media announced, on live television, that certain suspects were about to be arrested, giving the suspects time to escape. Here the media has no conception of security.'

He then said that, because of this, they would be apt to take chances, reminding them that in the Trade Center incident the various agencies had got their hands on the culprits relatively quickly. 'In spite of being lax in some ways, the American police force, the FBI, CIA and others were dogged in the apprehension of suspects. We must not forget that.'

Then he began to speak of the next targets they would attack. This time they would use the Semtex explosive that had been smuggled into the country almost two years before their mission. 'Tomorrow,' he smiled with pleasure. 'Tomorrow, the Americans will hear explosions.'

During the next twenty-four hours a car bomb exploded in the centre of Manhattan, during the rush hour, while a briefcase bomb shut down a portion of the subway for three days. There were forty deaths and over 150 injured, some maimed for life. Worst of all, a commercial airliner which had just taken off from La Guardia exploded in mid-air. Luckily the debris fell into the East River, but all forty-two passengers and crew died at 3,000 feet above the city.

Nobody claimed responsibility, but individuals with both the FBI and CIA counterintelligence departments knew that, in the end, these gross actions were their responsibility. They were stunned, looking grey, sick, their eyes carrying a haunted expression.

People on the streets had a similar demeanour; an anxiousness around the eyes, and a new-found hurrying step, as though they were determined to move quickly through the city and flee the impending doom of a terrorist act.

The President went on television that night, admitting that this was the worst terrorist action the country had ever experienced, and urging his fellow Americans not to be fearful of what might lie ahead.

In many ways, it was as though millions of American citizens were joined together in a collective mourning. Some had not felt the like since the dark days of the Vietnam war, which meant that many thousands were again feeling the soft stench of death's breath on their cheeks.

5

Herbie had been right about Gus's study, there was a
strange feeling in the room, as though the old interrogator still inhabited the place. The aroma of his pipe
had impregnated the curtains and his books, so that
Herbie felt he was surrounded by essence of Gus Keene,
bringing him back to the mind with frightening clarity.

Herbie walked around the room trying to rediscover
his old friend. This, he soon realized, was a disturbing
experience. As he wrote in his diary, it was disconcerting
for he heard the sound of the interrogator's footsteps,
imagined the door opening – it still had a slight squeak
of the hinge which, he assumed, had not been oiled for
a purpose. The way Gus had his work table set up he was
forced to sit with his back to the door. Gus never liked
sitting with his back to doors, so some kind of warning
was necessary, hence the squealing door which Kruger
recalled in dreams of the time he had faced Gus Keene
in this very place.

On the first night, the three of them – Bitsy, Ginger
and Herbie – drove into Salisbury for an Indian:
Ginger driving and not drinking which allowed Herbie
and Bitsy to knock off an entire bottle of unconscionably
ragged red with no pedigree. They also shared a chicken
vindaloo, and Bitsy became almost girlish about the heat
generated by the curry. In fact, they got quite chummy
and exchanged the names of mutual friends, both in and
out of the Office.

'Herb, you've lost a lot of weight, you know,' Bitsy
told him. 'You're not ill, are you?'

'Lost my appetite for a while, Bitsy. Getting it back
now.' He placed a spoon heavily loaded with chicken and

mango chutney into his mouth and chewed. To himself he admitted he *was* getting an appetite again. If truth be told, Bitsy could tell that Herb found her attractive, after a physical and lustful manner. As for Herbie, he allowed himself to flirt outrageously with Ms Williams. Later he chided himself. The thought of light, or even heavy, relief with Bitsy was not unpleasant, but he had vowed not to go through all that again.

Life, he had long decided, had a tendency to screw you. Under his breath he had muttered, 'The screwing you are getting ain't worth the screwing you get.' This was an adage – slightly fractured by Herb's English – passed on to him many years ago by Tony Worboys, when the world, and Worboys, really were young.

Bitsy was attractive in a manner difficult to describe: the hair was not brilliant – dark, though not the jet of a nightshade witch. Her face was slightly irregular, the nose just a trifle too big, though the eyes, large and brown, would widen, becoming disconcertingly innocent; while her mouth was moulded after the manner of Carly Simon – something which lit up Herb's libido like a marker beacon.

The interest did not go unnoticed, for she kissed him lightly on the cheek before retiring, and the faithful Ginger remarked that he should 'Take heed of the lady'. A strangely Shakespearean comment which Kruger put down to the fact that Ginger had done a lot of work with members of an old Office family – just as Kruger had – and to be with any of *them* meant Shakespeare was an obligatory second language.

Books surrounded him in Gus's old study, and he browsed quietly, noting titles. There was, of course, some fiction. *Crime and Punishment* nestled close to *Anna Karenina* and a Folio Society *Collected Plays of Chekhov*. Modern authors were also there: the more humourless espionage authors. Only the very good ones. No dross. Not a hint of the Bondwagon.

Inevitably there were the famed books on torture –

L.A. Parry, *The History of Torture in England*; Andrews, *Bygone Punishments*; Haggard, *The Lame, the Halt and the Blind*; Jardine, *The Use of Torture*; Duff, *A Handbook on Hanging*; *The Methods of the Inquisition*, ed. A.C. Keene. So, Gus had even added to the literature.

The bulk of the volumes, though, were required trade reading. Histories of the Office – as they called the SIS – both whimsically bad and inaccurate, and scholarly near-correct. Nigel West rubbed shoulders with Christopher Andrew. There were works on psychiatry and tradecraft; international diplomacy, plus obligatory tomes on intelligence services – Mossad, KGB, CIA, NSA and others in a similar line of business. Most of these were now period pieces, outdated in the rush to realignment since the main enemy had ceased to be, and the true menace lay under different patches of earth, in unfamiliar places.

He heard the line of some, once popular, song in his head, and he turned it around, as was his practice. Singing under his breath, 'I'll be seeing you, in all the unfamiliar places . . .'

In the centre of the room, an old, polished table, almost too big for the space, sat covered with items of work. It was a fine and wonderful table, probably worth a small fortune. Herb suspected that it was the real thing: a refectory table from some convent. *Get thee to a nunnery, Gus.* There was a laser printer at the fireplace end, next to a Macintosh Centris. To the left of the high-tech lay a small print-out of manuscript, about an inch high, while the rest of the table was taken up by piles of bulging ring binders, riding into a skyline.

On that first night, full of vindaloo and curried veg, Kruger looked only at one red folder carrying the word *Correspondence* on a laser-produced sticky label. The correspondence seemed haphazard, mainly between Gus and his publishers: for the most part a series of letters between the interrogator/author and a faceless editor with the unlikely name of Mark Collier. He flipped through the letters, noting the earliest dates had very correct salutations and sign-offs:

Dear Mr Keene,
I was delighted to learn that we have finally come to an agreement, via your agent, Mr De Monds, whom I have known for a number of years . . . et cetera, et cetera . . .
Sincerely,
Mark Collier

As things progressed, after a first meeting was arranged and kept – at The Connaught, no less – the letters became more relaxed. 'Dear Gus' and 'As ever – Mark'. The formal wooing was over and the honeymoon began. There was an enthusiastic piece about the title, *Ask A Stupid Question*. (So what was the twaddle Carole was giving me? he wondered.) Mark had written, 'It is absolutely right for a wide market, as it should appeal to the serious scholars of what you refer to as your trade, plus the huge readership of the more superior novels of espionage.'

Herbie pondered, sitting there at three in the morning, asking himself if Gus was pulling a fast one, with the connivance of the Chief. Producing a book of only near-fact, for who but the archivists – and Angus Crook – would be able to gainsay him?

The thought was banished when he came to a long letter bemoaning the news that it was unlikely Gus would be allowed to include the more juicy details of some highly sensitive interrogations in both Belfast and London, concerning operations against the Irish Republican Army. 'For instance, we could sell the book on Operation *Cataract* alone,' Mark had written more in sadness than anger.

Kruger nearly fell from Gus's comfortable chair at the mention of *Cataract*. His heart thudded, he could hear it in his ears; and a lance of alarm passed through his nervous system, for this had been one of the closely guarded secrets of the late 1980s. The simple fact of it being there, in an open letter, caused him to peer earnestly around the room as if to assure himself that nobody was peeping over his shoulder.

Unless he was very much mistaken, *Cataract* documents were classified at the highest level, and everything remotely touching on it was probably locked away in a nuclear shelter in some remote part of Norfolk, never to be opened until the last trump.

Herbie knew about *Cataract* because he had been involved, as had the Provisional Irish Republican Army, and the Special Air Service (the PIRA and the SAS), not to mention the Office: the SIS. Shame and scandal in the family that is the British Government would heap embarrassment on great names should any of *Cataract* become public property.

For the first time, Big Herbie fully realized that his investigation of Gus Keene's long professional life, and his fast, horrible death, would be like a trip down the Burma Road, or even the Ho Chi Minh Trail. Long and arduous.

He scribbled in his diary, which was more a way to quieten his own soul than apprise anyone else of his most secret feelings, and took himself to bed, where he dreamed of rolling green hills and a faceless man who had followed him with deadly intent. He woke, sweating and alarmed, just after five, before the advent of the dawn chorus, and went out onto the landing, trying to find his way, fuddled and drunk with sleep, to the bathroom.

Returning to bed, he could not sleep. Gus penetrated his waking thoughts and he found himself worried about the mountain that had to be climbed. Finally, he dropped into sleep again, awakened by Ginger with coffee. 'She wanted to bring it to you, sir. But I thought that might be a bit iffy.'

'Very iffy, Ginger. Thanks.'

'Breakfast in half an hour.'

'Great,' which he did not mean. Herb wanted to close his eyes and retreat under the covers. With that realization he suddenly sat bolt upright, wide awake now. Why did he want to sleep and hide from the day? Gus, he thought. Gus, or Gus's ghost, warning him off. *List! List! Oh, list.* He saw with a new clarity that this journey down memory lane with Gus Keene was going to be bloody dangerous. Particularly if Gus had originally planned to publish details of *Cataract*. He could not have done this, Herb thought. Never in a hundred years. But there it was, last night anyway, on a computer-generated page, a letter no less, coming from a London publisher – which meant lord knew how many people had seen it – the very word *Cataract*.

Before heading for the dining-room – having showered, shaved, and dressed in record time, Kruger returned to Gus's study where he opened the red file again, just to make sure he had not dreamed it. It was there, just as it had been there last night, in a letter dated 28 May of this very year. 'For instance, we could sell the book on Operation *Cataract* alone,' the unknown, as yet unseen, Mark Collier had written.

Big Herbie felt considerably edgy as he walked into the dining-room.

'Herbie dear, what've you been doing? I thought I heard you come down ages ago.' Bitsy Williams was all done up in an elaborate black two-piece suit, saved from being severe by many gold buttons and piping around the collar and cuffs.

'Had to look something up.' He knew that it sounded like a lie and he put on his big daft grin. 'I'm in charge so I can come down when I like anyhow.'

'Of course you can, but I brought your breakfast through.'

She had cooked him bacon, two eggs and a fried slice, all beautifully arranged on a plate. A photograph in a Delia Smith book would not have come amiss.

'What you all dressed up like a dog's dinner for, Bits?'

'The inquest. Eleven o'clock. I'm to represent the Office. Deputy Chief Worboys called while you were, presumably, in the shower. Wants you to give him a tinkle when you're free. I told him you'd call soonest.'

Herbie nodded and attacked the bacon and eggs, not giving his cholesterol a second thought. 'You want Ginger for the inquest?' he asked Bitsy, but it was Ginger who replied, 'Kenny Boyden's driving, and Mickey Crichton's going to mind her.'

'I thought Mickey was with the widow Keene?'

'He is, but she doesn't seem to want him. Prudence is with her all the time. Mrs Keene's not good, guv'nor. It's sunk in and she's grieving hard. That's the word from the guest quarters. I think they've put her on something to help.'

Yes, he thought. Prudence. Pru Frost, that was the name he couldn't put to the female nurse. Why the hell hadn't they sent two females? Mickey was in Ginger's class: very good with his hands, and exceptional with a weapon. Someone up the Smoke, in the Office, was worried about the widow Keene, even though she was surrounded by the highest possible tech security.

He drank four cups of excellent coffee, asking Bitsy if she was expected to do all the cooking. 'I like cooking, Herb,' she said. But he made a note to ask Worboys to send them a very secure chef, and lumbered off to the study to call him, as instructed, and then begin the long journey back with Gus. *Dance to the Music of Time*, he thought: then, the Long March through the Organs, which was how the old-style KGB had once spoken of the recruiting of their long-term penetration agents.

As he was leaving, Ginger asked if he had heard the news.

'What news?'

'Four large briefcase bombs on the London underground. Waterloo, Paddington, King's Cross and Victoria.' These are all main-line railway stations, each served also by the network of London's Underground.

'Many casualties?'
'At least sixty. FFIRA's denying it.'
'You bet they are.'

The FFIRA had every right to deny the bombs, for the London cell of *Intiqam* had begun work early. Hisham, the two youngest members of the group – Ahmad and Nabil – together with Samira, the more fanatical of the two girls, had left their house in Clapham at half-hour intervals starting at six-thirty that morning. The other two members of the cell, Ramsi and Dinah, who, by no coincidence, was Jamilla's sister, waited. Dinah had done a pre-operational job in London, similar to the work her sister had carried out in the United States – readying documents, passports and visas throughout Europe, but without having to resort to any honeytrap ops.

Ramsi was the bomb-maker: a short, rather stout little man. The kind of person you did not look at twice. He was the only member of the *Intiqam* teams whose complexion was totally white. They could all pass as Europeans, but Ramsi, by some strange mixture of genetics, had a perfect peaches and cream pigment. The girls hated him for it. But they hated him for a number of things – the fact that he preferred boys to girls being only one. Before they left for the operation, Hisham had questioned the wisdom of taking Ramsi because of his sexual preference but to no avail. It was not considered at all odd where they came from but Hisham knew that here the man would have to go out and search for company. There was danger in that from a security point of view.

The London cell had opted for a pleasant Victorian house in Clapham. It stood, with several others of the same vintage, in one of the up-market areas, surrounded by a red-brick wall, trees and a garden which the girls tended, and, during the summer months, they had all enjoyed – sitting in deck-chairs on the lawn, and having small parties in the warm early evenings.

73

The four who had begun to leave so early straggled back, their work done, at around nine-thirty. Each had left a briefcase at designated spots, well hidden behind seats and trash cans on the underground stations. For Hisham, Ahmad, Samira and Dinah the day's work had not finished. During the morning and afternoon they took separate flights to Paris, where they booked into modest hotels, in pairs. Four young people off on a naughty short vacation in the City of Lights.

Herbie found that Young Worboys was having calls screened – even on his red, secure, line – by the lovely Emma, PA and something else, unless Herb had lost his intuition.

'Got a message,' he growled when Worboys came on.

'Herb.' Bright and full of spiritual friendship. 'Herb, the very man.'

'How much is it going to cost?'

'Come on, Herb. No screwing around. You got positives on what was left of Gus's Zippo and the little stick pin, I gather.'

'Only insofar as he carried a Zippo and wore a badge which she says was British Legion, but I don' think so.' He was proud of the 'insofar'.

'All we've got, old Herb. Personal trinkets. You try out the watch on her?'

'That would've been a bit heavy. She's suffering, Tony.'

'Well, you're going to *have* to show it.'

'Why?'

'Because the anti-terrorist cops'll want to have details of a definite ID for the inquest, plus the medical people say there's nothing else showing from the body – skeleton really.'

'Can't they reconstruct the head, like in that movie, *Gorky Park*, or the TV thing with the female copper: Helen Mirren? They can do that, Tony. They can build up the head from the skull. Something amazing.'

'Something bloody expensive as well, and yes, Herb, they can build it from a computer model which is what they *are* doing. Take a while though.'

'And in the meantime?'

'You've heard what happened here this morning?'

'I heard. Bad.'

'Yes, very bad. But there's interesting news as well. The two car bombs the same day as Gus bought it . . .'

'What about them?'

'They didn't come up smelling of Semtex. Dynamite, Herb. Same as Gus, but I doubt if we'll get a match. It's going to be difficult to trace batches.'

'Better than nothing. What am I supposed to be doing, apart from raking through the ashes of old Gus's life?'

'The anti-terrorist people want a definite ID and you'll do the statement. Signed ID from Carole on the three items. I've faxed it through, and one of the girls is typing it up at the house now. All you have to do is show her the stuff, get an okay, and we can get a release. Everyone goes away from the inquest happy.'

After a long silence Herb said OK, he would do it. 'You faxed through a statement for me as well?'

'Of course. Be grateful if you'd give us a call when it's all done. Oh, and they're sending down a DCI from Anti-Terrorist as soon as we can do a clearance. You need much time before that happens?'

'A few days might be useful.'

'I'll stave it off for as long as I can without them smelling the proverbial rodent.'

'Tickety-Boo.' That was a First World War expression. An older member of the Office had told him once, a long time ago, and he did not have a clue what it meant but thought it sounded whimsical.

He went upstairs, unlocked his briefcase and took out the three evidence bags. Removing the watch he sat on the bed and examined it: a block of metal, but a child of four could have told you it was a watch. The face had gone and the movement had melted together, but the steel casing was intact, while the band, though fused, still showed the Rolex Crown on the clasp.

Herbie dropped it back in its bag, went downstairs and was about to lock the door to Gus's study when the internal phone began to ring. The main house wanted to know if they could pick him up for a visit to the Guest Quarters.

Carole was really very good. She was being watched like a surveillance camera by the omnipresent Pru Frost, a tall girl who moved like a giraffe, sandy hair cut short, every inch of her a nurse, and very caring – or so they said.

Carole gave him a big hug, and he made it as easy as possible for her, bringing out all three pieces and moving her through them, gently and firmly.

'Don't really know about the pin thing,' she said. 'Truly I never took that much notice of it. He only wore it occasionally, but it *was* in his lapel that night.' She was starting to distance herself, or it might have been whatever they were feeding her to keep her together until it was all over. 'But I guess that's the lighter, and that's certainly a Rolex. He always carried the lighter and wore the Rolex to bed. If that's all that's left, well . . .' She did break down for a moment then, but pulled herself together, signing the formal identification of her late husband's effects, using Pru and a girl from the main house as witnesses.

Herbie gave her another hug, told her, 'Courage,' and went back to the Dower House after getting the girls to witness his signature on the other document. It all took less than three-quarters of an hour, door to door.

Bitsy was still hovering, waiting for her car and escort, peeping constantly in the small circular mirror in the hall. Preening, Herbie thought. Woman's stuff.

'All done,' Kruger told Worboys on the secure line.

'Then you can expect some cops – coroner's court officers – in about half an hour. *You* don't need to be there – in the court, I mean – and one of the cops'll do a little statement to establish what the Americans call the chain of evidence.'

'I think we also call it that. Us Brits, I mean, Tony.'

'Probably. I just want all this done, then we'll deal with the funeral.'

'Yes, about that—'

'Later, Herb.'

'To hear is to obey.'

'That's it.'

'Oh, Tony, give a minute, uhu?'

'I have to get on, Herb.'

'We need a chef down here. Deaf, dumb and blind. Can't let Bitsy do all the housekeeping.'

'Why not?'

'Ever heard of liberated women, Tony?'

'Well, I can't promise, but . . . well, I'll try.'

The cops came in less than half an hour. They must have had the lights flashing and sirens on all the way, Herb thought. The transaction was very serious stuff. No smiles and only what might be called terse handshakes after Kruger had signed his life away in triplicate.

Once Bitsy had left, driven and guarded by the boys, like a gangster's moll going to a trial, Herbie considered, he went back into the haunted study and sat down at the long table.

Now, he thought, I am under starter's orders. Let us see what Gus has got squirrelled away here.

He picked out a thick ring binder at random – right out of the middle of one of the piles – opened it and almost stopped breathing. Here, in this house, admittedly within the protected circle of Warminster – Fenley Hall, if you wanted to be 200 per cent accurate – he was holding the entire detailed documentation of what had been called *Operation Cataract*. A tale so awash with moral corruption that it had power to harm even now, ten years after the event and, presumably, for much longer.

'What were you up to, Gus?' he asked the book-lined walls. '*Gott in Himmel*, what were you doing with these?'

6

The series of incidents which finally became *Cataract*
began in the January of 1984, while Big Herbie was
still officially a member of the Office, with his own
little cubbyhole away from the big steel and concrete
building which everyone knew was the hub of the secret
universe: Head Office. Herbie Kruger's operations ran
out of what they called the Whitehall Annex and he was
closer to going private – in plain language, retiring – than
he knew.

Kruger had already been through what many thought
of as a mid-life crisis. In a fit of pique, following an
incident in the field which had left him slightly
wounded, Herb had married his former agent Martha
Adler and put in his papers.

So, he had resigned from the Office and set up
a permanent home with his bride, in a pretty cottage
close by the New Forest. For several months things
were quiet. Then, almost exactly one year later, Herbie
was back at the front door, pleading to return to what
he described as 'a life of relative peace away from
relatives'. Later, he was to try and patch things up
with Martha, but the marriage had obviously never
really begun its take-off run, let alone got off the
ground.

Those who knew him best thought that Martha was
good for him as a companion, but there was little doubt
that, as a pair of lovebirds, life for the couple was really
a permanent squawking fight and feud.

So it was that, on this January morning, nursing a
cold and in a filthy temper, Herbie arrived at the Annex
some fifty-five minutes later than usual, the journey in,

from what they called his grace and favour apartment in St John's Wood, having taken for ever.

At that time, he was stuck with a junior officer called Vicki Grismer, a young woman of immense charm, a lot of guile – which, in the Service, is a compliment – and a heavy crush on Young Worboys who had recently been elevated to the field, his particular corner of which was Belfast.

'Mr Worboys's been on from Belfast, sir.' Vicki shook out her pretty blonde hair which she had been tending with a hand-held drier in what they laughingly called the kitchen. She had been soaked during the last long splash and scurry down Whitehall to the Annex.

'Tony Worboys?' Herbie made the noises of a puppy drying itself off. 'Sodding rain. Coming down like cats and dogs out there.'

'He would like you to call him back. He said urgent, on his second number.'

'Shit! Sorry, Vic.' He sneezed.

'I know all the words, sir. No need to be coy with me. Life is not PG.'

'And will you stop calling me sir. His second number?'

'That's what he said.'

'Hell.' Tony had obviously called the Annex from his one and only secure line, and now he was out and about with an iffy telephone. Herb dredged out the number marked 'Two', prised his bulk into a chair and began to dial. One of his new chores was fixer and liaison to Tony who ran things in the British province known usually as Northern Ireland; mainly from Belfast, but occasionally even from the bandit country of Armagh and County Fermanagh, along the border. Dangerous as hell.

The distant end bripped and Tony's voice said, 'Sutton, yes?'

'Wilf here.' Only Herbie pronounced it Vilf.

'Joker,' said Tony.

'Oh, shit. I have to?'

'Yes.' The line went dead.

Herbie grumbled and rummaged for biscuits and coffee in the kitchen, calling through to the delightful Ms Grismer, 'Vic, book me one return tomorrow morning. Air Linctus. London–Dublin, Dublin–London, all in one day. Tomorrow, Okay?'

'You get all the fun, sir – I mean, Herbie. Far away places with strange-sounding names.'

'Sure. What you do with those Custard Creams, Vic?'

'We're out. I had the last one yesterday.'

'Nobody ever tell you that you're a granite?'

'Never, and I think you mean gannet.'

'Whatever.'

At noon the next morning, Herbie sat in Bewley's of Grafton Street. The low-pressure system which had brought the freezing, pouring rain to London on the previous day had moved, overnight, to Dublin. Outside, a roof of umbrellas jostled up and down Grafton Street, and there was the smell of damp raincoat mixed with cooking in the warm, safe womb that was Bewley's.

Bewley's was the one thing Herb really liked about Dublin. Sure, on a sunny day the city had a charm of its own, and a lot to recommend it, but somehow he felt at home in Bewley's. He liked the waitresses in their brown and white uniforms and their blarney banter, and he loved the food. There were ketchup bottles and vinegar on all the tables and that was the kind of thing he appreciated. Once, he had read that Bewley's was the last bastion of the decadent fairy cake, those little tit-shaped concoctions, in corrugated paper with a half-cherry nipple on top. Big Herbie Kruger liked fairy cakes. Bewley's made up for the crack-of-dawn rise and the hour's ride in a 737 from Heathrow to Dublin International: focal point of the universe.

Tony Worboys' trip had been slightly more dangerous. People in his position did not like to advertise their presence in the South – in the Republic – so he had made a journey 102 times more dangerous. In fact he had moved, silent and alone but for two members of the

SAS watching his back, through one of the known illegal border crossings of Armagh where there was always the chance of coming face to face with a team of Provos up to death and destruction. On this occasion he had break-fasted in a grey bungalow castle of a place in Dundalk. A staging post for friends who had to make clandestine hops from north to south.

His return would be easier and even more illegal, for a military helicopter would dubiously nip across and lift him from a field.

Here and now, Tony walked into Bewley's, looking like a visiting farmer, hailing Herbie in a brogue you could have cut with a pair of blunt scissors.

They ordered from a cheeky waitress who was bent on telling them that she had seen that lovable little ET only the night before – and she did not mean at the 'filums' as she would have pronounced it. Bewley's employed a number of fey waitresses to supply atmosphere.

The huge plates of double fish and chips arrived, followed by pots of tea and piles of bread and butter. Tony spoke very low as they ate.

'This isn't a whisper, Herb. This is for real and it's bloody urgent.' He slid an envelope under the table, 'In case I get disintegrated.'

His story came from a source deep within the Provos; a source so secret that he lived in constant terror, but always came back for more, because the money was good and he really did not believe in the *Cause*. The source, plus what they called Elint – gee-whiz electronics that plucked conversations out of the air without the aid of wires and bugs.

'A new, specially recruited Active Service Unit,' Tony said in almost a whisper. 'Details in the envelope. Two men and two women. Hard as nails and all with a lot of experience.'

'We know when?'

'Within the month is all, but they *are* specialists, each

one of them, and their operation is called *Kingmaker*, work that one out for size.'

'Shouldn't I pass it to our sisters?' Herb meant the Security Service.

'Doubt it. These lads and lasses need stopping before they start. If our sisters get it, they'll put the Special Plod onto them and that means the usual bloody tie-down. Years in court trying to prove the impossible. These people've got to be stopped dead, if you follow me.'

'We do this off our own cricket bats? Pin them down, then bring in the plod?'

'No, you idiot. I'm suggesting that we take care of it quietly. Maybe a case of terminal accident. The last thing anyone wants is some cock-eyed arrest followed by indignant shouts and demos. Take it high up the chain but nowhere near the top if you can help it. This is *very* serious and we have an early warning, so we should make use of it. Could be done before they leave the North if necessary.'

They talked for the best part of two hours, then parted, right there in Bewley's with Tony leaving first, Herb ordering two fairy cakes, eating them, then paying the bill and pushing outside into the rain to get a cab back to the airport where he waited for two hours for a flight to Heathrow.

On the following morning, having examined everything in Tony's envelope in the privacy of St John's Wood, Herbie met with the group known as Co-ordination A. He had telephoned Head Office and used the word 'Amber' which was the way you did things in those days. The top brass were always careful not to get involved with an 'Amber' operation for they were usually what the Americans called 'Black' – in other words an operation which almost certainly broke the law.

Co-ordination A – one of those permanent committees always around to deal with things like this – consisted of Apted, a bellicose former field officer who knew the North and its troubles from way back; Archie Blount-Wilson, known in the trade as The Whizzer, a man with a penchant for splendidly tailored grey suits, and striped shirts with lots of cuff showing off gold links. The Whizzer sported iron grey hair and his contacts in Whitehall and government were legendary. He was their link with the mandarins of Whitehall. Last, there were two Fixers, Parsons and Deacon by name; called, for obvious reasons, the Church Militants, for they always worked together and had a dual reputation of taking short cuts but always coming up smelling of roses.

They met in a very secure basement room and Big Herbie told the story, showed the pictures, and brought forth the worried looks.

'Should really go to the sisters,' Apted began. 'But I can see why Tony's shy of that.'

'By all that's holy, we should bypass the sisters and go straight to the Minister who will probably seek refuge with the PM, then heaven knows what'll happen.'

The Church Militants remained silent, though their looks spoke of cutting corners and death by any possible means.

'Personally,' Apted was off on a short monologue, 'personally, if the target's as big as this, we should just get some of Tony's thugs to kill them where they are. The trouble is, though, that the Provos are bloody hydra-headed. Cut off an arm and they grow a more dangerous claw. Object of the exercise is really to let them get in, lay their plans, then take 'em out. More tricky, but the best solution.'

'We don't know exactly where or when?' The Whizzer asked.

'We know a lot, including the names.' Herbie touched the grainy prints. 'Names and records. These guys are dangerous.'

'Might I suggest the JIC . . . ?' The Whizzer began, and was howled down. Give it to the Joint Intelligence

Committee and they would still be arguing come Dooms-day.

'Look, Whizz,' Herbie's eyes became shifty. 'Whiz, old sheep, this is real world stuff. The target's clear enough and they're out for what they call a spectacular. Got to be stopped.'

'Then how if I idle along to the Minister and get the green light?'

'You mean do it ourselves?'

'Well, not exactly ourselves. I mean nothing on paper, but a nice nod from the Minister, and a wink from the PM's office.'

So it was decided. Wrongly as it turned out, but it seemed to be for the best at the time. From that moment on they all spoke of the target as *Rich and Famous*. The real name was never mentioned, not even in the dramas that followed.

From what little came out at a much later date, The Whizzer went to the Minister who immediately, in a careful moment of watching his own back and making sure that he would never take the fall – mixed, of course, with personal panic – decided that COBRA had to be informed. This was too serious a matter to be left to him.

COBRA, as everyone knows, is the acronym for Cabinet Office Briefing Room Annex and is the place where the government's own crisis-control committee meets to decide action when there is a national state of emergency.

COBRA had first shot itself into the consciousness of the general public in 1980, during the infamous siege of the Iranian Embassy, which ended in an effective bloodbath: the blood coming from the terrorists who had held hostages within the embassy for six days; the blood brought forth by members of the SAS who negotiated only with Heckler & Koch machine pistols, 9mm automatics and stun grenades; the blood called out by COBRA.

It was noted, at that time, that the SAS looked strangely like terrorists themselves in their black ski-masks and nondescript uniforms. There was no doubt, on that occasion, that COBRA had ordered the assault, just as the public were told exactly who sat and made the final decisions in the Cabinet Office Briefing Room Annex.

On *this* occasion, people could only presume, later of course, that men and women in very high places had authorized what became known as *Cataract*. No names ever appeared in the Press, nothing came out regarding who sat on COBRA, but authorization was undoubtedly given to the members of Co-ordination A, who were also never named – 'Thank God for political ambition,' as The Whizzer put it.

The green light came within twenty-four hours, though under the strange compartmentalism of the Office as it operated at the time, not even the Chief was told what might, and eventually did, happen. There were odd whispers that something was in the wind, but details were kept locked in certain people's heads, or in safes with particularly sensitive combinations.

So, now there were three definite kinds of performer in the drama: those who officially knew that the Provos were about to launch a very special Active Service Unit into the field – which meant the UK mainland – and could not deny their knowledge should anything go wrong; those who had the same information but, for one reason or another, *would* deny they knew it if there were some mishap; lastly, those who knew, whose real names would never come out, but who were in very definite danger by way of their enlightenment. These latter were now joined by a fourth contingent – Tony Worboys' dirty twelve; several police officers, who came in at the last minute; and the four members of the Special Air Service who only knew details a few hours before they went to do what they did best.

In the here and now, in the late Gus Keene's study in

the Dower House, Big Herbie Kruger turned the page and saw the documents giving the records of the four members of the Provisional Irish Republican Army who had been chosen to carry out what they called *Kingmaker*. In his head he saw them on videotape and during the final terrible moment in the West End of London, not a stone's throw from Oxford and Regent Streets.

He looked down the pages and did not even have to read the dossiers, for the facts surrounding the quartet were engraved on his memory like the songs he had learned in childhood.

All four were in their early thirties – children of the revolution; confirmed in the idea that the British Security Forces in Northern Ireland – brought in during the late 1960s to stop Protestant and Catholic from tearing out each other's throats – were an illegal occupying army, and the British people fair game for death, as they tried to pressure world opinion into the common cry of Brits Out.

Mary Frances Duggan. A lucid, vocal young woman whose quest for the ideal had made her a courier for the Provos at the age of ten, and almost certainly a bomb-maker of terrifying expertise by the age of twenty-two, for she had won a scholarship to Trinity College, Dublin, and crossed the border to read physics. A credit to her respectable family.

John Michael Connor. Born 1953. Intelligent, but with little schooling. Arrested as a teenage rock hurler. Known killer. Shrewd and practised in the art of guerrilla warfare Provo style.

Patrick Sean Glass. Schoolmate and cellmate to Connor. Suspected bomb planter. Known, but un-provable, close-up killer with knife and gun.

Ann Bridget Bolan. Provo groupie, father in banking and almost certainly one of the Provos' accountants.

These were the Gang of Four, as they came to be known among that little group of cognoscenti who had the ball of destiny in their hands. The quartet had everything going for them, except the fact that some long-playing traitor had already shopped them, and, through the miracle of electronic eavesdropping, they had also incriminated themselves.

Enter Tony Worboys' Dirty Twelve. Worboys' own private army of watchers and followers, none of whom realized they were in the pay of the British Secret Intelligence Service. They latched on to the members of the Gang of Four on the day after the Office gave Tony the thumbs up, and stuck with each of them, individually, either by stand-off eyeballing, or the more sophisticated microwave electronics, by spiking houses, directing mikes at windows, using the current Star Wars Technology – as it was known in the trade.

So, they had the lot; then Herbie's people waited for their arrival, well primed and with malice aforethought. In one case – Patrick Glass's – they knew so far in advance that the two-man team assigned to him had time for another beer before driving lazily to Heathrow and still had to cool their heels waiting for the arrival of the plane from Paris.

There was a lot of tradecraft employed by the Gang of Four. Too much, many said. Take Glass for a start. Out of Belfast to Orly. Whoring around Paris for two days, then a direct flight into Heathrow with a German passport.

Ann Bolan and Michael Connor arrived as a honeymoon couple from the Republic, straight out of Dublin and into Heathrow with the confetti in their hair and a first night of unbridled pleasure at the Post House Hotel, Heathrow.

Only the most dangerous, Mary Duggan, bomb-maker and zealot, almost had them snookered, for she disappeared altogether on the third day of watching. There one minute and gone the next. Tony was screaming and blaspheming at his private army, but that did no good and it was not until Mary Frances Duggan turned up at the house in the little cul-de-sac that everyone breathed a sigh of relief.

The team was there, gathered together in this tributary among the maze of streets running between Oxford and Regent Streets which, Herbie's people maintained, was obviously the bomb factory. They had listened, they said; they had used their sophisticated equipment, they said. Lethal stuff was inside the building and it was too close for comfort, in the centre of London's West End. The clock was ticking and Co-ordination A sat down in its bug-proof, sound-proof shelter to decide when and how they should strike.

The Whizz said, as they had the thumbs up and the complete co-operation of the Met, the sooner the better. Apted advised killing the buggers there and then, within the next ten minutes, and was backed up by the Church Militants, with hard faces and chopping motions. Herb wanted everything above board and insisted that The Whizz go to the Minister, and the Minister to COBRA, just to get the final nod.

The Whizz adjusted the cuffs on his Turnbull & Asser white and blue striped shirt, straightened his plain silk tie, and went off into the night to get the final go-ahead by word of mouth – 'Nothing in writing, Whizz,' the Minister was supposed to have said. 'Just do it, and let's all pray the Press applaud saving the target.' He did not use the codewords *Rich and Famous*, nor the true name, which – even after the event – did not appear in any official document.

It took three hours for The Whizz to talk with the Minister, and the Minister to alert COBRA, then give The Whizz the okay, so that when he returned to the little committee it was almost one in the morning. At one-thirty *Cataract* came into being. By one thirty-five it was up and running. Four members of the SAS were flying down from their base at Sterling Lines, just outside Hereford. The final briefing took place at four-thirty a.m.

Herbie remembered the tension, and recalled being surprised that one of the young soldiers, the captain in charge, smoked throughout. A Colonel came with them, and he became, together with a Commander of the Metropolitan Police, the eventual villains. It was stressed that the four SAS men should only resort to 'termination', as they called it, if their lives were in danger, and, only then, if they had been given the codeword *Bailiff* by either the Colonel or the Commander.

The area close by the West End cul-de-sac was owned by the police at around six in the morning, and Herbie sat, with Apted and The Whizz, in a communications and control van parked with police protection close to Liberty's in Regent Street, a quarter of a mile from the actual site of the bomb factory, yet with full colour and sound on monitors fed by three cameras brought in by what the Office euphemistically called Technical Support.

At just after nine, the door to the narrow little three-storey house opened and the Gang of Four came out into the raw cold morning air without a care in the world. The door was hardly closed behind them when the first two SAS men came into the picture, seeming to materialize from the far end of the cul-de-sac. At the time, Apted whispered, 'Christ, they can walk through walls.'

There was a moment of indecision. Of all the dramatis personae, Herb remembered young Ann Bolan's face running through a series of emotions ranging from surprise to puzzlement and, finally, to terror, as a voice off camera shouted, 'Police! Stop! Stand still!'

The owner of the voice, in fact the SAS captain himself, came into view a moment later, blocking the camera angle for a couple of seconds, but giving a full view on camera and tape of Mary Duggan reaching for her shoulder bag. Everyone heard the word 'Bailiff!' very clearly in their headphones, though, during the later hassle, nobody identified the voice.

On screen it was sickening and almost in slow motion. Mary Duggan was lifted off her feet, her chest exploding crimson and the shots hurting eardrums – the noise, in fact, blew out one of the mikes. The other three had all moved: Ann Bolan in panic, hands moving towards Patrick Glass, while Patrick seemed, in a reflex, to go for a gun that was not there. Michael Connor tried to run towards the only possible exit, blocked by the SAS captain and the fourth soldier. He ran two steps forward and then slid six steps back, his body whirling like a dancer, spinning in the crisp winter air to land, blood-soaked, across the body of Patrick Glass.

There were nine shots. Counted, heard and logged. Nine shots, four bodies. Then the SAS team disappeared, literally like magic, whisked away in police cars, while other cars and a pair of ambulances came haring in, sirens screaming.

One hour later, sitting in the Annex, with Vicki Grismer typing away as Herbie dictated, and Apted sat looking grim-faced, the telephone rang.

'We're going to need some damage control,' The Whizz said, and Herbie felt, rather than heard, the disquiet in his voice. 'There's nothing in the house.'

There was nothing: not a gun, not even a marble-sized piece of explosive; no primers, no wire, no batteries, no electronics, not even a child's cap pistol. The Minister and COBRA were busy denying everything, while the politicos from the opposition to highly-placed members of the government were screaming for a compete in-depth investigation by an outside team.

The Massacre of the Innocents? one hypocritical newspaper headline brayed that very afternoon, while, by the following morning, solicitors had already been retained by the families of the deceased Gang of Four. They were out to sue the British authorities for collective murder, and there was not even time or means to plant Semtex or weapons at the supposed bomb factory. The first Press Release actually called it a bomb factory and referred to the Gang of Four as known armed terrorists.

So, for the first time in that particular story, Gus Keene walked on, stage left – *a sinister* – and gave the performance of a lifetime.

Herbie riffled through the thick pages of documents which gave the true and complete story, and realized that this was only one small job in Gus, the Confessor's, life. Yet it was the one which, presumably, gave the IRA – or any of their successors – the right to make him a prime target even ten years later.

He heard the outer door slam and physically jumped, trying to make himself smaller, hearing again the terrible thud of bullets on that cold morning.

Bitsy Williams was back with the news that the Coroner had ruled in Gus's Death. Murder by person or persons unknown. Probably members of an unnamed terrorist organization.

'That make sense to you, Herb?' she asked. He nodded, and she then asked if he had heard the news from the States.

'What news?'

She related the three news stories they had heard in the car on the way back from the inquest. The car bomb in Manhattan, the explosion in the New York subway, and the awful tale of a Boeing 737 blowing up in mid-air.

'It's getting like Beirut and Bosnia,' he muttered. Then, as it suddenly stuck him, 'I wonder if they're the same crew that did the London underground?'

'Hardly,' Bitsy looked toffee-nosed. 'Look at the time factor.'

'You ever been on Concorde?' Herbie sounded like a man who had scored a good point.

7

Herbie recalled that afternoon, in 1984, as clearly as he could remember the conversation during dinner at the Indian on the previous night. He could smell the coffee, and Vicki's scent as she bent to the IBM typewriter, taking his dictation straight onto paper. Then there was Apted, and he realized that it was at some point during the long wait, getting a prepared statement down on paper, that he discovered Apted's first name – Cyril. Cyril Apted who, it turned out, knew more about the Provos than any of them, for he had watched the danger of the North from the beginning of the present troubles. That was 1969, when Protestant and Catholic met head-on in the streets of Belfast and Derry, and the blood-lust began again, for Ireland had been the UK's Vietnam since Good Queen Bess' Golden Days, and long before that. In 1969, 14 August to be exact, the Protestants tried to give the bum's rush to the Catholics. Tried to burn them from their homes. Tried to smash into their communities. Cyril told Herb that he had been there that afternoon, when it began, about teatime.

'Yes, it's Cyril,' Apted said with a sly smile. 'Could've killed my old man. Not a name I often own to.' He, as Herb knew, had owned to quite a number of different names in his time. At the Office there was a rumour that their sister service had Apted on their payroll as well. Cyril Apted, the Security Service's long-term penetration within the intelligence service.

'Best do a resignation as well, while you're preparing that statement,' Cyril said at one point. 'They're going to shoot us like fish in a barrel.'

'You sending in your papers then?' Herb asked between trying to work out sentences, with Vicki doing her best to correct his grammar.

'Me? Don't need to, old Herb. Me? I'm the cat with nine lives and I'm only on number five. Think I'll go for a stroll and see if I can tie up some loose ends. I'll see you later, so.' This last in a quick Irish brogue.

So Herbie prepared his statement, not knowing that Gus had already taken over and was sending people shooting around town doing good works; lighting bombs under them; doing, not just thinking; waving, not just drowning.

At around five, The Whizz called to say get the evening papers. 'Our bloody horoscopes prophesy death and disaster. Oh, yes. The Chief's gone off to the South of France and his closest Deputy's caught the first plane to Malta. No forwarding addresses.'

So Herb sent Vicki out to get the papers and she came back white-faced. Until then, Herbie had hoped that, by some miracle, the Press would trumpet a victory against the evil and illegal army in the North of Ireland, but they were taking the high moral ground. One of the evening papers had even hired a famous novelist, whose beat was the secret world and Whitehall, to put down the guidelines. 'Can we stand by and see murder done in our streets by trained thugs who hide behind the government's skirts, to shoot first and ask questions later? Questions *must* be asked now.' He went on to say something about seeing a glint of granite death in the eyes of policemen on the beat that day.

The lead story described the killings inaccurately and with an overabundance of gore, while the big news was that the PM had made a statement at two o'clock that afternoon. The words, as they often are, were fighting words, chock-full of reasonableness. A full and exhaustive inquiry would be undertaken. A judicial inquiry, by men and women who stood only by truth. 'London is not a boom town of the old Wild West,' the PM had said.

'If these deaths are, in fact, the result of illegality, and turn out to lie at the door of any government or police agency, then the true culprits will be brought to justice. But I suspect we shall find they can be laid at the door of the heartless and cowardly men of the Provisional Irish Republican Army.'

The Minister had stated that he had not been informed of any irregular operations being run against terrorists, and, no, certainly not, COBRA had not met for months.

Big Herbie Kruger prepared his second resignation. Then, around six in the evening, when he was wondering if it was worth while going home only to be called back in again, the Church Militants – Messrs Parsons and Deacon – arrived, their faces wreathed in smiles and their eyes glittering with hope.

'Got the buggers,' Billy Parsons said, as though that explained everything.

'Bloody Met. Should have done their job with more care,' from Dave Deacon.

'Which buggers and what care?' Herbie asked, a shade angrily. Parsons and Deacon were, in fact, on his payroll. His responsibility.

'We were sent back.'

'With a couple of senior police officers.'

'Couple of Chief Supers.'

'Told to pull the place apart.'

They were like a pair of old Music Hall fast comedy men – Boom-Boom.

'What place?' Herbie asked, suspicious to the hilt.

'Bloody bomb factory,' Parsons.

'Where the Micks got chopped,' Deacon, arms outstretched as though he were about to do a buck and wing.

'What you talking about?'

'We was sent back to the bomb factory. Scotland Yard, it seems, gave it only the most cursory going over.'

'So?'

'So we tossed the drum proper.' Again the boom-boom tag line from Deacon which, oddly, Herbie understood very well. It meant they had torn the place apart.

'And?' Herb asked.

'And we come up with the goods. Four nine-mill auto shooters, an Uzi and all their maps, plus some codewords, and a very interesting diary.'

'Very sloppy tradecraft.'

'Really?'

'Of course, really. In front of the two Chief Supers. They took Polaroid pictures, time and date stuff. All Sir Garnet.'

'Sir which?' For a second, Herbie was lost.

'All jonnick.'

'Honest,' Parsons finally translated. 'Honest, above board, Mr Kruger. Straight up, only they were under the floorboards.'

'And who told you to return, go back?'

'Mr Keene, sir. He's, like, in charge of what they're calling damage control. Good, isn't he, Bill?'

'Shit hot. Oh, sorry, Miss.' Vicki waved her hand, as though swatting a fly.

'Mr Keene told you exactly what?' Kruger lowered his head, like a charging bull, and gazed at the pair with an undisguised malevolence.

'He said he did not think the plod had done the place over thoroughly enough. Said it *in front* of the plod, Mr Kruger. Told us to go back and find something. Anything. The plod were to be witnesses.'

'And repeat what you found.'

'Four nine-mill Brownings and enough ammo to blow away the Horse Guards. Also a pouch full of maps and drawings . . .'

'And the diary with instructions and codewords for using on the blower.'

'They'd committed these things to paper?'

'Stupid of them, eh?'

At that moment the telephone rang and The Whizz

was on the other end, breathless. 'Herb, you heard the good news?'

'Which particular piece of good news we talking about?'

'The cache of stuff at what we thought was the bomb factory for starters. Then there's . . .'

'You got Gus Keene there, giving orders?'

'Gus's in charge, actually, thank God.'

'So.'

'So, he wants you to attend a little soirée he's holding over here at the witching hour.'

'You mean midnight?'

'Twenty-three fifty-nine to use army lingo, yes. Everyone's going to be there. Old chums' reunion.'

The Whizz sounded so relieved that Kruger could hardly believe what he was hearing. Though he never at any future point admitted it to anyone, there was always a lingering doubt in his mind about the cache discovered at the so-called bomb factory. If he reached deep into his conscience, he had doubts about a great number of things concerning the saving of *Cataract*, but one fact could never be denied. Gus Keene made all the right moves and saved the day magnificently.

They met, like plotters, at midnight at Head Office. Deep in what were known as the bunkers. To be exact, Briefing Room Two which was all done up like a private screening theatre, with plush seats, subdued lighting and facilities for everything. All that was missing was the organ that rises from the bowels of the earth, following the bouncing ball, and usherettes – as they used to be called – ready to serve choc-ices from those little trays hung around their necks by straps.

Instead there were coffee and sandwiches. Smoked salmon to be precise, and as The Whizz had predicted, *everyone* was there, including Tony Worboys looking content and more like a city broker than an Irish farmer, and the SAS team with their Colonel, plus a large contingent of cops.

Gus Keene was certainly there. Tall, imposing, his dark hair falling limply across his leathery brow. Completely imperturbable, and very much on the ball.

'We have to take care of certain matters,' he began. 'The general reaction to the quite lawful killing of four terrorists this morning appears to have boomeranged and it is our job to get the facts across. This I propose to do in the Coroner's Court, and I have already applied for anonymity for both members of my service and for the gentlemen from the SAS. Also for certain police officers. The Prime Minister may bleat about judicial inquiries, but we don't need them, and we *shall* avoid such a thing, even though the latest intelligence is that the families of the dead terrorists are planning legal action against HM Government. In Ireland the deaths are seen as overkill.'

He went on, carefully enumerating the weak points – 'The weaknesses of our case, and how they will be dealt with,' as he put it.

First, there was the time frame. Officialdom, to save their scented backsides, had openly divorced themselves from the whole business. This called, Gus maintained, for a defence which showed everything happened so quickly and in such a potentially dangerous order, that there was no time for the niceties of establishing a political chain of command. He brought on Tony Worboys, who carried with him a series of tape recordings: conversations filched from telephones and snatched from the air.

Herbie listened to these with a growing interest, for all four members of the Active Service Unit were heard planning the monstrous act, their voices captured, clear and unmistakable, by every kind of microphone that existed in the business. There was even a last-minute telephone conversation between Mary Frances Duggan and her Battalion Commander who was giving her the 'Go'.

'It's too fast,' she had remonstrated.

'It's the only chance you'll have to get *Lancer* in your

sights before the summer. I need this thing doing now, so do it, and get the bloody thing over with.'

Suddenly, as he listened, Herbie recalled from the trivia stored in his mind that their crypto – *Lancer* – for the target – *Rich and Famous* as they had nominated – was the crypto in use by the United States Secret Service for John F. Kennedy on the day of *his* assassination.

It was also clear that the argument was going to be that Tony discovered the operation a bare twenty-four hours before the attempted arrests. With amazement he realized that Tony's original telephone call, plus his own trip to Dublin, were being cut from the history which had been skilfully rewritten.

Gus next called in the watchers, alerted by himself, who had latched on to the four identified members of the Provos' unit. Gus was not just sorting things out, but making himself the major actor. The watchers, one by one, stood up to be counted, giving evidence of the way they had identified and followed the Gang of Four. The exception was the team – a man and woman – who had lost Mary Frances Duggan for several hours.

'This', Gus said, 'could now happily be accounted for. Cyril?' speaking to Apted who climbed onto the platform like a phantom and asked if the projectionist was ready.

That very afternoon, he told them, he had gone to see some of his friends in their sister service. He had remembered that he had a knowledge of a surveillance operation they were running on a house in Camberwell. The house was a suspected Provo safe house, and there was a tiny piece of evidence which could mean that explosives, and other bomb-making items, were being stored there.

His friends in the surveillance operation had been most co-operative and provided him with some photographs, and there, suddenly, like a surprise witness at a murder trial, were a series of grainy black and whites which showed Mary Frances Duggan arriving at the

Camberwell house. Then a tape captured by a stand-off mike which caught a conversation from vibrations from one of the windows.

The tape told them little, but that little could easily be worked up into damning evidence. Then there were more pictures, time and date-stamped like the previous ones, of Mary Frances Duggan leaving the house.

'I am pleased to tell you,' Gus continued, almost pushing Apted out of the way, 'that the Camberwell house was raided earlier this evening by Special Branch *with an SAS back-up team.*'

This was considered prudent when you bore in mind the events of the morning. Five people had been arrested and a considerable amount of explosives, together with all the other paraphernalia of bomb-makers, had been removed. The most interesting discovery had been a bomb in actual preparation, with an electronic remote control made from a converted walkie-talkie.

This, Gus claimed, was the bomb that would have been used on this very day to murder. He purposely did not use the true identity of the royal target, but gave the two cryptos: the Provos' – *Lancer*, and theirs – *Rich and Famous*.

Finally, he switched to the events of the previous morning, for it was now almost one-thirty in the morning of day two. He described how he, as duty officer, had received the news of the imminent threat together with the evidence that the assassination team were holed up in what they truly thought was a bomb factory in the middle of the West End of London.

'I shall simply tell the truth,' he lied. 'How a decision was made between myself, people on a committee within my organization, and a senior police officer at Scotland Yard.' He then played some further evidence tapes that were very real, and included conversations between the Gang of Four in their hide-out in the warren of streets running between Regent and Oxford Streets.

Herbie had already heard those tapes, and the evidence was damning if only because the four Provos had said, clearly and unequivocally, that their operation was on for that day. No coroner, nor – come to that – judicial inquiry, could possibly have a problem with those particular conversations.

The Commander from Scotland Yard went up at Gus's bidding and did his thing, saying that he had asked for, and got, a small SAS detachment from Hereford. It was his belief that the situation was, as he put it, 'Exceptionally dangerous and could possibly become a siege, which, in turn, could become a suicide bombing which might devastate a whole section of the West End. At that point, we all believed that considerable amounts of explosive were in *that* house. Therefore, I felt a fast-action professional team was essential.'

Gus did some cross-examination, which Kruger remembered as being tremendously professional.

'Are you aware of the rules of engagement regarding members of Her Majesty's Armed Services and terrorist groups?'

'Yes.'

'Then why didn't you seek out someone with the necessary authority? It appears that you, together with certain other officers, just went out of your way to exacerbate an already dangerous situation.' The 'certain other officers' were, of course, members of the Intelligence community, but in those days nobody ever said 'Secret Intelligence Service' aloud. There *was* an unspoken arrangement with the Security Service to the effect that, should an SIS officer have to appear incognito as a trial witness, the SIS brother or sister would be referred to as a member of the Security *Forces* – doublespeak-spookspeak.

'It was my opinion, and my judgement,' the Commander was very smooth, 'that a token force of SAS soldiers would be helpful in making certain the arrests took place with minimum danger to the general public.'

'In the final analysis, the danger was to the four poor

young men and women within the house,' Gus drawled, like a barrister making a big point.

'Because of what happened I am now doubly sure that I did the right thing.' Confident and relaxed. Absolutely convinced of being in the right.

The SAS Colonel was on next, and he was magnificent. Rules of engagement tripped off his tongue like deadly poetry. He was even able to justify their presence as, 'a perfectly normal operational requirement'. Adding, 'We did not expect to be forced to resort to violence.'

Gus played it this way and that, then brought in two P4 lawyers – P4 then being the branch of secret affairs which provided necessary professionals like doctors, lawyers, Indian chiefs and compliant senior fire officers when arson became a dangerous subject.

This pair laid into the policeman and the soldier, pulling tricks that they would never get away with in court.

Then, just about everyone had a go at the four SAS men who had done the shooting and it became obvious that they had not been chosen for their warlike skills alone. Each of them was bland, intelligent and, seemingly, very honest.

Last, about four in the morning, they played the video. Again and again the Gang of Four walked from their front door while the hooded pair of soldiers appeared from the end of the cul-de-sac and the words 'Police! Stop! Stand still!' echoed from noises off. Then the moves, and the word 'Bailiff'.

Gus froze the frame to ask who had said 'Bailiff', and what it had meant. The Commander and the Colonel both owned to what was basically an order to use force.

'Why?'

'You have eyes, sir, haven't you?' For the first time, the Colonel sounded sharp and piqued.

So, again and again they watched the grisly ballet. Then, to Herbie's immense surprise, after the SAS had disappeared as if by a warlock's spell, the cameras moved in close on each of the bodies. Two police officers, with an ambulance man in tow, turned over the corpse of Mary Frances Duggan and there, for everyone to see, was a 9mm Browning in her hand, slipping from the fingers onto the pavement. So with Patrick Sean Glass, only he had a small frag grenade.

The entire disclosure worried Big Herbie at the time, but everyone appeared to think this was exactly what happened, and you could not see the join on the tape.

Now, going through the papers in Gus's study by the glow from a green-shaded student lamp, it worried him even more because *these* papers contained a lot more detail. Payments made to certain specialists; logs which told of videotape being reprocessed and copied over a period of four and a half hours. Audio laboratory logs. Small ex-gratia payments to a pair of actors. All unexplained, leaving the odour of sulphur in his mind.

Twice, as he sat in the locked study, Bitsy Williams knocked on the door. 'There's food, Herbie. Come and have something to eat.' To which he replied, 'Later. Not now. Busy now.'

He remembered how things had gone in the Coroner's Court the next afternoon. How Gus, with his law degree that he never used, held forth; the SAS boys, Tony Worboys, and a couple of others giving evidence from behind screens with electronic voice-altering throat mikes. The faces of the four solicitors hurriedly engaged by the families of the four victims, as they took in the magnitude of the planned crime, and the honest, straightforward and legal methods used to entrap the team.

He heard again one of the SAS men responding to the Coroner himself. 'Sir, it is not an easy thing to do, kill another person close up. But we were cleared to take action and, as you've seen, we were in grave danger.'

While the Provos pledged revenge, and a small demonstration took place outside the court, the Coroner brought in the inescapable verdict: 'Lawful Killing,' on all four victims.

The incident remained big for some time, and security was noticeably tighter around *Rich and Famous*, or *Lancer*, depending where you were standing. Two books sold well. One from the Provos' angle by a Jesuit priest no less; the other by an in-depth news team from one of the Sunday heavies. Within the Office, the entire thing was noted as Gus Keene's triumph. Some said he was given a medal, and now Herbie saw from the documents that this was indeed the case. Why, though, he wondered? Why did Gus have what was virtually incriminating evidence in *his* files when the stuff should have been shredded long ago? He also recalled that it was only a year later that he resigned, for the second time, intent upon giving the marriage to Martha one last try. In the end, the Office helped put paid to that as well.

It was impossible to sleep, so eventually Herb went off to the kitchen and took a plate of Bitsy's sandwiches from the fridge, made coffee and carried the plate and mug back to Gus's study.

Gus himself seemed to be sitting across the desk from him, nodding and quietly telling him to get on with it. Herbie shuddered, for he could hear, in his mind, Gus's voice – 'You're on the right track, old Herb.'

In his time, Gus had been almost paranoid about security, and *Cataract* was something nobody talked about, once it was over. Yet here was the entire file, open and unashamed on Gus's desk.

At the time he recalled being very worried that Gus – a confessor by trade – had been called in for damage control, which he did wonderfully. Why Gus? he asked for the umpteenth time. Who called him in?

He flicked through the pages and, finally, there it was, the transcript of a telephone call – kept, no doubt, by Gus himself – stapled to a memo, signed and sealed, giving the job to Willis Maitland-Wood, First Deputy Chief. The old Chief's signature was scrawled at the bottom, with an instruction, direct from COBRA, saying, use the very best man. Gus was obviously thought to be the best man, for the transcript of the telephone call showed Maitland-Wood calling Gus at Warminster and saying, 'Gus, I want you at Head Office faster than light. There's something we need to take care of.'

'Can't it wait till tomorrow, Willis?'

'Now, Gus. They need you now. Christ, man, I've got COBRA waiting on the other line.'

'Give me a clue.' Herbie could just hear Gus lazily asking for the clue.

Then, the bit that really shook Herbie. No crypto, no telephone spookspeak. Maitland-Wood just came right out with it. 'SAS blew away four bad guys on Herbie's watch – Herbie and Young Worboys. Got to be put right, because nobody on the inside is going to take a fall. I have to fly out in less than an hour.'

Herbie leaned back, one huge hand clamped to his temples. He gave an enormous sigh, wondering if the Provos, or even the splinter group FFIRA, would come back and snuff Gus after all this time? The car bomb was very professional, though he had a solid intuition that this was not the work of the Irish extremists.

Out of the corner of his eye, he saw that the silent phone was blinking its little red light.

'Yes?' He picked it up.

'Thought you might be working, old Herb,' Worboys said from the distant end. 'You always were a night bird. Just wanted to tell you that I've got a watcher's van for Monday – Gus's funeral. The lot – son et lumière, and a beautiful parking place. Talk to you tomorrow.'

Herb sighed again, gathered up the *Cataract* file and dumped it into the small safe. Of one thing he was certain: he had one hell of a lot of digging to do in his travels backwards and forwards through Gus Keene's life.

★　　★　　★

While Herbie looked at this dubious past piece of secret history, the bombs were exploding in Paris. Four on the Metro, just as the early birds were off to work. Fifteen dead, twenty-four badly injured. One at Charles de Gaulle in a baggage hall just as passengers from a New York flight were collecting their luggage. There was also a shooting. A very senior army officer, leaving his mistress's apartment at four in the morning, was gunned down on the street.

There were no witnesses, though a waiter in a nearby café described a young couple who had dropped in for coffee around three-thirty. He told the police and the press that he did not think they had anything to do with it. 'They were so in love,' he said. 'I think they were on their way back to a hotel. I think they had only one thing on their mind.' Which in a way was true about Hisham and Samira who had taken a suite at the France et Choiseul in the Rue St. Honoré. Ahmad was already waiting for them when they returned. He had done the Charles de Gaulle bomb that morning, and was elated with its success.

'You should have seen the pig of a General go down,' Samira said almost before they were inside the suite. 'Ahmad, he spun around like a toy, you could see the jets of blood, like fountains, coming out of his back.' She was in a hyperactive state which Ahmad thought unhealthy.

'Samira!' Hisham's voice was like the crack of a whip.

'Yes?' Her eyes seemed glazed and she was flushed as though with fever.

'Calm down! Sit and calm down!'

'What's wrong? Why do you look at me like that?'

'*You* are what is wrong, Samira. In our work it is necessary to do things like this with a certain detachment—'

'But we killed a—'

'Yes, Samira, we killed. We took a human life. That

was our job, but you are supposed to be trained to remain calm at all times, and to carry out a job without becoming in any way involved with the target. You show disgusting pleasure at having killed. This is not the way we are taught to do things.'

'Hisham, even Ahmad here was happy after the bomb he planted . . .'

'Happy, yes. Proud, yes. But not revelling in the joy of killing. When you have carried out an order to kill you should not begin reliving that moment, for that way lies a kind of madness. Believe me, I have seen it happen. People who slowly come to see killing, not as a surgical necessity, but as a pleasant way of life – an enjoyment. The act of killing eventually takes over. It leads to a sickness of the brain.

'Where I was first trained, they removed people from the training if they started to revel in the act. To us, this is a job, like the job of a soldier. It is a matter of business and should never become personal.'

Samira lowered her eyes. 'I am sorry,' she whispered. 'I *did* enjoy the moment. I will try to be more calm and collected. What is your wish tonight, Hisham?'

He knew that the girl wanted to make a kind of celebration by going to bed with him, for he was her leader. He also would have liked to bed her, but his common sense as leader of this group told him that he should not spend the night with her. There were times when Hisham could be iron-willed, just as there were times when he could be weak. 'Take Ahmad to your bed, Samira. Treat him well, as a man should be treated.'

She looked up and he saw the disappointment in her eyes. She also knew of her faults. She knew that the killing of a target had become almost as exciting to her as the sexual act. She nodded, stretched out a hand to Ahmad and led him from the room, though, as a woman, she felt debased and, for a second, thought this was not the way a Western woman would be treated.

Hisham sat in silence. These two members of his team would never have guessed that his own mind was in turmoil, any more than they could have known that, in his own way, he was a traitor.

8

The *Intiqam* groups in London and New York were getting a great deal of media coverage. In London the TV news anchors gave the almost daily shootings and bombings their usual, almost diffident, matter-of-fact style; while the newspapers pulled out all the plugs – 'These cowardly acts of random violence can only stiffen the resolve of the British people . . .' was a phrase worked and reworked by editorial writers. The Prime Minister made several statements concerning what was obviously a campaign being stepped up throughout Europe.

Beneath the surface came the hints. The FFIRA were denying this new wave of attacks, but journalists – from print media and TV alike – sent a message, sandwiched between the lines of their stories, which bluntly said that they did not believe the FFIRA. Within the various agencies, including the Anti-Terrorist Department from Scotland Yard, SO 13, it was known that the FFIRA had an elusive Active Service Unit in the United Kingdom, so they tended to lean towards the possibility that this was a rogue splinter group which had no access to the most favoured explosive, the ubiquitous Semtex, in its various forms. Yet there was sophistication in the devices, and the most experienced officers claimed privately that the menace was truly new and came from the Middle East. There were pointers, they declared at conferences and briefings.

In the United States, there was, as the President said in a special Broadcast to the People, 'a heightened sense of concern that our enemies have resorted to these terrible and deadly acts which brought forth death and destruction'. He pledged that the wolves in sheep's cloth-ing which seem to be in our midst would be hunted down and handed over to those who dispensed justice. In the meantime every citizen; man, woman and child would have to be on their guard.

Privately, in the Oval Office, he fumed to his Security Adviser, together with the Director of Central Intelli-gence, the Director of the FBI, and the head of the NSA.

'I'm not going to allow the United States to become a hunting ground as the Brits have allowed their country to be used as a killing ground for terrorists. I won't have it,' he all but screamed. Then he questioned each of his experts in turn as to any leads they might have. There were none, except the certain fact that they were not being sucked in to the British Irish problem.

The consensus of opinion was that these attacks came from renegade Middle East groups.

'Well, track them down and kill them,' the President ordered. 'You could take a leaf out of the Brits' book. They know more about this kind of thing than we do.'

The men who dealt with security went away, renewed their efforts and talked at length to their opposite num-bers in London.

Also in London, early in the week, Detective Chief Inspector Olesker, having been rapped over the knuckles for losing sight of the FFIRA Unit, was told of a new assignment. The DCI would soon be working in harness with the spooks, for the recent wave of terror appeared to have begun with the assassination of one of their own. The DCI was not happy, having heard strange stories about the 'funnies' as the police usually called members of both the Security Service and the SIS.

Nobody had the slightest idea why Gus Keene wanted to be buried in the graveyard of a small country church, which served three hamlets lying in a triangle some seven miles west of Stonehenge. As far as they knew, Gus originally hailed from Berkshire, though this was a moot point these days because a section of Berkshire had been swallowed up by the hungry jaws of Oxfordshire in some political scheme which appeared to benefit nobody, but probably did.

On the Sunday afternoon, Big Herbie Kruger drove from the Warminster complex to take a look at what would be Gus's last resting place. The church itself was small and originally Norman, with a great deal of well-meant Victorian refurbishing: 'St James. All Welcome. Holy Communion 8 a.m. Sunday and Wednesday. Matins. Sunday 11 a.m. Evensong 6 p.m. Vicar: The Revd Brian Temple.' It was mid-afternoon and the west door was locked: a sign of the times in which we live that church doors have to be locked against possible theft and vandalism. The entire world, Herbie thought, will soon have to be locked against the mindless brutality and disingenuousness of crazy, morally bankrupt and uncaring people, and that did not count the terrorists.

Herbie scratched his head and did a slow walk around the building and into the churchyard. There he discovered three other Keene graves. Mother, father and, he thought, sister. That solved the problem. Gus wanted to lie next to his kinsfolk, and probably already had a plot marked out for Carole as well. Gus, if nothing else, was a realist. In life he always took care of things well in advance, if possible. When there was panic he was just about the fastest thinker on his feet. Old Ambrose Hill used to say that his brain did the two-minute mile – regularly.

At the top of the graveyard a splay of oak trees formed a demarcation line with a thicket of hedge running in front of them. Kruger walked up the gravel path, past the graves of Smiths, Hails, Martens, Graces and Collins – all local names, it seemed. At the hedge he saw exactly where Worboys intended to put his van. A long meadow, with hay already stooked, reached up a shallow slope to the horizon, and a tractor path followed the line of the hedge. He craned to right and left and thought he could glimpse a five-barred gate leading to a narrow metalled lane. They would bring the watchers' van up behind the trees, sort out the best views, shove directional mikes towards the grave itself, hack holes in the hedge for the telephoto lenses and the infra-red night stuff, and sit there for twenty-four hours.

He had asked Worboys, yet again, why he was so set on having the watchers out for the funeral and its immediate aftermath.

'Herb, old sport,' Worboys sighed wearily. 'I'm doing everything by the book: covering my bum if you like. Some odd mark turns up at the funeral, or comes visiting afterwards, I want to know because as sure as eggs *someone* will know and I'll be in the *potage*.'

'Shouldn't mess with *potage*,' said Herb, straight voiced and faced.

This was when Herbie called Worboys on the afternoon of the 16th – the Tuesday – with a mouthful of questions and desires.

He had gone quickly through the mounds of files on Gus's desk, discovering that most of them contained information which should have – as the argot said – gone out of style long ago, meaning it was ultra-classified; some of it flagged *Secure A*, indicating the take must not get into the hands of either their relatives in DC, or the sister service. 'Out of style' meant into the shredders.

'Tony,' Herb began, and Young Worboys became immediately alert, for he sensed in Herbie's voice the smoothness of some phoney mind-reader hearing codewords from his stooge.

'Yes, Herb. What d'you want?'

'We have a couple of problems. More than a brace, actually.'

'Speak.'

'Is what I'm doing, old horse. You know what Gus had down here?'

'Surprise me.'

'A lot of things that should be buried. Five fathom full . . .'

'Full fathom five, Herb.' At the distant end, Worboys bit his tongue as he heard Herbie chuckle.

'Sure. You got it. Anyway, old sheep, there's stuff here I don't want lying around.'

'Oh, come on, Herb. You're within the sacred circle there.'

'Is the bloody sacred circle that worries me, Tony. Everyone's after a piece of the action these days. Bitsy's a nice girl, but I don't even want *her* rooting through this stuff, so be a good chip and send something really secure, like one of those new safes that cannot be cracked even by experts. Get the okay from Homes and Gardens and have it sunk into the floor. Homes and Gardens haven't been lopped off, have they? We still own them?'

'Yes, but, Herb—'

'I'm serious, Tony. I mean it. I'm in charge of this and I don't want things lying around where the hired help can take a peep. Gus has nice locks on his doors, but I'm being careful.'

It took another ten minutes for Worboys to agree, then Herbie made his big pitch. 'Look, old sheep,' he began, in a way that made Worboys' hair stand on end. 'Look, you put me in charge, right? You said, go find the people who did Gus, right? Just for old times' sake. No pay, no packdrill, nothing. Then the Chief talked to me, private, person-to-person on a safe line, right? Repeated it. Read me my rights, okay?'

'Yes. Right.' Very tentative.

'Well, Tony, I want some paper.'

'What kind of paper?'

'I want authority to question people.'

'What kind of people?'

'From the past. Old Office people.'

'Such as whom?'

'Such as I ain't even going to mention on a secure line.'

'What exactly do you want, Herb? And is your journey really necessary?'

'Completely. I need a document of authorization that'll cut the red tape and make people talk to me. Something under the Chief's signature. Finding whoever did Gus is, I think, pretty full of importance, no?'

'Yes, for peace of mind. Yes.'

'Then you give me peace of mind, Young Worboys. You're covering your bum, I also want steel plates over my own rectum. You never know where this kind of thing can lead now that voices from the past are always popping up to haunt us. So, I want paper, the Chief's signature, stuff that everyone will feel comfortable with. *Verstanden?*'

Grudgingly, Worboys agreed.

'Send it down with the safe, eh?'

'I'll do my best.'

'Best ain't good enough. Send the paper down, either with the safe or by special courier. Remind the Chief what he said. Said I could have *anything*.'

'Okay, Herb. Something else you want? Like an unlimited budget or something simple like that?'

'Could do with use of one of your minders who's looking out for Carole. Just for the odd few hours occasionally. Like tomorrow morning. Maybe Sunday as well. Okay?'

'I'll let Mickey know that you might need him . . . What for, Herb? Really what for?'

'Sit across Bitsy's door when I'm away.'

'You're not happy with Bitsy?'

A long pause during which Herbie made some odd whining and grunting sounds. At last he said, 'Look, Bitsy's a nice girl. Got her knees brown, know what I mean? But, maybe I'm uncomfortable . . .' He stopped, a knee-jerk in his mind causing a small stab of pain. 'To be honest, I don't want her operational. If she'd simply agree to minding this place, like she does with safe houses, that would be okay. But *not* operational. You follow?'

In his office looking out on London, embraced by an unusual heat haze, Worboys knew what it was really about. Bitsy Williams had been the closest female friend of Herbie's now lost, and last love.

'Okay, Herb. Message received and understood. She is ecstatic to be working with you, though, so I'll keep her on until after the funeral. Then I'll put it to her in plain language.'

'Thank you many times over, old scout.' In the back of his mind, Herb wondered how Worboys knew Bitsy was ecstatic about working with him. Worboys' personal sneak, he figured. The school leper who sucked up to the staff. Worboys and the Chief, just keeping an eye on old Herbie. He could even hear the conversations –

'Old Kruger could be dead in the water, Worboys. I agreed he'd be the best man for the job. Agreed to bring him back with no paper. But . . .'

'Oh, I don't think—'

'He took one hell of a knock. Seen men stronger than Kruger go doolally from less. Shell-shocked, battle fatigue, LMF—'

'I don't think you could ever charge Herb with LMF, Chief.' Worboys was quite put out. LMF meant Lack of Moral Fibre, a term outdated in these days of political correctness, but still used by people like the Chief.

'Keep an eye on him, Worboys. Once upon a time he had odd tendencies to go aroving. Don't want to have him weighed in the balance and found wanting, do we?'

Herbie pulled himself back to the here and now with Worboys at the other end of the line. 'Just in case you're wondering, Tony, I still got all my marbles. Every last one, okay?'

'Of course, okay.'

'Good, then I expect the paper and the safe down here today. Seven o'clock latest. Right?'

'Any difficulties and I'll call, Herb.'

'If there *are* difficulties, I'm long gone before the night's out.'

There were no difficulties. First, the paper arrived, by a tall courier, leather-clad on a fast bike. A very official document charging anyone with knowledge of Office business, past or present, to assist Mr Kruger in every possible way. Doubts should be telephoned direct to Head Office. Time was of the essence. The legal department's fingerprints were all over the thing, and Herbie nodded his big head, smiled his daft smile, and chuckled with glee, silently so neither Ginger nor Bitsy could hear him.

Five men and a van turned up around five and took two hours fitting the safe into the floor of Gus's study, under Herbie's instructions.

'What on earth was that all about?' Bitsy asked over the cauliflower cheese and a nice hock she had somehow scrounged from what they were now calling the Big House, playing a little game in which they were the hired help for the young lordlings up the drive.

'You fancy a run out in the car tomorrow, Ginger?' Herbie spoke with a lot of smile, off-hand, casual as a pair of sneakers.

'Down the coast, Mr K, sir?' Joshing back, never quite certain when Herb was playing the fool.

'I come, Herbie?' Bitsy grinned and put her hand on his wrist. She was becoming an all too heavy touchy-feely person. Herbie did not really like being touched all the time, and kissed on the cheek – which he made certain of by turning his head when Bitsy aimed at his lips.

'No, Bits. Sorry, man stuff.'

'In this day and age. Year of the woman and all that?'

'That's how it goes. One of the nice gents from across the way will be in the house looking after you.'

She was genuinely offended by this. Her face flushed and her lips turned grey.

'Come on, Bits. Is work. Only I can do it, and

Ginger's been told to watch over *me*. Guardian angel style.'

'Then I can look after myself here, thank you very much.'

The daft smile from Kruger, and a tiny shake of the head. 'Sorry, dear Bitsy, but them's the orders. Someone here all the time in case Blind Pew comes in and tips you the Black Spot.' *Treasure Island* was one of his favourite reads and he had seen all the movie and TV versions. 'Har-Har, Jim lad!' He threw her a goofy smile attached to who-knows-what-the-future-may-bring eyes, which mollified her for the time being.

'So, where to, Mr Kruger, sir?' Ginger asked, the next morning when they were seated in the car.

'Long John Silver Awaaaay!' Herbie chuckled. 'Eastbourne, Ginge. Maybe we go sailing, maybe not.'

They found the house on the outskirts of Eastbourne, having stopped off for lunch at a Little Chef where Ginger insisted on sitting so that he could see the door, with his jacket unbuttoned.

'What you carrying, Ginge?' Herbie had asked.

'Bloody Glock, sir. Scared stiff of it. Light enough but the safety's iffy. A fellow could shoot his bobbit off.'

But now, they had found the house and Ginger parked down the road, well away, while Herbie slowly walked back past other houses, each with a nice three or four acres, some with mock Tudor façades, imitation leaded lights, the whole three-ringed circus, with names like Three Pines, The Grange, Manor Lodge and, last of all, the more restrained Oak House – the one he wanted. He had looked up the address by going on line from Gus's computer and using his own password, getting into the Registry files which were not closed to him.

The house was pleasant, unassuming, stippled white with a porch and an obligatory basket of flowers. The wide driveway, from the waist-high wrought-iron gates, was flanked by borders of flowers that he guessed were given instructions to stand to attention, even on a hot day. He followed the path around the house, glimpsing a lawn perfectly mowed.

'I help you?' She had come out of the front door, behind him. Tall, mid-forties, ash-blonde with just a hint of grey here and there. Daughter, he thought at once, then he vaguely recognized her from the past, and marvelled at her presence here.

'Looking for the master of the house,' Herbie grinned cheekily.

'We don't need anything you're selling today.' There was a glint of steel in her eyes. Then: 'I *know* you.'

'Shouldn't be surprised. I—'

'Yes!' A bark from the side of the house, and there he was, looking older, fatter, if anything a little more pugnacious, the face of a retired colonel crimson. Gardening trousers held up by what appeared to be an old Etonian tie, and a denim shirt. A battered and fraying Panama jaunty on his head, the short body in a boxer's stance. 'Good God in heaven,' he said suddenly, peering from behind the thick lenses of his spectacles. 'As I live and sneeze, it's Herbie. Herbie Kruger come to look up an old comrade in arms, eh?' Still the near-military bark, the words snapped out in small phrases like some kind of semi-automatic weapon.

'Just passing, Mr Maitland-Wood, sir.' Herb gave him the glad hand grin that said old comrades always stick together.

'Well. Well. Heaven help me, Herbie Kruger. You met the Memsahib, I see.'

Kruger turned and nodded to the lady, saying yes, in some kind of way he had met her, but was amazed at the discrepancy in ages, and the idea that Willis Maitland-Wood, the once-hated First Deputy Chief of the Office, had possibly known any woman in the carnal sense. In the old days, they had disliked each other with a hearty, near passionate hunger. Willis Maitland-Wood who, with many others, had helped to train Herbie and

118

had so often been the cross that Kruger bore, not gladly, but with a stoicism necessary for his own safety.

'Old chum, Willis? Old pal from the Cold War? I recognize the oaf,' said Mrs Maitland-Wood.

'Old chum indeed, Memsahib. Thought you put yourself out to grass, though, Kruger.'

'Came back for the good of my soul.' It was the sort of thing he knew Maitland-Wood liked to hear.

'Good for you, Kruger. Good for you. But, come on in. Come onto the lawn. Spot of tea, Mem? Possible, eh? Spot of Darjeeling and some of your Swiss roll. Makes a good Swiss roll, the Memsahib, Kruger. Best Swiss roll you could ever want.'

'Of course, Willis, if he's really an old friend. I seem to recall it differently.' She gave a neon wink of a smile, and retreated into the house, while Maitland-Wood led him onto the lawn with its geometrical stripes.

'You've a nice place here,' Herb ventured.

'Keeps me busy. Garden all bloody year long. Always something to do. Year-round business gardening. I garden, and am on lots of local committees. Chair some of them. Trick when they put you out to grass, keep busy. Keep a life going. This official?'

'I fear, official it is, sir. Yes, you might say so.'

Maitland-Wood gave a little nod, muttered, 'Mum's the word,' and led them over to a pair of deck-chairs in the shade of a fine chestnut. 'Have a little bit of body language to keep the Memsahib at bay. Still use the tradecraft. You recognize her?'

'She does have a familiar ring.'

'You probably knew her as Emma Paisley. Accounts. Been courting her for years. Amazed when she said yes when they retired me. She put in her cards and said yes, old boy. Yes, I'll marry you. Keeps me on a tight leash though.'

Emma Maitland-Wood, Emma Paisley as was – Herbie recognized her from the secret corridors of a decade or so ago – advanced on them bearing a tray loaded with tea and a large Swiss roll.

He saw Willis scratch his right ear and make sweeping motions with his left hand. He saw the former Ms Paisley give a stern nod as she said, 'I recall *you*, Mr Kruger. You got yourself wounded with that rake, Curry was it . . . ?'

'Curry Shepherd, yes. Going to look him up sometime.'

'Ah.' Maitland-Wood gave a series of small nods. 'He out to grass as well?'

'Not much call for his particular skills at the moment,' Herbie lied, for Curry Shepherd was only a few years younger than himself and had last been heard of trawling the Middle East in search of malcontents. According to Worboys he would be back in London at the end of the month.

'Like it strong, Kruger?'

'Please, very. With only milk a dash, afterwards, please. Just a pipette full, and sugar, lots. Death through the mouth, yes.'

'Have what you bloody like as long as you try the Memsahib's Swiss roll.'

'Big piece, please. Very partial. How do you make a Swiss roll, eh? Give him a push, yes?' He roared with laughter, stopping only when he met the former Emma Paisley's granite eye.

'If you're both happy, I'll get on with my chores,' she said. 'Nice to have seen you again, Mr Kruger.' She did not offer a hand, and made it clear that Herbie just had to do his thing then get out.

'Don't mind the Memsahib.' Maitland-Wood sounded a fraction off-key from the bully boy he once was. 'You ever see any of the other old boys? Tubby Fincher? Old Ambrose Hill? Anyone?'

'Tubby's in a nursing home. Bad heart thing. Ambrose lives a life of peace in – is it the Sheepland Isles?'

'Shetland. Shetland Islands. Just the place for old

Ambrose. Must be ninety in the shade by now.'

'I think early eighties.'

'Ah. Come on then, Herbie.' Was he softening. 'What's it all about?'

Herb had a mouthful of Swiss roll, so they both had to wait for a few seconds until he pronounced, 'Wonderful Swiss roll, sir. Best Swiss roll I eaten in yanks.'

'Yonks, I think you mean, old scout. Come on then, spit it out.'

'I'd like to chew it, then swallow.'

'I mean what you've come for.'

'So. Yes. Okay. Is about something right at the end of your time, sir. But I want you to know this is very official.' He laid a forefinger against his nose. 'Also very tight. Better read this.' He passed over the letter with the Chief's signature and all the fancy legal stuff.

'Old age.' Maitland-Wood drew out a spectacle case and changed his glasses. 'Intimations of mortality, what?'

Perhaps marriage had made him more human. He was still the bluff, bad-tempered old martinet, but softer. Herbie remembered him from earlier days, pushing his weight around, testing the envelope of his authority.

'Mind if I take up the offer in this?' He waved the letter.

'Phone away, Mr Maitland-Wood. Your privilege.'

'Quite right. Call me Willis, Kruger. No need to stick to formality these days. Just want to talk to Head Office because this gives you rather broad powers. What was it you had in mind particularly?'

'Tell you what, Willis, you make the call and I'll ask the questions, okay?'

'Yes. Right. Won't be long.'

Herb poured himself more tea and cut another unhealthy slice of the Swiss roll. He had finished by the time Maitland-Wood returned. 'You're working on the thing about poor Gus,' he said, almost accusingly.

'I know.' Herbie gave his more intelligent grin. Maybe he should re-tailor his attitudes. Spies and spymasters should be more sinister, darker, not jokey. He could not think of any of his colleagues who retained their dignity by being inappropriately light-hearted. Possibly he should rethink his entire approach. Bit late in the day though.

'So this is about Gus?' BMW asked, cutting himself another slice of the Swiss roll. Big Herbie had just remembered they always called him BMW – Bloody Maitland-Wood.

'Sure, about Gus Keene. One aspect anyway.'

'Shoot. I told the Chief I'd answer anything I could remember.'

'I came to you, because you were very high up the tree at the time. Quite near to your retirement though. *Cataract.*'

'Oh.' *Nobody* liked to hear about *Cataract*, but clever old Herbie knew that one of the answers could be prised out of BMW. 'Nasty, yes. But you know that. You were implicated as I recall, Kruger.'

'A little, sure. Willis, when things got really dodgy, when things began to unwind, they brought Gus down from Warminster.'

'Yes.'

'Why?'

'Why?' Mimicking. 'Why? Because he was the best man, of course. Best man for the job.'

'Willis, Gus was our Chief Confessor. The Lord High Inquisitor. Our private Torquemada. His skills were interrogation. This was big-time damage control. So, why Gus? I never figured it out, and now I've read the file, I still can't figure it out.'

'You think the Irish might have done Gus?'

'Can't tell you that, Willis. Just why Gus? Do you recall? You were close to the old Chief, and I seem to remember that both of you went off on fast vacations as soon as things got iffy. One of you must have recommended Gus, because I know, and the files say, that the thing was COBRA cleared. So, why an interrogator? Why Gus?'

Willis Maitland-Wood slowly pushed his Panama onto the back of his head. 'Yes,' taking up the slack in the waist of his trousers. It was not an old Etonian tie holding them up, but a tie that could be taken as old Etonian at five paces. 'Yes, the old Chief and I *did* go on little holidays, but let me tell you that was on the advice of COBRA.'

'Who made the recommendation, Willis?'

'To COBRA? As I recall it, we talked for a long while about it. You'll find nothing on paper, we had the bubblers on, no tapes running, and I personally went over to COBRA and said we should bring Gus in. The Chief briefed him.'

'Why Gus, Willis? Why an interrogator?'

The sigh sounded as though he were about to admit to some terrible crime. 'You read Gus's file yet? His jacket? His dossier?'

'Some. Events. Gems from his life.'

'A lot more to Gus than meets the eye. I mean there *was* a lot more.'

'That was obvious. He went through *Cataract* like the proverbial sheep through a goose.'

'I don't think you mean sheep, Herbie.'

'Maybe not, but was impressive.'

'Gus was a master of deceit, Herbie. But a master. He could look at you and make you believe black was white. One of the reasons we called him in was that he was most qualified to deceive people. Just trust me, Gus was a kind of camouflage expert, camouflage in words. Sleight of mind was his forte. *We* knew about it, about his expertise – the old Chief and myself – because he demonstrated it to us on many occasions. You see we all belonged to the same club at one time, and I'm not allowed to disclose any more than that. Not even to your current Chief, because this was something quite apart from the Office. Nothing to do with the Office.'

'Then tell me what you can.'

'I've told you. We knew that if anyone could manipulate a situation like *Cataract* it was Gus. He had the ability to make people think the sky was green, and grass was blue. Lots of clues in his dossier. Courses on mental as well as physical concealment. Highly qualified. You'll find the names of his specialist stuff if you look carefully in his jacket. That *truly* is all I can say, and all I could say under oath, Herbie. Slap a subpoena on me and the answer would be the same. It's all there if you look.' He peered through his spectacles and gave Big Herb a knowing and pleasant smile. 'You don't really think the old Chief and I would send someone in who wasn't qualified.'

'The stuff you can't talk about . . . ?'

'Yes.'

'The stuff *outside* his work for the Office.'

'Mmmmm.'

'Will I find any of that in his jacket?'

Slowly Maitland-Wood shook his head. 'It's purely civilian. Oaths were taken.'

'Like the Masons?'

'Not really, but again, yes, something of that kind but more entertaining. Now, I've said too much already. The facts concerning Gus's ability to turn that situation around, to clean the thing up, might not have been totally ethical. There *were* questions of morals, but it *was* essential, you'll agree there, surely?'

'Sure I agree. That's the job. Lie, steal, cheat, double-cross, mug, blag, pick minds, do a quick-change act, tricks on a trapeze even, do anything as long as it takes the heat off a difficult situation and provides information, stops people looking too close, yes?'

'Mmmmm,' grunted BMW, and with that, Herbie knew the interview was over.

They drove back under a pearly summer evening sky

with Kruger unusually silent, trying to work out the angles. A mystery within a mystery. It was all there in Gus's record, yet it was not quite all there.

He would not have the first glimmer of truth until the day after the funeral.

For the next couple of days or so, he went through Gus Keene's expanded dossier, using his brain as a fine-tooth comb. Yes, it *was* there. Courses on Psychological Warfare; Deception on a Military and Political level; the Strategy and Tactics of a *coup d'état*; The Optical Illusions of Deception (this last a special month's seminar, held jointly with US intelligence agencies in a highly secure old house in the Highlands of Scotland); the full Royal Marine Commando course, in the summer of '78, which made Gus a very tough *hombre*, because the Royal Marines always say they are the same as the SAS, with one exception – they are gentlemen. There were a number of other, smaller, but interesting retreats, conferences and restricted courses that *did* make Gus the obvious person to salvage *Cataract* and save both the Office and, more important at the time, the government from grave embarrassment. Unethical, immoral, sure – as Herb would have said – but that was the name of the game.

During this period, there was more death; bigger bombs. Two very serious ones in Rome; two shootings in Paris; a bomb in Washington DC, a shade too close to the White House for comfort. There were also four more serious explosions in England. One in Aldershot – another garrison town; one which actually destroyed an aircraft on an RAF base; and two more in London. The newspapers were starting to ask questions, and nobody could give any answers.

Like all good spymasters, and secret operators, Big Herbie Kruger rarely left trails unexamined. Old BMW, having hinted heavily at some other secret purely on the civilian side of things, made him think, cudgel his brains, seek out others, search through databases and even plunder a couple of sources restricted to him.

He was convinced that he could not even begin to do the long run through Gus's life – examining what Keene had already written, and what the notes and many files contained – until his friend's earthly remains were consigned to the dust from whence they had come. He would wait until after the obsequies, and, as obsequies go, Gus had a good turn-out.

It was a mild day. The undertaker was good, unless you counted the one pallbearer who was wearing sneakers dyed black, with his obligatory dark suit.

The Chief sent representatives, as did most of the Heads of Department, but – oddly – the Minister himself came, plus many old friends. Some known, some unknown, some looking like tough guys, which made Worboys remark that there was the touch of a Mafia funeral. Floral tributes were in abundance. Carole, between two of Gus's top assistants, bore up and even managed a smile for the really close old friends. The priest was bearded and a failed actor, but he made a very good stab at making the service mean something, which is quite a trick when you think about the Church of England. He spoke up, and did not muff his lines.

Only the cognoscenti, like Big Herbie, caught movements from the line of oak trees and the hedge forward of the trees.

They marched away, feeling that Gus had been done proud. Herbie also felt, very strongly, that Gus was physically present. He did not enquire of anyone else if they felt that Gus was there that afternoon – chuckling away at everyone – lest he be thought to be two sandwiches short of a picnic. But feel it he did.

The next morning, he settled down to work, opening

the inch or so of Gus's manuscript and beginning to read. Gus had a good opening line:

I have spent most of my adult life with crossword puzzles [he wrote]. Not the kind of puzzles that have neat patterns of black and white squares, and intelligent clues for One Down or Six Across. My crossword puzzles have usually begun with a couple of clues, a blank sheet of paper, and myself sitting opposite someone who is a clue in himself – or occasionally, herself.

Great opening stuff, Herb thought. Then the telephone rang and Worboys was on the line. 'I got something, Herb.'

'Not catching, I hope?'

'The watchers got something. It's really weird. Two guys paid Gus a visit around midnight. We have it on tape, and a lot of the sound is there as well. I'm driving down now so we can watch it together. Oh, yes, I'll be bringing someone with me.'

'Who's someone?'

'I can't keep them off any longer, Herb. I presume you got the other news? Bitsy, I mean?'

'Oh, yeah. Big drama queen stuff. Told me she'd do anything just to stay close to the operation.'

'See you in a couple of hours.'

Drama Queen stuff it certainly had been. 'Herb, they offered me some other godawful job.' She had brought the matter up just after the funeral. 'They've told me that if I want to stay on this I have to be down-graded. Chief cook and bottle washer. Well, I've been doing safe houses for a long time – that and catering for visiting firemen, so I'll do it for a real op. You'll eat very well, I promise, and *you* need good food, Herbie. You've got a lot of your old colour back already.'

'Sure, Bits. You're very good, and home cooking's just what we need. When it comes to nourishing food you're the tops,' he lied.

The Detective Chief Inspector from the Anti-Terrorist Plod, known as SO 13 in Scotland Yard's vocabulary, was in a different class.

Worboys had his own key, and gently called out, 'Hallo, anyone at home?' from the hall.

Herbie heard him first, and was out of Gus's study before anyone else knew there were strangers in the house.

He did a double-take, for there was Worboys, looking a shade too prosperous in a Whitehall suit, navy, double-breasted with a minute white stripe, cream shirt and a blue and white polka-dot tie. He wore a rose in his buttonhole and was accompanied by a young woman – well, in her late thirties, but looking twenty-nine. Medium height, short dark hair nicely done, pleasant face, not chocolate box pretty – the nose was a trifle too sharp, her mouth had a slight overbite. However, the eyes were large and brown and she was blessed with a dazzling smile, calculated to put a confirmed misogynist at ease. She moved with that kind of authority born of discipline, and carried a small suitcase which she put down carefully in the hall.

'Herb, this is Detective Chief Inspector Rebecca Olesker of SO 13. DCI Olesker, Eberhardt Lukas Kruger. Answers to Herbie, Herb, Big Herb . . .'

'And Mr Kruger sometimes.' Big Herb was pissed at Worboys. Why the hell had he not told him that the anti-terrorist cop was a woman?

'Just as I sometimes answer to Ms Olesker, Mr Kruger.' The overwhelming smile was like a trick from Special Effects. 'But I'd prefer Becka, Becky or Bex. I prefer Bex actually.'

'Like I prefer Herb, Bex.' His giant paw completely covered her hand.

'Well, we've got that over with. There is room for the DCI, isn't there, Herb?'

'Bitsy was doing something about that. Muttered something about another mouth to feed.'

'Well. Good.' Worboys was full of bounce, cocky with the look of a man who had just been proved right against all odds.

'You won the pools, Tony?' Herb still looked at Bex Olesker, giving her a cheeky wink.

'Maybe. Who knows? We won something.' He lifted a video-cassette and shook it like a trophy.

'We all going to see it?'

'Let Bex settle in. She's seen it, and I'm leaving this copy with you so you can cosy up and watch it together, discuss the wicked ways of the world.'

Ginger and Bitsy appeared out of nowhere. Herbie knew they had been listening and came in on cue. He took over and introduced her as DCI Olesker – 'But prefers to be called Bex.'

'Nice to meet you, Ms Olesker. I show you to your room?'

Bitsy bridled, 'Oh, no. I'm the housekeeper, Ginger. Let me do the honours.'

Bex did the floodlight smile, bestowing it in equal proportions on both Bitsy and Ginger. 'That would be nice. I'll see you later, then, Mr Kruger.'

'Herb,' he corrected, thinking that her voice could saw and weave around poetry: an actor's voice.

She gave him a little wink. 'Nice to be working with the pros.'

Herbie curbed his wandering thoughts and turned his mind on to things that mattered, lingering for a moment as the SO 13 officer walked away with Ginger and Bitsy.

'Very good,' Worboys said quietly when she was just out of earshot. 'One of their best.'

'Give me her history later. I want to see the product.'

'I warn you it's weird as hell, and the sound's a bit tricky. We don't get it all, but what we do get is pretty macabre.'

They drew the blinds and sat in front of the TV.

Side by side, like friends at the movies. 'You want a choc-ice?' Herb asked.

'No, I'll wait for the main feature. Here we go.'

There was a moon, and they had the infra-red on so the picture, while fairly sharp, was a grainy black and white. Not great definition, but the grave was instantly recognizable. In the lower left-hand corner there was the date, with a clock running. It said 12.23.31 – the last two digits clicking off the seconds: time going by in the fast lane.

Two shapes moved up the path towards the grave. They walked on the grass verge, gliding like ghosts so that Big Herbie felt his skin crawl. They wore what looked like old duffle-coats with the hoods up. The light made them appear as dark monks, highlighted against the sky.

The first words between them were incoherent, partly because whoever was doing the sound had not locked on, and the mikes obviously brushed against the hedge.

The two figures stationed themselves on either side of the mound of earth which merged into the darkness.

'You start.' That was clear. Male voice. Age impossible to tell.

'All right.' Another male who moved his head upwards and began to speak. The mikes were still not right, it was just a babble of sound as the audio operator struggled with his controls, finally bringing the words into focus, like a camera adjustment. Then, very clearly:

'Claudius Damautus is not gone. He has simply preceded us in mounting a stage upon which all of us must some day play a role. He has read a script which still remains unseen by those of us on this side of tomorrow's curtain. We join his loved ones in feeling that he has outsoared the shadow of our night and come so close that he may walk softly within our thoughts . . .'

More static, rustling leaves probably, drowning the words until –

'We men of earth have here the stuff of paradise,
We have enough,
We need no further stones to build the stairs to the
    Unfulfilled.
No other ivory for the doors, no other marble for the
    floors.
No other cedar for the beam and dome of man's
    immortal dream.
Here on the common human way is all the stuff
    to build a heaven.
Ours the stuff to build eternity in time.'

This last was spoken by the second man. The first raised something high above the grave, and as the figure turned, it looked like a small stick. He took up the words again.

'Since time immemorial, this has symbolized the power through which the miracles are consummated . . .' More interference until, 'His knowledge of the inner secrets of this timeless craft developed under the shield of this instrument. Without its master to control it, this is devoid of its vital force. It becomes but a stick of wood which others would sully were they to employ it.'

The figure's hand moved again, a knee came up and there was a crack as he brought the shape down across the knee, then leaned forward to push two halves of whatever it was into the soft earth of the grave.

The second man continued.

'Let us join in a closing moment of meditation:

'May we render a worthy tribute to our friend Claudius Damautus, by picking up the burdens he has laid down . . .' Again, and for whatever else was said, the mikes went crazy with static and even some other odd and uncanny sounds. They were almost certainly made by the equipment and the hedge, but Herbie felt the cold tingle as the short hairs stood up on the back of his neck. It was as though Worboys had set the stage on purpose, as if some eerie ritual were being performed, and the sounds, like animal cries and the creaking of branches, continued to play over whatever was being said. Presently the sound just turned into white noise, and the camera followed the two monk-like creatures as they walked softly away from the graveside.

The tape flickered, then went black. Cut to credits, Herbie thought. Words were leaping around in his head. Claudius Damautus. Claudius Damautus. Augustus Claudius Keene – 'His father was a history scholar. Roman Empire', part of the dossier had said. Who in hell was Claudius Damautus?

'What you make of it, Herb?'

'What they put in the grave?'

Worboys slid his hand inside his beautifully cut jacket and produced a thin packet of tissue, around six inches long. Carefully he unwrapped it.

It was made of wood, lacquered shiny black with an inch or so of white tip at each end. Cracked in two. The jagged crack fitted to make it a length of wood around a foot long.

Herbie heard Willis Maitland-Wood's voice again – 'We knew about it, about his expertise – the old Chief and myself – because he demonstrated it to us on many occasions. You see, we all belonged to the same club at one time, and I'm not allowed to disclose any more than that.'

'Masonic? One of those odd secret societies? Funny handshakes? Rituals? What you think, Herb?'

'I don't think funny societies. I think something different. I think a society, or even societies. But not funny in the sense you're thinking, Tony. You know what this is?' He lifted the two pieces of wood. 'You must've seen one. Is Magic Wand, Tony. Magic Wand, like with the magic tricks you see in clubs, or with Paul Daniels on

TV. Or David Copperfield, Siegfried and Roy, all those great people.'

'Oh, you mean conjurers?' Sneer. Curve of the lip.

'I think they prefer to be called Magicians. You see David Copperfield do the flying?'

'Actually, no. Don't really go in for that kind of stuff.'

'You never seen Copperfield fly? Should be ashamed. Sits there, wide eyed, says he's always dreamed of flying, then he does just that. Amazing. People all round him. Flies into a glass box. They put the lid on. Still flies. No wires. No strings. Then he flies over the audience. Picks up a girl and flies with her in his arms. Last he flies up and a falcon flies out onto his wrist. Moved to tears, and unashamed. Wonderful.' After the one operation they had given him a couple of years ago, Herbie had gone on vacation to the United States. He did not like gambling, but he still went to Vegas – mainly to see Siegfried and Roy. Copperfield had been playing at Caesar's Palace so he had taken in that show as well. Big Herbie Kruger had been a magic buff from before his secret life. His father had taken him to see The Great Bagheera on his tenth birthday. He had even had a *Zauberkästen* – a magic set – on that day. There was a time when Big Herb's great ambition was to be like The Great Bagheera and perform miracles.

'It's all a fake.' Worboys was still sneering.

'Maybe. But me? I believe, because great magicians do impossible things. I believe, and what have we got here? We got ourselves a dead magician here, Tony, that's what we got. The Great Gus Keene: Magic and Wonders. Smoke and Mirrors, that's what we got.'

9

Big Herbie wanted to start questioning people; the widow Keene to be precise, but the powers-that-be had said no, not yet.

'For heaven's sake, Herb, let the poor girl adjust. You've already had a little time with her.'

'Not enough. The first time she was coming to terms with things. The second was a quick ID of personal effects.'

'Give her a few days,' Worboys told him.

'Is correct to talk with her now; straight off.' Herb was frustrated, and feeling grim enough about the necessary inquisition. To him this was mere procrastination.

'You don't think she was hand in glove with the buggers who did this, Herb, so what's the problem?'

'The problem is that you made me a bloody detective, so I got to do it correct. I got to ask her if Gus was on edge; phone calls in the night; suspicious cars along the road or footpads near the scene. We don't even know what he was doing in Salisbury that night. Have no clue about the other guy seen with him by the roadside. Carole could shed light. Open a window. I need her now.'

'Couple of days, Herb, eh? Just a couple of days.' He was not asking, but giving an order.

Herb tried to put the bizarre scene at the cemetery from his mind and concentrate on the files and notes that Gus had left behind, but the more he tried, the more impossible it became. He had exhausted his choices regarding the files from the Registry mainframe. Even the ones into which he had peeked illegally had brought forth nothing of interest. In the end, though he did not like the idea of talking to Angus Crook, it was the only option left to him.

'Want you to do a wee favour for me, Angus,' he said on the secure line, carefully using the word 'wee' instead of 'little' in order to reach across the language barrier. The problem was that the 'wee' came out as 'vee'.

Angus grunted, so he tried a small threat, saying he could come down with the catch-all piece of paper the Chief had signed.

'Private lives,' he explained. 'Things that don't get in normal jackets. Trivia hidden from all the clowns who have no need to know.'

'Their *Blue Jackets*,' Angus supplied.

'Ja. Yes, that's the kind of thing.' Herb knew the files were called *Blue Jackets*. You had to have about twenty passwords to get at them on the computers, and what they contained was usually of no value to anybody: little sensitive secrets; skeletons in family closets; peccadilloes that had no true bearing on how they conducted their professional lives; shame and scandal in the family. People even asked for certain small nuggets to be buried in the *Blue Jackets*, and sometimes the request was turned down.

After all the fuss in what had once been the DDR, across the Berlin Wall when it was still standing, Herbie had asked for his major indiscretion to be buried in a *Blue Jacket* and they had said, no way.

'Whose *Blue Jackets* would ye be thinking of?' Angus asked with suspicion lacing his words.

'Former Deputy CSIS, Maitland-Wood, and the old Chief.'

At the distant end Angus sucked in breath through his teeth as though he were about to say that to do this was more than his job was worth.

'And Gus,' Herb added.

'Can't promise anything, ye ken.' Angus was back in his Rob Roy role.

'You ken that if you ain't doing it I shall come and thump you on your Scottish melon.' Herb hung up and waited, getting on with his reading.

Gus's manuscript was smooth and efficient – dealing with family, childhood and education in a matter of three pages which spread into the mind through the eyes at witty breakneck speed. Before you knew it, Gus was in the military and taking a course on interrogation with Army Intelligence, giving the reader just enough to whet the appetite but not enough to reveal the true secrets of the confessor's art.

There followed the story of his first interrogation, which, if you had known Gus, was relatively amusing. Some well-liked corporal working in immediate post-war Berlin – in a Quartermaster's office – had gone on leave, and then gone AWOL. He had been missing for a week when they discovered that about 200 ration stamps – worth around £500 sterling on the open market – had gone AWOL with the nice corporal.

The military police had picked him up in some den of iniquity deep in the heart of London's Soho. The corporal, impossibly named Tweets, who had always been thought of as a docile, rather shy man, had fought like a tiger and denied everything to the military cops. Gus was sent, from his unit in Berlin, to Aldershot where they were holding Corporal Tweets, ready to do the inquisition. Armed with all the best psychological ploys, plus considerable evidence, he prepared to face his victim as a monk would prepare for his final vows.

'Well, Corporal Tweets,' he began. 'You know they're going to charge you with theft, being absent without leave, selling government property and resisting arrest.' He thought it better to lay the case out straight away, and now prepared to break the man down into small pieces of gibbering jelly.

'Oh, yes, sir. I know, and that's fair enough. I'm guilty on all counts. Don't know what got into me. Never been to a court martial before. Should be quite interesting.'

Herbie chuckled over this, then his mind wandered again. Perhaps he should go through everything and check all files concerning Gus's various brushes with the Provisional IRA and the newer FFIRA, for they still seemed the most likely perpetrators.

He searched, flicking through the written pages, then Gus's notes. Eventually he came to a folder the first page of which said IRELAND. There it all was, and it made quite a horror story. Over one decade alone, Gus had travelled to Northern Ireland no less than a hundred times – and these were not mere day trips. The jobs were all detailed – names, reasons for interrogations, results. This was enough to make the man a legitimate target, but there was more: meetings with the Security Forces in London; interrogations all over the place. Some of the stuff was cross-referenced, and to go through it would take a long time. In fact the main cross-reference was to another file headed TERRORISM. This contained a whole mass of material which showed that Gus had either carried out, or assisted at, the interrogations of almost 100 known, or detained, terrorists. He had obviously had a great deal of knowledge regarding the entire spectrum of both overt and covert organizations: PLO, Red Brigade, various splinter groups, Black September, the Baader-Meinhof Gang. Gus had even assisted the Germans in the interrogations of those charming people.

In all, Gus must have been a marked man the world over, and on the hit list of a dozen organizations: there was a huge pile of information, and two draft chapters covering the anti-terrorist work, but Herb's mind, still jumping like a grasshopper, was not ready for that particular journey.

He returned to Gus's narrative. Back in Berlin he was sent to one of the outlying units dealing with the denazification process. Herb was just about to read this long and interesting section when the telephone rang.

It was Angus.

'What're ye actually looking for here, Herbie?'

'What you got? Multiple choices?'

'I can give ye a bit of sex scandal on Maitland-Wood.'

'You can?' Surprise, then he recalled the young Mem-sahib, formerly Emma Paisley of Accounts. 'Bit of the lad was he, Angus? Bit of a career lecher on the side?'

'Ye might say that. Comes as a wee surprise. I knew him, ye ken, and he always seemed ta be a pompous little fat fart to me.'

'To everybody, Angus. You are not alone in your amazement. Does not really interest me . . .'

'Aye, two long-standing affairs with girls from Registry. Much younger than himself. Nights in iffy motels; weekends in Brighton and Eastbourne. Ye ken about the marriage when he retired?'

'Yes, I ken, Angus. Some women like older men.'

'Aye, it's a funny old world right enough. The man had been tupping Emma for two years before he handed in his papers, so he must have had something the girls liked.'

'Probably a gleaming and beautiful soul, Angus. What else?'

'Only one wee funny thing.'

'Which is?'

'In civilian life he was allowed to use the letters AIMC after his name.'

'So what's AIMC?'

'Associate of the Inner Magic Circle. Ye have to take exams to get that, and there's only one higher order which is by appointment only. He was a conjurer on the side. Nobody knew that. Quite a high-up conjurer as well. Your Magic Circle doesna' take any riffraff. They're guy strict.'

'What about the old Chief?'

'Shared the same secrets as his deputy, except he was a humble MMC – Member of the Magic Circle. Never saw either of them do any tricks except in the line of duty.'

'Gus?'

'Nay a whisper. Nothing – unless you count the lang affair he had with Carole before his divorce.'

Herbie thanked him and said he might need more. Gus not on the Magic Circle list? That was odd, if only because of the pair of monk-like men doing the ritual over the grave. Perhaps Gus kept *his* secrets out of his *Blue Jacket*. He leaned back in his chair and smiled at the thought of Willis doing conjuring tricks. His eyes roved around the room, and his mind went back to the days when he spent hours here with Gus, his friendly confessor, always reassuring him that he was on his side, yet asking the really difficult questions when you least expected them. Gus was great on the throwaway lines, like 'You ever mention our American cousins to them, Herb?' Or, 'What about the *Hallet* business?' Worst of all, 'How much you tell 'em about *Birdseed*, Herb?'

Herbie had nearly gone crazy about the one black mark in his otherwise distinguished record. Against all instructions he had crossed into what was then East Berlin – a very big No-No – and, after several horrors, the East German security people had got him, banged up and at their mercy. Then the real authorities arrived so that, during the time he had been away, Herb had been put to the question by the KGB. He had done as well as could have been expected, for everyone breaks at some point. He knew what he had given to them. At the time he had been proud. It was only later that it was revealed to him – by Gus and Tubby Fincher – that two matters were still sensitive. Not just sensitive, but things that put a deep-seated penetration in the Kremlin in a very difficult position. He remembered this room with some horror, for it was here that he found out he had just about blown someone's cover with the *Hallet* and *Birdseed* material.

The agent concerned had been cryptoed *Stentor* and was the source of all good things from well inside what the Sovs used to call the State Organs. Kruger had truly compromised *Stentor*.

Now, as he leaned back in his chair and thought about Gus and his own old problems, he recalled something else. The room had changed a great deal, like the rest of the house. When he had been here before, with Gus being as subtle as a snake, there were two big mirrors, one on either side of the fireplace. Intuition had told him then that the mirrors shielded space; that the mirrors were not normal; that behind the mirrors technicians were monitoring his sessions with Gus. Audio on one side, together with someone taking notes, and video on the other. All those years ago he knew that behind the mirrors there were small rooms. Now, the mirrors had been replaced by bookcases stocked with leather spines.

He rose and went over to the books. They were real enough, but somehow he had the feeling that they had been bought by the yard as cover. There were titles here to which neither Gus nor Carole would have paid much heed.

Leather-bound copies of Jane Austen, the Brontës, and even Hardy were not Gus's thing at all. Gus was a biography and military history buff, not to mention arcane psychological journals. The books, Herb decided, were set-dressing, which meant that, behind the bookcases, the rooms were still in place.

He began to move the books, one by one, in the hope that some title activated a hidden catch. Then he realized that this method was pure Hollywood, and not the way old Gus would have camouflaged a lock. He examined the moulding around the shelves. Nothing, so Herb returned to the desk and began to examine the drawers, knowing this was something he should have done on the first day.

The top drawer on his right contained a revelation in the shape of a tape-deck rigged for long play/record, and a portion of the spool had already been used. A quick examination showed that the mike had been hidden almost directly in the centre of the desk; a tiny seed embedded in a fancy solar-cell calculator – an oblong affair on a small stand, with the glass touchpad working as an overlay to a hologrammatic background of coins.

Kruger rewound the spool and pressed play, startled as the voice came eerily from hidden speakers built into the two bookcases flanking the fireplace. Somehow, Gus had managed to hook this little machine into a larger stereo system, and the voice seemed to surround Herb: soft, a touch of amusement buried in Gus's familiar tones.

'If anyone's listening to this, it means I've either disappeared or quietly shuffled off this mortal coil. If that's the case, I'm sure a lot of people will demand explanations,' Gus began. 'Whoever you are, out there, you will already know that my life has been measured, not in coffee spoons, but in arcane crossword puzzles: the kind I mention at the start of my memoirs. I do not see why I should have all the fun. There are things about my life and times not known to many people at the Office. Those who do know a little about these matters are unlikely to come forward, so I will have to give you a push in the right direction.' The voice paused for a brief chuckle. Then:

'You are probably sitting at my desk as you listen to me, and you may, or may not, suspect hidden chambers, or even passageways. Without moving the telephone on your right, just hit 62442. Then touch the Redial button. Don't, whatever you do, lift the receiver. Just enter the number and hit Redial. Happy hunting, and if some secret idiot has seen fit to do away with me, I hope you nail him.'

Gently, as though it might trigger an explosion, Herbie did as the dead, disembodied voice told him. Over by the fireplace there was an audible click and the shelves of books to the left of the fireplace moved. A door opening up. Slowly he pulled himself out of his chair and walked towards the half-open bookcase, pulling it back to reveal a large U-shaped room, which ran right around the chimney-breast.

It was much larger than he expected. The main

oblongs on each side of the fireplace were at least 24 feet by 15 feet, while the space behind the chimney was around 8 feet wide – probably larger in fact, for practically the entire wall space was taken up with shelving, some of it glassed in with sliding panels.

It was a magic cave. He only had to glimpse some of the titles neatly lining the bookcases to see that: *Modern Magic*, an old book, obviously, but in mint condition; a row of slim matching volumes, *The Jinx*, each spine giving numbers of editions; another set, *The Phoenix*, again with numbered spines; books on advanced sleight of hand; books on magical history; books with titles that made no sense to him, some 2–300 titles in all. Ranged along the sides of the passage directly behind the chimney-breast were lines of videos – some obviously specialized instructional tapes, but some marked neatly in ink: *Damautus: Mentalism Live 1992*; *Damautus: Close-up Acts 1, 2 & 3 1991*, and so on, each prefaced by *Damautus*, then either *Stage*, *Close-up* or *Mentalism*.

The room to the right of the fireplace was the one where most of the shelves were protected by glass, and behind the glass, neatly piled little boxes or larger items laid out in a precise order: a pair of silver chalices; an oblong Lucite box with brass trim; glasses of various sizes. Right in the centre of the room stood a beautifully crafted table, its top inlaid with very high-quality green baize: the kind you would see in the better casinos. A triptych mirror was set on the table, with a chair neatly drawn in so that you could sit facing it.

Herbie stood there, mouth open, then wandered back and forth through the rooms, trying to take in everything, an impossible task at short notice. Why, he wondered, had Gus's secret not been in his *Blue Jacket*? BMW and the old Chief had been members of the élite Magic Circle. Why not Gus/Damautus?

As he moved back to the first room, a title caught his eye. Whaley's *Who's Who in Magic*. He slid the dark green book out of the row and turned to the Ds. There were two entries. First:

Damautus
(SPAIN: fl.1540s) A Spanish knight. Amateur Cardman who visited Milan in 1543 in the retinue of Emperor Charles V of Spain.[Ch;Dif].

Well, that for sure was not Gus, but the following entry most certainly was:

Damautus, Claudius MIMC
(Britain: fl.1975–) Birth and real name unknown. An exceptional close-up and mentalist performer, Claudius Damautus is a magical legend who refuses to announce performances or appearances – usually at major Magical Conventions – in advance. Has been offered the AMA Magician of the Year Award three times and refused. Offered the IBM Gold Medal which he also turned down. Author of several books, *The Mystique of Magic*; *The Secrets of Damautus*; *The Mystery of Mentalism*. Performs for charities, and gives limited lectures within the magical community.

'Curiouser und curiouser, said Alice,' Herbie muttered to himself. Magicians, he suspected, did not shun publicity, yet here was Gus, practising his usual deceits with the Magical Fraternity. He was mulling it over, trying to work out why BMW and the old Chief had their interest in the art of conjuring squirrelled away in their *Blue Jackets*, while Gus Keene, obviously a master of this craft, refused coveted awards and performed only when he chose the moment. He was thinking about this when he heard a light knock on Keene's study door.

Quickly he stepped back into the room, pushing lightly on the false bookcase until it clicked back into place. It was only as he did this that he realized the opening or closing of the door activated lights inside the secret rooms.

Walking to the centre of the study he called out, 'Yes? Come.'

Bex Olesker poked her head around the door. 'You free, Guv?' she asked, using the Criminal Investigation Department's – in all its forms from C 1 to SO 13 – abbreviation for a senior officer in charge of a squad or an investigation. Guv, or Guv'nor was standard among most of the British police forces, both central or local.

'Sure, Bex, come on in and I shall a tale unfold.'

She had the freckled grin of a sixteen-year-old, and closed the door gently behind her.

'It's Herb, not Guv.' In the pause, he reflected that the old devil lust had not invaded his brain when he first saw this woman from SO 13. His mind breathed a sigh of relief. Not a flicker of desire, not even a small twitch in the loins. The devil was perhaps dead, and a good thing if it was.

She nodded, and he gestured to the leather chair on the far side of Gus Keene's desk. 'But first, I would like you to unfold a tale to me.' Herb did his goofy smile.

'Shoot, Gu . . . Herb.'

'What's a nice girl like you doing in SO 13 and working in spook country?'

'That's what men are supposed to say to whores.' She did not smile, and Kruger got the distinct impression that, in some small way, he had offended her.

'Wouldn't know,' he shrugged. 'Probably put it badly. What I mean is how were you chosen to work with an old reprobate like me?'

'Reprobate? I was told that you were one of the best. A super-spook from way back.'

'Like athletes we super-spooks get out of training. You should know, DCI Bex, that I'm not even a member of the club any more. Blotted my copybook a couple of times; had a few nervous breakdowns. I'm doing this as an act of respect for an old friend. I have ID, and a few other things, but I'm a retired spook, now acting and unpaid. What about you?'

She told him; talked about the FFIRA Active Service Unit she had bottled up in a terraced house in Camberwell. How they had even spiked the place and had tapes running. How Billy Boyle the Bomber had turned up and how they listened to conversations until late in the night. Then how, after some three hours, the conversations and noises suddenly stopped. 'It was like someone had pulled a switch,' she said.

At first she thought one of their mikes had gone on the blink, but with some horror quickly realized that she had committed the cardinal sin of all surveillance operations. Because they had the place spiked, and well covered from the front, she had neglected the rear. 'There was no real way out of the back. No doors. Only one window that was big enough for an elephant to get through. The bloody house backed almost directly on to the rear of another terrace.'

Herbie nodded. 'So you had no way of knowing they'd rented the house behind, eh?'

'You'd have thought of that, wouldn't you?'

'Ah, but I'm an old man. Well, old in experience.'

'While I'll be lucky if I'm not back in uniform doing traffic if I don't make a collar on this one. The buggers had a big reel-to-reel tape-player running for half the night. They were long gone and away before we even knew anything was up.'

'So, you won't do it again. You been briefed on this thing of ours – Cosa Nostra?' he added, knowing it was quite a good gag, as gags went. She hardly smiled. Might go better second house.

'Up to a point.' She rummaged in her large leather shoulderbag and pulled out a thick manilla envelope. She opened the bag just enough to let Herbie see she was carrying a Heckler and Koch P9S automatic 9mm pistol. 'This is what they gave me.' She held out the folder. 'They said you'd fill in the gaps.'

'Okay,' Herbie gave an innocent grin. 'You show me yours and I'll show you mine.'

'They said you had a strange sense of humour.' Bex Olesker leaned forward and passed him the envelope. Again, she seemed a shade offended by Herb's remark.

During that first evening, while Herbie Kruger and DCI Bex Olesker were exchanging information, there was another meeting between the FFIRA and the London *Intiqam* team. This time, Hisham did not have to travel to Dublin or Belfast. Declan came to him, using a postcard and chalk mark, the aged tradecraft of dead-letter boxes – the kind of thing that the general public had thought outdated at the end of the Cold War.

They met in the stalls crush bar of the Palace Theatre, and sat together through *Les Misérables* – which they both found strangely emotional – doing their business during the pre-show and the interval.

'I've a personal matter I'd like you to think about.'

'Tell me. I'll do all I can to help you.'

'Well, this is *very* personal. Something I wouldn't want to take care of myself. You see, I was engaged to be married. Back in '84 that was. Ann Bolan, fought for the Cause. Died for the Cause as well. Was murdered right here in London.'

'You know who murdered her?'

'Ah, does it matter who? The usual SAS thugs pulled the trigger. Shot four of our people. Unarmed they were. Just shot down like sacks of flour.'

'We all take our chances.' Hisham sounded flat, completely oblivious to death. Whatever happened was the will of Allah.

'Yes, but she was young and there only for the experience. For Ann it was a training exercise.'

'You want us to wipe out the SAS?'

'No. There were four people very close to the cover-up – and I swear by God it *was* a cover-up.'

'You have names?'

'Oh, yes, we have names. One's a fella who did a lot of work in the North. An Inquisitor and Fixer. Gus

Keene his name was, and he was attached to the SIS –
the murdering bloody Brit Secret Intelligence Service, as
were the other three.'

'Whose names are?'

'Two of them still work with the spooks. Archie
Blount-Wilson, they nickname him "The Whizz" and
he has a nice little flat in Bury Street, St James, right
here in London.' He gave the number.

'The next?'

'Anthony James Worboys. They call him Tony and
he's First Deputy Chief. Lives in a big house called
The Hall. Harrow Weald. Used to be a clinic.'

'And the fourth man? Good title for a movie, the
fourth man.'

'He's retired, there's his address and the other
addresses,' slipping a file card into Hisham's hand.
'Keene's living in a little house the intelligence people
have in the grounds of their training, interrogation and
debriefing place up near Warminster; Blount-Wilson has
the flat in Bury Street; Worboys in Harrow Weald; and
the last one, Kruger, lives in this cottage just outside
Lyndhurst. You know where these places are?'

'My knowledge of England is, as they say in books,
comprehensive. You want these people taken out.'

Declan nodded. 'I don't want any tails coming back
to us. That's what I really want.'

'I'll do what I can.' Hisham's eyes registered sincerity
plus 100 per cent.

When he had arrived for the meeting, Declan was
not so much angry as put out, but Hisham promising
to service a dead-letter box at least twenty-four hours
before an event in the United Kingdom, and his promise
to take care of those four bastards, made life easier.

'We're still on for the putty?' Hisham asked him,
as though it did not matter either way.

'If you keep to the bargain, yes. End of next month.'
Declan shook hands and left Hisham among the crowd,
crossing the road and heading away down Charing Cross

Road. He was smiling to himself in a knowing way as he passed the corner building.

He was still smiling when the unmarked car drew up a little ahead of him and two plainclothes officers approached, blocking the pavement. He glanced around, hoping that Hisham was following and was the real target.

'Declan Norton?' One of the big men asked.

'Yes, that's me.' There was no point in trying to bluff it out with the Met.

'We're police officers and we'd like you to come up the station with us. Just a few questions.'

'About what?'

'Let's talk at the nick, Declan,' said the second man. By this time there were a couple of uniforms just behind him and people on the street were starting to look interested.

'Don't bump your head getting in the car. We wouldn't like to be accused of police brutality.' The first man laughed.

Declan wondered how they had got on to him. He didn't even suspect Hisham, who had been careful not to be seen in the street outside the theatre in the Irishman's company. When they had met in the bar inside the Palace Theatre, Declan had not even noticed that the Arab had removed the red silk handkerchief from his breast pocket and rearranged it.

Once they got going, exchanging information, big Herbie did not want to stop. This, inevitably, led to a small clash with Bitsy. He had called for Ginger and asked if they could have sandwiches and coffee in Gus's old study. So, back came the answer, quick as a flash, to the effect that Bitsy was preparing a three-course dinner, as a welcome for Bex Olesker.

'Sorry,' Herb shrugged at Ginger. 'We're too busy for the full soup and fish tonight. Tell her we're sorry, but we're hard at it.'

Bitsy's somewhat terse reply came ten minutes later. The only suitable food in the house for sandwiches was spam. 'I adore spam,' Bex said with a smile.

'Spam's okay by me, and don't hold the mustard.' Herbie was oblivious to the fact that his instructions had caused a major disruption in the kitchen – a disappointment that Bitsy took very personally – though the sandwiches did arrive, via Ginger, complete with sliced tomatoes to, as Bitsy put it, 'deaden the tastelessness of the spam'.

Herb then began a rundown briefing on all he already knew about Gus and his departure from this world. He included a précis of the confessor's progress through life, in particular the vast range of his job, carefully making sure that Bex knew about the constant arrangements that had been made to loan out his talents to just about every agency. He made a quick call to Worboys, at home, just to make sure she was *Cataract* cleared, before giving a slightly watered down version of that episode. He left out the latest magical revelations.

'So,' he chewed on a sandwich. 'Anything special you can add?'

Bex looked through her notes. 'I can see how the FFIRA might want him dead and buried, but, from what I've seen so far, the FFIRA had nothing to do with *that* bomb.' She said all the indications from the recent bombings and assassinations were that this was a relatively new organization, tuned to terror. There were two units – one in the UK and the other in the United States – and they both bore all the hallmarks of having come from the Middle East. 'It has a completely foreign handwriting. Definitely not FFIRA, but the feel of the thing's Arab. Gus have any Arab connections? Relatively recent?'

Kruger leafed through the relevant folder – the one which had given him pause when he saw where Gus had been used over the years.

'Yep,' his finger on the page. 'There you go. Three months. April to the end of June 1991, Riyadh. Duties: the interrogation of three captured senior Iraqi officers. Product Restricted 27, 28, 29. Deep Blanket.' He gave Olesker a shrug and a little smile. 'Means whatever Gus prised out of the Iraqis is put in an unbreakable safe, two hundred feet underground. Very limited access.'

'What would your best guess be?'

'The generals will now probably be living happy lives somewhere warm with a hundred interchangeable bimbos and all the spam they can eat.'

'Your best guess at what Gus gleaned from them?'

'Probably every site they knew concerning the manufacture of nuclear devices. Maybe every site for all – what do they call them? Weapons of Massive Destruction?'

'Mass Destruction.'

'Massive, Mass, what's the difference?'

'An Introit, Kyrie, Sanctus and a Gloria.' It was the first time Bex Olesker had even attempted humour.

'So, if it wasn't the FFIRA, and it came from the

Middle East, it has to be some well-trained terrorist team probably out of Iraq. Their Leader wreaking some revenge.'

'So what can we reckon they've done: Gus? Probably. Then the Italian intelligence officer in DC: the shooting.'

'He's on the list?'

'Both the Americans and ourselves think he was snuffed by the same people, if only because nobody has claimed it. Then we've got the Foreign Office man – diplomatic corps – and the third secretary at the American embassy. Both in London and both car bombs.'

'Then New York?' Herb suggested.

Bex nodded. 'All in one day. Large car bomb on Fifth Avenue; subway closed by a briefcase device; and the ghastly airliner explosion as it was taking off from La Guardia. Our American relatives started to panic after that. Big clampdown.'

'The London underground bombs at the tube stations – King's Cross, Waterloo, Paddington and Victoria. No takers, so it has to be the new boys on the block.'

'Right. We have a name for them at the Yard – at SO 13: the Shadows.'

'Old pop group: Cliff Richard and the Shadows. You also counting the two bombs in Rome, and the diplomats snuffed in Paris . . . ?'

'Of course, and the bombs in Aldershot and the RAF base – Boscombe Down, was it?'

Herb nodded. 'Good old English name, Boscombe Down. Trips prettily off the tongue.'

'We've had people working on links between the obviously murdered victims, not simply the random bombs. The guy from the American Embassy was Scowcroft's assistant during the Gulf War; the diplomat's name was Darlington – your FO man. He turns out to have been attached to the British Special Forces during the Gulf War. Ran liaison between them and London. The Italian in Washington was a co-ordinator between the Italian Air

Force squadrons and Schwarzkopf's Central Command at Riyadh.'

'And the two people dusted in Paris?'

'You do know that one of them was there from Kuwait? Discussing new arms proposals; and the other was a senior French officer – played a big part in rounding up suspects in Kuwait City.'

'So they're all tied to the Gulf War?'

'One way or another. The analysts all say this is their Leader's payback time. Two teams, they reckon. One out of London, covering Europe as a whole. The other based in New York.'

'Taking out specific targets, and using terrorist tactics. That's only of value to them if they eventually announce who they are.'

'We think they will; but they'll do it carefully. Describe themselves as a renegade organization. The Leader would wish to distance himself from them – in the early stages, of course.'

'Leaves a nasty taste when you talk of early stages. Makes you wonder what end game they plan.'

DCI Bex Olesker's eyes flicked up from the papers she held and gave Herbie a quick going over, as though questioning his ability. 'So, what do we do?' she asked.

'You're a sleuth, Bex. So we sleuth.'

'Starting where?'

'At the beginning. If my old friend Gus really is the beginning, we start with him and his lovely widow. You reckon he's a natural target, right?'

'Natural as the polluted air we breathe.'

'Well, I've a small problem with Gus.' He reached forward and went through the routine with the telephone so that Bex almost flinched at the click from the bookcase.

'What the . . . ?'

'Merlin's cave.' He gave the goofy grin. 'Gus's secret, and it's not a natural secret. Through there is the hidden part of his life, and I can't figure why he would want to keep it hidden. Why he should hide a skill.'

'What're you talking about, Herb?'

'I'm talking about Merlin; about Prospero, Bex, I'm talking magic here. You like magic?'

'What d'you mean by magic?'

'I'm talking of coins cascading from thin air; of levitation; of metamorphosis in full view – one person changing places with another; of empty boxes that suddenly sprout lightly clad ladies. I'm talking of childhood innocence; of wonder; of delight; of solid rings that link together and shuffled decks of cards from which one, only thought of, suddenly rises with no means of support . . .'

'You're talking about conjuring.'

'Call it that if you wish, like priests call out devils by saying, "I conjure thee to depart hence." I like to call it magic. Gus was a magician, Bex. The proof's through that artificial door. I think he was probably a very good magician but, though I knew him well, I did not know this about him, and neither did his close friends.'

'What're you saying, Herb?'

'I'm saying that Gus practised the old and noble art of entertaining with magic. I'm also saying that those of us who worked with him, close to him, did not know this. Don't you think that's kind of odd? Usually magicians perform for their friends, because that's what they like to do.'

'Yes, indeed they do.' Bex Olesker gave a long and weary sigh. 'My grandfather did that. Every time we went to see him – Christmas, Easter, whenever – we had to see his latest piece of deception. They're *tricks*, Herbie, and they drive me crazy. I'm a terrible sceptic. I used to be a pain in the bum to my grandfather, and I haven't changed. Nowadays you go to a restaurant and what happens?'

'You eat?'

'You try to eat. A lot of these places now have a resident magician; comes to your table and does his little tricks, then you tip him. Some of them are clever, but they still drive me crazy. I know they are *tricks . . .*'

'And you want to know how they do it?'

'Sometimes it's obvious how they do it. You can work it out by logic. If I can't see how, I go crazy trying to work it out. I *know* it's not magic, Herb. So I . . .'

'You sleuth. Figure it out.' He gave her a wan smile. 'Oh, Bex, you've lost your innocence. You should see these people with wonder in your heart.'

'I switch off Paul Daniels whenever he's on TV. Can't stand him.' She cocked her head on one side and did a passable imitation of Paul Daniels saying, 'You're going to like this . . . Not a lot . . . but you're going to like it.'

'Well, maybe you're not the right audience, but Gus left tapes in there and I think he wanted us to look at them.'

She raised her eyebrows. 'Why?'

'Because he kept his skill secret from all of us, and I want to know why he did that. It might just have a little bearing on the danger and the terror. It's inexplicable, why he should never talk about it; it's not as if it's the kind of hobby you leave hidden away.'

'I'll see how they're all done and I'll tell you,' she threatened, like a spoiled child.

'And I'll close my ears. Worst thing that can happen to a person is to lose innocence. You'll tell me next you don't believe in Santa Claus or the Tooth Fairy.'

'Don't be stupid, Herb.'

'God?' As soon as he said it, Herb knew he had touched a button.

'Yes, there's a God. Maybe that's the reason I don't like tricks. Only God can provide miracles. Magicians pretend to perform the impossible. There's a question of ethics as well. I've a feeling that magicians lie in order to entertain. I'm not sure that's right, any more than I think

154

a comedian pretending to be drunk is really moral.'

'Ah, I see.' Though he did not.

They passed through into Gus's secret cache of books, tapes and the things he used to perform his magic. Herbie chose the tape labelled *Damautus: Close-up Act 1*, taking it into Gus's work room and slipping it into the VCR.

'If it's the usual rubbish, I'm not going to watch.' Bex sounded formidable.

'Think you should, Bex. We're going to question the widow Keene – tomorrow, if I have my way – and she has said nothing about Gus's little secret. A wife would know these things. You ready?'

'As ready as I'll ever be.'

Herbie pressed the 'Play' button on the remote.

Hisham walked slowly back up Shaftesbury Avenue towards Piccadilly Circus, staying on the outside of the pavement. The car that pulled up just in front of him was a nondescript elderly Fiat. He increased his speed and the rear door opened so that he could duck his head and slide in next to the young man in the back.

'Welcome.' The driver turned and smiled at him.

'You can talk freely,' the young man sitting next to him said as they pulled away from the curb. As he spoke, he reached out and patted him on the shoulder.

'You take him?' Hisham asked.

'He was taken. You get any surprises?'

'Yes. He wants us to carry out four assassinations.'

'No future plans?'

'If you mean bombs, no. He was a little edgy.'

'Who does he want dusted?'

Hisham gave him the four names.

'One of them's gone already.' The driver was negotiating the warren of streets around Soho. 'Keene. Blown to pieces in his car. They think *you* did that, and with some reason.'

'Really? Keene's dead? Good riddance to him. I know him by reputation, and he did a great deal of harm to us, one way and another. So, that makes only three we have to do.'

'You're not to touch a hair of their heads, understand?'

'I'll make all three look like attempts. Have to. They're going to supply Semtex after the jobs are done.'

'And you're going to need the Semtex? More big bangs waiting for us?'

'I can't talk about that and you know it. That side of things is separate. Not part of our deal.'

'We're getting leaned on as well, Hisham. People are frightened.'

'With good reason. I said I would deliver certain people and I'm doing that. The deal was for what we call *Magic Lightning* to be called off and I'm going to do that, but I can't give you anything else.'

'What if we take the whole of your team in?'

'Then you'll get nowhere. There's a back-up group ready to come in over here and in the States, and you'll get no details of the American side of things.'

'You won't even give us a tip on how many and where they are?'

'I've told you. There are six, just like us. I think they operate out of New York, but I cannot be sure of that. You have all I can give.'

'We think you can provide a little more.'

'Maybe, but nothing at this time.'

'I think we have to insist.'

'On what?'

'On good, clean warnings for bombs or similar devices. Warnings that will allow us to clear areas. The civilian casualty figures are already too high.'

They had driven around the crowded Soho area, then doubled back, heading up Piccadilly and into Knightsbridge. Hisham made no comment regarding the last suggestion.

'What if we close you down, Hisham?'

'As long as I maintain contact with the FFIRA

you're not going to close me down. You know that, and I know it.'

'Keep looking over your shoulder, Hisham.' The car pulled over to the side of the road and the rear door opened for him.

'We could be ordered to close you down. Particularly if there are more casualties by unexpected explosions. So, we suggest that you call the number we're using. Give us the codeword Sacrifice followed by the exact place and time. If you don't do that, then the package will go to Baghdad. You have to understand that we have duties also.'

As Hisham stepped from the car, he spoke again. 'So, friend, just keep watching your back. You never know. And do as you're told.'

Hisham was unhappy as he hailed a cab and asked to be taken to Paddington Station.

The people who had chosen him in Baghdad had done so for many reasons, not least being his loyalty to his country's Leader and his familiarity with clandestine operations. He was one of several special operatives who had spent almost a year in Kuwait before the Iraqi army had moved in. During the war itself he had been part of the bodyguard detail for the Leader. They also took into account the fact that he had lived in Europe for two years and spoke excellent English. Through the bulk of that time he lived in London.

What his masters in Baghdad did not know was that, during those years, Hisham had committed a serious crime in London. Worse, he had been caught, and, worse still, it had been what they call a honeytrap.

On a Friday towards the end of July in that burning and beautiful summer of 1983, he had gone out into the West End of London, dressed to kill, with his beard neatly trimmed, and his Gucci shoes shined to such a perfection that, if he played his cards and placed his feet correctly, he could tell you the colour of a girl's underwear. In the case of Mary Delacourt it was black, but he did not find that out until later.

They met in a very smart nightclub, much haunted in those days by younger members of the Royal Family and their hangers-on. The meeting seemed completely accidental and Hisham never once really imagined that *he* had been picked up. Mary Delacourt was twenty-five years old, with long blonde hair that fell around her shoulders, a smooth sheen, so thick and flowing that Hisham immediately thought of some kind of gold mirror. She had clear skin, radiating good health, very light blue eyes, and lips that beckoned every time she spoke.

Once they had met and begun talking it was only a matter of time. When they left the club, it was Mary who laughingly asked him, 'Your place or mine?'

They went to her flat in the better part of Notting Hill, close by Holland Park, and made love in ways that until now Hisham had only experienced in fantasy.

She told him that she worked in a rather dreary government office and, within a week, they were inseparable to the extent that Hisham reached a point where he even thought of marrying her. Religion would be difficult but other men had successfully overcome that particular hurdle.

Exactly two weeks after they had met, at four in the morning the door to her apartment was broken down and they found themselves naked and facing four police officers and two somewhat sinister men in plain clothes.

The uniformed police drove Mary away in the back of a squad car, while Hisham was taken to a large apartment off Marylebone High Street where the two sinister men in plain clothes were joined by two more. They sat him down and played some lengthy video-tapes which showed Mary and himself appearing to reinvent the sex act.

Then came the questions.

Who was he spying for? What information had Ms Delacourt passed over to him? Who was his contact? How did he get the information out of the country?

Hisham was bewildered and alarmed, but for most of the time he was able to keep up at least a patina of outrage. His main problem was that the two years in Europe had been arranged by officers within the Leader's council. His occupation was the covert buying of artillery. The Leader himself had told him that this was Iraq's greatest need. Artillery and ammunition.

All his trips from London to Paris and, on occasion, Switzerland had been as an agent of the Leader's High Command, a fact that he was not about to share with the counter-intelligence officers who spent days and nights interrogating him.

Much further down the road, to the night he met Declan at the Palace Theatre, Hisham was to learn that the FFIRA wanted him to arrange for the death of one of his interrogators from back in the golden London summer of 1983. The man called Keene, who had almost been his downfall in that apartment off Marylebone High Street.

Keene looked like an English farmer; he would recall that all his life. Keene also seemed to know more than he, Hisham, knew.

What these men laid in front of him was the indisputable information that he was engaged in a close sexual marathon with Mary Delacourt. They also told him that the dreary government office in which Mary worked was a department of the Ministry of Defence. She had access to highly sensitive documents and they showed him several surveillance videos – taken both inside and outside the MoD – which proved beyond doubt that Ms Mary Delacourt had been stealing them blind: removing documents by day, taking them home to be copied, and returning them on the following morning. The one thing that had kept them from arresting her was that they could not tie down any specific country or agency to whom Ms

Delacourt was passing the many documents to which she had access. In the end, it was the man Keene who put the proposal to Hisham. What he said left Hisham in no doubt that the British knew exactly what he was up to in Europe.

'We're after slightly larger fish than you,' Keene had told him, leaning against an elegant marble mantel-piece. 'Frankly, we're not too happy about bringing Ms Delacourt under the floodlights of public scrutiny. We'd rather hush up the entire matter as I'm sure you would, also . . .' He left the comment hanging, with his pipe smoke, in mid-air.

'What are you suggesting?'

'Mmmm.' Keene gave a deep-throated chuckle. 'We have pretty pictures of you and Ms Delacourt. You've seen them. You know what they mean, and I'm certain that there are those in Baghdad who wouldn't be all that pleased to know the British Security Service had such tapes. I'm suggesting that we pretend none of this happened.' He paused and Hisham knew he had signalled through his general demeanour that he was greatly relieved.

'There is a price,' Keene had continued. 'It's a very high price for someone like yourself.'

'If it's reasonable . . .' Hisham spread his hands, a gesture of both supplication and haggling.

'We think it's reasonable.'

'Well?'

'There may come a time when we need someone who is trusted by the present Iraqi régime. If we ever do require such a person, we will call on you. When we call it could be for a small service or possibly for something slightly more dangerous. If you refuse us, then we will blow you sky-high by releasing the tapes, and some ancillary material which will suggest that, while you were here in Europe, you engaged in a little freelance work.'

They gave him twenty-four hours to think about it

and, being no fool, Hisham decided to take the offer. After all, he considered, Iraq was on good terms with both the United States and Great Britain. He could not envisage things changing in his own lifetime, which was a very grave and stupid mistake on his part. Within days of the *Intiqam* team arriving in London, the approach was made. First, via a young woman who bumped into him as he was leaving the real estate agency which had dealt with the Clapham house. He had felt her hand near his breast pocket, and later recovered the note she had left there. It was simply a telephone number, followed by the words, 'Call us or we'll call your superiors in Baghdad.' He was totally compromised, as was the entire London team. Oddly, they were not hindered from carrying out their planned acts of terrorism. Now, however, the screws were starting to be turned.

What Hisham never knew was that, in 1983, within twelve hours of him agreeing to the proposal, Gus Keene had sat down in a restaurant near Oxford. His companion was Mary Delacourt – though, of course, that was not her true name.

'All done, my dear,' he told her after the waiter left them with menus, saying he would give them time to make up their minds. 'A very good job,' Keene said, and the young woman smiled.

'I do assure you that the pleasure was all mine. Arabs are exceptionally good lovers. Very ingenious, innovatory, I think the word is. You cut everything off too quickly.'

'The way things go, my dear, and I have to warn you that, if you decide to freelance until we need you again, you'll have to keep clear of Islam. As it is, we feel that you should take a year's sabbatical – all expenses paid, of course. Where would you like to go?'

At that time, Gus Keene was under discipline also. When the Security Service had asked for his services they had put a couple of possible scenarios to him, then told him that, whatever, if he accepted the job, the facts should not be relayed to any other agency in the United Kingdom or the United States.

As far as anyone knew, Gus had died with that particular piece of information. It had occurred at a time when there was a great deal of competition between the SIS and the Security Service.

As he sat in a taxi, heading back to Clapham, Hisham began to become deeply concerned. Now they demanded warnings. How many bombs could he get away with before *Yussif* – the intelligence team watching and working with them – began to latch on to the fact that the British were being warned?

By the time he had left the cab and was walking the half-mile to the house, Hisham had made a decision. He would play for time: call the contact with *Yussif* and outline the deal he had been forced to make with the Irish. Maybe they would actually have to kill one of the targets. The man who lived near the New Forest sounded ideal. Kruger. That was his name. Possibly within the week they would take out Kruger for real.

Just as Hisham reached the house in Clapham, so, miles away, near Warminster, his first target, Herbie Kruger, was pressing the 'Play' button on the VCR so that, with DCI Bex Olesker, he could watch the magician, Claudius Damautus.

11

Herbie sprawled, undignified, in his chair. Bex Olesker sat straight, hands on lap, back like a ramrod, knees together. She sat like a very Victorian young lady, he thought, then turned his attention to the screen.

The titles rolled. *Claudius Damautus: Live at the Magic Circle*, then the usual parade of director, cameraman, etc., etc., etc. A voice-over quietly told them that this performance was taped by a professional crew, in front of an invited audience, none of whom were magicians. It was a performance only, and no camera tricks were used. Other magicians would recognize a lot of the material, but would find the routining exceptionally interesting in the hands of such a master as Claudius Damautus.

Fade to a long shot of twenty-five or so people sitting in chairs which all but surrounded an elegant oak card-table with an inlaid baize top. Low, in the background, came the sound of Manuel de Falla's *Ritual Fire Dance* from *Love the Magician*. Then a voice nearby said, 'Ladies and Gentlemen – Claudius Damautus,' and the music changed. Herbie did not know what it meant, the haunting, mysterious sound of Clannad singing *Na Laethe Bhí*, but it certainly built atmosphere. Then Claudius Damautus walked quietly from the right of the frame.

He wore Levis, soft, soundless moccasins, a white silk shirt, slightly bloused, and with the sleeves rolled back to half-way up his forearms. A tall, charismatic figure. It was Gus, but you would not know it. In life, the confessor had been around six feet in height, now he was at least six and a half. In life, Gus had dark neatly-cut hair thinning at the forehead; this Gus had grey-streaked hair which fell long to his shoulders and grew from slightly lower on his forehead. In life, Keene had the eyes of a hawk: could spot a movement a mile distant on a clear day; this Gus wore eye glasses and the colour of his eyes seemed to have changed.

Only a few subtle alterations, Herbie thought, yet he would have fooled friends in the street. Apart from the clever changes, his walk was not Gus's walk, which had always been one of long strides and a straight back. Claudius Damautus seemed to glide silently, his back stooped, just a tiny movement of the shoulders which Gus would never have made in his other life.

For the rest of the video the camera stayed mainly on the magician, keeping him and his table in the frame, and closing in on his hands or the items he used so that every twitch of the fingers or movements of his hands were seen in close-up.

The applause was hearty, sustained and welcoming. The audience obviously knew of, even if they had never yet seen, Damautus, who gently seated himself behind the table, smiling benignly. On the floor to his right was a deep briefcase which he opened, removing several items and placing them on the table: a small silver dish around four inches high and obviously very old; another, deeper, circular silver dish; a small dull brass cylinder with a cork at one end around three inches tall; and a beautiful dark blue glass stoppered Victorian scent bottle. He caressed this bottle with one hand and lifted the stopper to show the long glass rod by which Victorian ladies would transfer scent from the bottle to the body.

He looked up, smiled and spread his hands.

'I'm going to let you into a secret. It's a secret which goes back almost to the distant beginning of time.' Another smile. Even the voice was not Gus's voice. Gus had always spoken quietly; never seemed out of sorts; for ever calm and unruffled. In Damautus there was the same quiet peace, but the voice was pitched lower: a lover's voice almost, as though he were speaking to each member of his audience individually, gently seducing them.

'The secret concerns alchemy.' Pause, and light mysterious smile. 'The historians and, particularly, the scientists will tell you that there is no such thing, yet, centuries ago, our forefathers laboured over books that were, even then, ancient. They used their primitive knowledge of science, and their magic, which linked them to earth, air, water and fire. Later it connected them to magic symbols, particularly those we now recognize as the Zodiac. They worked hard in this attempt to turn base metal into gold. It was never accomplished. Yet, in some ways, it was. Let me show you.' He held up the dull and slightly battered brass cylinder, taking out the cork, tipping it over, pointing it towards the audience to show that it was empty.

'First, the base metal.' His right hand went to the deeper of the two dishes and rose, sprinkling a dark grey substance, so that it fell, like sand in an hour-glass, back into its container. 'Iron filings. A good starting point for base metal. And this . . .' the brass cylindrical vial, 'this is a vial which once, they tell me, belonged to Zosimus the Panoplite who lived around the fourth century AD.

'Even by then there was a mixture said to react with any metal to form gold. It consisted mainly of salt, mercury and sulphur. It is that same mixture we sometimes hear called the Vinegar of the Sages. In my own quest for the true substance, I discovered that one ingredient was missing. To complete the mixture one must add the tears of a twenty-one-year-old virgin – either masculine or feminine; one has to be politically correct. After a long search, I found these tears and so was successful in producing a small quantity of a mixture close to the Vinegar of the Sages. Let me show you. First the base metal . . .' He took several pinches of the iron filings, carefully letting them trickle into the brass vial.

'Next, a delicate mixing of the metal with the secret ingredient.' He lifted the glass stopper from the blue

165

bottle and transferred one drop of the liquid three times, then replaced the cork on the brass vial.

'It is well known that the Vinegar of the Sages must be used accompanied by certain words which I must keep secret.' His lips moved soundlessly as he held the vial in his right hand, placing it at various points on the table. A student of the occult would have recognized that the way he placed the vial followed the lines of the Pentagram.

'Now, it should be done.' Damautus uncorked the vial and tipped the contents onto the shallow silver dish. Instead of iron filings a stream of finely ground gold sandy material trickled from the vial.

Damautus shrugged and made a petulant noise. 'Not quite.' He looked up and smiled. 'A little more of the mixture, I think,' pouring the fine gold back into the vial.

Now he added one more drop from the blue bottle, placed the cork back onto the vial and went through the business of soundless mumbling and moving of the vial again.

This time, when he uncorked the vial and tipped it onto the table, three small hard golden nuggets rolled out.

'There. Base metal into gold.'

He waited for the scatter of applause and then picked up the three nuggets. 'The real trick is to make the gold into something one can freely use. Watch.' Lying the nuggets on the palm of his hand, Damautus reached out so that everyone could see the hand held only the trio of shining pieces. He closed the fingers of his right hand, blew on it and opened the hand once more. In place of the three nuggets lay a gold piece the size of a silver dollar.

Applause started. 'Wait,' he cautioned. 'There is one problem in turning base metal into gold using this method. Unhappily, the gold is unstable. Watch.' He flicked the gold coin into the air. Herbie was convinced that the coin altered as it reached its apogee, for when it fell back into Damautus's palm it had become a silver dollar.

'You see the dangers.' Damautus closed his hand into a fist again and this time turned the clenched hand, thumb upwards. Leaning forward he allowed a thin trickle of what could have been sparkling golden sand run from his fist onto the shallow dish. Only then, with a smile and a sideways nod of the head, did Damautus acknowledge the applause, showing the hand completely empty.

To Herbie, the fantastic part about what he had seen was that everything had been done in the open, with hands away from his body and the forearms naked.

'Is marvellous, eh?' He turned to Bex Olesker.

'Oh, it's clever enough.' She made a sour face. 'Very clever, but it's a trick. I'd like to know how he does it.'

'If it's a clever trick, you do it then,' Kruger almost barked, but on the screen Damautus, still sitting, had begun to talk again. 'There are, of course, other ways of making metal into currency.' He smiled, rolling a small cube of silver-like metal onto the table. The cube was no bigger than a Monopoly die.

'This way requires only the skill and knowledge of one equipped with the right incantations.' He covered the cube with his right hand, and started a rolling motion, his hand flat against the cube. 'Now see.' Lifting his hand he revealed that the cube had become a small sphere. 'The art is in making the metal into the right shape.' His hand was empty as he brought it down over the sphere, starting the rolling motion again, his lips moving as though he were concentrating on the metal under his palm. This time, when he lifted his hand, the sphere was replaced by a flat blank of silver which he flicked into the air and caught, offering it forward for the audience's inspection.

'It is from blanks like this that coins are made.' Another smile. 'The problem, however, is that one cannot control what kind of coin materializes.' The silver blank was dropped onto the table again, the hand shown empty and then placed over the silver disc and immediately lifted to reveal a rough, irregular-sided coin. 'A silver doubloon, or a groat or whatever it is,' holding the ancient coin between finger and thumb. 'The real object is to get its present-day value in usable coinage.' The old coin slid back to the flat of his open hand, in full view as he closed the fingers. Almost immediately, he opened them and slowly dropped four silver half-dollars onto the table.

'There, we might be able to use these. Four half-dollars. Two American dollars.'

The silver coins remained in view, spread towards the front of the table, as Damautus's hands moved quickly, clearing away the other items and replacing them with a wine glass; a packet of cigarettes; a small round silver box with a lid and an oblong glass casket with brass corner pieces. This casket was around seven inches by three, and about three inches deep.

'We've made a couple of dollars so far.' Damautus never once went out of character, and each word he spoke was as though he passed some confidential secret to each individual member of the audience. 'Let's see if we can keep the money this time.'

Picking up the casket he showed that the top was a hinged lid, then he placed it in the centre of the table.

'Smoking can damage your health,' picking up the pack of cigarettes, 'so I won't smoke.' He laid the packet across the top of the wine glass and covered the whole thing with a square of black silk. 'Let's cover all the glass, just in case we get a lightning strike,' throwing another black and silver cloth across the casket. 'Now, the coins.' He scooped the four half-dollars into his right hand and picked up the round silver box, clearly putting the four coins into it, one at a time, then dropping the lid on top. This he placed onto the covered pack of cigarettes, snapped his fingers and immediately picked the box up again, lifting the lid, turning it over to show the four coins had vanished.

'Into thin air,' he said, lifting the packet of cigarettes and the silk from the glass which was now filled with thick boiling smoke. 'Or thick smoke.'

For the first time that evening, Damautus rose and lifted the glass full of smoke. 'Maybe,' he said, 'if I pour the smoke towards the covered casket you might just see where the coins went. You'll certainly hear them.'

His hand holding the glass was almost two feet above the covered casket. He tipped the glass and the smoke poured downwards like liquid. The camera held both the glass and the casket in frame and Herbie swore that he saw at least two of the coins drift down towards the casket in slow motion through the smoke. He also heard the sounds as one by one the coins thudded and clinked against the casket, and the moment the fourth coin was heard, Damautus put the glass down and whipped the silk from the casket, picking it up and holding it high so that the four coins, now inside, could be seen clearly. In case someone was not quite certain, he opened the lid and took the coins out one at a time, tossing them back onto the table as he took his final bow.

'You see that?' Herbie was as excited as a schoolboy. 'Bex, did *you* see those coins drifting through the smoke?'

'I thought I did, but I bet it was a camera trick; they fell too slowly.'

'They said no camera tricks.'

'What do we know? They all lie, that's one of the things I'm unhappy about. The magician gets up there and does incredible things, defies logic, yet you know he's telling you one thing while something else is happening.'

'How do you *know* that, Bex. You tell your kids there's no Santa Claus?'

'I haven't got any kids.'

'So? So, you miss the fun. Me, I still believe in Santa Claus, and I believe in what old Gus did on that tape. Completely I believed it.'

'You're sure that was Gus?'

'One hundred per cent proof.'

'A good and clever disguise.'

'A very good disguise: a wonderful wig; a little change here and there, and he's a different person.'

'But you're sure it's Gus?'

'Completely sure. Know him anywhere.'

'But you said . . .'

'You want to watch another tape?'

'No, I'm ready for bed. What're we doing tomorrow?'

'We're talking to the good widow Keene whether Tony Worboys likes it or not.'

She stood, her eyes on him, an eyebrow cocked, the look one of disbelief. 'You believe in elves and fairies as well?' She was still harping on his delight at Gus's magic show.

'Not quite. But I think people like that . . . like Gus . . . can bring wonders into our lives. Entertainment, bewilderment. Maybe a return to childhood isn't so bad.'

Bex grunted. Then: 'Even if you're right, how does it assist in a murder investigation – probably a terrorist murder?'

'Probably because this is a part of Gus's life that none of his friends shared. I've known him for years, yet never guessed he could perform like this. It's a new dimension – that's the right word, Bex? Yes?'

'Dimension, sure. But I still don't see how it helps.'

'In the long run, who knows? All I'm saying is that until now I did not know what Gus could do. Maybe it has no bearing but, again, *nobody* knew and it's odd that someone who was a guardian of secrets led a second secret life. Somehow it jars.'

'Uh-hu,' she nodded. 'I understand that. What about the widow Keene? Hasn't she been given a once-over already?'

'Just lightly browned on both sides. The powers that be really didn't want her put to the torture until the shock of Gus's death had begun to wear off.'

'But . . .'

'But, I know, Bex. I know. Should have been done straight away. I tried, but it wasn't to be. We hit her tomorrow. You sure you don't want to watch another video?'

'I'm absolutely positive. I would like to use the telephone though. What's the situation regarding private use of phones here?'

'Whatever you like. Might have a trace on them. All art-of-the-state here. But you can ring your boyfriend, no problem.'

She coloured, a flash of anger crossing her eyes like a summer squall. 'I don't have a boyfriend.'

'Husband then.'

'You'd better know, here and now so that you won't put your foot in it again. I have a girl-friend, okay?'

'Sure. Okay. Fine. No problem.' So, he thought, what's wrong with that? Why the drama?

He went back into the Aladdin's cave and sought out another video, spending half an hour watching Gus, as Claudius Damautus, do impossible things. He named a word only thought of by a spectator leafing through a book; synchronized his wrist-watch with that of a lady, then asked her to just think of a time and write it down. When the time was revealed he showed that the hands of his own watch had moved to the time thought of by the lady.

He caused three finger rings, borrowed from his audience, to become linked together – each spectator identifying his or her ring – and then unlink; he did amazing things with playing cards – not just card tricks, but mysteries of impossibility where cards were simply thought of and then revealed to be missing from the deck; another card, merely thought of, was discovered under the person – on the chair upon which the man had been sitting. Gus, in his guise as Damautus, prophesied colours chosen at random; gave details of the contents of a woman's handbag and many other impossibilities.

Herbie went to bed, his mind reeling from watching

the Gus he had known, become a man he would never in a thousand years have truly known. Foolishly, he took a book from the secret library to bed with him and learned about the first stirrings of this art in the childhood of the planet. He read about people of whom he had never heard, for the book reached back through the sands of time to early religious magic, the conjuring up of gods and oracles in Egypt; the magical methods of priests in Greece and Rome; Dedi who lived 2,600 years before Christ and was reputed to have decapitated and restored the heads of geese and an ox; Zoroaster; Simon Magus; Elymas the Sorcerer; Apollonius of Tyana and the Oracle of Abonotica.

As he finally drifted into sleep he wondered at the knowledge Gus Keene would have had to acquire in order to perform these seemingly incredible feats. He slept restlessly, dreaming of sticks that turned into serpents and ghostly figures appearing on the walls of Greek Temples.

Out in the other world, *Yussif* was talking to the *Intiqam* teams.

12

Yussif, the Logistics and Communication back-up for the two *Intiqam* teams consisted of six men. Three hidden away in a remote cottage in the Hudson Valley, upstate New York, and another three living deep in the heart of rural Oxfordshire, near the thriving market town of Wantage. All six members of *Yussif* were highly experienced men. Four of them were former military intelligence officers who had served with the élite Republican Guard. The remaining pair – the leaders of each section – had worked in the West for some time as they had been drawn from the cream of the relatively small Foreign Intelligence Service.

All of them had that undeniable look of trained soldiers – the firm mouths and clear eyes which spoke of hours spent observing other men and women, across a waste of desert, or from windows overlooking city streets.

Even these men who received and passed on instructions to the *Intiqam* teams did not possess the full sweeping and demonic details of the master plan that was at the heart of *Intiqam*. Only one man carried all the facts, and he was guarded day and night in a pleasant villa outside Baghdad. He was also not known by name. The many people who made up the various teams called him the *Biwāba* – the Gatekeeper.

He was more than just the keeper of plots, this silent, secretive tall man with a huge hooked nose, and eyes which seemed to blaze into men's souls, making his immediate body servants consider him to be like some enormous bird of prey. He had heard himself referred to as a giant hawk, and he laughed at the description, for in many ways that was what he was – a night hawk, deadly and undetectable in the job at hand. The entire operation had been entrusted to him, and nobody else – not even the Leader in one of his many palaces or hiding places – knew the full scope. All they had been told was that the Gatekeeper could, and would, bring their old enemies to their knees.

He was laughing now, having just received, via *Yussif* in Great Britain, the news that the arrangements had gone well between his *Intiqam* squad in London and the splinter group of the IRA: the FFIRA. The 'putty' – the message said – would be delivered for the price of four lives. Only four? he thought. There was some irony there, for thousands of lives would be forfeit. The 'putty' was, of course, Semtex, and even that was a blind; naturally they would use it, but it was not the heart of the great terror that this one man was near to unleashing.

The decadent forces of the West thought solely in terms of bombs and assassinations. It was as though they could only see freedom fighters or revenge soldiers – terrorists as they liked to call them – as men and women who dealt death by dagger, pistol and explosive. Certainly, the Coalition Forces, during the Time of the Wars, had been concerned about what they called Weapons of Mass Destruction. Mainly nuclear holocausts, though there was a little panic in the United States now concerning the possibility that some troops had been in contact with biological agents.

The West was made up mainly of fools who could not see that nuclear warfare was a self-destructive way to go. For the years preceding the War the work in Iraqi laboratories had been concerned with neutron bombs, those which would kill men and women but leave the ground relatively intact. The Americans and British used propaganda which persuaded people to think that the countries in the Middle East – and in particular the organizations they considered as terrorists – were fighting to get their hands on nuclear weapons and the means to deliver them by rocket, if only to use as a powerful bargaining chip.

Certainly the Gatekeeper had a fair share in the development of neutron devices, but *his* first aim had been something he considered more deadly and less destructive.

When the men and women came to Iraq from the so-called International Atomic Energy Agency, they looked mainly at the plants in which work on the development of nuclear weapons had been going on. Of course, the nuclear road was one to be taken, yet the thinking within the powerful circle of military and scientific advisers to the Leader was that the old way – the great balance of power using nuclear arms as the compensatory spring – was now dead. In four or five years, they would be able to use a nuclear threat, complete with the means to deliver warheads to every major city in Europe and the United States, putting them on equal terms with what was known as the nuclear club. In the meantime, the West would become terrified and even more unstable by the use of other means.

As he started to draft instructions to both the *Intiqam* teams, the Gatekeeper wondered how long it would be before either the Americans or British would pick up on the real power he wielded. His country's enemies constantly referred to the fact that Iraq was bankrupt. They had not the wit to think of the old saying, 'When the money is gone you must make more to take its place.'

He was amazed that, when the IAEA had sent their men and women to sniff out nuclear plants, they had actually visited the modern building where the money was, in fact, being made. They had been told that this was a new printing plant for books: text books for schools. The Leader set great store by the education of children. The group from the International Atomic

Energy Agency had nodded gravely and left after twenty minutes. They had not descended to the lower floors where the four German forgers worked.

The making of money had begun almost six years ago, and they had searched the world for the people with the greatest skills, finding them in what had been the former DDR – East Germany. These men were so adroit that only in the past few months had the American FBI stumbled against the forgeries of $100 bills, and they had publicly admitted that this currency was all but undetectable from the real thing. Even with that announcement, the American and British media had played down the threat.

Already billions of the forged hundred dollar bills were circulating and in use in America and Europe, as, indeed, they had been during the time of Desert Storm. The forgeries had brought in billions of real currency, hidden away in banks, which meant it was simply great riches on paper. They could, as the Gatekeeper had told his Leader, buy anything they wanted. The great forgery campaign had given them the wealth of ages. With it, Iraq was the most prosperous country in the world. The trick was getting the weapons of choice over borders, across seas and through air space to beat the arms embargo. With time, and the *Intiqam* teams, there would be no problem in bringing anything they desired into the country. Then, the world, fractured by this current operation, would be held to ransom. Their time would come and the great age of Islam would be at hand.

If the truth were known, the Gatekeeper did not care much for their Leader. The man was, to his mind, unbalanced and not a person who was a true Muslim but that mattered little. What did matter was that Islam would at last become the leading religion of the world. It was of no consequence that people would be drawn into the faithful by fear. Fear was a good and holy weapon by which the decadent infidels and their leaders would seek the truth. To seek the truth they first must be humbled.

Big Herbie Kruger could not sleep. He dozed for a couple of hours, then got up again, showered, shaved, dressed and went down to Gus's old study. There, at the Confessor's desk, he read a book of magic history and learned about the eighteenth-century Isaac Fawkes and how he used an egg bag – a common device still in demand – from which he produced dozens of eggs; of his prowess with playing cards: how he would make pips change to court cards; and also how he performed the old Indian trick of growing a small tree in a matter of minutes. The book said that this made one wonder if there were any new tricks under the sun.

Also, he read of Matthew Buchinger, born in 1674 without legs, thighs or hands – simply a trunk with a head and stumps growing from his shoulders. He was most amazing because he could perform the cups and balls – magic's oldest trick – with amazing dexterity. Herbie had seen magicians doing the cups and balls. Balls appeared and disappeared from under and above three metal cups; finally a lemon or some such fruit seemed magically to have taken the place of the little balls. In Buchinger's performance, live birds would appear from the cups at the end of the routine. This strange, handicapped man also became well known for his drawings and calligraphy. The book had reproductions of some of his work which was so deft that you could hardly believe that it was done by a man with only malformed stumps and no hands.

Herbie considered there was far more to magic history than pulling rabbits from hats, making women appear from boxes, or escaping, like Houdini, from chains and strait-jackets. This was incredibly absorbing stuff.

At seven o'clock he heard stirrings in the house, but by then he was back into Gus's files, leafing through every contact the man had made with terrorist groups.

The telephone rang at just before eight. Worboys on the secure line from London.

'Herb, something damned odd is going on.'

'So what's new?'

'Our friends in the Security Service have been tipped that there will be four more bombs in London today. They even have the locations and times.'

'These IRA Freedom Fighters, or whatever they're calling themselves – FFIRA?'

'Our sisters say no. They're telling us the main terrorist group here, and in the States, is called the Vengeance of Iraq. Not the kind of thing we'd want to appear in the newspapers.'

'The ruthless Arabs, eh?'

'Iraqis, yes, but this isn't their style. They don't issue warnings. What would your opinion be? Our sister service receiving this kind of information?'

'You tell me where it's going to happen?'

'Sure. This afternoon, between six and seven. One at Piccadilly Circus underground, another in Bond Street. They also say there will be a big one at the base of Nelson's Column in Trafalgar Square; and a medium-sized bomb near Berwick Street Market in Soho.'

'And America? We know anything about Vengeance of Iraq in America?'

'Very nasty. One *inside* the Cedars of Lebanon Hospital in LA; a second one in New Orleans – the French Quarter; and a third in Grand Central Station.'

'We're taking it seriously?'

'Of course we are. But the Security Service has asked the police to be discreet. Discreet! I ask you!'

'Only one reason.'

'Tell me, Herb?'

'They've got one of the team on their payroll.'

'That's what we think, but it's irresponsible if that's what it's all about.'

'When did any of us get responsible, Tony?'

'As from this minute. We have a meeting with the DG

of the Security Service in the Prime Minister's office in an hour. We want the sites watched and the bomb placers pulled in.'

'They won't go with it, Tony. They'll want the credit for rolling up the whole team, and I'd bet the Americans are thinking the same way.'

'Well, we want the placers rolled up at least.'

'Let me know how it goes.'

'Any progress at your end?'

'We're talking to Carole this morning . . .'

Worboys began to say something, but Herb cut him off. 'Tony, don't you dare say not yet. We have to do it now . . .'

Instead of objecting, Worboys put on his quiet and conciliatory voice. 'Herb, yes. You must talk with her. I agree. It is urgent.' He paused and Kruger waited.

'The problem, as I see it,' Worboys continued without raising his voice. 'The problem as I see it is that all this other business – the Irish problem and the other terrorist faction – is starting to obliterate your main concern. Herb, your job is to find out what happened to Gus. Don't lose sight of that. Focus on it and keep *that* job in your sights. Okay?' He closed the line before Herbie could respond. Three minutes later, Bex poked her head around the door to say that it was breakfast time.

Carole Keene still looked stunned, but she at least remained calm. Those who staffed the so-called guest wing under the earth in the grounds of the estate were experienced in all manner of things, from nursing and TLC, to the psychological preparation for what Gus had called, 'Putting them to the question.'

She greeted Herbie with a hug, kissing him on both cheeks, and was remarkably friendly when he introduced her to Bex. Carole, it used to be said, had little time for women, and less for women with power.

On their way over, they had agreed that Bex would do the main questioning, while Herb would jump in with the revelation regarding Gus's involvement with

the performing art of magic which, he argued, was
something that had to be dealt with simply because
it was a secret part of Gus's secret life.

As it was, Kruger's mind reeled with what he had
read so far. The little nip of the magic bug in his
childhood had turned into a major bite during his
recent visit to Vegas. Now, seeing all that literature
on the art he had started to imagine himself as a
possible candidate for the magic wand. He wanted to
learn something: to pull showers of golden coins from
the air; to make chosen cards rise mysteriously from the
deck; to cut a rope and then restore it immediately
and in full sight of his audience. The Amazing Kruger,
Kruger the Magnificent, even The Great Krugini. These
were possible names that passed through his mind. Once
this was over, he would find out where he could get books
like those in Gus's secret library, and where to buy the
right equipment.

In this odd delirium, he truly saw a whole new career
opening up for him, though if any true psychic could look
into his mind they would chuckle at the very thought of
this ungainly, uncoordinated man being able to do even
the most simple sleight or self-working card-trick with
success.

The thoughts were banished once Bex Olesker began
her interrogation, for she proved herself to be a skilful
and shrewd practitioner of the inquisitor's art. Low key
to begin with, asking the immediate questions – Was Gus
nervous when he left home that night? Had he received
any mail which seemed to upset him recently? Had he
been acting in any strange, even paranoid, way?

At this last, Carole had actually laughed. 'Gus *was*
always paranoid, Bex,' she said. 'Few people actually
saw it though. He always appeared to be a man without
a care in the world.'

'But you saw a different side of him?'

'I had worked with him for a long time before we
first became lovers,' just a hint of wistfulness. 'Angela,

his first wife, just didn't understand the workings of his job. Gus taught me a great deal about the interrogator's trade, Bex, and Gus was a kind of prima donna as far as that was concerned. I was the only one who ever saw him get worked up about an interrogation. If it was a difficult one he would be jumpy, nervous.'

'He had doubts about himself?'

'All the good ones have doubts.' Carole seemed relaxed now. 'Gus was no exception. He'd be like an actor getting ready to play the lead. That's part of the job, being an actor and – for Gus at least – there is never a time when you can even think of failure. You just cannot fail. He used to worry about the great interrogators of the past – the men who couldn't crack Philby, for instance. They were the best, but nobody ever even shook Kim Philby.'

Philby had been one of the Soviet's longest-running penetration agents within the British intelligence community. One of the Magnificent Five as the KGB had dubbed them – Philby, Burgess, Maclean, Blunt and John Cairncross, all Cambridge undergraduates in the 1930s and all recruited by the Soviets as moles in the very fabric of the Intelligence and Security Services. In the end, while Burgess and Maclean were fingered by the authorities, they were never caught. Rather than that they fled to Moscow. Blunt did a deal, while Cairncross went to live in France and escaped the worst. Philby, however, was interrogated with great hostility. Eventually he also slipped the leash and ran to Moscow. No interrogator ever broke him.

'Whenever he became anxious during an interrogation,' Carole continued, 'he'd come back to the way Philby was never broken. He had a kind of complex about it.'

'But he was so good damned,' muttered Herbie. Even Carole, who had known him for a long time, could not tell whether he was playing with the English language or simply making a genuine error. Like others, Carole had noticed that, since his final operation, Herbie's mangled

English – which he used partly out of devilment and partly as a cloak to enlarge his dumb-ox exterior – had all but disappeared.

'So, Carole, you knew when he was really strung out?' Bex asked.

'I could tell as a rule, yes.'

'Had he shown any symptoms of that in the month or so before he was killed?'

'Well, yes. A little, yes. But I put that down to something else entirely.'

Bex immediately veered away from the obvious follow-up question. 'Any strangers? Odd mail? Cards? People? Anything during that month that seemed to be out of the norm?'

Carole shook her head, and Herbie took in the fact that she did not actually answer the question for the machines she knew must be taping her.

'Tell us, Carole. Don't nod your head. Just tell us if there was something,' he said aloud.

She looked uncertain, dazed, as though something was there in the front of her mind which she could not, or did not, wish to share with them. Herbie decided that this was the moment for him to step in. 'We know about Claudius Damautus, Carole. If it has anything to do with that . . . ?' He left the question trailing.

'Oh.' She gave a simple little sound of surprise. 'How do you know about that, Herb?'

'Took his room apart. Watched some of his tapes. He was very good.'

'He was more than good. He was one of the most brilliant magicians alive.' The tiniest of sobs on the word alive. 'He had that extraordinary talent which made people believe – or at least made them suspend their disbelief.'

'Count Bex out.' Herb did his daft grin. 'She doesn't like magicians. Can take them or leave them.'

'Then they probably threaten you, Bex.' Carole smiled brightly. 'That's how it goes with some people. They don't like to be fooled so they get aggressive about it. They won't go with the flow.'

Bex Olesker stiffened, even bridled a little. 'I just think it's a rather childish kind of entertainment, that's all.'

'Well, Gus would've disagreed with you. He said we now live in a new golden age of magic, because people've become so disillusioned with life, they want to see the impossible performed and the laws of the universe altered. It was Gus's life.'

'I thought the art of interrogation was his life.'

'Yes, that also, and several other sides of what the novels call the Secret World. Gus held that the tradecraft – the methods in the field – and the techniques of entrapment and interrogation run on parallel lines to the theory and practice of the performance of magic.'

'That why he kept so quiet about it? Why he didn't share it with his friends?'

'Mainly, yes. Gus knew more about magic than practically anyone alive. He was internationally known and revered as Claudius Damautus. Truly.'

'Yet he didn't come out of the closet. He was a closet magician.'

'To a certain extent, yes. There were some people in the Service who knew.'

'Like the old Chief and BMW?' Herb had the decency to smile.

'You picked up on them? I always knew you were good, Herb, but that's *very* good.'

'I got some help.'

'And you think it was because of the magic that something occurred during the period just before his death?' Bex gently brought her back to the real matter in hand.

Carole nodded again, then said, 'He was really hyped up all that week. The reason he was in Salisbury that night was to give a private performance and demonstration to a group of invited magicians.' She turned

183

to Herbie. 'I lied to you about that charred piece of metal. It *was* a small badge. One he wore with great pride – showed that he was a Member of the Inner Magic Circle.'

Herbie nodded. 'So, that week?'

'He always got stressed out before he performed – the same with interrogations.' She gave a little laugh, then added that his performances and interrogations were almost the same thing. 'You ever heard of Robert-Houdin?'

'Father of modern magic,' Herbie supplied with just a hint of superiority. Then a knowing smile spread over his craggy face. 'This is the French guy Houdini got his name from, yes?'

'Yes, Herb. Gold star and a green rabbit. You've been boning up on magic history.'

'Is interesting.'

Carole noticed that the grammar was not quite perfect. Mentally her guard came up. 'Well, Robert-Houdin once wrote that a magician is really an actor playing the part of a magician. There are a lot of people in the magic arts who don't believe that, but Gus did. I guess Gus also thought that about interrogators. In fact I know he did. He gave you a nice year of questions, Herb. You remember how he came at you?'

'Never three days alike.'

'Yes, he would chop and change the rhythm, but his style was always the same.'

'Sure.'

'Carole,' Bex was moving in close again. 'He was tense before this demonstration – performance – lecture – whatever it was, in Salisbury, the night he died?'

'That's what I said.'

'More than usual or less?'

'More. Definitely more. Gus rehearsed and practised every day of his life – and there's a difference to rehearsing and practising in magic. Just as to know how a trick is done does not mean you know how to do it. He was always a little strung out, but the whole of that day he was odd.'

'How was he the last time you saw him? When he left for Salisbury?'

Carole swallowed, and tears started in her eyes. 'He . . . Well, he . . . He was very demonstrative when he left. Old Gus was always a touchy-feely person with me, but that night, looking back, it was more.'

'How more?' from Herbie.

'Clung a lot. Held me very close. Longer than usual.'

The words floated into Herb's head and he just stopped himself from saying, 'The Long Goodbye.'

The silence between words was too long, so both Herbie and Bex began to speak at once, their words clashing, fast.

'Do you . . . ?'

'Carole, did you . . . ?'

Herbie gave way to Bex.

'Carole, can we go back a bit?'

'To where?'

'To something you said earlier. Maybe I haven't done my homework properly. Maybe this should be Herbie's question . . .'

'Then let Herbie ask it.' For the first time, Carole Keene showed a touch of antagonism.

'Okay. Let me try to ask it, and Herbie can take over. Gus was a full-time interrogator, right?'

'He was Chief of Interrogation, yes. He was also Officer Commanding Warminster. This place.'

'As Chief Interrogator of the SIS, how much would he have to know about the daily work of the Service?'

'Why do you ask that?'

'Because earlier you said that Gus viewed the theory of intelligence gathering in the field as parallel to the theory of magic as a performing art.'

'Yes.'

'What you're getting at, Bex, I think, is how much

does an interrogator have to know about life in the field? Right, ja?'

'Ja – Yes.'

'Let me answer that, Bex.' Herbie's face crinkled into a friendly, funny uncle kind of look. 'I can tell you, because I knew him. Gus knew every damned thing worth knowing about the collection of intelligence. Tradecraft; False Flags; Black Bag Ops; Surveillance; Cover; Multi-Layers of cover; Legends. You name it, Gus knew it, outside in.'

'Do you believe it then?'

'Believe what?'

'What Carole says about Gus. That the theory and practice of your job runs parallel to the theory and practice of magical entertainment?'

Big Herbie gave a giant shrug, his arms lifting and falling to his sides again. 'How the bugger I know, Bex? I know nothing about magic theory.'

'Better read it up.' Carole was really smiling now. 'Better still, Gus has written a long monograph about it. Two years ago he did a lecture for a very select audience. He didn't let on that *he* was a magician – used a disguise: even I didn't recognize him when I first saw him – but he was so damned clever. I have a copy somewhere – a copy of his lecture notes.'

'We have a look at them?'

'Better. We did a video at the time. His position was that if a very few, selected intelligence professionals learned the principles of magic as a performing art they would be able to function at a higher level in the field. He used to say that Operation *Fortitude*, the deception operation set up to disguise *Overlord* – the D-Day landings in Normandy during the Second World War – was one of the best pieces of stage magic ever performed. That, and the famous British magician, Jasper Maskelyne's work in the Middle East.'

'What he do, then, Carole?'

'Maskelyne? Many things. He moved the Suez Canal,

and shifted Alexandria Harbour several miles from where it really was. Had a unit called The Magic Gang out there during WW II.'

'You serious about this?' from Bex.

'Absolutely. I'll find the video and you can watch it. It's very entertaining. Gus suited his actions to the words: performed as he explained.'

'Okay, we'll take a—' Bex began, but the telephone in the room started to purr urgently.

'Ja?' Kruger picked up.

'You got a copy of *The Times* down there?' Tony Worboys asked at the distant end.

'No idea, but we can get one.'

'Do that. You're in the guest suites?'

'Sure.'

'Go back to the Dower House and call me when you have a copy of *The Times*.'

'Both of us? I got Bex here as well.'

'You're talking to Carole?'

'What else?'

'Leave the rest of that to Bex. I need to speak with you, okay.'

'I go, I go, look how I go.' Herb cradled the telephone. 'I got some funny business to attend to. See you for lunch, Bex, and see you later this afternoon, Carole. Want to watch that video of old Gus.'

There were copies of all the British dailies in what used to be called the Mess in the big house. Herb liberated *The Times* and walked quickly back to the Dower House where he called Worboys on the secure phone.

'Turn to the Small Ads.' Worboys sounded a trifle smug.

'Got it.'

'Second column of the Personals. Starts with the word Claudius.'

Herbie ran a big finger down the column. 'Yesu!' he said when he read the three lines.

'Interesting, huh?'

'Maybe a coincidence. Who knows, Tony? Coincidences happen.'

'I want you to go through his papers. See if you can pull the name out of his files.'

'I'll try. How you get on with the folks at "Five"?'

'The folks at "Five", as you put it, have agreed to share their product. The PM tore them apart. They've had an Iraqi in their pockets for some time and he's one of the team here. Tell you about it later.'

'So what's going to happen?'

'Compromise. Surveillance on the bomb planters. Follow them home then roll 'em up. But, before that happens, I want you to see if there's a link in Gus's files.'

'Gotcha.'

Herbie turned back to the newspaper. The Personal Ad in question read:

CLAUDIUS my king, I am here just as I told you I would be. The sands of time are running out and I long to see you again, just as I long to watch you work your magic. Just send me a sign and I will be there for you. Greetings, Jasmine.

13

The Police and Security Service surveillance teams were in place early. At two in the afternoon, men and women loitered, walked with purpose, or sat in the back of closed vans, covering the four target areas – Piccadilly Circus underground station, Bond Street, Trafalgar Square and Berwick Street in Soho. During the day, the latter was a clutter of stalls, forming the famous Berwick Street Market; selling flowers, fish and vegetables. At six in the evening it would begin to clear, though there were always quite a lot of people around.

The teams placed themselves at either end of Berwick Street, while a pair of watchers occupied an upper room above a butcher's shop, giving them a view of the entire street.

Bond Street was more difficult because of its length. In all they had twelve teams working the pavements, while pairs of officers visited each shop, warning managers and assistants regarding anyone who accidentally left a briefcase or package inside. It was an exciting afternoon for the staff of shops on Bond Street, as they were told to call a telephone number straight away, not to hang around but simply state the name of the shop, the article left by accident, a quick description of the person who left it, and a codeword *Tybalt*.

By the wonders of modern electronics, the message would immediately patch through to the earpieces of the watchers who, at one point, seemed to outnumber the actual civilians going about their business along this Mayfair thoroughfare.

They saturated Trafalgar Square and the large concourse of Piccadilly tube station, which is very big and almost impossible for ultra-safe surveillance. As one of the watchers was heard to remark, 'Trying to find a terrorist in Piccadilly underground is like trying to find the twelve of clubs in a deck of cards.' Apart from the many tunnels and platforms there is a great circular concourse around the ticket machines with small shops, entrances and exits to Piccadilly Circus. There are also the big banks of escalators and this underground station is reckoned to be the most used in the whole of London.

Changing shifts and places, twelve teams went onto the platforms, up and down the escalators, walked the passages and had the circular concourse covered completely. The operation was so large that the professional watchers of the Security Service had to be tripled by police officers trained in surveillance techniques.

It was the same in Trafalgar Square, and the entire business called for a lot of dressing up, the use of reversible coats, the changing of hats, briefcases, handbags, umbrellas and the like. The officer in charge of MI5's watchers complained that he was undermanned and really needed things as they were in the old days when he could bring people in by the busload. By one that afternoon, the Security Service had requested assistance from the Secret Intelligence Service, an action that made senior members of the SIS rub their hands with glee.

The message had been that the explosions would take place at an unspecified time between six and seven, which meant, with sophisticated timing devices, the bombs could well be in place before two, though the general agreement was that the Iraqis would not risk leaving the devices too early. They reckoned the mean time would be around four or five o'clock.

In the event, they were out by fifteen minutes. All the devices were placed during a five minute period starting at five-fifteen.

A dark young man who for the past hour had been sitting at the base of Nelson's Column stretched and got to his feet very slowly. He looked around and then started to saunter away. One of the watchers had spent the past fifteen minutes keeping him in sight and had moved quite close to him. He saw immediately that right next to where the man had been sitting was a bulky plastic yellow shopping bag with the Tower Records logo on it.

'You've left your bag, John.' The watcher called to him with a distinct cockney accent.

The young man glanced around, saw the yellow bag, shrugged and in good English said it was not his.

A second watcher moved in and began keeping a discreet eye on the man, who was young Ahmad, almost a boy. A woman in the same surveillance team fell into step behind the watcher who had already begun to follow Ahmad.

While this was taking place, one of the police teams – a male and female couple who had been strolling around the circular concourse in Piccadilly underground station – saw a lovely young woman with long dark and gleaming hair dump what looked to be a shoebox into one of the rubbish bins near the steps that led from the concourse to the bottom of Regent Street.

The female of the team fell in behind Samira, following her down to the main Piccadilly line platform, using a weekly pass – issued to everyone on this particular surveillance operation, which had been crypted *Cyclops*. Her male counterpart began speaking rapidly into the radio mike in his lapel.

In Bond Street, they were very lucky. Another pair of male and female watchers saw the youth, Nabil, pause beside the now closed door of a jeweller's shop and drop a Harrods plastic carrier bag. Plastic bags seemed to be the order of the day with this group of terrorists. The male officer followed and the female gave the warning.

In Berwick Street they were not so lucky. The two

officers watching from the window above the butcher's shop saw a tall youth slide a bulging plastic bag into a refuse dumpster. They immediately alerted the people on foot and two officers began to follow the young man.

All the alerts were in by twenty minutes past five, and the co-ordinators allowed ten minutes for the bomb placers and their shadows to get clear before police and bomb squad teams descended on the areas, moving people out and closing off all possible exits and entrances.

Dinah, cool, tall and elegant in a stylish navy suit with gold buttons, had been running a few minutes late and was coming up Rupert Street, ready to cross the road and head up the alley towards Berwick Street when the police cars and vans descended. She dumped her bomb with some litter outside an Indian restaurant. It exploded at three minutes past six, destroying the front of the restaurant, killing nine people and severely injuring another twelve, two of whom were policemen who had begun to fan out and look for the explosives, the bomb squad having identified the contents of the plastic bag as trash from a nearby office.

Ramsi, the bomb-maker, had done a very good job.

Eventually, all roads led to the house in Clapham. Young Nabil had gone to see a film in Leicester Square; Samira had an appointment with a hairdresser just off Piccadilly; while Ahmad made his way into the warren of streets bounded on three sides by Park Lane, Curzon Street and Piccadilly: the area known as Shepherd Market.

In Shepherd Market he made a telephone call which, they soon discovered, was to make an appointment with a prostitute. They even followed him to the whore's place of business and noted the small advertisement pinned below the bell push: 'Antonia. 2nd Floor. Special Services.' The services must have been very special and Ahmad obviously had money. He reappeared over an hour later, looking a very happy man, and treated himself to dinner at a small restaurant nearby. Eventually, he was the last member of the team to arrive back at the Clapham house.

Once they were all counted in, the final phase of *Cyclops* took almost an hour to put together. Members of the Special Air Service had been brought down from Hereford, and the raid took place ninety minutes later, after they had checked the entire area.

The police and the watchers were bewildered when, after the use of stun grenades and a lot of noise, the SAS team reported the house to be empty. After all, they had seen the bomb placers enter the house. A thorough search revealed nothing. No personal effects, no sign that the building had been recently occupied. Nothing. The final conclusion was that on their return each of the bombers had walked in at the front door and slipped out of the back – a move that would have taken only a matter of two minutes. They deduced that by the time Ahmad had returned everyone else had left, and that the house had been virtually cleared of personal items either during the morning or even the day before.

At the debrief everyone admitted that the Iraqi group had completely left-footed them by careful planning. Various senior officers had already started referring to them as the Keystone Cops. The only gain was the fact that they had surveillance photographs of three of the team. By ten o'clock that night, blow-ups of the faces captured by cameras in the act of planting the bombs or walking away were released to the SIS, MI5 and SO 13.

Shortly after ten o'clock, news began to filter through from the United States. Naturally, the information received that morning from the Security Service's asset among the Iraqi *Vengeance* group had been immediately passed on to the Americans, but, because of the different time zones, the explosions about which they had been warned would not hit their deadlines until much later by British time.

The first was Grand Central Station. The undercover

193

police, FBI and highly trained members of Delta Force, together with the fast response FBI team from Quantico, did not spot the planter. The result was that, as they neared the deadline, the authorities cleared the railway station and the explosion occurred at six forty-five Eastern Standard Time. Seventeen people were killed – mostly police and bomb squad experts – while there were about 100 injured.

The media began to ask awkward questions, and those who had been on the surveillance team were roasted, with righteous anger, by those in command. 'These people're running circles around us,' the Director of the FBI shouted, in the privacy of his office. 'Damn it, we're not part of a Laurel and Hardy movie. I want to see some arrests, and I want to see them now. People're dying out there, and it's our fault.'

At roughly the same time, in New Orleans, the local police, with some FBI Special Agents in tow, picked up Kayid with the bomb in a brown-paper parcel. It was more luck than anything else. One of the FBI people thought he looked shifty – but they pulled in a whole bunch of shifty-looking people. Unhappily for him, Kayid became very anxious – as well he might – as the timer only had around ten minutes to run when they finally got around to him.

Later that night, Kayid hanged himself in a police cell rather than risk giving away the rest of the American *Intiqam* team. He was the youngest member of the cell but showed great courage in taking his own life, though he knew that Allah would reward him. Suicide was something the *Intiqam* people had been instructed to do. The *Biwāba* had been specific about it. 'It would be better for one to take his or her own life,' the wise old man had said, 'than to risk the entire cell. The same could apply to an entire cell being put under great pressure. Follow your hearts and senses. If any of your comrades appear to be near fatally under pressure, or in imminent danger of arrest, then it will be up to the individual, or individuals, to see that those in jeopardy are put away from harm.'

At six forty-five Pacific time, two forty-five the following morning in England, Awdah and Jamilla just escaped capture at the Cedars of Lebanon Hospital in Los Angeles. They had been spotted in the Emergency Room as they walked out leaving a carry-cot behind. The carry-cot contained enough explosive to damage the main structure of the hospital, but was taken away in an armoured van and defused with only seconds to spare.

Meanwhile, Awdah and Jamilla had made it to their rented Ford Contour which they had parked two blocks away. Awdah, looking like a teenager, with his mop of unruly curly hair, was in the driving seat, heading out on the 340 East, then onto the 210.

'This isn't the way to LAX,' Jamilla sounded breathless, as though she had some constriction in her throat.

'They saw us. At least four of the people in the Emergency Room spotted what we were doing.' He appeared remarkably calm.

'So where're we going?'

'Ontario airport. The other side of Covina. It's within the commuter corridor so we'll get a flight out to some major hub. I'm not going near LAX in case they're already watching it.'

'Won't they be watching Ontario?'

'Maybe, but they'll close up on LAX, and maybe Burbank, first.'

They did not speak again for around four miles of dense traffic on the freeway. Then Jamilla surprised him. 'I'm terribly frightened.' Her voice was still breathless and she was almost whispering.

'You?' he said, moving over into the fast lane and overtaking two large diesel-spewing rigs. 'After all you've done for us in this country? You're frightened?'

'Suddenly. For the first time I think we're going to die and I'm terrified.' A pause, then, 'How do you know what I've done in the past?'

'It's common knowledge that you spent time here. They say you lived under an assumed name and religion in order to obtain passports and other things. Even the driver's licence I'm using.'

'Yes. Yes I did all that, but it was easy. There was no threat. Now, I . . .'

'Do not think about now, Jamilla. Allah will provide, and death should have no fears for one such as yourself.'

'I can't help it. When I was here before, it was like a game. Now . . .'

'Now, it's real life and real death. Courage. Stay calm.' In his head Awdah thought that he would kill her if she became truly hysterical. It was the only thing he could do if she got completely out of control.

They made it to Ontario airport and just managed to get two seats on a flight out to Chicago O'Hare. From there it would be easy to get back to New York.

Back in LA the authorities had circulated details of the terrorists, together with a police artist's drawing – made from the descriptions of those who had seen Awdah and Jamilla in the ER at Cedars of Lebanon. The drawings were uncannily good likenesses of the pair.

Pressure was beginning to come to bear on the two *Intiqam* teams.

While the surveillance and final outcome of the bomb threats was going on in London, Big Herbie Kruger sat down at Gus Keene's old desk with all the files, folders, manuscript and notes which had been destined to become the book *Ask A Stupid Question*.

His immediate task was to comb through material to see if there was any reference to the name Jasmine and he did not really know where to start. He checked the files for what were known as work names or cryptos and nothing showed. Then, more because it worried him than any other reason, he went back to the *Cataract* file: the killing of the four IRA members in central London in 1984, and the final cover-up conducted by Gus himself.

He now understood why they had brought Gus, an interrogator, down to oversee that bit of magic.

'Ten years ago,' he muttered. 'Ten years and is gone like a flash.' As he spoke, so his eyes alighted on a passage among the *Cataract* files. It was a memo, direct from Willis Maitland-Wood – Deputy Director of the Office – to Gus telling him to put a hold on *Faygeleh* and head to London straightaway.

What the hell was *Faygeleh*? he wondered, and started to go back through some of the other files, his eyes searching for *Faygeleh*. Eventually he came across it under Middle East Operations.

Under some of Gus's entries for October and January 1983/4 there had been reference to the recruitment of a high-ranking Iraqi officer by Mossad in Tel Aviv. As it is with intelligence operations, the word had come back via an asset in Israel that Mossad had turned the Iraqi, sending him back to Baghdad and using him as an agent in place.

At this point in the early and mid-1980s the more far-thinking intelligence analysts had already become concerned about the regime in Iraq. The Iraqi Leader had, over the past years, carefully built up a military dictatorship very much on the same lines as the Nazi Party had done in Germany under Hitler. There was a note, here, in Gus's files in which a witty analyst drew attention to the fact that the Leader and his government resembled the Nazis – 'but without their human warmth'.

Herbie, used to cross-checking documents and reading between the lines of field reports, became aware that the SIS's Middle Eastern Desk was doing its best to finger the Israeli agent, whom the SIS had code-named *Oytser*, from the Yiddish meaning treasure. Then, in December 1983, the tone of the notes changed. Instead of constant references to *Oytser* there was a new cryptonym, *Faygeleh*, Yiddish for a number of things, mainly 'little bird' or 'sweet little child'. It amused the Secret Intelligence Service to give Israeli-related cryptos in Yiddish. Insecure? Certainly. Childish? Of course, but boys will be boys and it was always over-looked.

Reading between the lines Herb would have put money on *Faygeleh* being an attempt by the SIS to recruit an agent of its own inside the Iraqi hierarchy. He looked at his watch; already he had been working through documents and notes for almost three hours.

He stretched, looked up, rubbing his eyes, and found himself staring at the computer screen. Why not? Already he knew that Gus had a sophisticated database in there, so he switched on the machine, logged on and asked it to search for *Faygeleh*. The screen blanked out, then started to ribbon-spread columns of names associated with *Faygeleh*. In the middle he clearly saw the name *Jasmine*.

'Wow!' he said, feeding the word *Jasmine* back into the Find procedure. Up came another message. *Jasmine*: final outcome of *Faygeleh*. Still active. Ultra secure. Cross under *Price 2*.

He tried *Price 2*. Nothing, so he tried *Price 1*. Still nothing. He switched off. A couple of seconds later it came to him. A blinding and sudden flash. The book he had been reading early that very morning still lay on the far corner of the desk. Its title blared out at him – *Magic. A Pictorial History of Conjurors in the Theatre*. By DAVID PRICE!! He picked it up and leafed through the heavy book. *Price 1*, he thought. Possibly Gus had another copy – *Price 2*. This one was in mint condition, almost brand-new and the dust jacket was carefully encased in cellophane.

He went through the procedures for opening up what he thought of as Gus's Merlin's Cave, strode over to the secret door and began searching the shelves. Sure enough, there tucked away on a bottom shelf was another copy of the book. He took it out and leafed through it. The last forty pages were a solid block with a recess cut in their centre. Inside the recess lay a computer disk marked *Jasmine*.

With the greatest care, Herb inserted it into the computer, then opened it up. It was a long file appearing quickly on the screen. Gus had dived straight in. The heading was simply *Jasmine* and his first words were:

JASMINE. Asset still current and close to the Leader of Iraq. Recruitment January 1984 while working on *Cataract*.

14

Herbie was about to read on, when there was a soft knock at the door and Bex put her head into the room.

'It's past eight o'clock, Herb, and all's *not* well. Bitsy's doing her nut. She did a cold lunch and only Ginger's bothered to eat. Now she's ready to serve dinner. She's pretty pissed because we're not keeping to her timetable.'

He gave a grunt of impatience. 'Timetables are for railways and airlines.'

'I think you should come, Herb. Just to keep the wheels running and well oiled.'

She stood there as he closed down the machine and slipped the disk into his pocket. 'Anything for a life of quiet.' He grinned. 'Worse than being married.' Then, to the amazement of Bex Olesker, he quoted from Holy Writ: 'Behold, how good and joyful a thing it is, brethren, to dwell together in peace and unity.'

'Amen,' she said automatically, then, recovering her composure, 'Any luck?'

'I think so, but have to talk to Head Office. You?'

'Not sure. I've run Carole ragged. I have to think it through. We talk after dinner?'

'Sure, why not. After I've spoken to Head Office.'

As if on cue, the telephone rang and there was Worboys at the far end, asking him how he was doing.

He waved Bex out, indicating that he would be through in a minute, then turned back to the telephone.

'I'm working on it. Gus was running an agent in Iraq. Crypto Jasmine. Leastways that's what I think.'

'That's what we *know*, Herb. It was highly irregular. Gus could be bloody secretive, and for some odd reason the old Chief and the Deputies cut him a great deal of slack. He *was* running *Jasmine*, but there's no details of paths to *Jasmine*, no contact procedures, no emergency buttons to press, and no ideas as to whom Jasmine is. Gus recruited and ran her – if it is a her. It's as though nobody wanted to know. It looks like a big secret.'

'Thought that was the name of the game, secrets. It couldn't be the asset that our sisters've been using?'

'No way.'

'So Gus had an agent on the books and he held him at arm's length?'

'Yes. Shared the product, but kept everything else up his sleeve.'

'Not done, that kind of thing.'

'Don't tell *me*. I know it was highly iffy. Gus was always treated with kid gloves, which was stupid, and I really don't know why. We eventually traced *Jasmine* to Gus after we looked at all the intelligence that he, she or it passed to us during the Gulf War. There must be something down there, in Gus's files.'

'I'm working on it. You be at home tonight?'

'Just leaving. It's not been an easy day.' He outlined the events and the disappearance of the *Intiqam* team.

'I'll get back to you.'

'I have something else to tell you. Serious.'

'Shoot.'

'Our friends at "Five" with their little Iraqi stool-pigeon have only just come clean on everything.'

'I thought that was done already.'

'Apparently not. One of the deals between this Irish faction and the Iraqis consists of taking out four targets, and Gus Keene is the first.'

'Who else?' Herbie thought he already knew.

'You, Herb. Me, Herb, and The Whizzer, Herb. Remember The Whizzer?'

Kruger's mind went straight back to 1984 and the damage-control situation following *Cataract*. Archie Blount-Wilson. The Whizzer.

'He still on the books? Still around?'

'Very much so. The eternal fixer. Has a nice little flat in Bury Street, St James's.'

'You told him about this?'

'One of my people is there at this moment. For what it's worth, "Five's" Iraqi friend has said he'll make sure that all attempts will be bungled. Said he'd see to it.'

'Oh, sure. How in hell's he going to do that? Tell his boys and girls that they've got to aim high?'

'Know what you mean, Herb. Just keep your powder dry and your bowels open.'

'What powder? My bowels are always open, especially when people shoot at me.'

'It's a saying, Herb.'

'Bloody stupid saying.'

'Well, nothing's going to happen tonight. The team in London are probably looking around for new lodgings. They're very professional, and Five says they seem to have lost contact with their friend but he'll come back to them like a homing pigeon. Got too much to lose.'

'Talk to you later, and will keep my powder dry.'

Herbie went through to the dining-room. Bitsy looked sour-faced, but put on a show of pleasure at seeing her entire brood around the table. She had spent most of the afternoon preparing gazpacho, fillet of sole with new potatoes and haricots verts. There were melon halves stuffed with raspberries soaked in kirsch as a dessert.

'My god, Bits, you done us proud.' Herbie attacked his food like someone who had not eaten for a week.

'You don't look after yourself, Herb. No lunch, working till all hours . . .' Bitsy began.

'Goes with the job, Bits. Things are dangerous – just like this cold soup is dangerous for my digestion.'

'Oh, I'm sorry, I . . .'

'Don't worry about it. I always live dangerously.'

Ginger piped up with the information that there had been a bomb in Rupert Street.

'Yea, I know. Blew out the front of one of my

favourite curry houses.' Herbie gave them a superior look, as if to say he knew the whys and wherefores of the bombing.

'Was it the people we're supposed to be dealing with?' Ginger again.

'Ginge, you shouldn't ask. Now let's change the subject. Bex, what was the funniest case you were ever on?'

'The funniest? Why?'

'Just to have a talk about things that don't have anything to do with bombs.'

'Funniest?' she repeated.

'Yea, funniest, like in ha-ha. Give us all a good laugh, ja?'

Bex smiled, then giggled. 'It's slightly indelicate,' she was trying to control the giggles.

'We're all grown men and women.' Herbie tried to draw her.

'Oh, well. It happened when I was just a plain-Jane policewoman on the beat. It was funny, but not for the poor devil who was the centre of attention,' she began.

She had been called, with her partner, to St Mary Abbots hospital around nine one night, and a somewhat embarrassed doctor explained the situation. A patient had got himself to the hospital in great pain and discomfort.

'He has a real problem,' the doctor told the police, 'and I think it should be reported to you in case he wants to bring charges of assault.' The patient in question was terrified of his wife finding out what had happened. He had been having a torrid affair which had got out of control. That night, he had gone to see his lover in order to tell her that it was all over. He could not go on cheating on his wife. The girl had seemed to take it well enough, and pleaded with him to go to bed with her just for one last time.

'They were apparently in the middle of things when

she reached out, grabbed a vibrator, and stuck it straight up the poor guy's rectum.'

'Serve him right,' muttered Bitsy.

Bex explained that the vibrator was one of those things with rubber ridges around it. 'They couldn't get it out without causing him great pain, but he insisted they should do whatever was necessary. They pleaded with him to have it surgically removed in the operating theatre under a general anaesthetic, but he wouldn't hear of it. If they gave him a general, they'd have to inform his wife and that was the last thing he wanted.

'We said if that was the case the last thing he would want was to bring charges against the girlfriend for assault with a deadly weapon. My partner went into the cubicle and tried to argue with him, but he'd have none of it. There was nothing we could do, and the doctor said they would get the thing removed but it would cause much anguish – which it did. You could hear the guy screaming all over the Casualty Department.'

'They got it out?' Ginger asked, laughing wildly.

Bex nodded. 'We were about to leave when his wife turned up. The girlfriend had called her on the phone, so we stayed on to try and avert any domestic violence.'

'And did you?'

'We managed to restrain her, but you should have seen the fellow's face when he came hobbling out of the cubicle – contorted with pain, then terrified when he saw his wife. I gather she forgave him in the end . . .'

Ginger guffawed. 'In the end is right,' he managed to say through his laughter. 'His girlfriend said goodbye in the end, and the wife forgave him in the end.'

'You got anything funnier, Herb?' Bex was starting to relax.

'Me? Nothing funny ever happens to me.'

'Come on, Mr Kruger. You must've had a couple of funnies.' Ginger had wiped his eyes and finally stopped laughing.

'Never had a vibrator,' Herb said, deadpan, which Ginger thought was no end of a joke. Kruger very rarely told people – even colleagues – stories, funny or sad, concerning his long career. There had been funny moments, certainly, but his experiences during the old long dark days of the Cold War would remain for ever locked away in his head and in the files of the SIS. Eberhardt Lukas Kruger, for all his bonhomie, was a very close bird who knew that the real adventures were not kiss-kiss, bang-bang, but mental exercises, deduction and analysis. Often dull and complex.

After dinner, they sat over coffee for a while before Herb bowed out, saying he had work to do. Bitsy once more became solicitous, saying he worked too hard and that he should relax.

'Bitsy, this is truly important. Let me tell you when I can take time off, then maybe we'll do some cooking together.'

This she obviously took to be more than an invitation to spend time in the kitchen. She smiled like the cat who had at last got the cream and disappeared.

'You're not really going to spend time cooking with *her*?' Bex said as they reached Gus's study.

'Keep her quiet, Bex. Me? I've finished with playing footsie with women. Age is catching up with me.'

'Nonsense, Herb. You're still an attractive man.'

'Sure, in the dark with light behind me, sure.'

When they had closed the door and were seated, he asked Bex about Carole.

'I didn't push too hard. Just had a long talk. I've got details about where Gus was the night he got himself killed. She was obviously very much in love with him.'

'True. First wife, Angela, was pain like your guy with the vibrator. Carole was one hell of an interrogator as well

205

as Gus. Once saw them working as a team. Incredible. They were like sharks. When one stopped pressing the other took over. Never knew if you were on your arse or Easter Day. Gus taught her the ropes.' He paused, looked at her and saw her eyes full of doubt. 'You got some reserves, yes?'

'Reservations, Herb, yes.'

'Why?'

'I've spent a lot of time with the bereaved. Seen grief and its side effects. Either Carole is a very tough cookie or she's in denial, or she's not grieving for some other reason. She knows something we don't, Herb. Can't think what it could be, but she really is holding back.'

'Maybe it's about the magic side of things. Gus obviously talked a lot to her. Before you came on the scene I talked with one of our retired Deputy Chiefs. Turned out that he was Magic Circle. Wouldn't even be drawn on the subject. Very close. Perhaps Carole's the same.'

'She can do no wrong in your eyes, can she?'

Herbie grunted. 'You don't know me proper yet, Bex. Nobody, absolutely nobody is beyond suspicion in my thinking. I had to learn that the hard way. Go ask Tony Worboys, he'll probably open up like a singing goldfish, but you could always ask him about Ursula. Then he just might tell you how I learned never to trust nobody – not Carole, Ginge, Bitsy, nor even Worboys. CIA man once called this profession a wilderness of mirrors. Quote from some poet, but he had the right word. It *is* a wilderness of mirrors. You always look twice, then again for the insurance. You always analyse what people tell you, even people you trusted for years.' Without a pause he changed the subject, veering off at a sharp angle. 'Where *was* Gus, and what was he doing the night he got blown to pieces?'

'Giving a magic lecture and demonstration to some Magic club in Salisbury.'

'We check that's true?'

'I have a name and number to call, yes.'

'Then call it now. Never put off the moment. Apologize for ringing so late, but push your police credentials.' He gestured towards the telephone.

The conversation was short and to the point. For once, the magician at the distant end was willing to talk. When she put down the receiver, Bex nodded. 'That was where he was. The chairman of the society said he was wonderful, couldn't praise him highly enough.'

'Gus certainly knew his onions. I watched another video last night. He did impossible things. Made me think he really had special powers, and I got a pretty logical brain. I think Gus could've made more money doing the magic stuff than he did as a confessor.'

Bex did not respond. Presently she said it was her bedtime. 'What're we on tomorrow? Another go at Carole?'

'Maybe. I have some files to read, then we'll see. Meet at breakfast, eh?'

'All bright-eyed and bushy-tailed.'

'Speak for yourself.'

When she had gone, he turned on the computer again and reinserted the disk. Slowly he started to page through the document on the screen.

After the rather formal introduction, Gus had written the story in his relaxed, slightly mocking style. He obviously thought that it might still make part of the book, and Herbie wondered if the man's great magic had made him believe in miracles. The only way that the story could be told publicly was if *Jasmine* had eventually run for cover and had 'gone off the books', as they said when agents were pulled out and given new lives, new Legends – those carefully constructed backgrounds given to people who had to disappear, or become invisible. When they were given Legends on retirement, they were usually referred to as ghosts.

To begin at the beginning [Gus had written], the activating of *Jasmine* happened at a very difficult time for me. I was already engaged in interrogating a number of people from the Middle East. The reports went straight to the Chief because we were looking for people who could be turned back in the main Mid-East countries. At that time, Iran was the big enemy, but we were also trying for someone close to Muammar Qadaffi in Libya and all the other Arab countries, including the Saudis, King Hussein of Jordan, and the Syrians.

I had a couple of tickles who just might be useful in Syria, and one we thought could turn out to assist in Libya. I recall that it was all very cloak and dagger with much screening going on in London among the Arab population.

There was always an in-depth appreciation of potential customers before they were brought down to me, and they usually arrived at night, suitably blindfolded. I used the underground facilities to both house and interrogate them and 99 per cent turned out to be quite useless. They were either too terrified to go back to their native countries, or just unsuitable for many reasons – mainly because their profiles did not make them into a reasonable risk. Some I even judged to be possible doubles anyway and I always reported this to London before they left. What happened to these individuals is unclear, though usually, I gather, they were quietly shipped back to their countries labelled *persona non grata*. Knowing the regimes under which these latter had to live, I did not fancy their chances when they arrived home. On the other hand, it must have become common knowledge that we were trawling for possible assets, unlike our American cousins who continued to carry on their stand-off approach in the Middle East, relying solely on the satellite and electronic intelligence, a situation which went on almost until the collapse of the Soviet regime in Russia.

I was forced to leave almost in the middle of a three-day interrogation of a Saudi prospect because of the *Cataract* business. This, as you will recall [Herbie momentarily smiled: Gus had an over-achiever's outlook; nobody would ever have allowed the *Cataract* business in his book], was, in effect, a damage control operation to cover up an unhappy incident in central London, where four members of an IRA Active Service Unit were killed.

I carried out the operation with the assistance of some very good officers and technicians, and it was at the SIS technical laboratory, where we were reprocessing videos and adding images, that I came across *Jasmine*.

She had been working for us, on the technical side, for five years since she was twenty years old. A member of an old and wealthy Iraqi family, she had been brought to the UK at the age of seventeen when her immediate relatives were threatened by the Leader's Secret Police. We got into a casual conversation about life under the current regime in Iraq and it immediately became clear that she was highly intelligent. She hated the political set-up in her own country and was clearly anxious to help against the ruling Ba'ath Party in any way possible.

I am not a saint as far as women are concerned and I made a date with her for the following evening, after the whole of *Cataract* was in place. The next afternoon, I went into Head Office and took a look at her file. She had been deeply vetted when she first applied for the job in the technical branch and there was already a tag against her name suggesting she could be developed – as the jargon of the day put it. In other words, Head Office had seen the potential and then immediately forgotten about it.

The Chief and his first Deputy were out of the country, so I decided to take matters into my own hands. On the next night I met with *Jasmine* and, not to put too fine a point on it, we were mutually attracted to one another. In turn, this led to me asking if she had ever thought of going back to Iraq and ingratiating herself with the establishment.

She took her time to think about it, and finally said she would need more details. A week or so later I called the Chief direct from Warminster on a secure line and put the position to him. He told me to proceed with caution, and a couple of weeks after that *Jasmine* was brought to Warminster where I worked with her for a week. She was a keen and bright young woman, and the challenge of what I was offering appeared to press the right buttons. In no way did I hold back the dangers of what she was being asked to do, including the possibility of her being tested by the authorities in Baghdad. I recall telling her that she might even be asked to kill someone.

Eventually she agreed on one condition which initially posed a problem. She would return to Iraq and do her best to infiltrate the higher echelons of the establishment, in particular their teams of so-called freedom fighters (aka terrorists). However, she would do this only if I remained her sole controller. In plain language, I was to be her one and only case officer. All intelligence gleaned by her would have to come back to me; all special instructions would have to be sent by me. She would in no way countenance a third party – even though she knew third parties would exist among those who performed analysis on the raw material she would send back.

From a personal viewpoint, this was not going

to be easy, so I went directly to Head Office and talked face to face with the Chief, who came to the conclusion that, should I feel able to take on the extra workload, I would be accepted as the sole runner of *Jasmine*.

Jasmine returned to Iraq the following year after an exhaustive course and briefings which covered every possible procedure. We had a series of methods to cover her getting information out, including a high-frequency radio which gave her the option of encrypted 'burst' transmissions; carrier pigeons which we supplied after she returned to Baghdad; and a dangerous direct encrypted-mail set-up in which she sent letters into Saudi Arabia which were then forwarded to me.

In the event of her ever being sent into the UK on any pretext, she was to get in touch with me through the Personal Ads in *The Times*. She would simply begin the ad with the word Claudius. I was to reply using the word *Jasmine* and telling her where to meet me by inserting a map reference disguised as telephone numbers, which meant that I could even set up a meeting in a restaurant if need be.

Over eighteen months passed between her return to Iraq and her first raw intelligence. We had, in fact, resigned ourselves to the fact that she had been taken, but once she established contact – using, first, the letters via Saudi – a steady stream of information began to come through.

During the Gulf War *Jasmine* went to great pains to get vital intelligence out of Baghdad. She managed, with ingenuity, to set up a mail service via Turkey and we later discovered that she was, by this time, working within the Iraqi secret police. Intelligence stopped abruptly towards the end of the Gulf War and we can only presume that *Jasmine* perished during one of the air attacks, or that she was discovered and was dead. This, however, is only a presumption, and she will remain on the books until the year 2000.

Herbie finished reading, closed down the machine and returned the disk to its hiding place. What they needed to do now was place a reply in *The Times* Personal Ads.

He wondered if he should call Worboys at this time of night and was debating the subject when the telephone rang.

'Herb,' Worboys was breathless. 'The buggers have just blown up your cottage. Sorry to bring you this news, but I think we should meet as soon as possible.'

Big Herbie Kruger spoke one obscene and unpleasant word.

15

Hisham had cursed the fact that his own stupidity, years before, had put his *Intiqam* team at risk. So far he had kept to his side of the bargain and let the British Security Service know exactly where the bombs would be planted. The fact that the security people had acted irresponsibly in Berwick Street was not his fault; just as he had taken every precaution to make certain his team would disappear, almost in front of the watchers' eyes. It would give them time to regroup. He also had another plan up his sleeve.

The disappearing act had been well worked out. When they first rented the house in Clapham, Hisham had also found a second house for rent in the Camberwell area of South London, quite near a well-known pub called The Grove.

He had kept this house in reserve. Money was no object for he had brought thousands of American dollars into the country, exchanging them, a little at a time, for British sterling. The whole team had taken part in the money-changing business, and later – in some cases over a year later – the forged hundred-dollar bills had turned up in other parts of Europe, even as far away as America itself.

While they were still in the Clapham house, the two youngest members of the team had carefully removed the floorboards in a downstairs cupboard and dug out a seven-foot-deep recess below the ground-floor level. They had lined this hiding place with plywood, and even put in a chair. Then they had refashioned the floor of the cupboard with great care. Even if you stood on it and jumped up and down, you would not detect that there had been any tampering.

They had also added some subtle touches. The cupboard contained brooms and mops, with some shelves high up, on which stood cleaning materials. The floor to the cupboard was now carefully hinged, and they left it open before leaving the house, balancing the brooms and mops on the edge of the trapdoor. So, when the last arrival returned he would enter the cupboard, close the door and climb into the hiding place. Now he only had to lower the trapdoor carefully for the mops and brooms to slide down into their usual positions.

Hisham was convinced that the British would latch on to at least one, maybe two, of his bomb placers. It was inevitable that they would follow them back to Clapham and begin surveillance on the house so, on the night before the bombs were due to be set, he called the whole team together. Those who had no specific jobs regarding the placing of the explosives would move out first thing in the morning, taking everything with them, including the personal possessions of those who were placing the devices.

The men and women who were to do the dangerous work by carrying explosives across London were put on a strict timetable. Hisham had worked out to the minute how long his people would take to get back to Clapham. He had factored into this the way in which the Security Service would operate. It was safe for three of the placers to return, enter the Clapham house by the front door and quickly walk through to the back door, then speedily leave the area.

The last arrival – Ahmad – would not be able to do this walk through so openly. Hisham thought, correctly, that by the time he returned the house would be surrounded. So it was Ahmad who let himself into the empty house and went straight into the hiding place they had prepared under the cupboard. He was chosen because he did not mind the dark and was adept at remaining very still for long periods, so Ahmad was actually inside the house when the SAS and police raided the place. Later he told of his fear, for there had been loud explosions and the front door had been broken in.

At three in the morning, Ahmad had gently raised the trapdoor and lifted himself out. As far as he could see, they had left only two police constables in the street, outside the smashed front door. An hour after coming out of hiding, Ahmad was making his way across London to their new headquarters.

Hisham had made another decision for that night. While he had told the Security Service of the four targets the FFIRA had picked for assassination by the *Intiqam* team, he was 100 per cent certain that nobody would expect an attempted killing on that particular night. He had also told the MI5 people that he would do his best not to allow the attacks to be lethal. They would, he had said, look like attempts that had gone wrong. It would be impossible to be 100 per cent inaccurate and he was determined that the assassinations would take place. Each, he thought, would succeed.

Terrified and in a no-win situation, with his loyalties cut in two by the fear, Hisham had now taken the step which would lead him into the even more dangerous game of trying to work both sides of the street. He played as best as he could, in a doomed attempt to keep his country and his secret masters believing in him.

So, when everyone was settled in the new Camberwell house, he issued instructions – Ramsi, Samira and Nabil would be on one of the early commuter flights to Paris. There, they would carry out the work already planned. From Paris they would fly to Rome and do similar jobs. They had been over these operations in detail. *Yussif* had issued information regarding where the explosives and weapons were cached in the French and Italian cities, and when it was all accomplished they would come back into London separately, going by slow and devious routes and coming back directly from Dublin.

For the time being, Ahmad was left out of current operations, ordered to stay on at the new house, to be certain that the place was secure at all times.

When he had gone over the briefings again, Hisham left with Dinah.

Early in the *Intiqam* operation they had bought two second-hand vehicles – a Previa, which would take all of them when necessary, and a Volkswagen Golf. Hisham and Dinah set off in the VW, drove to Lyndhurst almost in the heart of the New Forest, and checked into the Crown Hotel late that night. At around eleven Hisham had called ahead and reserved a room, saying they were making for Southampton for a business conference the following afternoon, but had been held up when their car had broken down. There were rooms available, and Hisham gave them a credit card number, saying they expected to arrive sometime before two in the morning.

Once on the outskirts of the New Forest, they turned off and headed towards Burley where they parked the car and set off on foot to reconnoitre Kruger's cottage which stood, isolated, by the roadside in about an acre of land a little over half a mile away.

There were lights on, and, as they approached the pretty little house, they could hear the sound of voices. Hisham was satisfied that somebody was at home, so they made their way back to the car, opened the boot and removed the four one-gallon cans of petrol which had already been prepared personally by Hisham during the afternoon. Each of the cans had three sticks of dynamite secured to the side with gaffer tape, and detonators, fuses and timers were in place. While they were still in the boot of the car, Hisham set the timers, with Dinah holding a pencil torch. These were crude devices compared with many that Hisham had used during the forty-two years of his life, but they should do what was required of them.

Each of them carried two of the cans, and when they returned to the cottage, the place was in darkness. Two of the containers were set close to the front door and two at the back – one against the door and another balanced on a rear windowsill.

They left quickly, driving to Lyndhurst and actually getting to the Crown just after one in the morning. A night porter let them in, showed them to their room and even brought them a pot of coffee with some cheese sandwiches.

As ever, Dinah knew what was expected of her. As ever, she also looked forward to a quiet time with Hisham. He was a good lover and the adrenalin which had been pumping throughout this mission – first with the bomb she had dropped in Rupert Street, and more recently setting the devices at the cottage – had left her ready for the most erotic of sexual encounters. Most of all, in the private part of her brain, she wanted the sex to be violent. The same obviously applied to Hisham, for, apart from the odd hour's sleep, they spent the night engaging in violent forms of sexual pleasure.

They had hardly finished with the coffee and sandwiches when Hisham took her, fully clothed, dragging her skirt up, pushing her underwear to one side and mounting her from behind as he threw her roughly across the bed. She followed his lead, and enjoyed the fierceness of his thrust.

Later she tried some of her own variations on Hisham, holding the strong, tough Iraqi down on the bed, her hands like twin vices around his wrists. Still only half-naked she rode him, occasionally releasing his wrists to slap him across the face. Hisham knew the game well and, while it was not manly to be dominated by a woman, he succumbed to it for the sheer pleasure.

Later, he turned the tables on her, tying her wrists to the bedposts, lashing at her silk-covered buttocks with his belt, so that she cried out in the exquisite pain, though not as loudly as she did when he entered her, again from behind as she grunted, 'Harder . . . Harder', and surrendered herself to the halcyon

217

moments which lay beyond the mixture of pain and pleasure.

It was while they were both enjoying the games of love that the cottage blew up.

The two petrol and dynamite bombs at the front blew a gaping hole in the façade of the cottage, sending a sheet of flame into the main living-room, while the two devices at the rear spread fire through the kitchen and brought a section of the upper storey crashing down in a puzzle of bricks and mortar.

It was the device placed on the rear windowsill that ruptured the gas main to the house, adding greatly to the explosion, which was heard as far away as Cadnam. The initial flame, from the gas inferno, was seen from a distance of ten miles. Within an hour, in spite of a fast reaction from local fire brigades, there was little left of the cottage.

In the United States, things had started to go badly early that morning when Awdah and Jamilla were picked up at JFK as they came off a flight direct from Chicago. Both of them had been reluctant to head straight back to New York, but the events of the previous evening told them they should get out of LA as quickly as possible. Awdah had reasoned that nobody had got a good enough look at them to make a positive ID.

Awdah was wrong. The FBI had released the descriptions taken from people at the Cedars of Lebanon Hospital, together with computer-generated pictures put together with the help of a highly sophisticated programme and worked on with eyewitnesses.

Plainclothes officers now watched all major air and sea ports on the East Coast, armed with descriptions and the computerized photofit picture. Those at JFK had no problem in identifying the pair of terrorists.

The NYPD officers, together with FBI Special Agents, had managed to keep the media off their backs. They had learned, from the 1993 bombing of the World Trade Center, to use diversionary tactics with them.

They had learned the hard way. Following the explosion on Friday 26 February, the forensic investigators had traced the vehicle used in the bombing to a Ryder Truck Rental Co. in New Jersey. The local Ryder officials knew who had rented the truck: a man called Salameh who had reported the vehicle stolen and wanted his $400 deposit back. The FBI instructed the Ryder Company to call Salameh and tell him that he could come and collect his money. This happened on the Wednesday following the bombing, and the FBI plan was simply to watch Salameh, putting him under close surveillance so that he could lead them to others involved.

The media, however, got wind of the plan and – in the interests of freedom of information for the general public – threatened to blow the story if the FBI did not arrest the man. In the end, it did not hamper police investigations, though the FBI were now thoroughly disillusioned with a media which did not understand the necessity of keeping certain information back to help investigators. They, rightly, felt that they had been blackmailed into making the arrest, and even had to allow the story that Salameh had been a loose cannon by reporting the theft of the van to be published. In fact, Salameh's action was an obvious piece of terrorist tradecraft. By making a fuss with Ryder Trucks about the theft of the vehicle, he had been attempting to draw the heat off himself and his associates.

This time, they remained watchful and maintained a very low profile. After all, the recent shootings and bombings had become a new dimension in the American way of life. Terrorism, until now, had been rare, and since the first explosions – the car bomb in Manhattan, the detonation in the New York subway, and the horrifying Boeing 737 explosion on take-off from La Guardia – the NYPD, and particularly the FBI, had remained close-lipped.

When Awdah and Jamilla were spotted at JFK they were virtually surrounded by a highly trained surveillance team, and with split-second timing the cab they entered outside the airport was actually driven by an undercover agent. By the time they paid off the cab – five blocks from the apartment building on Park Avenue – they were well blocked in.

They walked the five blocks, not sensing that anything was amiss. Within twenty minutes, the police and FBI knew exactly where the American *Intiqam* team were hiding out. It was only a matter of time before they would close in and make the arrests.

When his car drew up at what had once been Herbie Kruger's retirement cottage, Worboys could see the figure of Herbie standing, desolate, near the ruins. The big man wore a long black raincoat, fashioned to look like a nineteenth-century riding coat, long-skirted, with flaps like gills at the back. He wore it unbelted and the material billowed around him in the grey first light, shoulders bent in an attitude of hopelessness, and head slumped forward as though he were praying that this was a nightmare.

Tony Worboys had said he would meet him at the site, so Herbie had awakened Ginger, written a note to Bex Olesker, and called the main house to bring Kenny Boyden over to lie across the door – as the arcane argot has it.

The note had said: 'Bex, I got to be out for a while. Do not see Carole again until I come back. I know some good questions for her now. Not likely to be easy. In meantime, go and root out that magic man you talked to on the telephone. He must have been one of the last people to see Gus alive. *You* know the questions to ask him. Love and kisses, Herb.'

'He's taken it very bad, Mr Worboys.' Ginger was at his elbow, almost touching his arm. 'If I didn't know better, I'd have thought Mr Kruger was weeping, sir.'

'Just look after him when we leave, Ginger. This is bad, and it's likely to get worse.'

He moved forward and stood next to Herbie. 'You're well insured, Herb, right?'

The big head nodded, and the distraught face turned towards Young Worboys. 'Sure. I can build twenty cottages better than this with insurance, but I've lost a lot of nice bits and pieces from my brilliant career.' There was bitterness in the way he spoke. 'Shit,' he said. 'My own bloody silly fault. They thought I was inside.'

'How?'

'You know me, Young Worboys. Always fixing my own security.' A long pause followed by a great sigh which finally changed to a raw laugh. 'Did it all myself. Ran the place off a computer when I was away. One thing I remembered to do when I left here.'

'Alarms, you mean?'

'Sure, there were alarms, but I did more. The programme was computer-driven. Pulled curtains closed and open at certain times. Switched on lights in different rooms. Put the television on and off. Even played voices I recorded on a big old reel-to-reel. Anyone getting near the place would think I was at home.'

'Thank God you weren't.'

'You got to watch your back also, Young Worboys. You already warned me. Is The Whizzer fully briefed now? If not, you'd better tell him what they done to this place, yes?'

'Yes.' Worboys nodded. 'The Office'll see you have somewhere to live while you're sorting things out.'

'Should bloody think so, Tony.' He grinned, like a Hallowe'en lantern. 'Think of all the fun I have in building up my record collection again.' Then, as though it were an afterthought. 'Also, now I might do some dabbling in the magic, like Gus.'

'Lord save us from that, Herb.'

Presently, the local Fire Captain came up to them,

apologizing and saying that the explosions and ensuing fire looked like something deliberate.

'Tell me something I don't know.' Herbie did smile, though the words came out brittle and harsh.

'There'll still have to be an inquiry, sir.'

Worboys stepped between them and taking the fireman by the arm he led him a few paces away.

'Whenever you're ready, Mr Kruger.' Ginger came over from the car.

'Sure, Ginge. Let me have a few minutes with the good Mr Worboys. Alone in the car would be best, I think.'

'I'll stay out of the way until you've done, Mr Kruger. I'm so sorry about all this.'

'Don' be, Ginge. I got my life. I got my health. What more can a man want? Possessions aren't everything, you know. Don' worry.'

Worboys returned, saying that he had fixed the Fire Captain. The police he would deal with as soon as he got back to London.

'Tony, a word in my office, huh?' He gestured towards the car.

Once settled in the back of the car, with Ginger discreetly standing several paces away, Herbie told him what he had discovered about Gus and *Jasmine*.

'So, she's come alive again.'

'Looks very like it, Tony. Problem is meeting her. We have to give a map reference disguised as a couple of telephone numbers, which means some playing around. We do it the wrong way and she dives under the surface again. Neither do we know the tradecraft: which signals for safe and which for keep off the sodding grass.'

'It would be better if we could get around that. You say Gus had an affair with this one?'

'That's how it reads. He did some hanky-panky with her, that's for sure. I'm wondering how much Carole knew.'

'Well, for heaven's sake take care when you're talking

to her. Carole can be bloody volatile, Herb. Could get your dick caught in a mousetrap.'

'Ouch! Now you really scare me, Tony. You got absolutely nothing in the forbidden secrets department?'

'*Jasmine*, yes. Yes, of course we have. We've got the product. She was very good. Gave us indispensable intelligence during the Gulf War. Amazing stuff.'

'I mean how she was run?'

'It was Gus, and Gus alone.'

'Shit,' said Kruger, with a good deal of emotion.

'I'm so sorry, Herb.' Bex was waiting in the dining-room when he returned to the Warminster Dower House.

'It's terrible.' Bitsy was hovering, and the table was laid out with cold meats, hard-boiled eggs and seven kinds of salad. Enough to feed a couple of armies.

'Ach, is nothing,' Kruger grinned. 'What's one lousy house between enemies? The insurance'll make me almost rich. I can buy several houses with it. I'm alive. They meant for me to be dead, so we fooled them.' He helped himself to a huge plate of lettuce, tomato, cucumber, ham and hard-boiled eggs, waved away the wine that Bitsy suggested and asked for Perrier water. 'Kisses, cool as cucumbers,' he remarked as he placed the salad on his plate. Then:

'So, how was the Mage of Salisbury?'

'Nice.' Bex chewed on a hunk of French bread. 'Very nice. About a hundred and three, but he talked quite openly to me about Gus's visit to his magic society. They call themselves The Old Sarum Sorcerers . . .'

'Yesu!' Herb looked heavenwards.

'He said it was an honour to have Claudius there for the evening. Said it was one of the greatest experiences of his magic life.' Her tone was mocking.

'Don' extract the urine, Bex. These guys are mainly very serious.'

'Okay, but he went on a good deal about it. Even told me what Gus did for them.'

'Some other time. What about Gus's demeanour? What about when he left?'

'On very good form. Stayed for longer than most lecturers. Did you know there's a whole great lecture circuit in the magic business? Just about world-wide. He said Gus stayed, answered questions. Left on his own. Seemed to be in good spirits.'

'You got the time he left?'

'It was late for the Old Sarum Sorcerers. As he remembered, it was almost one in the morning.'

'That leaves about two hours unaccounted for – well, say one and a bit hours. Not a long drive from Salisbury to where Gus died. A lot of time missing, so we're none the wiser. We know he was there. We know that's what he was doing. Well, we know he left at around one, and the car blew up just after three.'

'Doesn't explain him standing by the roadside near his car, talking to someone as yet unidentified. Chatting one minute, driving off the road and blowing up the next.'

'No, it really doesn't explain a damned thing. I think we should have a little pry into the telephone logs. The big house and here.'

'They'd still log calls from here? Even though it was virtually Gus's private residence?'

'You'd be surprised at what they log. *Every* incoming and outgoing call. The lot. Must be on file somewhere.'

They finished lunch eventually and headed across to the guest quarters to have another chat with Carole. 'I do the talking on this one, Bex, 'cause you don' know the right questions. Just stand by to pick up Carole in case she gets the vapours.'

Carole was all sweetness. 'I thought you'd be over this morning.' She gestured to the chairs as though she were still the lady of the manor – which had been Gus's joke about her when he ruled the roost at Warminster.

'No, had a little problem,' Herb grinned. 'My house blew up, Carole.'

'You're joking.'

'I don' yoke about houses blowing up.'

'You leave the gas on or something?'

'No, someone put some explosives and petrol around the place and whoosh! Went up, ignited the gas line and boom, as in my house used to be here.'

'Oh, Herb, I'm . . .'

He held up a hand to stop her. 'Carole, you said there was a tape of Gus's special lecture to all those important people.'

She nodded. 'In the archives at the main house,' leaning forward and picking up a videotape from a side table. 'All yours, Herb. I got them to let me take it for you.'

'You did? Naughty, they should've asked *me*.'

'Well, I told them *you* wanted it. They know me well enough, and I'm not taking any risks.'

'Okay, we'll take a look later on,' and like a soccer player swerving and booting the ball away at ninety degrees he switched. 'Carole, tell me about *Jasmine*.'

Her face went hard as granite for a few seconds and he would have sworn that her eyes blazed anger. '*Jasmine*?' she asked.

'She was here at one time – 1984, I think. You gotta remember *Jasmine*, Carole. Old Gus was stuck on her.'

For a moment he thought he had blown it. Then Carole relaxed. 'Yes, Herb. *Jasmine*. Pain and grief, but Gus never knew. He was mightily stuck on *Jasmine* because of the potential. I'm pretty certain of that. You clever devil, Herb. Gus never knew but you dragged it out of the past, though I couldn't tell how you did it.'

'Just tell us about it, Carole, my dear.'

'Okay. The one and only time I was ever unfaithful to Gus.'

'Yes?'

'He brought this guy – an Iraqi, I think – down here. Usual business. He came at night, blindfolded. Gus said he was a possible recruit to do some bits of snooping in the Middle East. Said he had worked for the Office as a lab technician for some time. Now they wanted him to go back. It was risky. I remember laughing when I was told to refer to him only as *Jasmine*. Work name, I suppose.' Her tongue slid out and she licked her lips. 'He was a very attractive hunk, if you want to know.' She was almost belligerent about it. 'Gus had to be away a lot.' She sighed. 'Really never forgave myself for it. Gus said, keep him happy while I'm gone for a couple of days. Gus was my life, Herb. Why would I do such a thing? Never forgave myself.'

'It happens.' Herbie reached out and fondled her hand. She withdrew it quickly. 'I spent most of the first day just talking to him. We went for a walk, I recall. In the grounds, of course. The staff kept their eyes out for him – us. It was the second night. He was so attractive. Like silk, and with a beautiful voice, though what that has to do with it I don't know. Yes, on the second night I slept with him. The *only* time, Herb. I promise it was the only time I was ever unfaithful to my dear, dearest Gus.'

'And did the earth move?'

'As a matter of fact it did,' she snapped. 'But I wanted out. I felt filthy for days. Went through a routine of showering about three times a day. Even destroyed some of the clothes I was wearing. Please, Herb. Please, this hasn't got anything to do with Gus being dead, has it?'

'No. No, not directly.' He was away, trying to work out why Gus had left a document that was a direct deceit. Calling *Jasmine* a woman, with whom *he* had taken a trot around the park. 'No,' he added. 'Carole, Bex and I got to talk. We'll watch Gus's lecture and come back tomorrow. Long session tomorrow.'

As he rose, Carole asked, 'You don't think I'm a trollop, Herb?'

'Don' be stupid, Carole. You know I always lusted after you. No, you're not a trollop.'

226

Far away in the underground guest rooms a telephone purred. Instinctively Herb knew it was for him, and showed no surprise when the switchboard patched it through to Carole's room.

'Herb,' Young Worboys was breathless from London. 'You with Carole?'

'Yes.'

'Don't say a word, but I have a shock for you.'

'My house hasn't blown up again, has it?'

'No, Herb. Today's *Times*. There's an answerback.'

'What?'

'Go and read it yourself. Somewhere private. Certainly not in front of Carole.'

'Sure. Sure, Tony, I'll do that.'

'And call me back.'

'And when I've done it, I'll call you back.'

He almost dragged Bex out through the passage that led directly to the main house. All the way she pummelled him with questions, 'Herb, what is it? Please, Herb. Tell me what it is?'

There was a copy of *The Times* in the Mess. Kruger pounced on it like a huge bear wanting to do it an injury, tearing the pages apart.

It was in the third column of the Personal Ads:

JASMINE, my queen. Your news is wondrous and I can even smell your rich perfumes from where I am. Call me tomorrow night around seven at either 234-2210, or 234-2261. I yearn for you. Your beloved Claudius.

16

Earlier, in New York, Walid could not sleep. New York is the city that never sleeps, and Walid remained wide awake. First, Samih and Khami had made noisy love. To be fair, Khami had offered herself to Walid also, once the team's leader, Samih, had dropped into a deep sleep, but Walid had refused. He cared greatly for her, but hated the thought of her having been touched by Samih. His instinct told him that she would rather be alone with him, but what was instinct?

He still could not sleep, and realized suddenly at five in the morning that it was the silence that worried him. Even in the plush apartment building there was always noise. Twenty-four hours a day there was noise. The normal city traffic sounds of the day, and at night, if it was not the street-cleaning crews it was the wail of police sirens.

Now, here in the early hours, there was no noise. Quietly he climbed out of bed and went over to the long window that looked down on Park Avenue. With a jolt to his heart he realized why it was so silent. Below him, and on the other side of the road, the lights of police cruisers twinkled their red and blue strobes. There were three ambulances drawn up across the road and a pair of buses.

Walid reasoned that there was a SWAT team out there. Possibly negotiators, in case something went wrong, maybe even the FBI Fast-Reaction hostage team from Quantico. He did not know how long he had to get clear, and his first thought was to waken Samih as the leader, show him what was waiting for them, and take orders directly from him.

He must have puzzled at it for the best part of five minutes, and in that time he came to an unthinkable conclusion. They would not all get away: of that he was certain. Better for two to jump clear now, than all of them perishing.

Gently he woke Khami, placing a hand over her mouth and putting his finger to his own lips so that she would not be afraid. Carefully he led her to the window and saw her eyes open wide in fear, so he whispered to her, telling her to get dressed, that he had a plan.

Now, he also dressed and found one of the pistols which had a noise reduction unit fitted to its barrel. He told Khami to find a weapon and ammunition as he went about getting a spare pistol and even more shells.

Drawing Khami to the door he reminded her of what they had been told in Baghdad. If there was danger, particularly a situation were local police or intelligence agencies were likely to take the entire team, then one or two – no more than two – members would have to take the initiative.

Her eyes widened again. Those instructions had been given in graphic detail. If this circumstance arose, they would be cleansed of destroying their brothers and sisters, for the survival of one or two members of the team was essential, even at the cost of the others' lives.

Walid instructed her to go into the hallway which separated the two apartments. When she left, there was no doubt in her mind regarding what Walid was about to do. He did it by pressing a pillow quickly against Samih's head and firing through the pillow. With the noise reduction unit the shot sounded like a small popping noise, as though it had come from far away. Samih's head burst open, thick blood and grey matter flowering out from under the pillow.

He took the small briefcase in which Samih kept the bank account details, the cheques, credit cards, passports and over two million dollars in forged hundred-dollar bills. Outside, in the passage, he handed the briefcase to Khami and told her to go past the lift and through the emergency door which would take them down the stairs. She nodded and immediately did as she was asked.

Only when she had gone through the door did he lean on the bell beside the other apartment door. Eventually a voice croaked something about not making so much noise. It was Jamilla who had peeped through the little security fish lens set into the door. Jamilla, he thought, would be an asset to him, but he dared not allow her to live. He shot her between the eyes as soon as she opened the door, then, swiftly, he moved into the bedroom and saw Awdah sitting on the bed, dazed with sleep. He killed him, before Awdah even realized what he was about to do. One popping shot, to the head.

Walid was a meticulous man, and he checked the pulses to make certain there was no life left in them before he let himself out and closed the door behind him. Khami was at the top of the emergency stairs waiting for him. She touched his hand and then his face in an action meant to signify her sorrow for what he had been forced to do. He did not even think about it. The trick now was to get out of the building without the police catching them. After all, he would have to get a report to *Yussif*. Then, Khami would have to be told the real facts of life.

The emergency stairs, he realized, would not be safe, unless they could use them to get access to the twin building of the apartment block. Once the SWAT teams moved in, they would shut off the bank of elevators and come up these stairs. That kind of people did not trust elevators. He gave Khami an encouraging smile, to pass resolve and courage to her. Then he explained what they must do, and do quickly.

Big Herbie sat Bex down in Gus Keene's old study and laid out an overview of the situation. He needed her to listen, he said, and then tell him what conclusion she came to.

'First off, Bex, you're a cop; a detective, trained in this kind of business. You can probably make sense from nonsense. Okay?'

'If you say so, Herb.'

He went through everything that had transpired since the night Gus Keene's car had left the road and exploded near the village of Wylye. With great care he took her through the knowledge that there was an Iraqi terrorist team out for vengeance here in the UK, and another in the States. That his own life was threatened, together with Worboys and another officer. He did not mention that Gus had been included in the hit list. Then he gave her the complex details of Gus having recruited and virtually run an asset in Iraq for some years; how they did not have any handling details; how Gus had left a document giving the impression that the asset – *Jasmine* – was a woman with whom he had carried on an affair; and now, as she had just heard, it was Carole who had slept with *Jasmine* who turned out to be a man. Like someone explaining a difficult concept to a small child, he told her of the *Jasmine* notice in *The Times*, and now an answerback which, by all that was secret, should only have come from Gus Keene.

'So, what you make of all that, Bex?'

'These telephone numbers, which you say are supposed to be map co-ordinates?'

'Yes?'

'They mean anything?'

'Don't know, Bex. Haven't checked them out yet. I hope Head Office is at work on them now. In the computer age, you would have thought that'd be easy as falling off a leg.'

'Log.'

'What?'

'You mean log, Herb.'

'Sure,' he said with a grin, and Bex Olesker knew then, at that moment, that Herb was completely himself again. Deputy Chief Worboys had gone into Kruger's most irritating habits in some detail, and when she had first met him Bex had thought that Herbie was a broken man with all the bounce knocked out of him.

'Okay,' she continued. 'So we don't know if they work . . .'

'We will. Given time and a following wind, which with Bitsy's cooking shouldn't be difficult. Sorry, I embarrass you. The quick answer is we'll soon know if a map reference'll come out of the numbers.'

'You knew Gus for a long time, Herb.'

'Since I was first found in Berlin by the Office. Gus was Military Intelligence in those days. The Office talked with him a lot. I was present, often.'

'You want to tell me about Berlin? How they latched on to you?'

'Not really. My father was a Luftwaffe pilot, killed during Battle of Britain. I hated Hitler from then on, even though I was just a kid. Not even teenager. My mother was killed during battle for Berlin. I kept my head down. The Americans picked me up and interrogated me. Found I was anti-Nazi. The old American OSS put me to work. I trawled the camps they had for Displaced Persons. DPs they called them, which is pretty obvious. There were a lot of Nazis – real high-ranking Nazis – hiding out in the camps. They called me a ferret. Got a lot of them – not ferrets, Nazis.

'Then OSS was closed down – well, it stopped being OSS. Lots of guys went home, out of a job, but a lot stayed on and eventually became CIA. I was being run by a guy called Farthing. He left, but before he flew out he took me to an SIS friend, name of Railton. Donald Railton, though everyone called him Naldo – family nickname. Lives in America now. Retired. He used me for the same job a couple of times, then brought me out and the Office trained me. That's how it all began. Now I'm a dodo. I'm a dinosaur. Near extinction. Prowling around watching the end of an era, beginning of a new one. That's my history in a shell.'

'A nutshell.'

'Sure.'

'You really think of yourself as a dinosaur?'

'A little. Espionage, stealing secrets, is still very much in business, but there are new boys coming in all the time. Young Worboys was my junior – straight out of training – when I first knew him. They used to call the game the second oldest profession. But, now this is funny, Bex. I read in one of Gus's magic books that magic is second oldest profession. Interesting, huh?'

'But you know Gus from way back then?'

'Sure. Well, maybe I didn't actually *know* him. He knew me, though. Gus Keene had amazing memory. When I next time met him, he knew me. Said that we had met in Berlin in the late 1940s. Incredible with faces and names. Never forgot anything.'

'Would you say that you've always known he was devious?'

'Not always. No. Came to see it after my little spot of bother.'

'And what was that?'

'Worboys didn't tell you? Ha! I was naughty. East Berlin was out of bounds to me and the Office was letting an old network of mine go to whack and ruin. They tried to set it up again, running long range, but I flew over cuckoo's nest . . .'

'Wrack and ruin, plus flew the coop,' Bex thought, but did not fall into the trap of opening her mouth.

'I slipped over the wall. Bingo, got picked up by the Ks – KGB, that's what we called them. They dried me out and, when I got back, the Office had me down here for a year – in this very house; this very room. Gus hosed me down, cleaned me out. A year with Gus interrogating is like twenty years real time. Got to know him then . . . and when it was over. Spent a lot of time with Gus.'

'And by then you knew he was devious?'

'Sure. Devious like barrel of monkeys. Devious is

too good a word. Gus was the best. Guileful, shifty, underhanded, sneaky. That was Gus. Had all the good attributes for interrogator – confessor, like we called him – or for a case officer in the field. Yeah, I knew then how devious he was. Secretive also.'

'Secretive, like a magician.'

'Didn't have any idea about that. Not until I found out when he was dead. What you getting at, Bex?'

She raised her face, and for the first time, Herbie saw that she could look quite beautiful. A line of poetry slid through his mind:

And beauty making beautiful old rime,
In praise of ladies dead and lovely knights.

He thought it was probably Shakespeare, yet, out of context, it had a certain poignancy for him. 'What you getting at?' he repeated.

'It seems to me that your old friend Gus was even more devious than you ever imagined. The fact that he was a performing magician, under a pseudonym, makes a great deal of difference. He obviously thought like a good magician and, while I don't find that breed terribly amusing as entertainers, I *do* appreciate their certain skills. The thought has crossed my mind that Gus Keene's been leading us by the nose. He left a document where, if you followed certain clues, you'd find it. I'm talking about the *Jasmine* thing you unearthed. I also wonder, and it's just a kind of sneaking thought, if Gus the magician and Gus the Intelligence officer managed to disappear. To leap from the world in which you knew him, into another world.'

'You mean he could be alive?'

'Maybe. It's an option, isn't it?'

Herbie looked as if he were suddenly and completely fatigued with sorrow. 'There was a body,' he said, as though this were all he needed to prove that Gus had died in the inferno.

'So?'

'There was his watch; his Zippo; the stick pin. A body is a body.'

'Perhaps he met another body – coming through the rye,' she added.

'So that would make Gus a murderer. A killer.'

'In deceit he wouldn't have the stomach for *that*?'

Herbie thought for a long time. 'Yes,' he said, low and with a voice that seemed old beyond his age. Old and sad. 'Yes. Yes, I guess Gus was ruthless enough if the stakes were really high.'

'Then I'd put money on it as a possibility. Just a possibility.'

'That makes for more problems. Why, Bex? Why, if you're right, why would he do this? It couldn't have been sudden, like the spurs of the moment. Something like this calls for great planning. If you're right, he would have had to know what he was about to do for weeks before.'

'Yes.' Then quickly, as though reassuring him, 'It's only a possibility, Herb. Not necessarily true.'

Kruger grunted and reached for the telephone.

'Don't tell *anyone* yet.'

'Not going to tell anyone. Wait.'

He dialled the Office and they put him through to Worboys. 'Hey, Tony, you running those numbers through the magic machines yet?'

'Since we got them, Herb.'

'Make any sense? Got a match on some map reference yet?'

'No matches as yet, Herb. I'll get back to you as soon as we have anything – even if it's nothing, if you follow me.'

'Sure, Tony. Thanks.' Then, as though he had just thought of it, 'Can you get me the telephone logs for this place – big house and this one – over the period of, oh, a month before and a week after Gus died?'

'You're not thinking an inside job, are you?'

'Not going to tell you, Tone. Just get me the logs. Is possible, yes?'

At the distant end, looking out on the view of the Thames and the London skyline, Worboys thought, 'That's the old Big Herbie I know and love.' Aloud, he said, 'Okay, Herb. I can get the lot to you by the morning.' Privately, he thought, 'After I've had a sniff of them.'

'Not tonight?'

'No way, Herb. First thing in the morning. I'll get them to you by courier. Incidentally, I don't suppose you've seen or heard the news yet?'

'Which news we talking about?'

'Two car bombs. Big. One directly outside the Luxembourg Palais, the other close to the Palais-Bourbon. A lot of damage.'

'This is direct attack on the government then?'

'That's what it would seem like.' The Luxembourg Palace was home to the French Senate, while the Bourbon is the meeting place of the French lower house of parliament – the National Assembly or Chamber of Deputies.

'Responsibility?' Herbie asked.

'Nobody as yet.'

Kruger responded with his favourite obscenity. He replaced the receiver and turned to Bex. 'Let's go to the movies,' he said.

Ramsi, Samira and Nabil had left London on an early British Airways flight to Paris. They hired a car and drove in from Charles de Gaulle. They left the hire car in the underground park near Notre Dame and took a taxi across to the Gare du Nord where they picked up the explosive devices – two heavy steel cases left for them in two different lock boxes.

Samira and Nabil ate lunch at the station while Ramsi went off and stole a car – a small elderly British Austin. Samira took one of the cases, set the timer and left the car as close as she could get to the Luxembourg Palace. She then headed back to Notre Dame, which was shrouded in scaffolding. Half Paris seemed to be under reconstruction, but the great church was open and she passed the time inside, while Nabil was stealing a second car – a Citroën this time. Nabil and Ramsi both took the second car to the Bourbon Palace, set the bomb and took their time to find an empty parking slot.

Both bombs were set to explode at six p.m., and by then all three of them were on an Alitalia flight to Rome where they checked into the Cavalieri Hilton. All three were smartly dressed and carried expensive overnight bags. In the Cavalieri Hilton they were invisible.

Later in the evening they watched the Sky Channel on television and saw the police and rescue services dealing with the bodies and devastation in Paris.

Walid and Khami went down to the ground floor. They could hear the police talking with the night doorman.

'So there's only one way out? This way?' The voice conjured up too many nights of booze and smoke. Rough, as though he was telling the doorman, not asking him.

'Only way.' The night man spoke very halting English. 'No back way out. Have to come out front here.'

'Well, thank Christ for that.' The cop gave a laugh. 'Means we don't need to put anyone in back of the place.'

Walid took Khami's arm, pulling her back towards a little bathroom at the rear of the building. Being a very careful man, Walid had checked every possible entrance and exit. The bathroom – for the staff – had a small, unsecured window, low above the toilet. He climbed up and opened it, then helped Khami out. Below the window was a narrow alley which ran behind the building, and one further block. When they reached Park Avenue they could see the police were concentrating on their building. Nobody had thought of its twin, even though they must have plans of the whole complex.

'What now?' Khami asked.

'I must telephone *Yussif*. Also we have to get new clothes and luggage. The best thing for us is to hide in plain sight at a big hotel.' They stopped at the first bank of public telephones they came to, and from there Walid called The Parker Meridien on West 57th near 6th Avenue – which is what all New Yorkers call Avenue of the Americas. This hotel had been recommended by Baghdad, as being luxurious, large, well appointed and ridiculously expensive. Always best, they had said, to hide in plush and expensive American hotels. One of the briefing officers – who was now part of *Yussif* in the United States – had said that the Americans rarely suspect freedom fighters of staying in vast comfort. According to this man, the agencies in America would look in down-at-heel places first. Staying at very cheap hotels had been the downfall of many so-called terrorist groups the world over.

Walid reserved a suite, in the names of Mr and Mrs Jaffid. He knew they had passports and Legends – cover stories – in those names. Now, he told Khami, they would have to wait until morning, then do some shopping.

They passed the time by finding an all-night deli on West 57th Street, where they ate eggs and drank coffee. There were several other customers, even at this time in the morning, and Khami was, at first, outraged because this was a Jewish eating place – 'That's why nobody will even bother looking for us here,' Walid told her firmly.

At nine in the morning they took a cab to Saks where they both went on a shopping spree, buying dresses, suits, shoes, shirts, underwear, socks and every possible accessory. Four items needed alterations and Walid asked for them to be sent to them, under the name Jaffid, at the Parker Meridien. They also bought Louis Vuitton luggage into which they loaded most of their purchases. When they left the store, Khami was wearing a dark blue business suit, while Walid looked every inch a businessman on vacation: grey slacks, good shoes, a navy double-breasted blazer with white shirt and a tie which looked suspiciously like the tie of a well-known British regiment.

They took a cab to the Parker Meridien and – because of the exorbitant cost of the suite – were treated like arriving royalty.

The moment they were left alone in the suite, Walid turned on the CNN Headline News. After fifteen minutes the anchor cycled back to the police raid on two apartments in the building on Park Avenue. The police spokesman said they had raided the two apartments following a tip-off. They had found two men and one woman dead from gunshot wounds. There were pictures of the bodies being carried out in bags.

Walid immediately punched in the telephone code for *Yussif*, America, and far away in the Hudson Valley one of the group picked up.

'Better Bread Company, Joe speaking, how can I help you?'

'Joe, it's Bobby Jaffid here.'

'Yes?' Startled.

'You've seen the news?'

'Yes. The price of most commodities will rise, I reckon.'

'I'm here, at the Parker Meridien in New York, with Sylvia. We're not getting the full story. We were out and about until the early hours. Peeled off when we saw the action. I think the fox killed the chickens. Anyway, we're ready to take on anything you might want overwritten. We'll be here for a week or two. Here and waiting.'

There was a long pause. Then:

'We have work for you. Quite a lot. Glad to hear you're okay, we'd already figured that the story wasn't quite true. I'll get something couriered to you. Probably tomorrow. We'll try to bring in other help, but it will be difficult, okay?'

'We'll be waiting.'

Downstairs, at the Bell Captain's desk, one of the

young porters remarked on the fact that Mr and Mrs Jaffid's luggage had no tags on it. 'In fact,' he said, 'it looked like the stuff had just been bought. Not even an airline label.'

'Well, some folks are funny about that kinda thing,' the Bell Captain replied. 'I know wealthy people who get the tags clipped off their luggage the moment they arrive any new place. Baggage thieves go for bags that have lots of stuff hanging from the handles.'

'Yeah? Well, there wasn't no little bits of string left on those bags. Not a dent in them. Not a scratch neither.'

'Live and let live, Barney.' As he said it, the Bell Captain thought to himself that this might warrant a report to the Duty Manager. Just in case they had got a pair of hustlers in.

The Duty Manager merely shrugged and said that the husband had given them a Platinum Amex card. It had been swiped and come up grade A. Prosperous.

In England it was the middle of the night now, but neither Big Herbie Kruger nor Detective Chief Inspector Bex Olesker could sleep. The video of Gus Keene's lecture had contained things that might puzzle the most astute intelligence officer.

17

The first shots on the video showed the audience. The camera zoomed in on particular people, and Herbie muttered something about high-powered talent. He recognized faces of men and women he had not seen for years. People he thought long dead. The Chief of the Secret Intelligence Service was there, of course, as was the Director General of the Security Service, MI5. There were also politicians and ranking officers of other services – notably the American CIA and NSA. The main body of the people there were outstanding field officers and people who had worked in dangerous secrecy during the Cold War. Men like Oleg Gordievsky, who had escaped the old Soviet Union by the skin of his teeth, having been a British asset within the KGB for over nine years. Kruger saw that the camera held his face for a few seconds, as it did with two other exceptionally well-known former agents. Gus had drawn a capacity crowd of highly select members of the secret world.

Herbie did not recognize the theatre, but thought it was probably a facility below the old SIS HQ in Century House. It certainly was not in the new building – Vauxhall Cross on the South Bank. Wherever, any terrorist group wanting to blow away some of the Western world's best members of the Intelligence Community would hit the bull's-eye here.

The video was obviously directed and shot by a professional team – again, Herbie considered, probably one of the three crews the SIS used for these things. His mind drifted back to the videos shot and tampered with at the time of *Cataract*. Once more he saw the bodies of the three victims. He saw again the wrecked corpse of

Mary Frances Duggan being turned over to reveal the Browning pistol. A magic trick, he thought. A magic trick that had turned back on itself and now had led to himself, among others, being sought out as victims for revenge.

The old Chief rose from the front row – 'Lord,' Herb thought, 'he really *did* look old.'

Climbing onto the stage, the Chief beamed around the room and the buzz of conversation died.

'This is a very special evening,' the old Chief's voice had a thin, reedy quality. 'This is graveyard stuff, being given to us by a man whom I have known and worked with for many years. You'll not recognize him, but I can tell you that his knowledge of the way we operate in the field is encyclopedic. Heed him well and, as I say, it's graveyard. You do not speak of this to anyone outside this room. Never. Please understand that.' Again he gave his beaming smile.

'Of course,' Herbie thought. 'The old Chief, like Deputy Maitland-Wood, was Magic Circle.' The pieces were beginning to come together.

'I am simply going to introduce to you . . .' the thin voice rose. 'Ladies and Gentlemen, The Great Covert.'

Then, the house lights went down and there was an undeniable sense of expectancy among the audience. It was as though they were about to watch a theatrical performance – which, in many ways, was exactly what they would see.

Softly the familiar music began – Falla, the *Ritual Fire Dance* from *Love the Magician*. This must have been Gus's signature music.

The curtain went up to reveal, centre stage, a large solid-looking chest with locks, brass corners and hinges. A man appeared from stage right, dressed casually in black evening trousers and a white, open-necked silk shirt. Gold flashed at his wrist from watch and cufflinks. At first, Herbie did not recognize him as Gus. It took him a minute to realize that it was, indeed, his old friend.

The disguise was exceptional. Not the one he used as Claudius Damautus. This was completely different: the man looked the very model of an old-time magician. A little like the great performer Dante. Herb had only seen photographs of him – white hair, beautifully groomed goatee and moustache. Straight-backed and completely in command of his own universe.

The music went on as he dragged the chest around in a circle, knocking heavily on the sides and top. Herbie recalled his first meeting with Carole after Gus's death. How she had locked herself in the main living-room of the Dower House and played the *Ritual Fire Dance* again and again.

As he thought of the moment, Carole appeared from stage left wearing a very skimpy costume which looked like leather bikini briefs and bra. Only this was not the Carole Herb knew. This girl was taller – lifts in her shoes, he thought – and had long platinum blonde hair reaching to her shoulders. For a few minutes, Herbie could even forget that it was Gus and Carole. Their appearance was wonderful to behold.

Gus flung back the lid of the chest and Carole pulled a bright blue sack from within. She held the sack inside the chest while Gus climbed in, Carole pulling together the sack's mouth, binding it closed with strong white rope, then padlocking the rope, the ends of which were fitted with metal eye sockets.

She pushed on Gus's head as he lowered himself into the trunk, then she slammed down the lid, knocked down the brass clips on the front of the trunk and slapped large padlocks through the fitments, finally sealing the lid with a long steel rod.

Carole then picked up a cloak of thin, silky black material, mounted on to the lid of the trunk, and lifted the cloak above her head. At the moment the cloak stopped rising, it was violently torn in two and there was Gus standing where everyone had seen Carole just one moment, less than a second before.

Gus yelled in triumph, 'Operation *Fortitude!*' Leaped to the stage, slid out the steel rod, undid the padlocks, threw open the lid, clicked the key into the padlock attached to the sack, unwound the rope and helped Carole out of the trunk. All the time he yelled, 'Operation *Fortitude!* . . . Operation *Fortitude!*'

The audience had audibly gasped, then, as his meaning became clear to some of them, they laughed.

(Herbie leaned towards Bex Olesker and whispered, 'Best people I ever seen do that were Pendragons. Good Illusionists. Fastest in the world.' He smiled, because Bex had obviously also been stunned.)

Gus, bowing charmingly, and pushing the applause towards Carole, came downstage and began to talk.

'Operation *Fortitude*', he began, 'was, as you know, the catch-all final name for what had originally been Operation *Bodyguard*, the deception operation for *Overlord*, the dramatic and courageous assault upon Hitler's Fortress in June 1944: *Bodyguard* having been first chosen because of Winston Churchill's remark in 1943, only months before *Overlord*, "In wartime, truth is so precious that she should always be attended by a bodyguard of lies."

'Operation *Fortitude* is, for me, one of the greatest pieces of Intelligence magic ever performed,' Gus continued. 'It worked – which is the main thing in its favour. You just saw my assistant and myself change places in a magical manner, which is an illustration of how *Fortitude* was constructed. We made the enemy believe that we had armies amassing in two different places, through the use of the Nazis' senses. Their eyes and ears. We sent out a lot of *en clair* radio chatter between army corps and battalions which did not exist. We filled fields and roads with dummy tanks, transport, aircraft. We used his own spies, turned by our notorious and exceptional Twenty Committee System – aways written with the Roman XX: the double-cross – to tell him what was not true. Just as, a moment ago, you thought I was in that trunk and my assistant was outside.'

For those who could see, Gus had carefully plucked four red billiard balls out of the air and now held them between the fingers of his left hand. 'Tonight,' he said, 'I am not giving a lecture in the usual sense of the word. Rather, this is a demonstration of the principles we use as intelligence, and counter-intelligence, officers, to glean information, or to watch and monitor things we are not supposed to see, even though they are going on right under our noses.'

By this time the billiard balls had vanished, one at a time, until he had only one left in his hand. He tossed the ball into the air, where it apparently changed colour, becoming a white ball. As he continued to speak, so the white ball was joined by a bright blue billiard ball, then a yellow, and finally a green ball, so that the four balls were between the fingers of his left hand.

'We rely on subterfuge,' Gus said. 'We rely on tricks of the light, misdirection, psychological advantages, and on electronic and optical secrets which, under the threat of great danger, puzzle the enemy and make him turn away just when we need him to be looking in another direction.' The multi-coloured balls in the left hand were now joined by the original red balls which reappeared, one at a time, between the fingers of his right hand.

'We steal, we misdirect, we draw attention away from agents or devices so that when our target looks again he sees nothing.'

He displayed the balls in both hands, brought the hands together and they were suddenly gone, a cloud of confetti appearing in the air in front of him.

As he began speaking once more, Carole brought a table and a couple of other items onto the stage behind him.

'These are the tricks of our trade,' said Gus. 'They are also the tricks of unfriendly intelligence and terrorist organizations. The secrets, the theoretical rules by which we go into the field to filch the secrets of others, all run parallel to the theories I am demonstrating to you now. For instance,' Carole walked on stage and handed him a book, 'for instance, who has read John le Carré's *The Russia House?*'

A sprinkling of hands came up. 'I want someone who has not read this book, but is interested enough to wish to read it. A show of hands would be nice . . . sometime today . . .'

Some hands came up in the front row and Gus passed the book down to a lady whom Herbie recognized as a former field agent who had once worked in the Soviet satellite countries.

'That book is yours,' Gus continued. 'Yours as a gift, and you will be able to read it from cover to cover, but not while you are here. I want you to help me; do something for me. First, how many pages are there in this book?'

The woman riffled through the pages and called out, 'Three hundred and fifty-three.'

The house lights had come up and Carole was down amongst the audience, carrying a file card, an envelope and a throwaway pen.

He addressed Carole first. 'I want you to move as far away as possible from the lady with the book.' She walked to the rear of the auditorium, and Gus picked up what looked suspiciously like a brick. 'To make absolutely certain that I am not in collusion with anyone here,' he began, then turned quickly back to the woman officer who held the book, 'Madam, we are not in collusion, are we? I want you to tell the audience truthfully that you are not working for me as a stooge.'

'Certainly not.'

'Good. I'm going to hurl this brick at one of you, and then I want that person to throw it backwards, over his head. Whoever catches it then, and remains unhurt, will be asked to do something very simple.' He paused for the mild chuckles before saying, 'It's a rubber brick. Don't worry,' as he tossed the object to the Chief of the Secret Intelligence Service sitting in the front row. 'Sir, I want you to chuck the brick without looking. Just toss it hard over your shoulder, towards the back of the audience. This will get me off the hook if anyone *does* get hurt.'

The CSIS threw the rubber brick over his shoulder and it was caught by a man whom Herbie recognized but could not put a name to.

'Sir, you have the brick. I want to ask you, are we in collusion? Are you operating under my control, to use language we all know? Tell the truth.'

The man with the brick shook his head vigorously and said that he was definitely not in collusion. Carole went to him, handed him the card, envelope and pen, retrieved the brick and disappeared through an exit at the back of the theatre. The camera showed her leaving.

Gus now told the spectator to take the card and write on it a three-digit number between 100 and 353, which he pointed out would cover all the three-digit numbers in the book. He then asked him to place the index card in the envelope, seal it and have that envelope passed forward to the lady with the book. He stressed that it would be impossible for him to know the number contained in the envelope.

When it had made its journey to the lady with the book, he explained, 'The number inside that envelope is the number of the page I would like you to use. Don't let me see it, but open the envelope, and look at the number. You can show it to those near you. If you like, you can lift it up so that the gentleman at the back can identify it, but do not let me see that number. In fact, I will turn away until you have done this and found the page.'

He turned his back to the audience, and even the camera did not pick up the number. The female with the book put the card back in the envelope and marked the page with it, then told Gus that all was done.

Gus retreated behind a rather beautiful card-table

with inlaid green baize. Herbie recognized this as the table he had seen in one of the previous videos. A pad of paper lay on the table and a group of around four pieces of laminated card, held together with a bulldog clip, rested against the right side. The cards measured around two feet by eighteen inches. Gus picked up a pen and began to speak again.

'First, Madam,' looking at the lady with the book, 'I would like you to concentrate on the number of the page which has been chosen at random by another member of the audience. Good. I need complete silence during this, because it is not the easiest thing to do. It requires great concentration. Now, Madam, would you simply think of the number. The number of the chosen page . . . Think harder . . . Try and imagine that you are thinking of the number so hard that you can see that number hanging right here, right in front of my eyes . . . Good . . . Good . . . Yes, you're very good at this.' He jotted down something on the pad, picked up the larger cards, removing one from the bulldog clip, turning it sideways on and at the same time picking up a black marking pen. He started to write something on the card in front of him, saying that he thought he had the correct number.

'Now,' he continued, 'I want you to read – to yourself – the first line of the chosen page. Tell me when you've read it and then concentrate on the first few words. That's it . . . Do it as you did before . . . Think of the words hanging just above my eyes . . . Good. Yes . . .' He wrote on the laminated board. 'Good. That's it. Now, would you tell me, was the page number three hundred and twenty-seven?'

The spectator looked surprised. 'Yes.'

'Sorry I could not get all of that first line, but it begins "trawl that was worth a damn".' He turned the board to face the audience, and there it all was, written in large black marking pen. 'Page 327. trawl that was worth a damn'.

'Yes.' She looked even more bewildered. 'Yes . . . How the . . . ?'

'Watch your language, madam.' Gus wagged his finger at her. 'We have some very reserved gentlemen here. For those who believe there is no need for an explanation,' he said with a smile. 'And for those who do not believe there is no need for an explanation.'

The applause was long and hard, so that Gus finally had to stop them. 'That is how we must be seen to collect intelligence. It is how we must be seen to have secrets passed back from field agents to case officers. We all know that the old-fashioned agent in the field is back as flavour of the month, because electronic or satellite intelligence cannot look into the minds of those who would be our potential enemies, just as the wonders of electronics cannot see things that are truly well disguised and hidden. What I am showing you are demonstrations of devious means which should activate your senses, start your brains working. Think about this . . .'

He picked up a boxed deck of cards and threw them out into the audience where they were caught by a beefy looking man three rows back. 'Okay,' Gus stared unsmiling at the man. 'Take the cards from their box. Now cut them and complete the cut. Take the top card. Do not look at it. Just put it into your pocket. Look through the cards just to be sure that is an ordinary pack. Now put the pack back into the box.'

The beefy man did as he was instructed.

'In order for me to find out what card is in your pocket, I would have to either get you to take it out, or go through the pack you are holding. Right?'

'Correct.'

'Even you do not know what the card is. Right?'

'Correct again.'

'Then how do I know it is the seven of spades? Look and see for yourself.'

The spectator, and almost the entire audience, laughed nervously and broke into more wild applause as the man held up the card in his pocket showing that it was, indeed, the seven of spades.

'Keep the cards. A gift from me – and a club I know who really owns them.'

He continued, talking about the way in which their agents should be invisible, and repeated that what he was doing was really a demonstration in the secret arts. 'You probably think I am simply doing magic tricks or conjuring, but this is important. I have no need to give away any secrets for you to realize that the theory behind what I am doing is that same theory which has been drummed into the heads of intelligence, and counter-intelligence, officers from the beginning of time. The Craft of Intelligence is also the Craft of the Magician and Illusionist. We are both the second oldest professions in the world, and we rely upon mundane things like misdirection – as we saw in the Second World War in Operation *Fortitude* and, incidentally, in the Gulf War when Saddam Hussein's officers disguised trucks as missile-launchers, and Scud missile-launchers as trucks. The Iraqi military played an exceptionally good game of deception. Almost as good a game as the British Magician, Jasper Maskelyne, played when – using tarps and lights, fires and a strobe on a pole – he made the Italian and German night bombers think that the harbour of Alexandria actually lay a mile up the coast in the bay of Maryut.'

He proceeded to perform several other baffling pieces of magic, including a silver ball that floated across the stage, around Gus's body and even right out into the audience. A beautiful illusion. (Herb looked it up in one of Gus's books later and found it was generally known as the Okito Floating Ball, supposedly invented by Theo Bamberg, the great Dutch magician who performed as an oriental, calling himself Okito – a slightly garbled anagram of Tokyo. Okito came from a long line of Dutch magicians, but in truth the beautiful illusion was created by David P. Abbott, a magician and loan shark from Nebraska. As Herbie said, 'Each day I learn more about the magical history.')

He also performed a small piece on his table, down stage so that it could be seen by everyone, introducing a small covered stand which contained a seven-inch Samurai sword, locked between a pair of wooden posts. Borrowing a ring from an American intelligence officer in the front row, Gus vanished the ring from his hands and, upon taking the golden covering off the stand, showed that the ring was now threaded onto the Samurai sword – an impossibility as the sword had to be unlocked from its stand to remove the ring.

All the time, he talked of how the performing art of magic as entertainment mirrored exactly the way in which the tradecraft of intelligence gathering had evolved over the decades. He reminded them that at least one American illusion builder had been employed by the American service to build hiding places into cars and other vehicles to smuggle documents, and even people, out of the old Soviet Union, and how this could well happen again as the world was now more dangerous than it had been during the iceberg days of the Cold War. Finally he came to the end of this extraordinary demonstration.

'Always think of the psychology of deception; the use of optical illusion, the manner in which to hide in plain sight, and move invisibly.' He lifted a hand, twisted it in a circle and threw it down, dramatically. A sudden cloud of smoke covered him, and as it cleared all that appeared to be left was a butterfly with a wingspan of approximately four feet. The butterfly seemed to hover in the centre of the stage then break up before the audience's eyes into hundreds of red and yellow butterflies, fluttering in a great cloud, then they too vanished. In their place was a dove. The dove flapped its wings and flew out over the audience, high up to perch somewhere behind the camera's eye as the tape slowly faded to the inevitable music again – the *Ritual Fire Dance*.

Big Herbie looked at Bex whose manner had changed. She saw him staring at her and snapped, 'All right, Herb. So I was impressed. It *was* wonderful, but they're still only tricks.'

'Sure,' Herb scratched his head. 'Sure, they're tricks. But these are the kind of tricks you can translate into the work we do every day of our lives. The man's a bloody genius.'

There was a long pause, then Bex spoke.

'You realize what you just said, Herb? You said the man – Gus – *is* a bloody genius.'

'Was? Is? What's the difference?'

'Life and death.'

Samira, Nabil and Ramsi settled their bill and left the Cavalieri Hilton in Rome at just after nine the next morning. This was a relatively easy job. Through contacts in Italy, the *Yussif* team had arranged for the complete bombs to be left in a camera shop within the Stazione Termini – Rome's largest railway station. The bombs were large and packed into two aluminium camera cases. One was destined for the American Embassy in the Via Vittorio Veneto, while the other was to be placed inside Bernini's Palazzo di Montecitorio – the seat of the lower house of the Italian Parliament.

A lot of plastique was crammed inside the chunky solid cases and, if set correctly, would cause a great deal of damage and probably many deaths.

They arranged for Nabil and Ramsi to go into the shop and collect the bombs while Samira watched from some distance. There was an operational rule among the *Intiqam* teams that only two members of the cell should be together at dangerous moments. They did not realize how dangerous this particular moment was really going to be.

At eight o'clock on the previous evening, a call had come in to the main police headquarters in Rome and a female voice told the operator that the people who had planted the bombs close to the Luxembourg and Bourbon Palaces in Paris were now in Rome. Two of them would be picking up bombs the next day. She gave the exact location of the camera shop, spoke flawless Italian, assured them this was no hoax, and was off the line before anyone had a chance to trace where the call came from. The caller ID showed it was not placed in Rome itself, and all indications were that the woman was telephoning from somewhere overseas.

The Italian authorities never treat any terrorist tip-off call as a possible hoax. Because of Italy's complex political history – plus terrorist attacks ranging from the first Red Brigade Units to Italian Fascist extremists – their anti-terrorist organizations have been organized and reorganized again and again. Nowadays most anti-terrorist operations are dealt with by a unit within the paramilitary Carabinieri, and it was the Duty Officer of this section of the Carabinieri who was called in to listen to the recording of the woman's telephone warning.

So it was that, on the following morning, when Nabil and Ramsi went into the camera shop they were under surveillance, not only by Samira, but also by a large force of unseen Carabinieri. Once the two members of the *Intiqam* cell were inside the shop, armed uniformed men surrounded the whole of the railway station, while another group, in civilian clothes, moved in towards the shop. The general public were ushered away by uniformed police officers concerned lest the terrorists exploded one or both bombs in a last desperate suicide act.

Samira saw what was happening and walked away, distancing herself from the two men. If the worst came to the worst, she knew it would be up to her to make a run back to London.

As Nabil and Ramsi emerged, carrying the two heavy aluminium cases, pistols and automatic weapons appeared in the hands of the plainclothes men, and one officer shouted for the two *Intiqam* men to stop, put down the cases and place their hands over their heads. Ramsi, suddenly terrified by what he saw, forgot all his long training. By trade he was a bomb-maker, happy to spend his time in some cellar or back room building devices that would cause death and horrible injury. He knew what his speciality would eventually accomplish but, like a pilot aiming his smart bombs from thousands of feet above the target, he was, by the nature of his work, detached from face-to-face combat where instant death lay in the pistol in your hand. Ramsi was also at another disadvantage. He had been angry when briefed for these missions in Paris and Rome. Hadn't he been sent with the team to build the bombs that would be used against their enemies? Hadn't he received special training to arrange explosives, fuses and timers? Hadn't he been given the most important job of teaching other members of the team to plant bombs, to set timers, to handle the explosives safely? Now he had been sent out to pick up bombs assembled by others in order to carry out the missions.

During the previous day in Paris, he had insisted on checking that the devices would do the job. He had intended to do the same thing today in Rome. So it was Ramsi who did as he was told, placed the case on the ground and slowly straightened up, placing his hands over his head.

Nabil did not hesitate. He turned and started to run, knowing that they would probably have to hunt him down to catch him, banking on the fact that they would not take the chance of firing at him while he was carrying the case. He was ten paces from Ramsi when he glanced back, saw his comrade had given in and, with a loud curse, pulled his pistol and raised it to kill the traitor, Ramsi.

He was riddled with shots from the Carabinieri. The case he was carrying crashed to the ground, and, for less than a second, everyone seemed to pause, flinching away from the huge explosion that could follow. But nothing happened; the pause went almost unnoticed as Nabil's chest was ripped away by bullets and his body seemed to spin in the air like some whirling children's top, then lifted, finally hitting the paving with a crunch.

They closed on Ramsi, frisked him – two bomb-squad men pulling the case away – and handcuffed his wrists. In a daze the bomb-maker was led away.

Samira saw all this and was filled with fear. She now knew what the word dread truly meant and she willed herself to walk slowly away. Finally she hailed a cab and asked to be taken to Rome's Leonardo da Vinci Airport.

During the flight back to Heathrow she calmed down, her mind going through the many problems that faced the *Intiqam* team in Britain. Samira was the most fanatical of the entire group and her momentary lapse into panic caused her grievous embarrassment. I have worked for the good of my country, the Leader and Allah, she thought. Now was not the time to be afraid of anything. The picture constantly replayed itself in her head – Nabil's blood filling the air around his whirling body, then Ramsi being seized, looking bewildered. Ramsi was the main concern. The man was the weakest link in their chain. Like as not he would talk to his captors. Little tubby Ramsi enjoyed making bombs, she considered, but he treated them with great respect, so it was possible that he did not care much about the end result of the weapons.

The more she pondered on this, the more Samira became anxious and angry. There was little they could do about Ramsi now that he was in the hands of the Italians, but they had to go forward and carry the work through with even greater effectiveness and stealth than before. She was certainly ready and willing to die for the cause.

In a blinding flash, which seemed to light up her brain, she knew for certain that she was going to die for the things she held dear. This fact she embraced with all her heart and mind. To believe was, for her, the only thing that counted. If she were to die now it was the will of Allah and that was why she was on this earth. Death held no real fear for her.

By mid-afternoon she was back in London and heading towards the Camberwell house. She took great care and made the journey by underground, taxi and bus; changing several times and finally walking the last four or five blocks through a light drizzle of rain. Yet, in the distance the sun was starting to break through. There was a rainbow shimmering in the air, and that seemed to reflect her own feelings of happiness. Now it was up to the four of them: herself, Hisham, Ahmad and Dinah.

It was only when she let herself into the house that she was told by Dinah – who had been left behind – that they would be moving to yet a new location and that there had also been trouble in the United States. The story had been on the television news and, while the *Intiqam* teams were not cognizant of each other's roles, the fact that only two of the original American team were still at large upset both the women.

They left the Camberwell house in the early evening and Dinah led her to their new quarters: a large service apartment just off Kensington High Street.

Far away, sitting in the garden of his villa overlooking Baghdad, the *Biwāba* – the Gatekeeper – was alone as he contemplated the situation. His team in America had been decimated. Two of the British team were out of the game – one dead, the other in custody. It was Ramsi, the man being held in Rome, who worried him most. Ramsi, he had always considered, was the one who might crack under the pressure of hostile interrogation. Hisham would certainly move the British team to another safe house so there was little information Ramsi could give on the question of location. Neither did the bomb-maker know the final moves of the plan – the moves they called *Magic Lightning* – so that was safe.

256

The fact that only two of the original team were left in New York caused him even greater concern. To succeed and carry the entire design to its natural conclusion would now be very difficult as security forces would be more alert. The original scheme had called for acts of violence to take place throughout the summer months so that the culmination would be when the various governments returned to their seats of power when the long vacation period was over – two weeks to go.

He sat and thought over the matter for almost two hours. Finally he came to a decision. They could not wait out the two weeks until the main targets would be in place. He would have to bring the targets back to their cities. To London, Washington, Paris and Rome so that the *Magic Lightning* could play on them and so destroy all effective governments.

He went into the house and put a telephone call through to a number in Switzerland.

In a room leading from an underground laboratory on the outskirts of Geneva the telephone rang. It was picked up by a young biochemist who, with two other equally brilliant young men, was being paid a fortune to develop something which, once let loose, would be more lethal than any poison or nerve gas.

'This is the Kingpin,' the *Biwāba* said, in his soft, slightly threatening voice. He spoke in English.

'Pestilence,' the young biochemist replied.

'How long will it take you to complete the packages?'

The young man laughed. 'A day. No longer. As we told you, the work is not arduous. It is a relatively simple matter.'

'Then make your final preparations. I shall have couriers with you in the next forty-eight hours.' The *Biwāba* closed the line, and then called the *Yussif* teams in both England and the United States. They talked in a code which told these men in Britain's beautiful Oxfordshire countryside and in the Hudson Valley that they were to prepare for new and very special instructions that would reach them in the usual manner.

With luck, the *Biwāba* would have things ready for the final horror in a matter of hours. If everyone concerned did exactly as they were told, a week would see it done.

18

Once more, big Herbie Kruger found it difficult to
sleep. Perhaps it was the complexity of the case, or,
possibly, the atmosphere of the Dower House, once
his own private hell during the year of interrogation.
He raided the fridge and found some tasty fish paste
which he spread on a couple of pieces of bread, taking
them through to Gus's study, together with a large mug
of coffee. Only later did he discover, from Bitsy, that the
fish paste was a well-known brand of cat food. Bitsy had
started feeding every stray cat that came her way.

Earlier he had tried to send himself to sleep by reading a book from Gus's library, *Conjurers' Psychological
Secrets* by S.H. Sharpe, but instead of lulling him, the
work wakened him up. He was amazed, for it could just
as well have been written as a manual for Intelligence
and Security Services. Gus, he considered, had been
right. The techniques and methods of the performing
magician ran parallel to the techniques of what was, in
intelligence, called tradecraft.

In the study he tried to gather his tangled thoughts.
It was exceptionally difficult to focus everything on the
how and why of Gus's death, when they now found
it appeared to be dovetailed with the recent terrorist
activity. The FFIRA and the hostile Arab cells seemed
almost to have been designed to lead them away from
the truth, pulling efforts into tributaries which beckoned
them from the main target – Gus's killer, or killers.

He was also depressed as there was something funny
about Gus having run the agent *Jasmine*. To add to this
concern, he was now 99 per cent certain that he could not
trust Carole, and that hurt him, for he had been almost

like a father to her. Slowly he came to the conclusion that he had no option but to interrogate her again, with great hostility.

So, through the night, Herb worked his way through several layers of Gus's dossier and the tangled web of notes for his memoirs. At around eight in the morning he had another shock. This time it was a private file, red flagged and marked *Mr Keene Only. No Subscribers.*

After reading only a few lines he picked up the telephone and called Worboys, who was also in the Office early.

'Tony, the asset that "Five" latched on to?'

'The one who gave us so much grief?'

'That's the fellow. One they didn't give up without a struggle. You got his name?'

'Sure. Hisham Silwani.'

'This can't be *Jasmine* by chance?'

'Definitely *not Jasmine*, Herb.'

'He got a crypto? With the Security Service I mean?'

'Yes.'

'Let me have it, Tony. Be a good old chum and share it with me.'

'Share it, Herb? Share it? For heaven's sake don't go all American on me. The damned American Service are always wanting to share things with me when, as they say, they have a visit with me. I'll do better than share it, Herb, I'll give it to you.'

'Wait.'

'Wait?'

'Sure, let me have a shot at reading your mind.' He had watched Gus doing his thing on video, so now Herb was in the psychic business. 'I sense that this man has a crypto which is Biblical. It is a Bible name beginning with an I . . .'

'Cut the crap, Herb. Yes.'

'It starts with an I and the name is Ishmael, like in *Moby Dick* also – "Don't call me Ishmael, I'll call you." '

'No, Herb. Ishmael as in son of Abraham and Hagar. Recipient of a divine blessing. Our friends in the Security Service have a sense of humour, Hisham Silwani was the recipient of their divine blessing. They turned him.'

'Wrong, Tony. I got it in front of me. *Gus* turned him.'

'What?'

'You heard me. Gus turned this guy for the Security Service. Same as Gus got hold of this asset *Jasmine*. Very close fellow our Gus.'

'You're sure? I mean 100 per cent sure?'

'250 per cent sure. Proof positive. Might even be able to get DNA.'

'Stop horsing about, Herb. You're really serious?'

'I told you, Tony. We lent Gus to "Five". Gus turned the guy and never told us. Like "Five" never told us.'

'Shit!' said Worboys with feeling.

'While we're at it, Young Worboys, what did you get from the telephone numbers in *The Times* answerback ad?'

'Damn all. Those telephone numbers make no sense at all.'

'You tried other cities as well as London?'

'They tracked the entire United Kingdom, Herb. Nothing. Zero. Zilch.'

'Okay, why not try it world-wide? You see, Tony, they have big silver birds these days. Carry people over oceans.'

'I think we have them doing that already – I mean a global search.'

'Good. So what about the telephone log in and out of here and the big house?'

'On its way to you now by courier. A couple of interesting things there. But you really have got Gus's fingerprints all over Ishmael?'

'Told you, Tony. Give you full report later in the day. Trouble is these islands are full of noises and full of silence. Now we got committees running things, left

261

hand doesn't know what right hand is doing half the time.'

'We really only want to know who blew Gus away, Herb. This is getting more complicated.'

'Sure, I'll give you full complications later. You could give me the full story, Tony. Okay?'

Herbie had it there in front of him. Chapter and verse. A long notation giving all the facts.

The Security people had come to Gus in 1983 wanting to lay their hands on yet a new Middle East asset. They had put the man, Hisham Silwani, under surveillance and considered that he was not – as they said – kosher. Gus had the notes of his first meeting with the two officers who really wanted the man. 'You're good at turning and burning, Gus,' they had said. 'Can you do this one for us? Discreet. Closed mouth. Strictly *entre nous*.'

Gus had noted in the file: 'They took me out to watch Silwani today. Playboy Arab on the surface, but he has contacts which a playboy would steer clear of. I was with them on the following night, and it was very obvious that Mr Silwani liked playing with the ladies. To be fair they liked playing with him also. I told J and B that I could set it up. I thought Mary Delacourt would suit very well. I said that if I baited the trap the actual burn would be up to them. Then I'd come in and turn him when they had softened him up. They said okay.'

The next comment was made almost a week later. 'Our brothers at "Five" have decided to give Mr Silwani a shot. They called me in for a meeting, and C has given permission for them to use me without having the details from them. I am not elated over the fact that our brothers and sisters are not going to share the product, so to speak. However, it is a go, so we go.

'Last night I had a long talk with Mary (Delacourt). She said things like, "Oh, yes!" and "Yum-Yum." So I Yum-Yummed her, just for the practice, and she is going to latch on to him sometime this week. The boys will then do their stuff and I shall be called in to spin him.

It all appears to be straightforward. Mary is a Sloane at heart, and she mentioned some club where the younger royals can be seen at least twice a week. She has an in with the management and they will send Brother Silwani an invitation – a free week of temporary membership, then he can decide if he wants to pay ten grand a year so that he can go out with aristocratic young women, and get the occasional glimpse of Di and Fergie.'

Another two weeks passed before Gus made further reference. Then:

'Well, Mary did the work and they felt Silwani's collar yesterday morning. It appears that he is fearful to the extent that he is without excrement. I am on standby and they're going to let me listen to the tapes before I go and burn him good and proper.'

Three days later Gus turned and burned Hisham Silwani in the apartment off Marylebone High Street.

When he had laid out the terms, playing a very hard man from the word go, Gus had said, 'That's it, pure and simple, Mr Silwani. You throw in your lot with us, or we explain certain things to your superiors. I realize that this puts you at a disadvantage whichever way you decide, but with us at least you get to go on living.'

It took Hisham Silwani only thirty minutes to make his decision, and it had not been all bad because the Brits had been generous with money for expenses.

Now, in Gus's room at the Dower House, Herbie listened to the sounds of the place coming alive for a new day. He locked the files away and went through for breakfast.

In the new Kensington apartment, Hisham had also suffered a night of sleeplessness. After the news that Nabil was dead and Ramsi in the hands of the Italian authorities, all Hisham wanted to do was dig a hole and hide.

During the night, he struggled with his conscience and tried to work out his options. All Ramsi could tell them was the size of the team. He could also give them descriptions and names. Names – that had always been a weak point. They should have known each other only under code-names.

From Baghdad's point of view there was no problem, but Hisham had a slightly different vantage point. The British Security Service had him by the balls. They knew his name and had told him what he should do. If he did not do as he was told, they would make things more than uncomfortable. If *Ajax* had still been alive, he would have bypassed the people who made direct contact with him and thrown himself on *Ajax*'s mercy.

Ajax, as he knew only too well, was the man Keene, who had already been blown to heaven before they began *Intiqam*. For Hisham, or *Ishmael* as the British knew him, there was no way out. He also wondered how much the man Declan, from the FFIRA, was telling his interrogators.

He wanted to run, but had nowhere to go. If he did not carry out his orders and report to the British, they would come for him by reporting him to Baghdad. If he went on and did the real jobs allotted to him, the British would still bury him. He assumed they had blown the target Kruger into little pieces, though the news segments on television had made no mention of a death when they reported on the explosion near the New Forest. Like all intelligence and security services, the Brits liked to keep quiet about things like that. It was sometimes better for them to remain silent.

There was still some time to go before the day of *Magic Lightning*, and what he required was time. Perhaps some half-hearted attempt at the other two targets – the official Worboys and the man with the strange name, Archie Blount-Wilson – might buy him a few more days.

By six in the morning, Hisham had made a kind of decision. They would go for the other two targets. No botched jobs. Straightforward assassinations, with dead bodies at the end of the day. That would at least keep him on the right side of the FFIRA, who could be mightily bad enemies.

After that? Well, maybe it would be time to run to the Security Service and beg for their mercy. Surely they would have to do something to help him. Everything else was in hand. He had sent, in code, their new hiding place to the *Biwāba*. He did not expect any instructions for major incidents, as they liked to call the placing of bombs, for some time yet. Today he would instruct his team on the assassinations of the two targets and he would leave tomorrow's problems to look after themselves.

Once again, Hisham was being pushed into that dangerous area of self-deception which made him walk, not just on two sides of a street, but three – if you counted the Irish.

It was the middle of the night in New York, but Walid and Khami were awake in their sumptuous suite at the Parker Meridien. Khami – as Walid had long suspected – really cared for him. During the previous afternoon, *Yussif* had telephoned them – right there in the suite. It had worried him because the call came in through the switchboard, but *Yussif* had been careful; asked for Mr Jaffid, and went into a long and very punctilious monologue which, in the end, had told him that they should stay and wait for instructions. It was possible that *Yussif* himself – by which the voice meant one of the team – would visit them and give new instructions. In the meantime they should act as normally as possible. 'Enjoy your stay,' the voice had said.

Walid took that literally. He knew, from past times, that Iraqi women who became Westernized liked nothing better than to go shopping. He had noted on earlier visits that Westernized Iraqis could easily squander thousands of dollars, and they were always very happy to do this. So, he told Khami to go out and buy herself a lot of frivolous things, giving her a credit card in the name of Fatima Jaffid. 'Be bold,' he said. 'Buy things that will please you, and me also.'

On Khami's return they had called down to room service and had a huge meal sent up to the suite. 'We are living like kings and queens,' he told her. 'Enjoy this while you can, Khami. They will certainly give us more work to do soon.'

After they had eaten, they bathed together in the Jacuzzi, then Khami told Walid to go and rest as she had many beautiful things in store for him. He put on a towelling robe and stretched himself out on the bed.

Presently, Khami, also dressed in a robe, came into the bedroom. She appeared to be shy and modest as she approached the bed. 'Walid,' her voice was soft and throaty. 'Walid, I would like to come to you as a bride on her wedding night . . .'

Walid tried to reply, but she shushed him. 'Listen to me, my prince. I would like you to forget all the indignities of the past weeks – when I have been with Samih in the same room as yourself. You can never know how base, coarse and inferior that made me feel. On that last night I longed to be with you, and knew that you rejected me because of Samih. Now, I ask your forgiveness.'

'There is nothing to forgive, Khami. Not a thing. Like me, you were under discipline. We are still under discipline . . .'

'Yes, but tonight should have nothing to do with the discipline of *Intiqam*. I want this to be for us, for both of us.' The robe slipped from her shoulders and Walid saw that she was dressed in the most sexy underclothing of pure silk, trimmed with a fine and delicate lace. 'Fit for a bride?' she asked.

'Indeed, fit for a bride on her bridal night. Come.'

'No,' she shook her head. 'I shall make love to you, Walid. Tell me if you like what I do.'

She then stretched her body over his, the tips of their tongues met between their conjoined lips and she

266

teemed kisses all over his body as a prelude to what was to be the greatest night of love-making Walid had ever experienced.

Now, in the small hours of the morning, she lay in his arms and they spoke of the love they bore one for the other.

Presently she asked him about the killing of the other members of the *Intiqam* team. 'Did you intend to do that, to end all this, from the beginning?'

He lay silent for long seconds. 'I always knew I was capable of doing it, and I suppose I knew that, if there were no other way, I would not shrink from it.'

'Then you think the *Intiqam* is wrong? That revenge is not the way?'

'I did not say that, Khami. But I am not happy about what I have done. Nor am I happy about the things we may be called to do.'

'But you will still do them?'

'We have pledged. What we are ordered to do must be done.'

'Of course. I would expect no more and no less.'

They made love again and she felt as though her heart would burst as Walid entered her. She cried out both when he came inside her and when she reached the peak of her satisfaction.

They lay in the dark, very close, feeling content as the sweat from their bodies mingled. After a while she asked if she could go shopping again. 'In the morning?' she asked.

'Of course, my Khami. If you return as ready for love as you did last time.'

'I shall be better than ever.' Her hand strayed to him and he began to become aroused for the fourth time in that one night.

The courier arrived with the telephone logs just as they were finishing breakfast. Bitsy Williams had been even more difficult than usual this morning. She had cooked an elaborate meal, placing various things in silver dishes on warming plates set on the sideboard: bacon, kedgeree, eggs, both fried and poached, sausages, and toast in little silver racks. Obviously she had been digging around in Carole's and Gus's cupboards.

'Bit too uppity for me, Bits,' Herbie had said.

'It's how we used to be served breakfast when I was a girl,' she volleyed back.

'Looks like something out of that movie, *Remains of the Day*.' Herbie gave her an innocent smile. 'You see that movie, Bex?'

'Wonderful,' said DCI Olesker. 'But everything Anthony Hopkins does is wonderful.'

'I specially liked the scene where he had the words with Emma Thompson about not calling his father by his first name.'

'You're right, Herb. This is like dining in a grand house in the twenties or thirties.'

'As Bits says, like when she was a girl.'

Bitsy Williams stamped out of the room with a stifled little mewing sound.

'Bit cruel, Herb.'

'Needs to be moved down a peg or two.' He paused. 'You really gay, Bex?'

She gave him an odd little look. 'Me? Gay? What gave you that idea?'

'You. You had to go call your girl-friend first night you were here.'

She gave a tinkling little laugh and pushed the hair off her forehead. 'Mmmm. Yes, I did, didn't I?'

'You soitenly did, Rebecca, you soitenly did.' Herbie's imitation of Laurel and Hardy was reasonably good considering his German background.

'I always do that when I think a man's going to become . . . well . . . dangerous.'

'I am an old man, Bex. An old man in a dry month. A hollow man. A stuffed man. Never could I be dangerous. I have forsworn wenches.'

'Have you now?'

At that moment the doorbell rang. The courier arrived and Herbie tore open the envelope and began to go through the lists of calls covering the period just before and after Gus's death.

'Is interesting here,' he pointed. 'And here also.'

Bex Olesker, leaning on his shoulder so that her cheek was dangerously close to his, pointed with a long finger, 'Not to mention here.' She stabbed at the print-out.

'Let's go and get her. No good and bad cops, okay? Just both bad cops.'

'Very bad cops.' Rebecca Olesker touched his cheek with hers as she straightened up.

As they were opening the front door, the telephone purred in Gus's study and Herb hurried to answer it.

'Got some news,' Tony Worboys said.

'Good, bad or indifferent?'

'Don't know really. The terrorist they caught in Rome. Guy by the name of Ramsi al-Disi.'

'What's in a name?'

'The Italians are turning him over to us.'

'You mean *us* as in SIS, or *us* as in Brits in general?'

'Both. They're flying him back today. Private jet. All hush-hush. We've agreed that you and DCI Olesker, plus Martin Brook, can clean him out.'

'Very nice of you, I'm sure. Talk later then, Young Worboys. We're off to clean Carole out.'

'Just thought you should know. It's all under wraps. No press release. Nothing.'

'Until my baby comes home,' Herb crooned.

'What the hell . . . ?'

'Old nice song. Vintage, Tony. Before your time. No love, no nothing, until my baby comes home.'

'Ah.' You could almost hear him shaking his head.

19

Carole was waiting for them, in the guest quarters.
She looked rested, wore a crisp blue dress, the colour
of the Mediterranean on a good day, and her hair was
pulled back, almost flat, tied into a severe bun at the
nape of her neck. For a second, Herbie was reminded
of a woman in prison garb: the plain dress and the hair
short as prisoners are made to wear it.

'Any news, Herb?' Though she asked a question
she did not look at him, as if she already knew the
answer.

'No news is good news, right?' Herb pitched his voice
flat and tranquil. Carole looked up sharply. She knew the
tone, had used it herself before this, and had learned it
from her loving husband. 'Let them know if it's going
to be tough,' Gus used to say. 'Let them know about it
straight off. Keep the voice level; never sound pleased
to see them; never give ground. Remain neutral all the
time.' She looked at Bex and said, 'Good morning.' A
shade stiffly.

'And to you, Mrs Keene.'

'Oh, Christ,' Carole thought. 'No good cops here
today.' She wondered what it meant.

'We have to ask you some hard questions, Carole,'
Herb began.

'Very difficult,' Bex added.

'Has something happened? Something new?'

'Nothing really new, Mrs Keene.' Bex sat in a chair
at right angles to Carole, while Herb took a seat directly
opposite her, so that he could see her eyes and hands.
Always watch the hands and eyes, they taught interrogators. Carole already knew all there was to know about

inquisitions so it would not be easy for Herb and Bex if she had something to hide.

'Is like this, Carole,' Herbie began. 'Got to ask you about certain telephone calls.'

He thought he caught a very slight movement in her eyes, so tiny that it was difficult to tell. 'First, on the night Gus was killed, you took a call from a public phone box at just before two-thirty in the morning.' He looked down quickly at the telephone log attached to a clipboard, his pen poised, like a schoolmaster ready to tick things from a list.

'Two-thirty in the morning? Yes. Gus called me to say he was on his way back. He was later than he had expected to be.'

'Two-thirty in the morning?' Bex queried.

'Yes, it was around half-past two. I had been slightly worried.'

'Did he say where he'd been?' Herbie again.

'You know where he had been. At a meeting of the Old Sarum Sorcerers. I told you . . .'

'He left the meeting at one in the morning, Carole. Did he say where he had been *after* he left?'

'Not that I can recall. He could quite easily have gone for a drink with one of the bloody Sorcerers.' She was cool, but the use of the word bloody signified a disquiet in the back of her mind, even though her voice did not rise or take a different tone.

'The Sorcerer you put us on to said he left alone. They had a good evening, he said. Even apologized to Gus for keeping him so late.' This from Bex. 'I spoke to him. Gus said he was going straight home.'

'You see, Carole, we have a little time problem. Gus left at one in the morning. Then he calls you at two-thirty. Hour and a half not accounted for.'

'Perhaps he had some bird stashed away in Salisbury.' She smiled, signifying this was a joke.

Herb made it clear it was no joke to him. 'He have birds stashed away, Carole? Gus, was he a ladies' man outside your happy marriage?'

'Don't be bloody silly, Herb. Gus was honest as the day is long.'

'Days can sometimes be short.'

'The answer is no. No, I am pretty sure there were no extra-curricular activities.'

'Then how you account for missing hour and a half?'

'Simple. I can't.' She took a breath, as though about to say more, then changed her mind. Took another breath, and said, 'I can't, Herbie, but you knew Gus. He always had little things going on the side – I don't mean women.'

'When he was Service. Before he went private, yes. Yes, he always had little deep side. Secretive. Things he did on his own until it was time to talk about it with the Section it concerned. But he was gone private, Carole . . .'

'He was working on his book, Herb. He *did* see people. I knew that. He saw people in London, so it's quite possible that he saw someone in Salisbury. It's not unknown.'

'Still, we've got to account for that missing ninety minutes, Carole. You can't help us there, no?'

'No. No, I can't. Sorry.'

'Okay.' Herb referred back to the telephone log. 'There was an incoming call at five-thirty in the morning.'

Carole sighed, touched her face and bit her lip. 'The law,' she said. 'The place was swarming with cops by then. They arrived around four. Woke me up . . .'

'Swarming?' Bex asked.

'Well, a pair of plainclothes guys arrived to break the news to me. A couple of uniforms turned up soon afterwards. They had use of the telephone. There were a number of calls out. Three, four maybe. If they got a call back, it didn't register with me. I wasn't exactly in the mood for taking calls.'

Herbie nodded, 'You took one at five fifty-seven.'

'The Chief called just before six, yes. I took that one.'

'But you didn't take the five-thirty call?'

'I have no memory of a call then. Why?'

'Because, as you well know, Carole, the monitors are very good. Both here and in the house. The five-thirty call came from a rest stop on the M4 Motorway. About four miles from Heathrow. You know the one? Video games, shop and a couple of restaurants? Greasy spoon type food.'

'Yes, I think I know it. We'd stop there for a pee if we were driving to London.'

'So, who could have stopped there for a pee at half-past five in the morning on that day? It *was* answered at this end. The cops call from public phone boxes, do they?'

'In this case they must have done.'

'Then the Chief called?'

'Yes, just before six. Said he was on his way up. Nice. Very good of him.'

'He get here before seven?'

She gave a deep sigh. 'I really didn't take note of the time, Herb. When you've just been told that your husband's been killed by a car bomb, you don't exactly sit around looking at your watch.'

'You took a call around seven-seventeen. It's logged here, and shows as answered manually. Not the answerphone. Seven-seventeen on the dot.'

'I have no memory of that. The Chief was here by then – I think. I think he was here.'

'This call – seven-seventeen – came from a public telephone at Heathrow Airport.'

'Don't remember it.'

'Who'd call you from Heathrow at seven-seventeen, Carole?'

'For heaven's sake, Herb, I don't know. There were a number of calls in and out. I know the Chief made several calls and took one – from Tony Worboys . . .'

'That's right. Tony called him at eight-twelve. He

called from my cottage, which isn't a cottage anymore.'

'Lots of people called. Even that bitch Angela called . . .'

'Not until after she heard it on the news. Angela, the former Mrs Keene, called from her home at nine-twenty. Who else called?'

'Herb, I didn't take count. There were various calls. I didn't log them in and out.'

'No, but the machinery did.'

'Then ask the damned machinery.'

'That what we're doing.'

'I didn't even know the Dower House was linked to the telephone computer in the main house.' She all but shouted in anger.

Herbie made a hurrumping noise. 'They probably forgot to unhook the Dower House phones. Accident, but we got a complete log.'

'So you don't remember the seven-seventeen call?' Bex pressed.

'No. Bitsy was here by then. Ask her. She could've taken it.'

'We're going to ask her. Thought we'd do you a favour and talk to you first.'

'Well, I can't remember every call that came in on that day. It was like a mad house, and I was in no condition . . . Oh, Herb, I'd help you if I could.' She caught his eyes with her own spaniel eyes. Pleading, don't be too hard on old Carole, Herb.

'Two-thirty the next morning. Middle of the night.'

'What about it?'

'Two-thirty – Chinese dentist time . . .'

'What?'

'Tooth hurtie.' Herb grinned the Hallowe'en grin, did not even get a flicker of a smile from the bad joke. 'Go better second house.' He switched off the grin. 'Call at two-thirty in the morning. That was answered. You answer that one, Carole?'

'I don't recall one at two-thirty.'

'Funny. It was picked up at this end. They show it as picked up quickly, within a couple of seconds. The machines are all-knowing, omnipotent, but you know that.'

'Of course I know it.'

'Two-thirty was picked up very quick.'

'Very quickly, Herb,' Bex corrected him.

'Sure,' he nodded to himself. 'You pick up the one at two-thirty, Carole?'

'I don't remember. Perhaps the log's wrong. Could be a call going into the main house.'

'Definitely not,' he shook his big shaggy head. 'Two-thirty, Carole? This one's important.'

'Why so?'

'Came in from overseas. Abroad. Out of the country. America, we think. Maybe New York.'

'Who the hell would call me from New York at that time of night?'

'That's what we need to know.'

'No memory of it.'

'Then get your memory into gear, Carole. We're doing all this work to find out who blasted old Gus from face of the earth. Need your co-operation.'

'You've got my co-operation, Herb. I want to know as much as you.'

'Two-thirty from New York?' Bex prodded.

'Don't recall it.'

Herb, watching her hands, saw the involuntary twitch. The fingers of the right hand giving a little jump as they lay over her left hand. Bull's-eye, Herb thought. A hit, a palpable hit.

'A call from overseas in the early hours of the morning and you don't remember?'

'The doc gave me a sedative. Said I needed some sleep.'

'You took this sedative?'

'Of course I took it, Herb. What's this all about anyway? You think I offed poor old Gus?'

'We got everyone as a suspect.'

'Oh, grief. *Me?* You'd suspect *me?*'

'Everyone, Carole. You know the form.' A tiny conciliatory tone from Bex.

'You also made a call from the main house the other morning.' Herbie looked at her as though she had committed a truly cardinal sin.

'I did?'

'You know you did, Carole.' Bex again. 'You were seen making it and it was logged.'

'Okay, so I made a call. In fact, I went over to the main house to get that video of Gus's lecture and demonstration. Nobody seemed to mind.'

'Good video. Very puzzling and really good theory.' Herb paused. 'You made a call to Martin Brook at the Office.'

'What if I did?'

'Why, Carole?'

'Because Martin's a good lad. Gus brought him up in the ways of the world – the old world.'

'So you called him on a whim?' Bex asked.

'Not really. Bitsy told me he had called the Dower House. Bitsy's been very good. She's been over to see me almost every day, which is more than can be said of you, Herb.'

'So what you talk about? Old times? The changing seasons of the world of secrets?'

'No. If you want to know, I asked him if I could give the tape to you.'

'Why would you do that?'

'Martin, if you hadn't heard, is the Lord High Inquisitor designate. Which also means he'll be in charge of everything down here.'

'Didn't know that, Carole. You get it straight from the Chief or what?'

'Tony Worboys.'

'When?'

'Last time he was down here.'

'Came to see you?'

'Came in for what he called an informal chat. Told me that Martin's appointment would be approved before the week was out.'

'So you called him to say, well done, Martin?'

'More or less. I knew he wanted the job. Nobody's really been in charge since Gus retired. Temporary people all the time. Temporary and unpaid from what we heard.'

'So you said, well done, Martin? That all?'

'I tried to be honest with him. Said I was handing over one of the tapes and asked if that was okay.'

'And what did he say?'

'Follow your own judgement. He said do anything if it would help get the people who murdered Gus.'

'He know what the tape was?'

'No. The Fat Boy – that's what we used to call him – did not know about Gus's talents.'

There was a pause of around a count of twenty. Then Herb said they would put aside the telephone log for a while. 'Want to ask you other things, Carole. Unpleasant things. Your little dalliance with *Jasmine*.'

'Your affair with *Jasmine*,' Bex added.

'It wasn't an affair. It was a one-night stand. Not even that. A one-afternoon stand, and I felt so bloody guilty that I just kept away from him after that.'

'What actually happened? We know Gus was away, but how did it really happen?'

She shook her head, eyes brimming and the corners of her mouth quivering. 'I don't want to talk about it.'

'I'm afraid you're going to have to talk about it.' Bex being very firm.

'I told you. When Gus brought him here he asked me to make him comfortable. Keep him happy. You know Gus. When he was working on someone he liked to get the atmosphere right. Make the target feel at ease. That was partly my job.'

'And you fancied him straightaway?' Bex again.

Carole shook her head, not a negative shake, but a

277

movement that looked as though she was trying physically to get rid of cobwebs in her brain. 'In a distant kind of way. You never felt that, Bex? When you're promised, or tied, to another you see a guy and something inside your head asks you what it would be like with him?' As she asked, she automatically glanced at Bex's left hand to note if there was a wedding or engagement ring.

'I know what you mean. What'd he look like?'

'He didn't look like an Arab. That was the first thing. Yet he was a fine-looking man. A hunk as they say. Very tall. Six two. Six three. Somewhere around that. Muscular. You felt that he could break someone with his fingers. Enormously charming. Oozed charm. Of course we were all younger then.'

'So you thought, what would it be like with this rather striking man?'

'Yes, but it was innocent. You never made a list, Bex? A list of guys you know and would like to do it with?'

'No, but I know what you mean. A list of blokes that you would like to try out and then rate on a scale of one to ten?'

'That's it . . .'

'Like the band of the Royal Marines,' Herb said to nobody in particular.

'It's odd, thinking back. I loved Gus. I loved him like never before. We used to say that nobody had ever loved each other more than we did . . .'

Herbie turned away. *That's* what had happened to him. Twice. The feeling that the beloved and the loved were somehow mystically joined in a way that no other two people had ever been, or ever would.

'But?' Bex probed.

'Difficult to explain.' They had Carole now. They had really got her attention. 'Very difficult. It was summertime . . .'

'And the living was easy,' thought Herbie.

'Summertime. Early summer. For some odd reason,

I remember that I was terribly randy. Couldn't get my mind off sex. It was as though everything that happened had some underlying sexual content. Even what I ate and drank. I remember that it was like a subtext to my life. Sex reared its lovely head in every action, in things I read, trees I touched, flowers I gathered for the house.'

'And?'

'And . . . Well . . . Well, Gus was very busy. Tied up with a lot of things, and . . . Well . . .'

'You weren't getting any.' Bex sounded crude, and Herb knew what she was doing. This woman is good at playing with people's heads, he thought.

'If you want to put it like that,' Carole bridled.

'Gus wasn't paying you much attention, is what Bex means.' Herb stepped in.

'That's about right. Poor lamb, he was so busy. Dashing around like a scalded cat. Didn't have time for anything outside work.'

'He was a lot older than you, Carole. Never forget that.' Herbie again.

'I never forgot that!' Again she bridled. 'Don't you ever remind me of that again, Herbie Kruger. I had been with Gus a long time before we married.'

'He was your morning and evening star, I know this, Carole. But at that particular time there weren't enough hours in the day?'

'You have a row with him?' Bex remained almost callous.

'No. No . . . Well, not exactly. Just a bit of a tiff. Something and nothing.'

'And he left town, so to speak?'

'He was away for two days, yes.'

'So, when did it happen?'

'The first day. I spent the whole day with *Jasmine*. He was charming, luxuriously charming. Told me tales, flattered me. He was very subtle in making his move. Had me like a cobra has a mongoose. His sexuality hypnotized me.'

279

'Where'd it happen?' Herbie again.

She bit her lip, then looked away. 'Don't want to talk about it.'

Bex dug deeper, 'But it's getting you sexually worked up even thinking about it now.'

'Shut up, Detective Chief Inspector. Shut the hell up!' She was near screaming. Bex had pressed the right button.

'Go on, Carole. Tell us. We're not peeping Tims.'

'Toms, Kruger. Don't play those tricks on me. I know you and your damned ways.'

'Okay, but just go over it once.'

'Do I have to do this?'

'Afraid so, Carole.'

'And if I refuse?'

'Then, dear Carole, we get the cops in and tell them you been lying to us. Tell them you're withholding information. They probably take a dim view and take you down the nick, questions, questions, questions. With us, you only have to go over the thing once. Then we finish.'

'Promise?'

'When I ever let you down, Carole? We been good friends. Now, you going to talk to us?'

'Okay.' A very small voice. 'All right, Herb. You'll think me terrible.'

'I been pretty terrible in my time.'

'I gave him lunch. I even remember what we ate. Lamb chops, new potatoes, beans, a salad. Then chocolate mousse. I was having a chocolate fad at the time. Couldn't live without a chocolate fix.'

'Know what you mean. The sweet tooth can be a real problem.'

'There was nobody about. The guest rooms were empty. The security staff were around, but that was it. I want to get this over, Herb.'

'Go on. Fast as you like.'

'I think, maybe I had drunk a bit too much at lunch. We got to the door and he . . . Well, he kind of trapped

280

me in his arms. Kissed the hell out of me. I said, no, and all those things a girl does, but the kisses got stronger and I began to respond. We walked over to the room he had – down here. Kissed again inside his room, then bingo. I was telling him to do it in sixty-five different positions. I'm trying to be honest. I just couldn't stop it and it was like losing my virginity all over again. It was like having a man for the first time.'

'And you've never really got it out of your system, have you?' Bex's voice incredibly comforting. Soft. Nearly the cooing of a mother to her baby.

'I've never forgiven myself. Didn't see him again. Sent a message to him the next day. Told him I had no time, that something had come up. Gus came back and I even avoided him. Couldn't tell him. You know what was funny?'

'Tell us.'

'For the first time in weeks, Gus made love to me again that night. He came back around three. Had been to London and came back all excited. Went to see *Jasmine*, then said things were moving fast. Elated, that's the word. Gus was elated, and that night – I was going to confess, but he made such glorious love to me. Gus was always so inventive. I read a book once – espionage fiction. There was a guy in this book. Creative. A very creative lover. The author had him and his lady dressing up to make love, or reciting *The Owl and the Pussycat* while they were at it. Great book, because Gus was just like that.'

'He dressed up?'

'I dressed up. Sometimes. Turned him on. No, he set up situations. He was my white knight and I was the lady in distress; he was . . . Oh, lots of things. Mostly it was poetry. We'd recite things line for line as we were . . . you know. We did it in . . . No, you don't need to know. That was the only time I was ever unfaithful. Ever. Couldn't forget about it. You know, when they came and told me, after I had taken it in – to begin

281

with I said there had to be a mistake. Anyway, when it sank in, when I really knew, that was the first thing I thought of. Christ, I thought, I never told him.'

'Two-thirty,' Herbie began. 'Two-thirty in the morning. Morning after Gus was killed. You took a call, Carole. It was from New York. Who'd be calling you at two-thirty in the morning from New York?'

'For God's sake, Herb. I told you. I have no memory of a call from New York.'

'Okay,' Bex leaned back. 'We have all the time in the world, Carole. Let's start from the top again. Two-thirty in the morning – the morning Gus was killed. You had a call then. You say that it was Gus, and if it was we've got one and a half hours unaccounted for.'

Carole gave a long sigh and nodded.

They had not been able to hold Declan. The police were in constant touch with the Security Service people, but Declan's brief turned up. A lawyer they knew of old. Good solid Sinn Féin lawyer. 'Charge him within the statutory time, or I want him out.' The lawyer knew how to play them.

They got a search warrant for the room he had been staying in. Nothing there, and nothing on him. At the magistrate's hearing they showed the photographs to the magistrate only. Nobody wanted Hisham's picture on public display. They got reasonable cause to hold him for a week without bail. Struggled for a week and got a bit more time, but, eventually, he was out. Released. No charges.

The security boys had a team on him very fast and the lawyer banged in an injunction citing police harassment.

They pulled off, but put in six of their best people. People Declan would not have a hope of seeing or taking action against.

Declan was what they referred to as a live one. He knew every dodge in the book. Within twenty-four hours the ace team lost him. They alerted airports and seaports. Tight as a drum. He still slipped them, happy in the knowledge that they had no clues as to where he was.

While Big Herbie Kruger and Detective Chief Inspector Rebecca Olesker interrogated Carole Keene, Declan sat in a safe house in Paris. He also sat on several hundreds of pounds of Semtex, and had set up its transfer to the Iraqis in London. He had called off the Active Service Unit in London. They were taking a well-earned rest in Scotland. Money was no object, for the FFIRA – and Declan as its Quartermaster – provided weapons and explosives for the *Intiqam* teams on both sides of the ocean. Some, such as the Semtex, would be for services rendered. Four assassinations, well, three because someone had already snuffed that bastard Keene, and he presumed they had got Kruger in his cottage though the press had not announced the actual death. Never mind, they would do it and it would be carried out properly.

Declan smiled to himself and thought it was about time he had a jar. He would go down to the café on the corner. There was no risk.

'She's stonewalling, I know it.' Bex dropped into a chair in Gus's study. 'I don't know what it is, Herb, but the barriers are up and she isn't talking.'

They had spent six hours with Carole, going over the same ground again and again; pressing and pushing, following the usual route of hostile interrogations. Herb nodded his big head. 'There are a couple of nuggets – and you're right, Carole holds some key.'

'What nuggets?'

'She's inconsistent. First time she told the story – the other day – she told us the hanky panky took place on the second day she was alone with *Jasmine*. Now she says it was the first day. Also she's not talking *Jasmine*. I've no doubt she had the little fling with the guy, but I think she's talking about *Ishmael*. For some reason she's switched the two. It's *Ishmael* she's talking about. I got to call Worboys. See if they have any results in about *Ishmael*. Security Service tags him with Gus, and what's he done for them? Like to know that.'

'And I guess a lot of people'd like to know it as well. What's the use of an asset if he isn't working for you?'

Herb was about to pick up the telephone when Bitsy tapped at the door and came straight in.

'Ach,' Herbie gave her the big smile. 'Just the person we wanted to talk with.'

'Well, that makes a change.' Bitsy smiled at Herb and gave Bex a freezing shoulder, not even acknowledging she was there. 'I wanted to make certain you'd be in tonight. I thought of doing a curry. You liked it so much that night we all went out . . .'

'Sure, Bits. Curry okay for you, Bex?'

'Brought up on it. Mother's milk to me.'

'Okay, so it's curry and chips, Bits.'

'Don't be so damned stupid, Herb. What did you want to see me for?'

'Talk about telephone calls. You were here that first night, yes?'

'The night after Gus was killed? Yes.'

'The calls in and out of here are logged. They kept the telephones wired to the main house's system. You recall the telephone ringing around two-thirty in the morning? Almost twenty-four hours after Gus died?'

'I remember. It would be about half-past two, yes.'

'Who picked up?'

'It woke me. I was just dropping off to sleep and the damned phone woke me. Rang twice, then Carole must've picked up. I was just reaching for it when it stopped. Didn't intrude.'

'You'd swear that under oath?' Bex, all police and hard as nails.

'Of course. I was here, and it happened.' Her face changed, a touch of panic mingled with shock. 'Carole's not . . . ?'

284

'Not what, Bitsy?'

'Not, well, not in any trouble?'

'We don't think so, Bitsy.' Calm Bex again. 'But we need to check something out regarding that call. Don't tell anyone we even asked.'

Bitsy went off, shaking her head, the concern showing.

For the second time, Herbie reached out for the phone. His fingers were an inch from the instrument when it began to ring. Somehow he knew it was bad news before he even picked it up.

'Herb,' said Worboys from Head Office. 'They've got The Whizzer. Got him ten minutes ago. Shot down on the street. Dead before he hit the ground. The bastards'll answer to me. The Whizzer, Herb. Gone.'

20

The Whizzer, Archie Blount-Wilson, had fallen into
bad ways and was constantly committing the cardinal
sin of all old field agents. He had become a man of
habit, something he would never have been before the
alarms came off when the USSR closed up shop.

Nowadays Archie was still on call; still attended briefings; even went into the Office a couple of times a week.
Apart from that he had become a creature of custom:
one who moved mainly to a set routine. In the old days
they were reminded constantly of Moscow Rules, which
meant always behave as you would in the field; always
act as though they had you under twenty-four-hour surveillance. Always, particularly in the bright little, tight
little island nation of Great Britain.

Yet The Whizzer, great fixer that he was, usually
left his bachelor apartment in Bury Street at around
six in the evening. He would turn right and walk down
to King Street where he would take a left, then a left
again into Pall Mall. He would wait to cross the road,
and so walk up to The Travellers' Club where he would
normally find other friends of a similar persuasion.

Friends was the operative word. For decades, members of the Diplomatic Service always referred to members of the SIS as 'The Friends'. One of their favourite
watering holes was The Travellers' Club.

On this particular evening, he did as he was wont to
do. He got as far as crossing to the correct side of Pall
Mall. There was a steady flow of traffic coming towards
him, as there always was at this time in the evening.
The one-way system filtered into St James's carrying
passengers up into the fleshpots of the West End.

He took no notice of the taxi-cab which slowed down almost at the door of The Travellers' Club. He did have time to notice a young woman fumbling in her handbag for the right change to pay off the cabbie. It was the last thing he saw. A violent pain seared deep into his chest, the last remnants of his dying brain signalled heart attack. The rest was silence and dark oblivion.

The porter at The Travellers' came running down the steps, followed by one of the younger servants. One pedestrian walking a few yards behind The Whizzer gave a detailed account to the police. The cab had pulled up, and just as Mr Blount-Wilson came abreast of it, the young blonde woman passenger wearing sun-glasses had leaned towards the lowered window and shot him twice with a pistol to which a silencer was attached.

The cab's number-plate was obscured. Some said by mud and dirt; two other witnesses claimed it had a rag half covering it, but it did not matter to Archie Blount-Wilson who was dead and gushing blood onto the pavement.

In the cab, Dinah bent low to remove the blonde wig and shades, while Ahmad pushed up the speed, slalomed through the other traffic and took to the side streets. They abandoned the taxi ten minutes later in a narrow street temporarily empty of traffic and pedestrians. Then they parted company, separately making their own ways back to the Kensington safe house.

It seemed that Tony Worboys had been distanced from the hierarchy at the Office and was now running the events in the aftermath of Gus's death. Ginger was left at Warminster, and two cars were sent down to pick up Herbie and Olesker. They were crammed with minders, most of whom, Herb thought, were now working for the Office on a temporary basis. Herb and Bex travelled in the second car; the first contained the traditional three-man team, two up front and an observer in the back, all armed to the teeth.

The first thing Kruger noticed in their car was a short Heckler & Koch MP5K in a clip between the driver and shotgun passenger up front. It was an indication of how seriously they were taking the situation.

'Our lives in their hands,' he muttered to Bex, nodding towards the weapons.

'I loathe guns,' Bex wrinkled her nose. Then, 'This man who's just been killed? He a big noise? Is it very serious, his death?'

'The Whizz was The Whizz,' Herbie was being almost coyly uncommunicative about Archie.

'What's that supposed to mean?'

'Long Service career. Knew his stuff, but must have dropped his guard for a moment. Archie was a great fixer. In essence – that's good, eh? In essence? Good English? – he was a very private person which is excellent in this business, as you must know, Bex. In police you have the informers, yes?'

'Grasses,' Bex grinned, again wrinkling her nose.

'Like people smoke? The grass?'

'No, a grass is a police informer. You're saying that Blount-Wilson ran a lot of grasses?'

'He had contacts in all kinds of places. Called him The Whizz because he was a wizard at seeking out experts, briefing them and coming back with the eventual take.'

'Such as?'

'Such as once, I remember, in Switchbackland . . .'

'Where?'

'Switzerland. My mangled English calls it Switch-backland when I decide to use it.'

'You turn your fractured English on and off like a bloody light switch, Herb, right?'

'Only when I can't make it.'

'So what does *that* mean?'

'Means I turn it on and off like a neon sign. Getting old hat nowadays. The old hands know what I'm on about. The younger, and less subtle people, pretend they don't understand. They're like critics, these new guys. Always

288

pretending they don't know when you're being subtle. Everyone's a critic nowadays.'

'You were in Switzerland.'

'Sure. I needed to get a very delicate job done. Time was short. I needed two new Swiss passports and some other papers. The local resident didn't want to know, and the guy we usually used had gone on holiday. South of France. Bloody technicians. They're like policemen, Bex, never there when you need them.'

'I'm here.'

'Sure, but do I need you, Bex?'

'I hope so.'

He wasn't certain, but he could have sworn that her shoulder moved into his shoulder and stayed there.

'Yeah, well. There I was, DCI Olesker, out of time, in a country that gives new meaning to the word brusque, and with a great need for papers. What do I do?'

'You get on to The Whizz, or I suspect that's where you're leading me.'

'Gold star and green rabbit for you, Bex. I call The Whizz from a public telephone. Tell him what I need. In twelve hours I have a courier at the hotel and they're "Paging Mr Kruger". Or at that time it was "Paging Mr Klause". I was using work name, Klause.' He gave a little puerile chuckle. 'As in Santa Klause.'

'What other wonders could The Whizzer do?'

'Anything. You wanted it, The Whizzer provided. They used to say he could get a Witch Doctor to change the weather if you needed it. Great saying about The Whizz. He could get a Witch Doctor . . .'

'And change the weather. Yes, I *did* understand.'

At Head Office the minders crowded them, as though they were Heads of State. Kruger recalled the time he had been sitting at a sidewalk café in the Place de L'Opéra in Paris, when the legendary, very tall, President Charles de Gaulle turned up. Cars offloaded around twenty tall men who bunched together and headed up the steps. At each step he had seen the

French President's head bobbing up from the middle of the knot.

'We can't go around like this, Tony!' Kruger almost shouted as they got inside his room. It was high in the building, and they had passed down corridors where young men and women hurried about with set faces, on secret business.

Worboys' room was decorated in salmon pink with paintings on the walls that made Paul Klee look like a designer for romantic novel book jackets.

'They gunned Archie down in broad bloody daylight.'

'So? We have to go out only at night? Turn us into vampires, Young Worboys.'

'I wasn't going to take any chances, and I didn't want to set up a meeting in some safe house. One thing's for sure, Herb, we're next on the list. They must've figured out by now that they didn't get you at the cottage. Gus down, Archie down. Now it's us.'

'Watch your back then, Tony, and I'll watch mine.'

'Just sit down, Herb, and let's get on.'

'With what?'

'They found the cab.'

'Good. We all go home now and I get on with trying to solve poor Gus's murder.'

'I think that's what we're doing, Herb. Just listen. No, I'll give you some good news first. I've a cheque here for three-quarters of a million. I threatened all kinds of mayhem if the insurance people didn't pay up promptly. Buggers tried to say it was an act of war, your cottage going up. This is an adjusted sum. You do a list of contents and value and they'll up the ante.' He passed the envelope across the desk.

'So I'm rich. Anyone for champagne?'

'Just listen.' Worboys' temper was wearing thin.

Kruger took the hint and sat down, looking like an obedient schoolboy, his big hands folded around the envelope containing the cheque.

Worboys went through the obvious information first,

talking about the two terrorist teams; their links with the FFIRA as far as the UK team were concerned; the probability that, going by the American evidence, there were now only four of the team left in the UK. In the United States, they reckoned on only two being still at large. 'The analysts're convinced that there's some kind of end game both here and in the States.' Worboys sat behind his desk, fingers laced to stop him fiddling around with his hands – a habit to which he was prone when either frightened or angry.

'We have no idea what this end game could possibly be, but in Europe they could be badly stretched because they seem to have been operating both here and in France and Italy. We're taking it as read that these people did for Gus . . .'

'Why?'

'Because of the style. Their bombs have been mainly old-fashioned dynamite, except for the occasional Semtex used on the continent, which indicates that they have access to plastique in small quantities. The explosive used on Gus was dynamite. We know these people are Iraqis . . .'

'Sure.'

'We're getting more information about Hisham Silwani.'

'Want to ask you about him, Tony.'

'What in particular?'

'"Five" had him on a rope since when? Nineteen eighty-three?'

'Eighty-three, yes.'

'Buggers didn't share him with us—'

'They got severely rapped over the knuckles for that—'

'I'm sure. Go away, don't be bad boys again. Now, Young Worboys, they recruited him in '83. In all those years what was he doing for them?'

'Most of the time *Ishmael*, as we're now supposed to call him, was providing priceless information regarding the Irish problem. That's why they baited a trap for him, and that was their main objective. *Ishmael* has links inside the Irish terrorist factions that we couldn't get near in a hundred years. Apart from the time of *Desert Shield* and *Desert Storm*, he was passing high-level intelligence to "Five" that really paid off. He *was* very important to them and, having seen some of the product, I can understand their reticence about sharing him. For instance, we are aware of two murders in the North of Ireland which were carried out in error. Because they thought they'd fingered informers inside the organizations concerned. They hadn't. The informer was *Ishmael*. Simple as that. In the Baghdad pecking order, friend *Ishmael* handled liaison between their Leader and a number of what we call terrorist groups – Abu Nidal, PLO, and certainly IRA. You've no idea how much these people talk to one another. *Ishmael* held a lot of secrets which were passed on to us. For that alone, *Ishmael*'s a hero.

'Our main and biggest quibble with "Five" is that they ran him through a senior officer from our shop – Gus. If this had come out while Gus was still alive, there'd have been hell to pay. We'd have probably docked the man's pension.'

'And *Jasmine*?' Herbie asked.

'That's what I'm coming to, Herb. We know that *Jasmine*'s not here in the UK. So we had another go with those phoney telephone numbers. They computed. The meeting place was being set up in New York.'

'Ah.' Kruger's big hand went up to his chin. For a second or so he looked like a caricature of Rodin's *The Thinker*. Then:

'So you really think *Jasmine*'s in New York – or the States somewhere?'

'What I think is that she was one of the team working out of New York. Which also means she's either dead or she's one of the two who escaped and are holed up somewhere.'

'He or she,' Bex said softly.

'What d'you mean, Chief Inspector?' Worboys' forehead creased and he looked ten years older.

'Was going to tell you about that, Tony.' Herb did his Hallowe'en grin, reserved only for special occasions. 'If you read Gus's reports, *Jasmine*'s a she. If you listen to Carole, it's a he that she had a little fling with and never forgave herself for.'

'You're joking.'

'Wouldn't joke about something like that to you.'

'You mean there's a genuine doubt about the sex.'

'Oh, there's no doubt there was sex.'

'I mean the gender.'

'There is doubt, yes.' Kruger was getting into his stride. 'Doubt, but what we think – what Bex and I think – is they both had a little hokey-pokey.'

'Both?'

'Sure, and you know that's wrong, hokey-pokey?'

'What're you talking about?'

'The song and dance. The hokey-pokey. The real name is Hokey-Cokey. Second World War song. Americans learned it over in the UK from us Brits. Took it back home and got the wrong words. Now they all sing hokey-pokey and it's really Hokey-Cokey.'

'Herb,' Worboys tried to sound patient. 'Will you get on with the sex business. You say they both – Gus and Carole – had sex with *Jasmine*?'

'No. No, we think Carole strayed from paths of righteousness with *Ishmael* and Gus made the beast with two backs with *Jasmine*.'

'Beast with . . . ?'

'Shakespeare,' Herbie sounded pleased and lofty. 'Othello. Bard of Avon calling.'

'Then who was playing silly fools? Gus or Carole?'

'We think possibly Gus. We think Gus trained *Jasmine* somewhere else, without telling you. Typical Gus. Had a devious mind. I think he took *Ishmael* to Warminster and did stuff with him, then went away for a couple of days and *Ishmael* got his leg over Carole. That's what we think.'

'We do?' Bex queried.

'I do, and I think you'd go along with it eventually.'

'Eventually's right.'

Worboys cut across all the conversation. 'Please, the two of you. Just work it out between you, and know that here the money's on *Jasmine* being either dead or alive in the USA – we think alive, naturally. Also, there's no problem about finding out what sex *Jasmine* is, or was. Gus, as I recall, recruited *Jasmine* from the Technical Department. We had changed over to computerized records by then. All I have to do is look it up. I'll have to use one of the sensitive machines, but it shouldn't take long. Back in a couple of minutes.'

Worboys left the room. Herbie twiddled his thumbs and sang, 'Oh-Oh the Hokey-Cokey, Oh-Oh the Hokey-Cokey, Oh-Oh the Hokey-Cokey, that's what it's all about.' Then he turned to Bex and said, 'Young Worboys thinks *Jasmine*'s alive, naturally.'

'Naturally,' Bex repeated and they both retreated into silence.

Worboys was out of the office for much longer than five minutes. Herbie, who was counting, by constant glances at his watch, made it thirty-seven minutes before he came back, looking irritated and slightly red in the face.

'Impossible,' was his first comment. He sat down behind his desk. 'Jesus, Herb, old Gus really had things tied up as tight as a—'

'Careful, Tony, you got ladies here. What's the score?'

'The score, as you call it, is that everyone's been cut out of the loop. *Jasmine* shows in the active database cross-referenced with CSIS *No Subscription* files, and that's exactly what we have. No bloody subscription. There're half a dozen files under the old Chief's work name, and they're empty. Transferred to the present Chief. Took me ten minutes to work out *Jasmine* and that's disappeared. There is a cross-ref to *Ajax*, and *Ajax* is Gus. The file's empty. So, I went through the normal personnel files. Checked on people working and active in the Technical Department. *That* database was set up in early 1984 with a nice little tag which said "No previous lists available", which means, Herb, that the old Chief and Gus had a pact with the Devil. The Old Man saw to it that all references to *Jasmine* were filleted from the database. The only records of people working in that department go back to '84. Nothing before then. Together they wiped out the lot. There's no way we can get at who *Jasmine* really is, or was. All we know is that he, she or it was handled solely by Gus, and he's not around to tell us any more.'

'Neither is the old Chief, Tony. Gus wore rubber pockets so he could steal soup. Lovely man. Great professional, but dead cagey. Silent as the grave.'

'Well, that's that. I think we should talk about our friend Ramsi al-Disi whom you'll have to put through the wringer.'

'When's he coming to us?' from Bex.

Worboys looked at his watch. 'With luck he'll be there by now. The idea was to get him quietly into the guest suites – well separated from Carole – while you were up here.'

'What did the Italians get?'

'Sweet damn all. But we've seen the transcripts, and we think that Mr al-Disi knows more than is good for him. The problem is that we also think the man isn't aware of all the information he has piled up in his head. He has to be coaxed, and you have to do the coaxing.'

'He knows but he doesn't know?'

'Herb, *you* know what I'm talking about. He *has* said that both teams were together in Iraq for a year or so before they left for London and New York. The very fact that they were together means he has a mountain of information. The Italians, I fear, did not persist but, give them their due, they felt we could do better. Get more out of him. So, it's up to you to do the real probing.'

'Play magicians' psychological tricks,' Herbie Kruger said, low and to nobody in particular. Then: 'He speak any English?'

'Quite good English actually. Very correct.'

'Good.' Herbie gave a massive shrug. 'Wish I spoke good English. Make life easier.'

In New York, Khami had taken Walid up on his offer and gone shopping again. She was out until mid-afternoon and brought back a mixture of garments frivolous and sexy, together with a small pile of gifts for Walid which included two sets of handcuffs, a beautiful grooming set and a large box of male colognes, aftershave and similar items. Her best gift for him was a dark blue silk robe.

'I liked the colour,' she smiled. 'This blue will suit you, Walid. I also buy you a pair of very fine driving gloves. Feel the soft leather.'

'Where am I going to drive, my peach?'

'Probably nowhere, but the sensation of soft leather against my skin is very appealing.'

He wanted what he called an undress parade straight-away, and they were just getting started when the telephone rang.

Walid made a dive for the phone and answered with a curt, 'Yes.'

'This is Yussif. I'm downstairs. I wonder if I can come up to see you. It's most important.'

Walid made shooing motions to Khami, signalling that she should get into the bedroom and put more clothes on. 'Please, yes. Come straight up. We were hoping you would visit us today. In fact we've been lost without you.'

The man who called himself Yussif was tall and distinguished-looking, with a striking hawk-like nose and brilliant pale blue eyes. This member of the *Yussif* team was, in fact, the leader: one of the men who had lived for at least a decade in the West, working for his country's intelligence service. He was very formal to both of them and they called room service for coffee and some cakes.

It was not until the food had been delivered that Yussif began to talk in earnest.

'It is a miracle that you have been spared,' he began. 'The police still stick to their story that your comrades were dead when they arrived, when the police arrived.'

'That cannot be true.' Khami now wore a modest dress which covered her shoulders and reached almost to her ankles. 'They were all alive when we left. On our return, the police were swarming all over the place.'

'We know they tried to fight back. In their press statements the NYPD say that some had weapons in their hands.'

'It is a catastrophe.' Walid made a motion meant to convey horror and grief.

'No. We have the pair of you, and I think you will be able to do all that is necessary. Two people can, at a stretch, carry out *Magic Lightning*, but we have to plan now. See, I have brought the necessary information. The tools you will need for the work will be made available when you get to Washington.'

'*Magic Lightning* is to take place in Washington?'

The man from *Yussif* smiled, nodded, and then did something incredibly stupid. As he spoke, he realized that he was giving away information not meant for their ears. 'Washington,' he said, 'Washington, London, Paris and Rome. It is all being co-ordinated. This must all happen within the next four days. See.' He brought out a map of the centre of Washington DC, and the plan of a building.

There were to be two major bombs, he told them. Two in very high-profile places. Many would die as a result. He showed them on the map that one bomb would have to explode at the Lincoln Memorial and the other at the recently refurbished Union Station.

'It is possible,' he said, 'that we may require another pair of smaller devices. If so, they will be timed to go off within minutes of the two major explosions.' His finger traced the map. 'One here and one here.' He pointed to the Executive Office Building, close to the White House, and the National Museum of American History on Constitution Avenue. Then he turned to the chart. It was a plan of the United States Capitol, the building with the large dome which dominated the city.

The plan was simple, though traced around with red lines. 'These', he said, pointing to the red lines, 'are the ducts for both heating and the air-conditioning. You will see that they have small access doors which for some odd reason are not locked. Any person finding himself alone in any of these ten areas,' again his finger stabbed at ten different points on the plan, 'could easily slip something within the ducts, and you see where they lead. All of these small roads lead into the House and Senate Chambers. Think in terms of tear gas – and you will have something far more lethal – and consider what even tear gas would do. It would seep along the ducts and finally spill out into the two seats of government. They are far apart, at opposite ends of the building, but if these ducts are used,' he pointed again to the ten specific access points, 'if a gas, or some other such, is placed into any of these areas, it will fill the two chambers very quickly. In a matter of minutes.'

'So, what will we be putting into the A/C units?' Walid's eyes had a fearful look deep in their irises.

'When the time comes, you will know, and the timing is of great importance.'

He looked from Walid to Khami and back again. 'After you have set *Magic Lightning* in place, and after it begins to take effect, there will be other matters for you to attend to.' He smiled affably, as a devoted father might smile at his children.

Earlier on that day, in the Kensington house, a man from the British end of *Yussif* was explaining similar things to Hisham, complete with similar plans. The plans in this case were of the London Houses of Parliament, plus the seats of Government in Paris and Rome. Hisham had already been told where their bombs had to be placed. One close to the Foreign Office in London's Whitehall, another directly opposite Buckingham Palace. This latter would rip apart the great fussy and ornate Queen Victoria Memorial which stood in the centre of the circle joined by The Mall, Constitution Hill and the short twin roads leading from Birdcage Walk and Buckingham Gate.

The sites of the explosions in Paris and Rome were also chosen with daring, and meant to give the people of France and Italy cause for deep anxiety.

Hisham was also extremely worried. With his team depleted, he had no idea how he would be able to carry out the attacks as planned. Apart from himself, there were only Ahmad, Dinah and Samira to call upon, and even at this moment Samira was out of London.

After Ahmad and Dinah had so brilliantly assassinated the man called Blount-Wilson, Samira had volunteered – even demanded – to carry òut the killing which Hisham and Dinah had botched a couple of days ago. Not that it was their fault, but Hisham felt ashamed that it had not been done properly. He prayed that Samira would deal with the matter.

Later that same evening, Big Herbie Kruger would feel the brush of the Angel of Death's wings.

While all these things had been happening, Declan Norton, the virtual leader of the FFIRA, had gone a'roving, spending time in some of his old haunts. In Belfast he took one risk, going into a bar near the Falls Road. The bar was a regular meeting place for members of the Provisional IRA, and some of the iron men of the old Army Council were often to be seen there. Norton had no desire to run into anyone highly placed within the Provos, for the leaders of the PIRA were more than serious this time. Like the British, they wanted the ceasefire to hold and lead everyone into a righteous solution of the age-old Irish Problem.

Yet Norton took the risk, for he knew an old friend of his was a regular in the bar. The man, Shamus Doherty by name, was there and greeted his friend with warmth and the offer of as much booze as he could drink. Declan declined the drink, for even friends could not be trusted in these difficult times. He simply asked Shamus the whereabouts of Margaret Mary Walsh, whom he described as an old girlfriend. He knew the Doherty family and the Walshes were close, and his friendship with Margaret Mary had fizzled out years ago. Shamus knew exactly where the Walsh girl was living and passed over the information without hesitation.

As soon as Declan left the bar, Shamus was on the telephone to the Intelligence Officer of the Army Council, warning him that, as he put it, 'The renegade Declan Norton is after visiting with Margaret Mary Walsh. If you want to close him down you'd best send a couple of hard men over there. He may even be on his way now.'

This was exactly what Declan wanted. He knew the Provos would like nothing better than to close down the FFIRA, and he was never truly safe in Belfast. If they could be made to look in one direction, then he could proceed – with some caution – in another.

In fact Declan Norton had a nice little business running on the side. Unknown to his former brothers-in-arms with the Provos, Declan ran a strong-arm extortion racket against a number of car dealerships in and around Belfast. The car dealers and garage owners thought they were helping the Cause by shelling out money to Declan's boys. In fact the bulk of the cash – around £2,000 a week – was going into Norton's own pocket. The remainder paid the salaries of his two lads, the Dolan brothers: twins, apolitical, and known as Prancer and Dancer.

They were big lads and were known in the criminal underworld on both sides of the border. Both were exceptionally good at prancing and dancing on human bodies, leaving many a good man with broken ribs, legs, arms, heads, and, in some cases, worse than that.

The very fact that Norton had been running this non-political sideshow for several years meant that he was forced to make frequent visits to the North in general and Belfast in particular in order to collect the money earned by his little team. On this occasion, he met with Prancer and Dancer many miles away from the fiercely Provo area where Margaret Mary Walsh lived. He took his money and arranged that future payments should be deposited in an account set up at the Ulster Bank in Dublin. He was wanted on both sides of the border and on the mainland, but it was the North he feared most, for his old comrades there would not simply get him arrested and put in jail: they would kill him for disobeying Army Council orders, so he was safer in the Republic and even in England. A strange situation for him, but one which had to be faced.

He was not spotted in Belfast, and on the next evening he crossed the border into the South without any trouble, heading for the fleshpots of Dublin, for, as he often remarked, 'A fella can have a grand time in Dublin, what with the strong drink and the eager women.'

So, he indulged himself for a time, knowing that soon he would be returning to London. He and his lads had plenty of work to do, with both the Brits and the Iraqis who were holed up in the British capital city. As yet he had to learn about the rout of the London-based *Intiqam* cell.

21

Samira wore a wig similar to the one Dinah had used for the assassination of Archie Blount-Wilson, though Samira's wig transformed her into a brownish redhead. She also put on granny glasses and a long summer dress of flimsy material. The American passport she showed at the car rental agency gave her name as Cronin. Delphina S. Cronin, the same name she had on the international driving licence and the American Express credit card which she used to pay for the rental.

She filled in the papers in a neat round hand which bore no relation to her own writing. It was one of the skills they had all learned from the *Biwāba* during the long training period.

Hisham had given her an accurate map, so she set out from London heading for Salisbury, pulling in at the first service area to get a sandwich and change into jeans, a black T-Shirt and a dark denim jacket. It would be ironic, she felt, to hit the target Kruger near where the man Keene had died. She knew there was plenty of time, because their contact at the place they called Warminster had said Kruger would not be back until early evening. At the service area she had called the Kensington safe house and Hisham had given her the code which meant Kruger had yet to leave London. She called again, from a public booth in Salisbury, and the word was that he had just left with some firepower in a chase car. Hisham said that Kruger would be in the second car.

She did not even bother to think about how Hisham got the information, all she knew was that he had someone on the inside who passed him stuff – inconsequential information, as far as his contact was concerned, but life or death matters to a leader like Hisham. He had once told her that his person within the British Intelligence was an unwitting agent, and there had been plenty of those around during what the West called the Cold War.

Throughout her journey, Samira kept repeating to herself, 'I am the Angel of Death. I am the Angel of Death.' Hisham had reminded her that chanting something which described your operation was a way of fixing the mind, keeping focus. It was almost hypnotic.

It was dusk when she reached a stretch of open road with no houses in sight, and flat country on either side. Flat unless you looked hard and had a soldier's knowledge of cover. There were two little rock-strewn hillocks, bumps really, about a foot high. They were close to the road around fifty yards from where she had pulled off onto rather soggy ground.

Samira worked quickly, changing the car's number plates, putting her duffel bag into the boot and opening the zip to uncover the grenades and the Polish-made PM-63, not the ideal weapon for the job as it was known to have an erratic muzzle movement and required a shooter to hold it in a tight two-handed grip to fire a complete magazine of eighteen 9mm rounds in one burst. Samira was really relying on the grenades. If she timed things correctly, she could get both cars. She had personally set the grenade fuses to five seconds. It all depended on her judgement. Samira was good with weapons and was confident that she could handle the timing. From where she now lay it would be possible, even in near darkness, to roll two grenades, one after the other, so that both cars would get the full impact. 'I am the Angel of Death,' she thought again, knowing that as soon as the grenades had left her hands she would have to flatten out, as though digging herself into the earth, for she would be lying in the lethal zone when the grenades exploded. When that was over she could finish the job by moving up and using the PM-63.

Now, she only had to wait and hope that no passing

303

motorist, or thief, took it into their heads to give her car the once-over.

'I am the Angel of Death . . . I am the Angel of Death . . . I am the Angel of Death . . .'

Big Herbie Kruger stayed behind for a few minutes, talking alone with Worboys in his office. They had been joined by Martin Brook who waited with Bex and the muscle outside in an ante-room. God in heaven, Herbie thought, Young Worboys even rated an ante-room these days. Only a handful of years ago he was Herbie's gofer, running errands and playing around with the female staff. How times had changed. Nowadays if you complimented one of the female staff on her appearance, like as not she would scream sexual harassment. Maybe he could have Bitsy Williams on sexual harassment charges. Should work both ways, but this politically correct business had taken so much harmless fun out of life. What everyone needed was a good dose of male liberation, Herb reckoned.

He talked with Tony Worboys about Ramsi. 'He being co-operative?'

'Ramsi? Yes. Yes, very co-operative. You'll have to go in at the back door, search his subconscious a bit, meddle with his mind. He's in a kind of denial over the whos, whys and whats, but it shouldn't be difficult.'

Herbie switched subjects. 'You pinpoint the locations in New York? The map references given in the phone numbers to *Jasmine*?'

'Yes, as a matter of fact we did.'

'And?'

'Passed them on to the anti-terrorist boys. Too late if they were for real.'

'Where were they?'

'The locations? One was a bookshop – Barnes and Noble – on Fifth Avenue. The other was outside St Pat's Cathedral. They put watchers on, but came up with zero. As I said, too late.'

'Or maybe the watchers got spotted and they called off the meet.'

'Whoever they were, yes, could be.'

'Also the meets could have had double meanings. Like we used to do with times on open telephone lines. Subtract four hours, or add six. Stuff like that.'

'Yes, but who was playing *Claudius* to *Jasmine*? Maybe we'll never know. Your job is Ramsi now . . .'

'And Carole. We haven't cleaned out Carole yet. Not completely.'

'You'll have Martin Brook giving you a hand.'

'Sure, how do I stand with *him*?'

'You mean can he outrank you?'

'Outrank, yes.'

'No way. He knows the score. He's taking over Gus's old job on a permanent basis, but he knows you're running this op.'

'Good. He gets out of line, I call you.' Herb grinned, raised a hand and headed towards the door. 'Watch your back, Tony. We're both targets now, so watch your back.'

'Don't worry. I'm going to earth. Wife and kids're already in this building. We're using the Infirmary. The kids think it's a great lark; always asking to see the minders' guns. Wrap these buggers up tight, Herb. Get Gus's killer and close the thing down as quickly as you can.'

The journey back was noisy and a shade cramped. The Fat Boy, as they used to call Martin Brook, had slimmed down greatly. Bex sat between him and Herbie in the back of the Rover, while the chase car constantly switched positions. Sometimes it would be behind them; at other moments – if its crew didn't like the look of a car overtaking – it would pick up speed and get behind the vehicle, riding in front of Herbie's car while the observer in the back of the chase would punch registration numbers into a laptop secured to the back of the shot-gun's seat. The laptop's modem ran through the car's radio telephone and details of the owner of any queried car would ribbon out on its screen within seconds.

The two-way radios between the cars were on constant chatter.

'Hardy One. There's an old Jag coming up fast and overtaking. We will follow.'

'Roger, Hardy.'

'Hardy One, we're coming up in front of you now. Ease back.'

'Wilco, Hardy.'

'Think they're bloody fighter aces,' Herbie muttered. He did not like it, because it made them more visible. The technical advances had brought drawbacks with them. Kruger was not always happy with advances in technology.

They skirted Salisbury and prepared for the final leg, down the Wylye Valley. Inevitably, Herbie thought of Gus's last journey to Warminster. He wondered again what had really happened? Thought of the man seen talking with Gus beside the car. Or was it Gus? he asked himself. Was Gus already out of it, unconscious in the driver's seat? Had there been other people, unseen by the witness, crouched beside the car, waiting out the headlights raking them? Men who joined Gus and read him the death sentence before they fixed things up, ran the car off the road and blew it, melting into the night once it was done.

Big Herbie also thought of the various other permutations. The old Chief and Gus had covered all the tracks to *Jasmine*. Had another person been in the loop? BMW for instance? Had Willis Maitland-Wood really retired fully, or was he the new *Claudius*? He thought he should give Willis a call. See if he was still gardening away with his Memsahib in darkest Eastbourne. Or was he heading down a wrong tributary? Was there a serving officer who had been culled by Gus to take over the running should he shuffle off the mortal coil?

Who? He wondered. Who would Gus choose to walk steadily in his footsteps?

He glanced up and saw they were nearing the bend through the village of Wylye, and the headlights behind them were suddenly very bright.

The radio crackled. 'Hardy One, there's another Rover coming up like the clappers. The guy's either drunk or wants to kill himself. On our outside now. Overtaking. Watch him, we're going to pass you. Get in between.'

'Roger, Hardy. Got him.' The shotgun in front moved slightly, grabbing at the H&K Herb and Bex had noted that afternoon. He turned. 'Get down,' he said firmly but calmly. 'Right down in the back.'

In the darkness, Herb caught a long slice of thigh as Bex groped down between him and Brook.

In the chase car, the observer had noted the registration and typed it in as they were passing the car they were minding.

'It's okay. Belongs to a doctor in Warminster.' He read the details from the screen as they slid between the cars. Then the hell broke loose.

Samira heard them, was aware of the lights before she looked up and was dazzled by the headlights. Shit, she thought, they've put an extra car in. Her brain computed the situation. The really heavy muscle would be in the first car, while Kruger would be sitting quietly in the middle car. The third car might be a problem.

She automatically took in the speed of the approaching convoy, pulled the pin on the first grenade and rolled it into the road. Then the second grenade. There was an instant, the fraction of a fraction of a second, when she realized that her timing was way out. Then the first car came abreast of her and the two grenades exploded. One directly under the first car's engine and the second – the throw badly timed – blew out the back of the same car. The middle and last two cars both did expert handbrake skid turns, ending up side by side across the road.

Samira stood up, yelled at the top of her lungs, 'I am

the Angel of Death,' and began to pull the trigger. As she rose from the ground she felt the spasm of pain in her lower legs where the pieces of grenade cut a swathe through her shins, just below her knees. Then the stat-stat-stat came from the rear car. As she was raised up by the impact of the 9mm bullets from the Heckler & Koch, she yelled again – 'I *AM* the Angel of Death!' She felt the ground as her back thudded onto the grass, then she seemed to drift away. From above she saw men running, forming a tight, protective circle around the last car. In the white light she also saw herself, lying on the ground. Then she was lifted higher and higher into an unbearable brightness.

The chase car stayed for the police and ambulance, though there was little left of the doctor who had been rushing back from a Salisbury hospital where he had been seeing a patient moved from Warminster hospital that evening. He had a dinner appointment and was late.

The woman lay cut to pieces by the grenades she had thrown and by the bullets fired by the shotgun in the front of the car under protection. She looked young, and had once been pretty, before the grimace of death had taken her. There was a wig lying near her head. Most of her chest was gone, and the legs had almost literally been sliced from under her.

There was a lot of chatter on the radios, and the car carrying Bex, Martin Brook and Herbie only stayed for less than five minutes. The chase-car minders moved around, automatics and sub-machine-guns ready and swinging from side to side.

Later, Bex said that she only became frightened when she saw the minders, for they had pulled ski masks over their heads and looked like a terrorist team.

They dropped Martin Brook off at the main house, while Bex and Herbie were driven straight to the Dower House. Even there, both the driver and shotgun climbed quickly from the car, weapons in hand and ski masks still in place as they shepherded their charges to the door.

When she saw the party, Bitsy started a little weeping and wailing act, but Ginger appeared behind her and roughly pulled her back into the house.

'You okay, chief? And you, guv'nor?' Ginger fussed around them as they went straight towards the dining-room.

'Bits,' Herb shouted. 'Bitsy Williams, we need booze and food.'

'Shit,' Bex slumped into a chair. 'I think I'm beyond food.'

'Try the booze then, Bexo.' Herbie was getting back into his stride.

'What the hell happened? I knew I should have been with you.' Ginger sounded genuinely concerned.

'Some babe tried to take us out.'

Bitsy came into the room looking grey around the gills and acting like a Victorian girl about to have an attack of the vapours. 'You called, Herbie?'

'Booze, Bits. A vodka-tonic for me, and . . .'

'The same,' Bex nodded.

'You *will* eat, won't you?' Bitsy seemed to have slipped into her mother hen mode again.

'Sure we'll eat, Bits. What you got for us tonight, chopped liver?'

'Christ, Herb!' shakily from Rebecca Olesker.

'I've got some nice steaks and new potatoes, followed by a Charlotte Russe. How about that?'

'Nice girl, young Russian Charlotte.' Herb had taken the vodka and put it away in one. 'Feels better.'

'What exactly happened?' Ginger asked.

'Will you eat now?' Bitsy's query overlapped Ginger's.

'Yes, we'll eat now, eh Bex?'

Bex nodded and took another sip of her vodka.

'Before you serve up, freshen this, would you, Bits?' Herbie handed over his empty glass, then launched into a graphic description of the attempt on their lives. He was just reaching his climax when the telephone rang and Tony Worboys, sounding shaken, asked the same questions.

They sat down to eat about thirty minutes later. Bex mainly pushed her food around, but Herb tucked in, making short work of the tender steak. 'Come on, Bex. We got more work to do tonight. You're going to need sustenance. That right, sustenance?'

'Absolutely, Herb.'

After they had eaten and Herb had complimented Bitsy on her cooking – 'You'd make someone a good wife, Bits, if that's not politically incorrect to say' – he called Martin Brook at the main house to tell him they would be over shortly.

'This guy, Ramsi? He settled in okay? Plenty of space between him and Carole?'

'Carole doesn't even know he's here.' At one time, Martin Brook had been very smitten with Carole. Since then he had always treated her with care and respect. 'Our visitor seems very pleased with his quarters. You need me tonight?'

'Would like to have the tapes running so you can listen before you join any interrogation.'

'It'll be done.'

At around ten-thirty, Herbie and Bex entered the area of the Guest Quarters allocated to Ramsi al-Disi, who appeared to be very relaxed. Herbie introduced himself and DCI Olesker, asked him if he was comfortable and being treated properly. He was ecstatic, and told them he had not lived in such luxury since the days when he was with his father and mother, long ago now.

'And you seem to speak English very well?' Bex's remark was half query and half statement.

'Yes, I speak English very good indeed.'

'Lucky for us,' Herbie smiled. Ramsi was a short, somewhat tubby little man, who had a strangely pink, European complexion. He also spoke a lot with his hands.

'Sit, Ramsi.' Herbie realized, as he said it, that it was like giving an order to a dog, but he let it ride. 'We're going to ask you a lot of questions in the next few days, but I can promise you that, if you co-operate with us, we can almost certainly grant you complete immunity from prosecution.'

'But I am bomb-maker.' The little man pushed out his chest proudly. 'It is because of me that many have died. I was a major force in the *Intiqam*.'

'And what exactly is *Intiqam*?' Bex asked, as though she had never heard the expression before.

'I will co-operate,' Ramsi cocked his head on one side. 'I will co-operate and put myself in the hands of Allah. You must deal with me as you see fit.'

'If you give us what we want, we'll give you immunity, Ramsi. I've already told you.'

'What exactly is *Intiqam*?' Bex repeated, seeing the drift in conversation as Ramsi's first attempt to tread water.

He turned towards Bex, and looked her straight in the eyes. '*Intiqam* is Vengeance of the highest order. Members of the Teams of Vengeance were especially chosen from among many. We were sent here to bring terror and revenge on behalf of the Leader.'

'Revenge for what?'

'Naturally, revenge of the highest order for the humiliation you heaped upon our Leader and our people in the war. Our soldiers, sailors and airmen fought bravely. You know as well as I that they held out until the last man in some cases. They flew great sorties against you. But you – by which I mean all the countries who ranged themselves against us for no good reason – you had superior forces and more men to call upon. We killed you by the thousand and you kept on coming. You British, the Americans and the other countries, were not concerned with loss of life. You just sent more men and machines, so you eventually overcame us. The Leader called for revenge and I was lucky to be chosen. Happy to take part in the Vengeance, which our Leader says will bring about a complete subjugation.'

'You believe all this bullshit?' Herbie asked with a laugh.

'No, of course I don't believe it. But I am sworn to the Leader. I kept from trouble and was chosen to do the work. A man has to do some work. I am good bomb-maker. Besides our rewards are to be great.'

'How great, and what rewards?' Herbie sighed and leaned back in the armchair upon which he had perched until now.

'When the governments of Britain, America, Italy, France and the other powers who stood against us, are overcome, then we will be rich men and women.'

'Rich as in money?'

'Of course. The Leader and our country is very rich in money.'

'Would you be surprised if I told you that your country is almost bare-arsed poor? Excuse me, Bex.'

Ramsi smiled broadly. 'I think this is first real question you are putting to me. We have billions, trillions of dollars. This is true. The leaders of the Vengeance teams brought great wealth with them. I have seen it in London, and I know there is more.'

'Secret bank accounts in Switzerland and that kind of thing?' Bex was making notes.

Ramsi laughed as if he were really enjoying himself. 'Oh, Ma'am, no. The money is made in our country and then exchanged by the banks all over Europe and America.'

'Made in Iraq?'

'Of course. I know that the authorities are aware of this money, but it is indistinguishable from the real thing. I am telling you this so that you will know I am sincere.'

'Okay, Ramsi. As I said, we have a lot to ask you, but let me take you one small step along the road. What is the name of your leader here in Britain?'

Ramsi nodded, quite happy with the question. 'Our leader here is a man called Hisham Silwani. A good fighter and with many weapons.'

'Sure,' Herbie thought, '*Ishmael*. Great. Very strong on weapons.' Aloud he asked, 'Name some of his weapons.'

'You expect me to say the bomb, the gun, the knife, the strangling cord, but I won't say those things. They are obvious. To prove beyond doubt that I am willing to tell you all I know, I will give you his greatest weapon. This place you have brought me to. It is called Warminster by you, yes?'

'Yes.' No harm, if he already knew, Herb considered.

'Well, know this, sir. Hisham has control of someone right here at this place. This person is providing him with information, though the person does not realize our cause is being assisted by what is told to Hisham.'

Both Herb and Bex told each other later that they both only just restrained themselves from blaspheming aloud.

'You know a great deal, Ramsi. You know my name?'

'Would you be the Mr Kruger who is on our death list?'

'That's me, large as life, Ramsi. One of your people tried to do for me tonight.'

'Ah, but you escaped?'

'I wouldn't be sitting here now if I hadn't escaped. Ms Olesker here, she wouldn't be sitting here on her pretty little . . . Ah, no . . . Sorry Bex.'

'I'm flattered.' She gave him a friendly, knowing look, then turned to Ramsi again. 'You know all the names on this death list?'

He nodded. 'Yes, but you are our targets so that we can receive a favour from FFIRA – you're conversant with FFIRA?'

'We've heard of them.' Herb looked a shade blank. What he called his dumb ox look. 'So, tell us the names on the death list, Ramsi. Just to humour me.'

'Certainly, sir. The list was four names. Yourself, Mr Kruger; a man called Blount-Wilson; another – an officer of some kind – by name Anthony Worboys; and a fourth, Mr Augustus Keene.'

'And you're the bomb-maker?'

'That was my role.'

'So you're the bastard who made the bomb that exploded in Mr Keene's car.'

Ramsi looked bemused for a second, then his face cleared. 'Oh, no, Mr Kruger. You see, when we were given the list we knew that Mr Keene had already been killed. I did not know it was a bomb. But we didn't have to bother ourselves with him because he was already dead.'

22

They had concluded the first session with Ramsi almost directly after hearing that Hisham had some kind of penetration into Warminster, the indication that the Iraqis had vast sums of almost undetectable forged hundred-dollar bills, and the fact that, according to the little bomb-maker, the British *Intiqam* team had nothing to do with Gus's death.

They eased out of it gently, of course, bearing in mind the rule that, when you have picked one small bone clean, you do not let the subject know he has passed on vital facts.

Big Herbie immediately called Worboys, telling him what their first trawl had gleaned and asking for extra minders at the Warminster facility. He, of all people, knew that, even though the electronic warning system had been beefed up, the huge grounds surrounding the Main House, not to mention the Dower House, could still be dangerous. There were always gaps through which determined fanatics could penetrate.

Herbie's constant nightmare returned to the time, only a few years ago, when he had been called back to deal with the inquisition of the world-famous orchestral conductor, Maestro Louis Passau. On that occasion there *had* been a breach of security, and people had been shot to death in the grounds. In London, they still argued about the Warminster security.

Worboys was clear on the subject. He would have to get the nod from the CSIS before the manpower could be released.

'I'll try and get someone to you before tomorrow,'

he said, his voice sounding weary. 'I feel like a prisoner here.'

'So you should.' Herb paused and then became almost Shakespearean. 'Soft you, Tony. They're running out of manpower, but they'll still try to get you. Stay safe.'

'If they try my home, they'll be in for a shock. The Old Man's let me have some of the lads standing by there.'

Herbie also said he wanted the latest telephone logs, covering the past three days. 'Is most important, Tony. We got a pigeon's stool here, and I want to know if it's Carole. There's something not quite right about the widow Keene. She knows something we're not privy to. Nothing surprises me any more.'

'If the Iraqis didn't blow Gus to pieces, who in hell did?' Worboys was musing aloud.

'Maybe the Irish. Maybe not. It's always possible that it was done private, if you follow me.'

'The bloody bomb had these Vengeance people's fingerprints all over it.'

'Handwriting, Tony, not fingerprints.'

'What's in a name?'

The minders who had travelled with Kruger to and from London were *not*, as he had first thought, freelance old hands called back for temporary work. He had felt the fear, tasted the bitter wormwood and gall of near death on the road to Warminster, just as Gus had tasted it for the last time.

It had been so sudden that he had to sit quietly and reconstruct the events in his head. The two sudden flashes and detonations in the car which had overtaken them. The smell of explosives. The calm words of the man travelling shotgun in their car – 'Get down. Right down in the back.' Then the flash of thigh as Bex's skirt rode high and the softness of her body, her hands grabbing him as they lay there. The roller-coaster feeling as the car squealed sideways. The stutter of the Heckler & Koch, then the view of the men from the chase car, plus the driver and shotgun of their car, circling in the road. They had put their three charges first, not even going to see if they could assist the driver of the private car which had borne the brunt of the explosions.

The ski masks, and the soft unhurried way in which the minders had closed ranks around the car carrying him, Bex and the Fat Boy, had a recognizable deadly choreography. It was in the way they moved, the tension, the readiness. These were SAS officers, troopers and NCOs. Things had to be at a high crisis level for the CSIS to get the okay to use the Special Air Service men as bodyguards.

Herbie was pulled from his daydream by a soft knock at the door. Bex Olesker came into the room looking shaken, her face still pallid from the experience earlier that evening. She had gone through the interview with Ramsi like the pro she was. Now, the fear had set in, and she looked terribly vulnerable.

'Sorry to bother you, Herb.' Her voice was soft and throaty.

'You never bother me, Bex.' He saw that she was trembling.

'Delayed shock, I think.' She sat down and rested her head against the back of the high chair, breathing out as though letting go a long sigh of relief. It was now that she told him she had felt no fear until she had seen the men with ski masks surrounding the car. 'I thought we were finished. The first time in my career that I've felt real fear.'

She said that, up to then, she had done surveillance on known terrorists, and had even been at the sites of three terrorist actions within minutes of the bombs or guns doing their deadly work. 'But this really had me terrified. I don't honestly know if I should stay with SO 13.'

'You get use to it, Bex. Is like any other job that has danger at its heart. Hours of boredom punctuated by moments of fear. You think I wasn't frightened?'

'You didn't seem to be. Nor did Mr Brook.'

'Martin? Martin's a confessor; an inquisitor. Trained by Gus. You notice he didn't show any sign of wanting to be with us when we talked to Ramsi? My guess is that he was too busy throwing up.'

'You really do get used to it, Herb?'

'Matter of having to get into the swing of things.' He gave a laugh that sounded like broken glass, then moved softly across the room, stood behind her chair and put his fat arms around her, his forearms resting on her breasts, and his big rugged lived-in face buried in her short black hair. Her hair smelled of sunshine. It was the only analogy Herb could draw from the scent.

'Thanks, Herb,' she choked. 'I'm still bloody frightened.'

'You got me, babe,' he crooned, remembering, through the smoke in his brain, some 1960s pop song: back in the days when Cher was Sonny and Cher and not an actress with a picture in the attic.

'I've got you babe,' she said softly. 'That's a voice from the past.'

'For me, most things are voices from the past.' Big Herbie Kruger closed his eyes and breathed in the sunshine.

At the house known as The Hall in Harrow Weald, on the outskirts of the Metropolis, three two-man teams from the SAS HQ at Stirling Lines, outside Hereford, lay in wait. Two watched the rear of the property, two lay in cover which gave them excellent views across the drive and the gardens that led up to the house. The last pair was actually in the house.

They had set up portable sensors in a ring some hundred yards from the place, plus a small infra-red TV camera which they controlled with a joystick, watching the images of the night as they swept it in a 180° arc. They lay quiet, almost unmoving except for one of the men softly humming 'Music of the Night', as they watched and listened.

Hisham, against his better judgement, had sent Ahmad and Dinah out to Harrow Weald before the news of Samira's botched attempt had come through. Now, at two in the morning, Ahmad lay in the thick grass next to Dinah, well inside the grounds of the Hall, watching and waiting for some sign of life.

They knew that the target's car was there. Not even in the garage. The Range Rover was parked in the turning circle right in front of the house, and had been there since they had crawled into position. They had watched the lights go on and off in various parts of the building, and now only one bulb was burning in what they took to be a bathroom on the first floor.

All this, of course, was courtesy of the SAS team inside the house. Now, one of the troopers inside had quietly climbed the stairs and switched off the light in the master bathroom. Waited for a minute so that his eyes could adjust, then returned to his partner in what was normally Worboys' study at the front of the house. The curtains were drawn over the two windows facing the drive, so that the tiny diffused light from the TV monitor would not be visible from outside.

It was just on two-thirty when one of the men beside the monitor heard two distinct clicks in his radio earpiece. One of their comrades in the grounds had spotted movement, so they slowly traversed the camera over its full 180°. They picked up the first figure, crouched by a line of rhododendron bushes near the end of the drive, almost at the edge of the turning circle right in front of the main door.

The clicks on the radios, they hoped, indicated that their people outside were tracking whoever had penetrated the grounds. They moved the camera very slowly so as not to alert the intruders. There were two of them, black shapes carrying what looked to be automatic weapons, and they came quietly towards the front of the house, one on each side of the drive. Then, one of the shapes detached itself from the bushes and moved towards the Range Rover, knelt down and unslung a satchel, placing it by the front offside wheel. The figure had moved like a woman, and her companion joined her for a moment whispering softly and then making his way to the back of the car, covering her, looking in the direction of the house as she carefully turned onto her back and slid under the vehicle.

Did they think they could get away with a car bomb in these days of red alert? Every possible target would examine the underside of their personal vehicle before getting into the driving seat. So pondered the officer in charge of the detail as he lay, unmoving, less than fifty yards away.

This was the moment, he decided. As long as there were only two of them. With one occupied under the Range Rover and the other watching the front of the house, they might even bring the pair in unharmed. His thumb came down on the send button of his Pace Landmaster transceiver. He gave a rapid series of clicks and, before he had even stopped sending, the portable floods came on.

They had placed the floods while there was still plenty of light. Twelve portable high-intensity floodlights, secured at intervals in a crescent around the front and side of the building. The sergeant who controlled this battery of lights had switched them on the moment the rapid clicks had started to come through his earpiece.

'Stand still. Police. Do not move . . .' the officer in command shouted in vain.

Dazzled by the sudden brilliant light, Ahmad had reflexed, turned in his crouching position and let go two bursts of automatic fire from the Uzi tucked into his hip. He died instantly, an SAS man rushing from the bushes and putting four bullets into him from a 9mm Browning.

Dinah pushed her heels into the gravel and shot her

body backwards from under the Range Rover. As she moved, she grabbed for the Mini-Uzi lying beside the satchel. She brought the weapon up in one hand and fired three short bursts turning between each burst, then getting to her feet, realizing that her only chance would be to blow out the searing blinding lights.

She got no further than two steps from the car when the same SAS NCO took her out with two fast pairs of shots.

They heard her go down onto the gravel, but waited for a minute in case any other trespassers had not broken cover. After a minute, the officer in charge had shouted a command for those in hiding to come out or be shot down. There was no response, so, after another minute, the SAS team rose and went about clearing up the mess.

An officer trained in bomb disposal eased himself under the Range Rover and examined it with a small torch held between his teeth.

'Bloody clever,' he muttered to himself. The limpet bomb secured magnetically to the underside of the chassis had been shaped like a small pipe, with ends at right angles, and covered in dirt, oil and grease. It had been placed carefully next to the crosswise bump in the underside of the chassis, covering the front axle. A cursory check would reveal nothing.

As he began to prise the magnetically attached pipe from the car, he moved too quickly. The mercury switch within the pipe slid down and made the connection to the batteries. A stab of power hit the electronic primer and nine pounds of explosive became unstable and blew a funnel of flame and destruction upwards. The officer died instantly and the whole of the forward section of the vehicle was destroyed.

As the echoes died, so police and ambulance sirens could be heard as they raced to the scene of a reported series of shots, called in on 999 by a neighbour.

Hisham watched the News at Ten, and so got the

first indication of Samira's attempt going wrong. The account was terse, an outline confirming earlier reports of a terrorist incident in Wiltshire. There were pictures of a wrecked car and a form covered by a tarp by the side of the road, while police and forensic experts worked nearby.

The anchor took a feed from a local news team at the site. The reporter was a woman trying her best to appear as a tough, unfazed media person.

'The police are being very tight-lipped over this,' she said, looking a shade shifty herself. 'But it has been confirmed that there was an attempt to kill two senior intelligence officers and an anti-terrorist police-man who were travelling from London. The car that took the brunt of the explosion in fact belonged to a well-known local doctor whose name is being withheld for the moment until all relatives have been notified.

'The VIP intelligence and police officers escaped unharmed, and the one terrorist was shot dead by security forces. It is of interest that this happened very near to the spot where a former retired intelligence officer was killed – it is thought by a terrorist bomb – some three weeks ago. Police will not confirm if there is any connection between the two incidents, but this latest atrocity comes at a time when the security forces on mainland Britain, on the continent, and in the United States have been on a high state of alert following several bombings and shootings. Informed sources tell us that a Middle East terrorist group has been responsible for the acts of violence both in Europe and the United States.'

Hisham left the television switched on and pondered his position. He now had only Ahmad and Dinah at his disposal for the final push – not that he had as yet decided to let the horror they called *Magic Lightning* go ahead. His immediate problem was what to do about his own situation. He would have to report to *Yussif* who, in turn, would be in instant contact with the *Biwāba*. What would he, Hisham, do if he were in the *Biwāba*'s shoes?

It depended on how many trustworthy people he had at his disposal. It was possible that he would send in a new team and, should he decide on that option, Hisham might be told to continue with the operation. On the other hand, the *Biwāba* was a great strategist. He was also a realist. In all probability he would have Hisham recalled and that would mean only one thing. He would be immediately handed over to the truly dreaded Secret Police – *Amn-al-Amm*, known by a frightened people as the AMAM – and so would disappear.

In the back of his mind, Hisham could really only see one way out of his dilemma. He should call one of the two numbers he had been given under his *Ishmael* cryptonym. He had no illusions about what could happen then. The British could easily deny him because of what he had already accomplished, or they could bring him in, turn him inside out and then throw him back to the *Amn-al-Amm*.

He waited. The TV programmes finally ended for the night, and he switched to a portable radio, listening to the news updates each hour. As the time dragged on and Ahmad and Dinah did not return, Hisham became more concerned. Then, at just after three-thirty in the morning, the DJ broke into his programme saying there was a news flash.

That was it. A terrorist attack on the house of a very senior intelligence officer in Harrow Weald. There was talk about a car bomb explosion which had killed one army officer. Then, almost as an aside, the newscaster announced that two terrorists, a man and a woman, had been shot dead after they opened fire on security forces.

The whole of the British *Intiqam* team, except for their leader, had gone. One in custody, he presumed, wrongly, in Rome, the rest dead.

Hisham put on a light raincoat against the chill of the morning air and left the flat, going to the nearest telephone booths up near the Borough of Kensington and Chelsea Public Library.

Using one of the telephone cards, he dialled the *Yussif* number in Oxfordshire. They told him to stay put. There would be instructions. Probably tomorrow morning. Wait, they commanded, and he had to admit that the man in Oxfordshire sounded as though it were an order he must obey at all costs. By this one action, Hisham realized, he had broken off his ties to the British. Or had he? Hisham was a frightened and confused man who just could not make up his mind.

It was late afternoon in Baghdad when they got the message through to the *Biwāba* – the Gatekeeper. As usual the old man took the bad news calmly. He told his staff that he did not wish to be disturbed, and walked out into the garden to sit in his favourite spot, looking out over the city which he had known all his life.

Realist that he was, the *Biwāba* knew it would be absolute folly to pass these new tidings on to the Leader. His mercurial character was sometimes difficult to bear, for he was the kind of leader, moulded like the great kings of old, who would punish the messenger for bringing reports of setbacks or the catastrophic results of a lost battle.

This was a battle which could continue, the *Biwāba* knew. Logic told him that the operations in Europe were probably dead for the time being. Yes, he had some well-trained people he could send in, but these things required time and great patience to bring about. He thought of Hisham as a good commander who had stumbled and come up against bad luck. Perhaps the best thing would be for Hisham to join Walid and Khami in the United States. Over there, *Magic Lightning* was slowly going forward. He would leave matters for twenty-four hours, but prepare Hisham for a possible journey to America.

After an hour of meditation, the *Biwāba* returned to the house and wrote a short message which was to be sent straight away to Hisham in London. *Yussif* would have to deliver the news personally, and nothing must go wrong.

Big Herbie only managed a little sleep that night. He had spoken to Martin Brook, calling him Fat Boy to his face, which was a daring thing to do at any time. It turned out that Martin was really not interested in sitting in on further interrogations of either Carole or Ramsi. He, not unnaturally, was getting things organized for his move in as Warminster's commanding officer.

At around midnight there was a message from Worboys saying that a troop of SAS were on their way to assist in making Warminster more secure; also the most recent telephone logs were on their way by courier. They had a short spat of words about the telephone logs, Herbie arguing that, as they were made up here at the Warminster complex, they should be passed over to him directly instead of this bureaucratic nonsense of being sent to London, copied, and then sent back.

'Herb, you know the rules as well as I do. Now that Whitehall oversees every damn thing we do, it's more than my job's worth to slide them over to you directly.'

Herb argued for a while, then decided it wasn't worth his time.

That night, though Kruger never admitted it, he almost got to the point of asking to be relieved of being detective in residence, attached to the Gus Keene murder case. It was but a phase, so he turned his mind to the question of what they could accomplish in the morning. He thought it might be a good thing to have another go at Ramsi. He had to examine the telephone logs. Maybe they would show that Carole had been making calls out. It could, he supposed, be her, or Bitsy, Ginger, Kenny Boyden, even Mickey Crichton or any one of the other half-a-dozen staff knocking around.

Whoever he turned up, he would play hell with the guilty party. After all, what they had reported to this man Hisham Silwani, aka *Ishmael*, had almost caused him to be killed. They had caused the death of an innocent doctor, and given great anxiety to DCI Bex Olesker. He was very angry about that. Bex had swallowed a large glass of medicinal brandy – the fact that it was Remy Martin did not make it less medicinal – before going off to bed. She had given Herb a big hug and a little peck on the cheek before she went. All this had left him slightly unnerved, and he could not for the life of him understand why.

Yes, Ramsi tomorrow. First on the list.

He went into Gus's secret magic cave again where he found an excellent book by someone called Milbourne Christopher who, it appeared, had been National President of the Society of American Magicians from 1957 to 1958. It was called *Panorama of Magic*, and he went through it from cover to cover, fascinated by the drawings, engravings, reproductions and photographs, not to mention the text, from which he learned a great deal.

Finally he fell asleep in Gus's chair, only to be wakened by the telephone. He blundered out for it, found that it was Worboys and the time was seven forty-five.

'Well, they tried,' Young Worboys said.

'Tried what? I just woke up.'

The Deputy Chief went through the events in the middle of the night at The Hall, Harrow Weald.

'Have to buy yourself a new Range Rover then, won't you? I got to get shaved.' As long as it was only the car that had gone and not Worboys, Herb was happy. At the time he knew nothing of the young SAS officer who had been killed.

The representative from *Yussif* arrived at the flat off Kensington High Street at a little before ten in the morning. He was serious and did not smile once during his discussion with Hisham Silwani. The instructions were very clear. He was to get the first possible flight out of London to New York. Once there, he should use a public telephone to call a number which had to be committed to memory. Things would take shape after that. He would join what was left of the *Intiqam* team in the United States and make sure that *Magic Lightning* was carried out in Washington as soon as possible, taking instructions from the American team leader, Walid.

After the emissary from *Yussif* left, Hisham sat for the best part of thirty minutes. Then he gathered together a few belongings, left the apartment and headed once more for the bank of public telephones near the library. His hand was shaking as he dialled the number. Panic stricken, he had once more swerved in another direction, all logic gone.

In the guest facility at Warminster, Herbie and Bex were just getting into their stride with Ramsi. They had learned that the American team was, as far as he knew, the same size as the one sent to the United Kingdom. They even got some names and secure passwords, and they also discovered that both groups were being handled by someone called *Yussif* – 'I think, however,' the stout little bomb-maker said, 'this *Yussif* is not just one man but several. Also, I think one *Yussif* is here and another in the United States. I even know the telephone number for the one here.'

'Really,' Herbie tried to sound as though he were not interested in the slightest, so Bex said, 'Better give it to us, just for the record,' and wrote down the number in her little black notebook.

She was just about to put the next question to Ramsi when there was a tap at the door and Martin Brook looked in.

'A word, Herbie, in private. Rather urgent, I think.'

Kruger excused himself, prised his body, now almost back to its old weight, from the chair and lumbered out of the door.

'We've an odd call on the line,' Brook told him, walking quickly towards the room that used to be Gus Keene's office. 'There's a fellow in a public callbox.

London, I think. Says he's *Ishmael* and will only speak with *Ajax* or someone who knows his work. I thought it might be up your street.'

'Jesus.' Herb pounded along the passage into the office and picked up the telephone.

'*Ishmael*?' he asked.

'Who's that?'

'A very old friend of *Ajax*. You want proof?'

'That would set my mind at ease.'

'The name Mary Delacourt mean something to you?'

'If you know about her, then you know about me.'

'Yes. What can I do for you?'

'I want to come in. I'm in a very difficult position.'

'Yes, I should be imagining that you are, now that you're alone.'

'I told you. I want to come in. There's more I can do, and I'll do it. Just get me out of sight for a few hours so that we can talk.'

'Okay,' Herbie tried to sound normal and unexcited. 'Now, where are you?'

Hisham told him.

'Anyone on to you?'

'No. I don't think so anyway.'

'Spend the next half an hour checking that out, then go to St Mary Abbots Hospital in Marloes Road. You can get to it easily from where you are. You know Marloes Road?'

'I think so.'

'Be certain nobody's on your heels. Wait by the entrance to the hospital. A car will stop and a man will ask you if you're from the Society for Stray Dogs. Got it?'

'For stray dogs?'

'Yes. Tell him you have a dog called Hagar. He'll have you on the way to me as quickly as he can.'

'Hagar?'

'You've got it. Any problems, put your right hand in your pocket. If things are okay keep your hands in sight. You carrying anything?'

'Small suitcase.'

'Off you go then.'

Herbie cradled the instrument and immediately began punching in numbers that would get him straight through to Worboys. He was breathing hard.

23

They gathered in what had once been the main briefing room in the big house: Worboys representing the CSIS, Big Herbie Kruger, DCI Olesker and Martin Brook.

Tony Worboys was the last to arrive, having waited until Hisham Silwani had been picked up at St Mary Abbots Hospital and taken in an unmarked car to Warminster. Only then was Worboys driven down in one of the Office cars. When he came into the room he was in what Herbie later called 'a flurry'.

'This is not strictly any of our business,' Worboys began.

'Okay, *you* call the Security Service and we'll throw him to them,' Herbie said brightly.

'He *is* their asset.'

'He was Gus's asset, and my job is to find out who blew Gus away. This guy is – or was – the leader of a terrorist team operating in Europe out of the UK. Let's see what he has to offer. If he's just your usual run-of-the-militia terrorist, we'll toss him back. No harm done. You pick up the phone and say, "Stella, we've got one of your bodies. Please send a spare van for him." '

'I know Gus ran him, but he did that under MI5's authority.'

'Oh, shut up, Tony. I need to talk with him.' As far as Herb was concerned, the matter was over.

'You do have him secure?' Worboys looked hard at Martin Brook.

'Houdini couldn't get out.'

'I'm not thinking of Houdini. I want to be certain the bomb-maker – Ramsi – doesn't bump into him taking a morning stroll.'

Herbie laughed. 'Tony, it's Carole you should be worrying about, and they're all well separated.'

The underground guest facilities had four holding units which could be opened to each other or closed off. If they were closed, nobody down there would even know anybody else was quartered near him.

Each unit had been built with an eye to comfort, and they were like small suites in a luxury hotel: sitting-room, bedroom and bathroom. In the same facility they had two interrogation rooms – one for hard cases, bare and uninviting; the other for the soft sell with calming paintings on its walls – sea views and sailing ships – deep, comfortable leather armchairs and not a single No Smoking sign.

There had been some peeves about the latter from the vociferous many, but Gus, a pipe smoker to the end, had overruled everyone. His argument was that the second-hand smoke lobby did themselves more harm by walking the streets of any big city and, if you completely prohibited smoking, it would be necessary to do away with alcohol and sex also – both being just as dangerous in the long run.

Worboys changed tack quickly, asking if the extra security had settled in.

'They're happy as sandboys,' Brook told him. 'We've given them free range and their two officers dashed around the place setting a watch.'

'I'm going to need three or four of those blakes—'

'Blokes, Herbie?'

'Sure. Three or four of those blokes in civilian clothes.'

'They're all in civilian clothes.'

'That'll make things nice then.'

'What for, Herb?' As the senior man from the Office, Worboys felt out of place in the presence of Kruger, who had no rank but was in charge of the investigation. He could not blame anyone for this, as it had been his idea to bring Big Herbie back to do the dirty work. The CSIS had agreed without reservation, for any investigation of Gus's death would be dangerous.

'We still got that room upstairs? The one with the two-way mirror?' Herb asked of Martin Brook.

'Yes, and all the gear.' By this he meant audio and video machines which could take pictures or preserve conversations from behind the mirror which looked into a room containing only a table and half a dozen comfortable chairs.

'What for, Herb?' Worboys repeated.

'Ask no questions and you'll get no lies, as my old grandmother used to say.' A statement that was highly improbable as Big Herbie's grandmother, on his father's side, never spoke English in the whole of her long life. He gave the Hallowe'en grin, then said that before he even began talking with Hisham he wanted him put in that room – 'looking respectable and with four SAS faces'.

'Going to be difficult to make *them* look respectable, Herb.' It was Bex speaking for the first time.

'You have to work with what you got, Bex. When this is all set I want to bring Carole up to take a shiftee at them through the mirror.'

'Shufti . . .' Worboys corrected, then saw Herb's grin. It was like old times, he thought. Herb had the bit between his teeth and probably smelled blood. Maybe he was close to the truth.

It took almost an hour to set things up. The SAS were a little difficult about being in what was virtually – as Herb explained to them – an identity line-up. They finally settled on the right four and brought a tired Hisham over from the guest facilities.

Herbie, Bex and Worboys were behind the mirror, and Martin Brook came over with Carole. The booth behind the mirror was soundproofed, so none of the five men in the ID room heard a word.

'So what's this, Herb?' Carole sounded edgy.

'Just want to rule out a couple of things.' He patted

her shoulder in an avuncular manner, something that Worboys rightly interpreted as a bad sign for Carole. 'Today we're going through the oblong mirror.' Herb was aping a children's TV show in which the anchor would take toddlers through triangular, square or oblong windows out into a fantasy world behind them.

'Take a very careful look, Carole. Just let me know if you recognize any of the men out there.' He then turned and watched Carole rather than the men sitting uncomfortably before them. He watched her closely, his eyes flitting between her eyes and hands. He detected no sudden revelations so was not surprised when she said no. 'Nary a one, Herbie. None of them mean anything to me. Never ever seen them before.'

'Okay,' Kruger sounded a shade too bright. 'Tell you what, Carole, Bex and I'll be down to talk a bit later.'

'Well, I hope you're going to tell me when I can get on with my life and leave this place.' She was serious and did not even smile.

Worboys made his apologies, saying he had to get back to the Office and left with a flourish of minders. This gave Brook plenty of time to get Carole back to the set of rooms she occupied in the guest facility, then they broke up the party and took Hisham back to his suite, from where they soon removed him to the soft interrogation room.

Bex went back to the Dower House with Herbie, and they looked over the most recent telephone logs which showed calls in and out of the main house, Dower House, and even the guest facility.

'Interesting stuff, here.' Herbie pointed to half a dozen calls.

'You want to talk with her now, or later.'

'Later would be best. Let's give Hisham/*Ishmael*, a marathon going over before we talk with the lady.'

'Whatever you say, oh Genie of the Lamp.' Bex gave his arm a little squeeze and they both laughed. Herbie was not quite sure why they laughed, but he was not in the mood for any lengthy analysis at this point.

Fortified with coffee, they started what would be a crucial interview with the Iraqi.

'Now, Hisham, old sheep,' Herbie began, all bright, happy and friendly. 'We need to go over a few things with you.'

'Anything. Whatever you want to know, I'll co-operate.' Herbie thought that, for loyal Iraqis, both Ramsi and Hisham were not the people he would have chosen. He nodded at Bex, who took over.

'I'd like to ask you one or two things about 1983, when you became an active agent for our Security Service under the workname *Ishmael*.'

'Yes.'

'And I should caution you that we have a lot of information regarding your activities both as *Ishmael* and leader of the Vengeance team in Europe.'

'You'll get the truth.' Hisham was almost belligerent in his tone, as though shocked that Bex might think him to be dishonest with them. 'I came to you,' he added, as if this made matters clear, 'I came to you in order to tell you the truth.'

'Good.' Bex sounded like a bright schoolteacher. 'First of all, would you tell me the name of the man who did the final interrogation, and instructed you under the workname *Ishmael*.'

'His name was Keene. He told me to call him Gus, then later, when we got down to the worknames, I was to call him *Ajax*.'

'Never *Claudius*?'

Hisham shook his head. 'No. Always *Ajax*. I used the name when I telephoned. *Ajax* was my control.'

'But you knew who you were working for?'

'For your Security Service.'

'And over the years you provided some excellent information regarding the activities of other terrorist groups.'

334

'I gave *Ajax* all I could, and more. It wasn't easy, and—'

'It's never easy,' murmured Herb as if he were sharing part of his own secret life with the target.

'Particularly when I was appointed to lead a group under cover here in Europe.'

'An *Intiqam* group, we understand?'

'Vengeance, yes. You'd call it Vengeance, or Revenge.'

'Good. Now I'll tell you something. Mr Keene—'

'Is dead. They told me that.'

'Yes, he's dead, but I was going to tell you that he was not a regular officer of our Security Service. He worked for our Intelligence Service. *This* is an Intelligence Service facility. Occasionally, Intelligence loaned him out to Security. He recruited and ran you from the Security Service. We did not find out about you until quite late in the game.'

'So?'

'So, when Mr Keene was coaching you in your successful role as *Ishmael* did he ever bring you here? This place is known as Warminster. It's also sometimes known as the College. Ever been here before Hisham?'

'No. *Ajax* went through things with me in London. After I became an agent for him, he thought it best that I should carry on with the work I was doing for the Leader of my country. We would meet in a flat near Marylebone High Street. He would coach me there: communications; tradecraft; paper; signals. All that I did under the cover of meeting a young woman.'

'Did you *really* meet a young woman there, Hisham old sheep?' Herbie sounded as though he had just awakened from a long sleep.

'Oh, yes. She was a good friend of Mr Keene's – of *Ajax*. *Ajax* was very professional. Said that it was no good just pretending that I came to the flat for what you people call a bit of nookie. If I came here to see him, I must always have the bit of nookie.'

335

'You speak good English,' Herb grinned. 'A bit of nookie is good.'

'Thank you.'

'Always the same girl?'

'Always. She said she was under discipline to *Ajax*.'

'You get her name?'

'Sure, she was called Betsy. I think it was her real name.'

'Can you describe her, after all these years?'

'Difficult, but I try.' He described her. Later, when the session was over, Herbie said to Bex that Hisham must have enjoyed her greatly. 'That's just about what she would have looked like in the early '80s.'

'Still waters run deep.' Bex nearly giggled. 'Just think of it.'

'Next, Hisham, I want to ask you about certain things connected with your dealings with the Security Service when you came in with your group – your *Intiqam* people – on this trip.'

Hisham nodded, looked unhappy and then shrugged, as if to say it was all in the line of duty.

'Did you make contact with *Ajax*?'

'No. The Security people contacted me, and I thought I had got into the country unnoticed.' He told them about the woman bumping into him outside the Real Estate office and the note she had slipped into his breast pocket – 'Call us or we'll call your superiors in Baghdad.'

'Not very sporting,' Herbie laughed. Then: 'We understand that you said certain things to the people who began to handle you. For instance, you told them that, should they take your little cell out, there would be others to take its place immediately.'

Hisham remembered the night they had pulled him into the car after he had seen *Les Misérables* with the Irishman, Declan. 'Yes. Yes, I told them that.'

'The real question is, was *that* true? *Is* there another team waiting to come in?'

Hisham gave a little soapy smile and shrugged again.

'I really don't know. There were plenty of people under selection, but the infiltration process takes a long while. My team came in separately. Then we lived in one place to blend in with the scenery. The *Biwāba* called it becoming chameleons.'

'And who's the *Biwāba* when he's at home?' Herbie made it into a throw-away question.

'The *Biwāba* is a very wise man. He is also a holy man. In our language *Biwāba* means Gatekeeper. He is the Gatekeeper to our actions against the West. This will sound offensive to you, I know. But the time of Islam *is* coming again, and the *Biwāba* is the one who prepares, trains and chooses those who must first go out and fight the spiritual and political battles against the unbelievers.'

'You believe all this?' Herbie recalled asking a similar question to Ramsi on the previous night.

'It is not a question of belief or unbelief. I am a Muslim, but my faith is not as it should be. I suppose I am a Muslim agnostic. I have lost touch with what is true and what may not be true. I have grave doubts about our Leader and his methods. He rules by constant fear. This is one of the reasons I came to you as a final recourse. I know what would happen to me if I returned home. The *Biwāba* would speak on my behalf, but it would be to no avail. I would simply cease to be.'

Bex nodded. 'You're an experienced man, though, Hisham. You know the way your freedom fighters are being prepared. We are simply asking your opinion. In your opinion, is there another team ready to move in?'

He hesitated slightly. 'To be truthful, I think the *Biwāba* would counsel a waiting period. In fact I believe he has already made up his mind. He will let the American operation run its course and leave Europe for some time in the near future. This is why I have my orders to go straight to New York and link up with the *Intiqam* there. I *know* the American team was exactly the same strength as mine, and like mine they have been drastically reduced.'

'Okay. You've promised to tell us the truth now, Hisham. You've made a sacred promise. You told the Security people that you would not, or could not, tell them the truth about *Magic Lightning*. Can you, in fact, tell us anything?'

'Even what little you might know,' Herbie said in a flat voice.

'I will tell what I know.' Hisham took a deep breath. '*Magic Lightning* is the end of our joint operation. First the bombings and shootings. Next the complete disruption of important Western governments – your own British government, the American government, the French and the Italian. There was to be a serious softening up, using large bombs. Here there were two major bombings arranged – the statue of your Queen Victoria outside Buckingham Palace was to be obliterated.'

'A worthy action,' Herb laughed. 'A lot of people would think that statue is a monstrosity, but don't quote me on that. Where else?'

'Also your Foreign Office in Whitehall. These were to be two huge bombs.'

'With what object?'

'To make sure that your government – your House of Commons – would be called to a special sitting.'

'And then a bomb for them?'

Hisham shook his head. 'No. For them it was to be something else. Something which would, in all probability, strike them very quickly and leave the country without a solid leadership. Don't ask me what *Magic Lightning* really is, because I don't know. I only know that it is the unleashing of something very unpleasant, to cripple the government. The same was to happen in France and Italy. As far as I can see, it is still going to happen to the American government.'

'Okay,' Herbie shifted in his chair. 'You had a deal with our Security Service. Two deals in fact. First you were going to alert them to any bombs, giving the place

338

and time – and with enough warning to let them take remedial action.'

'Yes, and I would have kept that promise.'

'You would?'

'Of course.'

'Then why didn't you keep your other promise?'

'What other promise?' Hisham's legs turned to jelly.

'The FFIRA, in the person of Declan Norton, promised you a large shipment of Semtex if you assassinated four targets.'

'We didn't really need the Semtex. It was a deal to get them off our backs. They wanted plenty of warning regarding when we would carry out bomb attacks or executions. The Semtex would have been handy to provoke more fear once *Magic Lightning* had occurred, but the promise was made to calm them down. I have had very good contacts with the Irish for a long time. These people – the Freedom Fighters – are men and women out of control. Yes, I agreed to their terms . . .'

'You even carried them out.'

'I told the Security Service people that I would have to make it look good.'

'You made it more than good, Hisham. For one thing you killed an old friend of mine, Mr Blount-Wilson; you tried to kill me by burning my fucking cottage down.' He was standing up now, and raising his voice, as though the calm reasonable character had been taken over by some terrible demon. 'And to cap it all, you very nearly killed DCI Olesker here, last night, and you were within an ace of killing me – for the second time. Then you have the audacity to try and blow one of the deputy directors of our Intelligence Service to kingdom come.'

'They were not meant to happen. Not meant to be successful.'

'Well, I don't know what your idea of success happens to be, Hisham, but from my viewpoint you had a serious go—'

'And ended up with no team. Ended up running to you for protection.'

'Yes, indeed, and, by God, you're going to need it. First, these *Yussif* people. I want confirmation of the telephone number you've been contacting, and I want it now.'

Hisham looked stunned at what was an exhibition of violence – for Herbie had banged the table almost shattering it, and kicked at one of the stand chairs, sending it skittering across the room. 'I want that telephone number now. This minute.'

Hisham reeled off the number. Twice, then a third time, very fast just for good measure. 'I said I would do anything.'

'Good, then let me tell you what you *are* going to do. You are going to get onto an aeroplane and fly to New York, just as *Yussif* told you to do. Then you are going to telephone the number he gave you. After that you're going to telephone one of *our* people in New York and he'll advise you. I'll get you on a flight late today, and you'll have *my* people on your back all the way. Understand? Hisham you sonofabitch child of a syphilitic whore, you dense cretinous coward, you pig-faced, evil, murdering, unholy low-life bastard. You understand?'

In a very small voice, with his head nodding like one of those appalling toy dogs people put in the back of their cars, Hisham whispered, 'Yes, I will do all you ask.'

'Damn right you will. If you don't, then we'll pick you up, tie a label onto you, pack you in a crate with a recording of this conversation and everything the Security Service has on you, then send you sea mail to your pissant little country.'

'That was impressive,' Bex Olesker said, sounding happy, as they made their way back to the Dower House.

340

'I'm great when I'm roused, Bex.' The goofy grin as he looked down at her, his hand resting on the small of her back. He noticed that she did not try and remove it.

'Oh, you're back late. I've had a nice soup and some smoked salmon and salad ready for you since 1 o'clock,' Bitsy greeted them as they came through the door.

'Couple of things to do.' Herbie picked up the pile of Gus's mail that lay on the table in the hall. Every day since it had begun, his practice was to go through the mail, sort what required diverting to Carole, and giving the rest a quick once over.

Bex went upstairs to wash and tidy herself up for lunch, while Herbie sat at Gus's desk and went through the day's bills, circulars, junk mail and magazines.

Not much today. Then his eye caught one of the magazines. It was simply titled *Magic* and it had come from the United States. He removed the wrapper and began to flick through it. He had already seen copies in Gus's secret Merlin's Cave so he turned to an article by someone called Max Maven who, he thought, wrote a fairly erudite column. While trying to find it, his eye caught a double-spread advertisement. He looked at it with some kind of bewilderment. Then grabbed the telephone and dialled a number in Virginia.

'Collector's Workshop,' said a friendly female at the distant end.

'I am calling about your convention,' Herb tried to keep his voice level.

'The World Magic Summit, yes? You want to register?'

'Only if your ad in the current edition of *Magic* is correct.'

'Yes, it's quite correct.'

'You say that among those appearing in the Grand Show is Claudius Damautus. Is this true?'

'Yes, he's definitely going to be there. I spoke to him only yesterday. He's doing a new act called *The*

History of Magic in Twenty Minutes. Paul Daniels is going to be there *and* The Pendragons. I'm sure you'll enjoy it, Mr . . .'

'Kruger. Eberhardt Kruger, but I answer to Herbie.'

'I'm sure you'll love it, Herbie. Where're you calling from, Germany?'

'No, I'm in London,' he lied. 'But you can put me down for two registrations.' He gave her his name again and a credit card number. 'Don't forget to book the hotel accommodation yourself.' She gave him a number. Then, 'I'll need an address.'

'Can I pick the tickets up at the hotel?'

'When you come in to register, of course. And I'll need the name for the other registration.'

'Olesker, I'll spell it. O-L-E-S-K-E-R. Rebecca Olesker.'

'We'll see you at the World Magic Summit, then, Mr Kruger. Look out for me – Jane Smith Ruggiero.'

'Look forward to it.'

He went through to the dining-room, beaming and looking generally as though he was a cat who had just licked all the cream.

'Bex,' he said quietly, leaning over to whisper in her ear. 'I know who killed Gus.'

'You do? Who?'

'Not now. Later. We're going to the States.'

'Both of us?'

'Very necessary. We can book tickets when we deal with Hisham's bookings after lunch. Also we have to talk to Carole.'

'And someone else, I think,' she said pointedly as Bitsy came in carrying the tray with three bowls and a tureen of what looked like pea soup.

'Potage Longchamp,' Bitsy smiled, serving them.

'Pea soup,' Herb grinned. 'Nothing like a good pea soup, eh, Bits?'

'I like it. Made it from the ham stock. That piece of ham we had the other evening.'

'I like a good slice of ham as well,' Herbie continued to grin at her. 'You like a little cut off the joint, Bits?'

'Oh, I . . . What do you mean?'

'Question time, Bits.'

'Question ti—?'

'Don' worry, Bitsy. No names, no pack drill, as we Brits say. Just need the truth, whole truth, nothing but truth. We won't say a word if we get the truth.'

'What're you talking about?'

'Questions, Bitsy, you ever work with Gus?'

'I did safe houses. Did some for him, of course. I also handled visiting firemen from time to time.'

'What you mean by "handled"?'

'Just the usual. Made sure the cars were at the airport. Booked the rooms, if that was necessary.'

'Ever keep any of them happy, Bits?'

'Keep any of them . . . ? What do you mean exactly, *Mr* Kruger?'

'What I mean is, did old Gus come to you one day. 1983, maybe '84, but who's counting? Did he ever come to you and say, "Look, Bitsy, I've got this Arab asset in that safe house in New Cavendish Street, just off Marylebone. He needs a bit of classy nookie. Will you provide? Gus ever say that to you, Bits?'

24

'That's insulting, Mr Kruger. One of the most insulting suggestions I've . . .' Bitsy Williams could not seem to find the right words, her face turned beet red, and her eyes had that glint of rage one can just catch in the eye of a doomed bull ready to charge during a corrida.

'Not as insulting as hearing it in an open court of law, Bitsy.' A stillness came over Herbie, and his voice, while not unfriendly, assumed a hard, rocky quality – the voice of a man with whom you did not trifle. 'That's where it'll all come out, if you don't co-operate. Understand?'

'Kruger the unstoppable,' Bex thought. She also realized why this big, seemingly uncoordinated man was so attractive. It was not his looks or manner, but his dependability; his gift of being able to focus on a situation, cut through the dross and lance straight to the heart of the business in hand.

When she had first met him, Bex Olesker had little idea of how the man operated. The brass at Vauxhall Cross had painted a picture of a man who was a legend, a cerebral giant.

'If Herbie can't solve the problem, nobody can,' one of the senior members of the SIS had told her. 'He works, like God, in mysterious ways. This business is one of 90 per cent boredom and 10 per cent action and fear. Don't believe what you've read in the novels, because it just isn't true. Most of the time you're a laboratory assistant, working to rule. Don't blame the novelists, they have to spice it up a little. They have to please their readers. Old Herb may be almost over the hill, but he has the ability to see through the jumble of life's follies and cut straight to the centre. That brain may seem slow, but it's blessed with a kind of logic that's ideal for this sort of job. He also has incredible intuition, which is, of course, born of experience.'

She had detected none of this when she first met him, but slowly it had dawned on her that Kruger had a tenaciousness coupled with a comprehension unrivalled in this kind of work.

'Come on, Bits,' he said now. 'No harm's done, except one terrorist girl got herself killed. I'm trying to help. Look, I knew from the start that you wanted to be in on the Gus investigation, that you were desperate to stay attached to the op. I guessed you had some reason, maybe – I thought – you were a shade concerned that you might figure as a walk-on in Gus's book. Well, you don't appear in the book, Bitsy. I be honest, I don't think old Gus ever wanted the book published. I couldn't work out why you'd take a job like chief cook and bottle-washer here. Then I got it. You needed to be on hand. You . . .' He stopped.

Bitsy was hunched in her chair, miserable, tears just visible. 'He talked me into it. I was between boyfriends; needed some kind of reassurance, so I whored for Gus. The bastard could charm snakes from baskets and birds off trees. I whored for him, Herb.'

'No, you did something that was needed.'

'It wasn't even a honeytrap. I could feel better if I had done it for my country . . .'

'You did, Bits. Did it for country and helped keep an asset sane. Now, I need you to identify him. Sorry, but is necessary.'

She nodded, sniffed and then nodded again.

'And while we're at it, Bitsy, I suggest you give us the full story. Sure, you opened your legs for an asset Gus was burning. Then it became a little more than that.'

Bitsy looked down. Looked at her plate. A lock of hair fell across her forehead. When she spoke, her voice was so soft that they both had to strain to hear her. 'Yes. It became something more.'

'Like what?' Herb's question cracked like a revolver shot. She stayed silent. 'Like what, I asked, you dumb bitch?'

'Herbie, I . . .'

'Cut the Herbie. I'm Mr Kruger to you. Strictly, you're a fucking traitor, Bitsy Williams.'

'But he was working for us. On our side. I didn't think—'

'You didn't think nothing, you silly, stupid limp-brained idiot.'

'He *did* work for us. I was there. Was there when Gus was turning him. I heard so much of it.'

Kruger let out a long sigh, as though he was somehow deflating. 'Look, Bitsy,' his voice kinder now. 'Look, tell you what I'll do. I'll bury the evidence.'

'What evidence?'

'The telephone logs.'

'I only used the house phone twice. Two calls, lasted about a minute each.'

'I know that, but you should've known better. They're logged and we've got the number you called. I'll bury it for you. Keep you out of court.'

'Why would you do that?'

'You've been led by the charms between your legs. You know what they say about the guys we sprang honeytraps on? They say that they get led by their gentiles . . .'

'Genitals, Herb.'

'Sure, Bex. I know. Only they don't use such a polite term.' He leaned towards Bitsy. 'You were also led in the same way. I don't for a minute think you meant to betray, get me killed, get anyone killed; but you very nearly did. How did you work it? That damn telephone box down on the corner, near the Army camp?'

She nodded, lips quivering.

'Okay. Just tell me, true or false. You gave sexual comfort a long time ago to someone Gus turned. Then things got out of hand. Right?'

'Yes.'

'You told him you loved him. He said he loved you. Right?'

'Yes.'

'You pleaded with him to come back to London as often as he could. Right?'

'Yes.'

'And every time he came back, you saw him, met him, screwed him, and talked to him on the telephone. Right?'

'Yes.'

'How often did he come back?'

'Couple of times a year. Sometimes for two months. One year he came back for three months. Summer of '88.'

'Then, bingo, he came back and said you must be quiet. Only telephone him at certain times. You realized it had something to do with Gus. That it?'

'I didn't think he had killed Gus, but I wanted to be around the investigation. Just to keep an eye on things.'

'He asked you to do this?'

'Yes.'

'And you knew his crypto.'

She nodded. '*Ishmael*.'

Herbie nodded. 'Bitsy, is *this* true? Were you in so deep with him that you gave him information about the comings and goings here because you thought, with Gus dead, he might not have a friend in the world – *our* world?'

'That's it exactly.'

'So you let him know when I was going somewhere, or when Young Worboys was coming down here. You gave him a chart, a flight plan, every time anyone moved. That it?'

'It's what I did, yes.'

'Because you thought he might be out on a limb?'

'That, and the fact that I loved him.' Then, quickly,

347

'Not any more. I couldn't care less. In fact I'm mixed up. Can hate be so close to love?'

'Hate is *very* close to love, Bitsy. I know. I've been through all that.'

'Will they charge me with . . . ?'

'I don't think they'll charge you with anything, Bits. I think you should leave the Service. Early retirement. I'll put in a good word, even though you nearly got me killed. Okay?'

'Whatever you say, Her . . . Mr Kruger.'

'Good, we'll get it over with, then you can get on with your life. Let me make a call, set it up . . .'

'He won't see me?'

' 'Course he won't. We do a through-the-looking-glass game. Which is good because the guy still really doesn't know which side he's on.' He bit down on a piece of French bread, took two large spoonfuls of soup and was away, lurching out of the room.

In Gus's study he called the main house and just caught Worboys as he was about to leave. Five minutes later they were both behind Gus's locked door and Herbie was laying out a plan of campaign.

Worboys listened to the theory, asked a couple of questions, tested two of Herb's statements, then listened again as Kruger outlined all that needed doing immediately.

'Need it all now, Tony. Have to move like a force ten gale. Lot to do.'

'And I carry the can if anything goes wrong. You realize that?'

'Sure, but it won't go wrong. When I ever let you down, Tony? You know *me*. I taught you to swim in these shark-infested waters. Now you've got to show some trust.'

A very long minute passed, then Worboys nodded. 'It all makes sense. Okay, I'll back you. Let me use this telephone.'

'Take all the time you need, as long as it's bloody

quick.' He went back to the dining-room, where Bex was talking to Bitsy, calming her, reassuring, as Herb said, 'like a Dutch aunt'.

He finished the soup which had cooled off, then demolished a huge plate of smoked salmon, talking Bitsy down as he chewed.

Worboys stuck his head around the door. 'All set, if you have a minute, Herb.'

'Sure.'

'And they have him up in the viewing room.' Worboys looked pointedly at Bex, who rose, put a calming hand on Bitsy's shoulder and spoke softly to her.

'That DCI's worth her weight in gold,' the Deputy Chief said as they reached Gus's study door.

'Her price is beyond rubies,' Herb quoted. Again it shook Worboys, for he quoted from the Bible, and he just stopped himself from automatically doing the old schoolboy joke about what was Ruby's price?

Seated in the study, he went over each step, made Herb repeat telephone numbers, told him about the deal he had made with the American agencies, and the big cut they had demanded in return for Herbie and Bex operating on United States' territory. 'You're still not really their flavour of the month.' He chuckled. 'The last time you ran an op there it wasn't a completely spectacular success for them. They have long memories, but this thing's so important they really can't say no.'

'You bet they can't. I have to see Carole, as we agreed, then do the final session with friend *Ishmael* and time's running out.'

'Go, then, Herb. And good luck.'

'It's not luck I need, Tony, it's solid facts and making the right pieces fit. I don' even know if all the pieces are in the box. If they're not, then we won't solve the puzzle.'

'Knowing you, Herbie, you've some extra pieces hidden on your person.'

Kruger smiled. 'How you guess that, Young Worboys?

Hope I see you when I get back – if I get back. Maybe, this time, I run out of road.'

'Don't even think it.'

Bex and Bitsy were coming back through the front door as the two men emerged from Gus's study. Bitsy, red-eyed, quickly made for the staircase.

'It's him. No doubts now. She feels unclean.' Bex jerked her head in the direction of the stairs.

'Then she shouldn't. She's not the first person who had to screw for Queen and Country and she won't be the last. Bex, we're out of here within the hour. I have one more thing to do, then throw some clothes into a case. You got enough stuff for an extended trip to the USA?'

'Just about. What a good thing I always carry my passport with me. Do I need to report in to the Yard?'

'Been taken care of, Bex,' from Worboys.

'Go pack, Bex. See you in half an hour.' Herbie was gone, his hands swinging the wrong way, left to left leg and right to right. He was whistling 'The British Grenadiers' as he lumbered from the house, heading for the guest facilities.

'When's this farce going to be over, Herb?' Carole did not even stand up when Big Herbie came bulldozing into her room.

'For you, Carole, my dear, it's over. I come personal to give you the news.'

'Then you know who did for Gus?'

'We think we know, Carole. We certainly know that it wasn't you.'

Her cheeks flared with anger. 'You didn't think for a minute it was . . . ?'

Herb's giant shoulders moved almost to his ears in an overstated shrug. 'Who knows what evil lurks in the minds of men and women? The Shadow knows.'

'Don't try the funny papers on me, Herb. You didn't really . . . ?'

'People are guilty until proved innocent.'

'It's the other way around.'

'So they tell me, but that's in the real world, little one. Seriously, Carole. You are greatly loved, and we're all devastated about Gus. We think we know exactly what happened and we're going after the bastards, though I fear they've flown the coupé.'

'Coop, Herb, as in hen coop.'

'Oh, really? Well, it doesn't matter now, does it? You're free to go. You get your passport back, and you can return to your house because we're leaving.'

'Really? It's true? I can really go?'

'You think I'd lie to you, sweetie? Who knows what—'

'You just did that one, Herb, but you're a darling.' The smile faded. 'Be honest with me, Herbie. Are you going to get them?'

'Depends.'

'On what?'

'On whether any of them are still around to be got. I do my best for you, eh?'

There were tears in her eyes and she gave Kruger a massive hug, which was rather like trying to hug a bear. 'I can really go?' she asked again.

'Really. I should take a holiday if I were you.'

'Maybe I will. Maybe that's what I need.'

Even as they talked, people like Ginger, Kenny Boyden and Micky were packing papers into boxes in Gus's study. Later a security van would take them to London and they would be deposited at Vauxhall Cross to await the tender mercies of the analysts.

They caught American Airlines 107 out of Heathrow at six o'clock. Hisham would be on the BA flight 179 leaving at six-thirty. Ginger, in the guise of a taxi driver, was taking him to the airport and there had been many confidential telephone calls from Vauxhall Cross and Warminster to make certain that Bex and Herbie did not bump into Hisham in the Terminal.

The aim was to get Herbie Kruger and DCI Olesker

into JFK before Hisham. The way had been smoothed at that end also.

Before leaving Warminster, Herb sat down opposite Hisham and put matters to him in an unfriendly, austere and brutal manner.

'If we could use someone else we would, and you'd be dead and buried without anyone being the wiser,' he began. 'Hisham, don't doubt for a moment that you'll be watched all the way. If you deviate or fail to report to us, then we'll close you down permanently. You understand that?'

Hisham made it very plain that he understood. He was a terrified man, and Herbie bothered him almost more than the thought of being thrown to the *Amn-al-Amm* in Iraq. Herb detected the fear, like a wild beast scenting terror from a human. He warned Hisham that he should – as he put it – 'act as normal. Be yourself. Don't hint to any of those clowns you'll be working with. Just keep it light. Do as you're told by them, and also do it right for us. I tell you, Mr Silwani, that the slightest deviation will mean you're out of the loop – for ever.'

On the flight over, they talked and, for about two hours, Bex Olesker went to sleep, her head dropping sideways onto Big Herbie's shoulder. At one point she almost came awake, but grunted, made a mmmmming sound and snuggled closer.

Herbie did not get any sleep, but vastly enjoyed the time he spent with Bex's head in close proximity. She smelled, he thought, of wild violets, but what the hell, he told himself; what do I know about wild violets?

In England, while all three players were rumbling across the Atlantic, a team of SAS soldiers arrived on the outskirts of the village of Cowley in rural Oxfordshire. They were backed up by police and four members of the Security Service, plus Tony Worboys, who was kept well back out of sight.

A trace on the telephone number given to them

by Ramsi and confirmed by Hisham had pinpointed an old farmhouse, recently renovated, on the outskirts of the village.

They went in at nine o'clock, just when the three men who were *Yussif* had been taking their evening meal. Only one of the men bravely tried to go for an Uzi which was lying on a chair a few feet from the table. He died instantly, and his body was removed quietly in an unmarked van.

The remaining pair – one ex-military intelligence officer, and the other an agent of the Iraqi Foreign Intelligence Service – stood straight-backed, but with heads bowed. They looked like proud senior officers surrendering themselves to their enemy.

The SAS stayed on to act as guards, while two of the MI5 officers, both women, remained behind to interrogate the two men who were left. The inquisitors were exceptionally good and had read both Arabic and Hebrew at Cambridge. They began by completely breaking down the pair of *Yussif* men, telling them all the information they had on the *Intiqam* teams in both the UK and the USA.

The young women also did a subtle piece of second guessing, based on the fact that the number had been tapped by the Security Service from the moment it was traced. They knew – so they said – that there were constant monitoring calls made from Germany and Switzerland. They indicated that they also possessed all the codewords used between *Yussif* and their monitors.

The pair of men who were now the only link *Intiqam* had left in Britain complied with all the requests made by the inquisitors. For them it was humiliating to be questioned like this by women, but the alternatives offered to them – such as public humiliation, or word passed to the Leader of their country, together with their live bodies – were more terrifying.

From that moment everything was done by the book. Local people did not detect anything wrong. They did not even see any troops in the area. Life went on as placidly as usual.

What nobody knew at that point was a meeting between *Claudius* and *Jasmine* had taken place early that afternoon. Part of the coded ad in the London *Times* had indicated a four- to five-day wait before any contact should be made.

They met outside St Patrick's Cathedral, and walked together across the road, and down to the crowded area in front of the Rockefeller Plaza.

Jasmine gave *Claudius* a detailed account of the state of play, including the fact that there was a possibility they would be moving to Washington DC very soon. 'Then it's really going down?' It was a rhetorical question from *Claudius*.

'It looks very like it. If you have a number, I can call you once we have the complete information. You'll need to know the exact times and the nature of *Magic Lightning.*'

Claudius gave *Jasmine* two numbers, only to be used in an emergency.

The entire meeting lasted twenty minutes, then *Claudius* wandered off while *Jasmine* stayed a little longer, bathed in the sticky heat and watched the rollerblading going on below. In a couple of months' time this would be a skating rink. *Jasmine* wondered if death or worse would come between now and then.

American Airlines Flight 107 landed at JFK ten minutes early, at eight twenty-five on a clear warm evening. At the jetway they were met by one of the Embassy people from Washington DC, and a pair of FBI Special Agents who hurried them through the usually interminable immigration and customs checks, helped with the small baggage, and then drove them into Manhattan. On the way through the airport they checked the arrivals monitors and saw that Hisham's British Airways flight was also on time. He would be going through the endless routines with Customs and Immigration in around half an hour's time, which meant they could not expect his call-in for around an hour.

They were to stay in an apartment in the luxurious Trump Tower, often used by the British for short-stay diplomats. Their own people from DC had readied the large and comfortable flat that afternoon, putting in extra telephones, colour-coded so that they could immediately know which direct and safe line they were on – one to Vauxhall Cross, another directly to the Resident's office in DC, while a third and fourth were local, for dealing with the people on the ground.

The first call came in just as they had chosen rooms, unpacked, and generally settled in. The man from the British Embassy was still with them as he had been instructed to stay until they knew all the equipment was working properly.

The call was from a section of listeners, holed up in a cramped apartment off East 57th. Hisham had followed orders to the letter. The two remaining members of the American team were, it appeared, living in style as Mr and Mrs Walid Jaffid at the Parker Meridien Hotel. He had been instructed to check in and contact them in their suite – 6102. Hisham had also confirmed the number he had been given was definitely the telephone number for the *Yussif* team in the United States.

'So, we're off and running,' the man from the Embassy said. He received a curt nod from Herbie, who was not about to pass on any extraneous information to anyone outside what he considered to be a charmed circle.

As soon as the Embassy contact left to take the shuttle from La Guardia back to DC, Herbie put in a call to Vauxhall Cross. He was patched through to Worboys who was at home. They spoke for some fifteen minutes, after which Herb decided they should get some food sent up.

'What you fancy, then, Bex?' he asked, giving her the big open smile.

'About sixty hours of sleep.' She looked as though she had been run ragged. 'Then I'd like to go out and splurge on clothes and stuff I'd never even think of in England.'

'Maybe your day will come. Seriously, no food?'

'No food. Seriously. I need sleep.'

'Then I think I'll have a Reuben on Rye with fries and some coffee. Maybe also apple pie à la mode.' He turned the room service menu upside down and reached for the phone.

'Just a snack, eh?' Bex gave a winning little laugh and tottered towards her bedroom.

In the Parker Meridien, Walid and Khami were indulging in their favourite indoor sport when the telephone rang with a message from *Yussif* saying that help was on the way, very near at hand.

'There is an English saying,' Walid groaned as he gave Khami the news. 'Two is company. Three is a crowd.'

'He won't actually be sharing this suite, will he?' She sounded panic-stricken.

'Not if I have anything to do with it. You want the handcuffs off?'

'No, my prince. Just have your evil way with me . . . Please, Walid! Please!'

Hisham had done everything they had told him to do. Now he took a cab to the Parker Meridien where there was a room reserved for him under the name of Dr Sa'dun Zaidan.

They showed him his room and he thought, 'This is the greatest luxury to which I have ever been exposed.' He then put a house call through to suite 6102.

'My old friend, Walid,' he said. 'This is just to let you know I am here, in the hotel. Have you any plans for this evening?'

'I'm afraid I'm going to be tied up for most of the evening. But we *do* have things to talk about, so perhaps we could breakfast together.'

'Certainly. What time?'

'Let's say noon, Sa'dun. Noon would do nicely. I fear we do not have much time left in New York. I think we will soon have to leave for Washington.'

'Really? How soon?'

'I suspect either tomorrow evening or the day after.'

'I have never been to Washington.'

'There's plenty to do there, my friend.'

'So I've been told. Tomorrow then.' He replaced the receiver, then lifted it again and punched in the number he had spoken to after making the obligatory call to *Yussif* from New York's JFK Airport.

Down in the vast marble lobby of the hotel, an FBI Special Agent was talking privately to the Duty Manager. 'No, no there's nothing to be alarmed about,' the Special Agent responded to an anxious question. 'The Jaffids are very close to the royal family of their country and they, in turn, have been concerned about their well-being. They get jumpy these very rich Arabs, and it appears that they disapproved of the Jaffids being in New York without the usual bodyguards.'

The Duty Manager was checking through the Jaffid account and the staff notes. 'I'm glad to hear that,' he said, still sounding a shade uncertain. 'The Bell Captain *did* put a query in to management. It says here that the bellboy who dealt with their luggage drew attention to the fact that it all seemed to be brand-new and had no trace of an airline tag on it. In fact no tags at all.'

'Probably their security advisers.' The Special Agent sounded unconcerned about the matter. 'Some security experts think it is best to remove all traces of tags and labels from luggage. Anyway, sir, do not be alarmed if any of my people come into the hotel to keep a discreet eye on them. We don't want to alert them. I dare say they wouldn't take kindly to their relatives poking their noses

357

into what is really Mr and Mrs Jaffid's own business. After all, they're paying us so we should stick around.'

'It won't go further than this office.' The Duty Manager rose and extended his hand.

That same night a carton which had obviously been packed with professional care arrived at JFK from Geneva. The instructions were for forwarding to Washington National to await pick-up by a Dr Ali Duba. The carton was not heavy, but it was well labelled as *Medical Supplies. Do Not Open. Do Not Subject To X-Rays*. It had been cleared from Geneva and bore the official stamp of Schtubble Laboratories, Rue de Lyon, Genève. The Customs authorization claimed the contents included material which could be damaged by exposure to the air.

An hour earlier a call had gone to London's Heathrow Airport from a Dr Jonathan Schtubble, of Schtubble Laboratories, Geneva, and was forwarded to the Air Freight offices. Dr Schtubble was obviously agitated, and wanted the status of a similar package. He quoted the waybill number and impressed upon the manager of the Air Freight office that the package was extremely important.

After a short wait, he was informed that the carton had arrived twenty-four hours earlier but had not been picked up. 'I shall see what can be done,' the doctor told the manager of the Air Freight office. 'There has been a serious error. The package should have gone to a Dr Ali Duba in New York. I'll try to get someone to come down to you and sign the requisite documents so that it can be forwarded to New York.'

The biochemist put down the telephone in his office at Schtubble Laboratories in Geneva. 'What'll be the best thing to do?' He looked at the other two men, wearing white lab coats. 'You realize this fellow who calls himself Kingpin gave us the okay to dispatch the packages. We've done all the work . . .'

'And been paid a million each in American dollars,' added one of the three-man team. 'I think we should at least try to get back to Kingpin. After all, Jonathan, both those parcels had this address and *your* name on them.'

'I think we should definitely get hold of Kingpin.' The third man sounded even more anxious. 'For heaven's sake, that stuff is dangerous. A dozen special canisters filled with enough Toxic Strep A, heavily loaded with necrotizing fasciitis enzymes, to kill half the population of the UK are not the kind of things we can leave hanging around at Heathrow – especially with this address on it. Call Kingpin now. There's no option. We *have* to talk to him.'

25

The *Biwāba* was angry. He did not vent his anger at
either of the *Intiqam* teams, or those who handled them
through *Yussif*. The *Biwāba* was a very fair man.
He vented his anger on the one to blame – himself. He
meditated on the problem and placed it squarely at
his own door. He should have waited until both teams
were absolutely ready. He had not even anticipated the
complete collapse of the British team, but in his haste he
had issued the orders to the Swiss scientists to go ahead,
finish the items and dispatch them.

The idea was sound, and had come to him through
reading various medical journals and newspapers. The
Biwāba was a considerable linguist. The newspapers had
made much fuss and dubbed the bacteria as a 'mystery
killer virus which had the power to eat flesh'.

As the entire reason for *Intiqam* was to destabilize
the governments of Britain, America, France and Italy,
he had reasoned that if you could expose them to the
so-called mystery virus, it might just kill off some 50–60
per cent of the people concerned. So, he had sent for a
notable Iraqi doctor who had been trained in Edinburgh.
A man called Aziz Jibril who laughed heartily when he
talked of the 'Mystery Virus'.

'There is no mystery,' Dr Jibril said. 'In the West,
the medical profession has been aware of this since
the seventeen thirties. The problem is that the normal
Streptococcus Group A lies in every human being, and is
sometimes capable of becoming deadly. There are several
thousand strains, but only a minute percentage produce
deadly enzymes. The relatively harmless strains produce
unpleasant things like a strep throat infection or an ear

infection. There is a link to scarlet fever and to what used to be called puerperal fever. They are also sometimes the cause of meningitis.

'In Britain, it is normal practice to hit any potential strep infection with powerful cocktails of antibiotics, but the real problem is diagnosis. We do not really know how the Strep A bacteria become infected, but when they do undergo a change it works very quickly. They can produce enzymes of a gangrenous type called necrotizing fasciitis which finally contribute to the destruction of fat and tissue. The bacteria do *not* eat flesh, they poison it, and if not diagnosed very fast can kill rapidly. Hence the use of large quantities of antibiotics at the first hint of a strep infection.'

'Would it be possible to reconstruct this deadly type of Strep A?' the *Biwãba* asked innocently.

'Very simple indeed,' the doctor nodded. 'Original Strep A bacteria can have enzymes added in sterile laboratory conditions. It would be potentially very dangerous, but this can be done – probably *is* done for research purposes.'

'I am concerned,' the *Biwãba* tried to sound off-hand, 'I am concerned that this might be the kind of agent used in germ warfare by our enemies. Would it be possible to deliver this virus?'

'Probably,' the doctor scowled in a concerned way. 'It could certainly be put under pressure in a vacuum. Like an aerosol spray. I do not see it being of much use in conventional delivery systems, but the spray would work excellently if you could feed it into air-conditioning or heating ducts. Something like that would be very effective – and also very cruel, my friend. You could bring many enemies down on to your head. You're not really thinking of experimenting with this, are you?'

'Of course not,' the *Biwãba* replied smoothly. 'It would be diabolical.'

During that time, he thought more and more of the possibilities. If the toxic form of Streptococcus A could be introduced, via specially constructed sprays, into the heating or air-conditioning ducts of the House of Commons in London or the Capitol in Washington while the governments were sitting, there was a chance that 100 per cent of the men and women who were members of the government would become quickly infected. The further possibility was that around 50–60 per cent would die in a matter of twenty-four hours.

His main precaution would have to be making the introduction of the bacteria foolproof and untraceable back to Iraq. Money, he was certain, could buy the necessary technicians, but they would have to be dealt with at arm's length.

Money was no problem. The forged hundred-dollar bills had already proved to be undetectable and the *Biwāba* had access to huge amounts in banks around the world. All he had to do was buy himself the people who could do the work under safe conditions.

He chose Switzerland because of the Swiss reputation for secrecy, and it took only two weeks for his agents to discover the Schtubble Laboratory in Geneva. The biochemist who ran Schtubble was the grandson of the man who had originally started the business. He was also the man who had run the Schtubble Laboratory into the ground.

To the passing tourist, Geneva is just a beautiful lakeside city, noted for the wonderful view of Mont Blanc's shimmering white cap, and the famed Jet d'Eau which rises some 150 metres high from the lake. It is also renowned for its great hotels and restaurants. Tourists may not realize that Geneva is also the prestigious last resort of many very wealthy families, which makes the city a target for class consciousness. The weekly trippers and packaged visitors do not even begin to scratch the surface of the varied strata of rich, famous and infamous who use Geneva as a playground.

Entrance to society in what was once the centre of Calvinism – with John Calvin running his own secret police, which included children informing on their parents' lapses of morality – now has its clubs and cliques, its balls and parties, sometimes on a Bacchanalian scale.

It was Jonathan Schtubble who, for a short but memorable time, dug deeply into the profits built up over the years by his grandfather and father to become a playboy of this section of the Western world. Alas, he awoke one morning to discover that his current income from the modest laboratory was all that was left of a considerable fortune.

The *Biwāba*'s agents unearthed this in a couple of weeks, for two of them were wealthy Iraqis with access to the high-flying set of Geneva. The *Biwāba* was informed, and within a month, one of his glib-tongued assistants sat with Jonathan Schtubble over lunch in the Parc des Eaux-Vives, gently bringing him round to the matter of a toxic Strep A bacteria.

At first, Jonathan was appalled, and wanted to know why anyone would want to produce a toxic product such as this. He was told that new laboratories would soon be operating in London and New York as part of a research project concerned with the detection and fighting of necrotizing fasciitis. They were willing to pay a great deal of money for samples to be made up in droplet form within aerosol-type sprays.

The word money brought Jonathan's moral scruples toppling from the high ground. He would need at least two associates and money to create the correct sterile conditions in his laboratory, including clothing and incinerators. He would have to see exactly what kind of cash they were talking about.

The *Biwāba*'s agent mentioned one million for each person involved, plus the outlay on whatever new equipment was needed. It was an offer Schtubble could not refuse. He knew the names of two associates who would do very well. Over coffee and a fine brandy he shook hands on the deal.

Now it was all done and the aerosol canisters had

been shipped in very secure packaging. Indeed, the aerosols would not even work, as they were sealed to the top of each unit and could only be operated by a special device being made by a company in England: a company which imagined it was assisting with AIDS research. The *Biwāba*'s problem was that the dozen units shipped to the United Kingdom were sitting, uncollected, at Heathrow. There were two things that needed doing and he dealt with the first by making a secure telephone call to Switzerland – not to the Schtubble Laboratory, but to a telephone number miles from Geneva. To a villa on the shores of Lake Lucerne.

'Richardson,' a voice announced at the Swiss end, the one name clipped out and sounding very British.

'I'm sorry,' the *Biwāba* spoke slowly, as though he were bemused. 'I am sorry. I think I have got a wrong number.'

'Who did you want to speak with?'

'An old friend of mine. A Dr Akkur. A-K-K-U-R.'

'Sorry, old chap. You *have* got a wrong number. Wish I could help you.'

The man who had called himself Richardson put down the telephone. It was early afternoon, the sky was clear, and from where he sat Richardson could clearly see the 7,000-foot triangular crag which is Mount Pilatus.

For a moment he thought of the legends of Mount Pilatus – that, after Christ's crucifixion, the devil flew into the mountain with Pontius Pilate leaving his spirit to wander aimlessly around. The other story was that Pilate, overcome by remorse at sentencing Jesus, had come to this place, climbed the mountain and thrown himself down a deep abyss.

Richardson did not like leaving his charming lakeside villa, but there was always a need to make more money in order to keep up his preferred lifestyle. He rose to his feet, stretched and returned to the house. Within three hours he was on a train that would take him to Geneva.

Back in his villa, the *Biwāba* made another call.

This time to Germany. He spoke quietly for several minutes to the female voice that answered. In turn, the young woman who had taken the call – in Munich, as it happened – punched out the country code for the United Kingdom, followed by the area code and the number of the farm in Oxfordshire.

The two members of the *Yussif* team who were still alive had not understood why the military men and two of the officers they took to be part of the British Security Service had not taken them away and put them in a secure prison. When the telephone rang they both realized why these people had held them in the farmhouse, fed them, and been generally forgiving towards them.

One of the officers took out an automatic pistol and asked which of them would normally answer the telephone. The older of the *Yussif* team nodded and pointed to himself, noticing, for the first time, that a tape machine and a pair of headphones had been attached to the instrument and the other security officer was hurrying to put on the headphones.

'No tricks,' said the one with the gun. 'No messages. If you deviate from your normal practice, I will simply shoot you through the head.'

The Arab reached out for the telephone.

'One more thing,' the man with the gun put the barrel to the Arab's head. 'We know all your codes. We will know if you try to alert someone at the other end.'

'Yes?' said the Arab into the mouthpiece after he picked up the handset.

'Is that Yussif?' asked a female voice in English, but with a thick, not unattractive, German accent.

'Sure. This is Yussif. Who . . . ?'

'I have a message from the Kingpin. My name is Legion. There has been an error. A box of the things which were to be used for that last experiment is waiting for pick-up at Heathrow Air Freight. It has been sent to a Dr Ali Duba for collection in London. It should have gone to Dr Duba in Washington. Kingpin says you should go to the Heathrow Air Freight office and deal with the paperwork. Have it sent to Dr Duba for pick-up at Washington National, via JFK New York.' She then gave the air waybill number and broke the connection.

'Do either of you know what this is about?'

There was a long pause, before the elder of the two men hesitatingly said that this consignment would be connected to the codewords *Magic Lightning*. Earlier, they had both admitted to knowing the words but not comprehending their meaning. 'It is the end game of the *Intiqam* operation,' the younger man had volunteered. 'But we have not been told what this entails.'

The two *Yussif* men were taken into another room while the Security Service people spoke to their Head Office. The outcome was twofold. Within the hour they began to pack up and leave the farmhouse. The two Arabs were hurried to a detention centre near Wimbledon, usually referred to by MI5 as Centre Court. There, they would be under a constant watch and, later, a marathon debriefing inquisition.

Also within the hour a modified Land Rover arrived at the Air Freight area at London's Heathrow Airport. The rear section of the Land Rover was encased in thick armour plating, making a bomb-proof shelter on wheels.

There was considerable activity at the Air Freight area, following a call from the Metropolitan Police Bomb Disposal Unit. The entire set of warehouses had been cleared, and the duty manager had marked exactly where the package from Switzerland was located.

One member of the Bomb Disposal Team entered the warehouse which contained the package. He wore the standard heavy anti-blast suit and helmet, making him look like an old-fashioned deep-sea diver. The package was placed inside a bomb blanket and carried to the Land Rover, locked into the secure blast-proof rear and driven away to a disposal and testing site five miles from Slough. To the cognoscenti, the place was known as the Friendly Bomb Complex – from the former Poet Laureate's, the late Sir John Betjeman's, poem which began, 'Come friendly bombs and fall on Slough'.

They X-rayed the package in the large open, rough field behind the buildings and immediately discovered that there was no apparent explosive content. To be certain, they smelled it with electronic sniffers, and when they were certain it was free of anything that might go bump in the night, they opened it up.

The twelve aerosols were padded and packed between foam egg-crates, with extra foam taped around each one. The removal of one aerosol showed that it should contain *Brutus – The Friendly Hair Spray for Unfriendly Hair*, but they did not believe a word of it, except the legend that it was 'Made in Switzerland'.

After further examination it was decided that the entire twelve aerosols should be sent, immediately, for tests at the one Chemical Warfare Centre that remained in the UK. The consignment was driven overnight. Testing started on the next morning, though it would be some days before the full analysis came in.

Carole left the Dower House at around three that afternoon. She took two suitcases and a pair of briefcases with her. She drove her own car, one of the new Saab 900s, and within thirty minutes knew she was not alone. It was just as she had expected.

On Herbie's instructions, backed up by threats from Deputy CSIS Worboys, they played it very long indeed, using the relay tactic.

Carole counted three motorcycles changing position every fifteen minutes or so. She even pulled down the sunshield on the passenger side to give herself an extra mirror, but knew, within the hour, that they would be waiting for her when she arrived at Heathrow.

For the layman, who watched this kind of thing on television and the movies, an airport or a railway station was the easiest place to run a surveillance. You simply loitered around and, once the target had been picked up, it was a matter of child's play.

Maybe this is true of the unwitting target, but Carole was cognizant and had taken precautions. She checked in for BA 179 to JFK New York, feeling the hot breath of a team very close behind her.

They were still there when she went through security on to the air side. After that she vanished, but the team remained happy that she would soon be on her way, posting four footpads at the air-side security to be certain she did not come back into the ground side again. Carole had simply gone into the ladies' rest room and disappeared.

In the restroom she dumped one of her briefcases, turned her reversible raincoat, put on a pair of horn-rimmed spectacles, retrieved the blonde wig from the dumped briefcase, set it in place and topped the whole thing off with a soft hat. She even passed one of the team as she came out into the concourse and was not recognized.

She had squirrelled away an extra pair of passports from her time in the service, and the one she now used carried her own name with a tarted-up photograph wearing the blonde wig. She simply headed to the air-side desk for BA 179 and pulled her switch, as they used to say in the bad days of the Cold War, spinning a believable story that she had just received a call which changed all her plans. Had they got room on the 5.45 p.m. Concorde to Washington Dulles? – knowing very well that there was at least one seat, for she had cancelled a booking in the name of Hacking from an air-side telephone only a few feet from the Concorde lounge.

Yes, they said, there was room available. They would even get her baggage brought over from BA 179 which took off on time, with the surveillance team wrongly assuming that Carole had to be on board. They called New York, alerted their people at that end, then went back to the Office satisfied that – though they had not actually seen her board the aircraft – Carole was on her way.

When, several hours later, the news came back that Carole Keene had not arrived at JFK, there was fury in Vauxhall Cross. Some said they had never seen nor heard Worboys in such a vile temper.

When they finally checked and cross-checked they came up with the answers, and one of Worboys' aides called Kruger who had reached New York by then: but that was in the future.

At about the same time as BA 189 – SST to Dulles – was beginning its take-off roll, the telephone rang in Jonathan Schtubble's private apartment in Geneva. He was dressing prior to taking a spectacular red-headed girl out to dinner and what he hoped would be a more physical dessert.

'Schtubble.'

'Dr Schtubble, I have something for you and your two colleagues.' The caller spoke in French, the language of choice in Geneva.

'You have something for me?'

'You and your colleagues. Mr Kingpin is very pleased with your actions regarding the consignment that went astray. He has authorized me to hand over a bonus of one million dollars to each of you. In cash.'

'He has?'

'I have it here, and I'd like to deal with the matter as quickly as possible. Can you get your colleagues together now, tonight? I would suggest we meet at your laboratory, in, say, half an hour.'

'Well, I'll try to get them, but I don't—'

'I have to leave by a late flight, Dr Schtubble. It would be most inconvenient for me to delay this matter. I do require signatures from each of you.'

'I'll do what I can.'

'And I will be at your laboratory in half an hour. I will wait for twenty minutes. If you haven't arrived

369

by then I shall leave. I will not be back in Geneva for another six weeks.'

'Wait. We'll be there.'

He caught his colleagues at their own apartments, and they both postponed plans in order to get to the Schtubble Laboratory as fast as cars and taxis could carry them.

Richardson watched as they arrived. He sat quietly in the back of his rented Mercedes parked some distance from the laboratory, and did not leave the car until he had counted them all in.

He wore a smart dark business suit and carried a pigskin briefcase. His hands were encased in black, soft leather driving gloves. They let him into the building almost before he rang the bell.

'I'm so glad you could all make it,' he told them. 'It would have been inconvenient to have come back, even in six weeks' time.'

They all shook hands and Richardson put the briefcase onto a small table which he moved in front of the chair he had been offered. They were gathered in the small recreation room off the main laboratories.

'Please, gentlemen, sit down. I am a notary public and will require signatures on certain documents I have here.'

'A million each?' Jonathan Schtubble still sounded incredulous.

'You used your initiative.' Richardson looked up and smiled at them. 'Our friend Kingpin is a generous man who likes to repay good common sense.' He opened the briefcase, and smiled again. Not even looking down, he lifted the weapon from its hiding place.

The Ithaca Stakeout is a short weapon, only 13.23 inches in length, but based on the Model 37M shotgun. It is easily concealed, has a pump action and comes in two calibre sizes – 12-gauge or the more manageable 20-gauge. The Stakeout only fires shot-loading cartridges, as heavy slugs would make the recoil very difficult to handle.

Richardson started on his left, and fired three 20-gauge cartridges at high speed as he moved, shot, pumped, moved, shot, pumped, moved and shot again. There was very little left of the faces and chests of the three victims and the room reeked of smoke and blood. Calmly he walked to the exit, being careful to step over any blood splatters. In the laboratory he removed the other item from his briefcase; a device the size of a beer can. He tapped in the timer so that it would explode in fifteen minutes, spreading a Napalm-like flame which would engulf the laboratory in seconds after detonation.

He then returned the shotgun to his briefcase and quietly left the building.

At the railway station he found that he had half an hour to spare, so he used a card-operated public telephone to call the man he knew as Akkur. In a few hours he would be back in his villa on the shores of Lake Lucerne. By that time the distinctive, short-barrelled shotgun would be at the bottom of the lake, and he would be a million dollars richer. It was good doing business with Akkur. You always knew exactly where you were with him. The money would be in his Zurich numbered account by the morning.

Jasmine, as arranged, telephoned Claudius late that evening.

'It's going down this week, beginning on Tuesday,' *Jasmine* told him.

'It's going to be tight. The Labour Day holiday comes up at the end of the week.'

'They say that's why it has to start on Tuesday. They want people to be as jumpy as neurotic fleas, and it'll probably force a special session at the Capitol.'

'Well, I'll no doubt see you there. Good luck.'

They never stayed on any telephone line for longer than a minute.

Declan Norton had slipped into England unnoticed.

He wore a very simple disguise, and came via the Isle of Man. Nobody looked at him twice.

The two other men who, with Norton, made up the Active Service Unit were back from Scotland and waiting for him at the new safe house he had arranged for them in Camden Town: a five up and five down desirable little detached place with a small garden and a row of four poplar trees at the far end. The other member of this particular unit – Billy Boyle, their bomb-maker – did not return with them. While in Edinburgh one bright morning, Boyle had gone for a walk. He did not return, and for a while the other two FFIRA men were concerned lest Boyle had been arrested.

They need not have worried. Days before, Billy Boyle had decided that it was wrong for him to carry on what had been his life's work. He was an intelligence man and felt that the ceasefire between the Provos and the Brits should be held. For a number of years he had been seeing a young Scottish widow in Aberdeen. Now he took the plunge. He had hung up his detonators, fuses and electronic timers for the last time. A month or two later Boyle married the widow, under an assumed name. They presumably lived happily ever after, for he was never heard of again.

The weather was mild and they had the windows open as they sat around after their evening meal, talking strategy.

'What're the targets, then, Declan?' Sean asked. Sean O'Donnel was young and full of the fire of enthusiasm.

'If it's bombs you're talking, you can forget about it.' Declan knew exactly what he wanted out of these two. 'That Eye-rackian lot had about as much terror in them as a spider has to a whore in her bath. I wanted to get them to do the real job and finish the people who were behind the business in '84, but they botched the whole damned thing. They got one of them, and that clever bugger Keene got his before any of us started. Now we might have to go further afield.'

'But isn't that more in the line of your own private settling, Declan?' Fergus was the oldest of the bunch and carried a lot of old-style Provisional IRA baggage with him.

'Now, see here, Fergus.' Declan had about him that thick toughness born of the years of struggle and anguish. 'There were men and women in the Provos that I made a pledge to when I came in with you boys. *They* felt the Provos hadn't extracted revenge for those deaths during *Kingmaker*. That was to have been the spectacular of all time, and what happened? They got nowhere. Four young people shot down like dogs, then the thing covered up by the bloody Brits. I stand by my original promise. We have to do away with the last two. The feller Worboys, and that fat German oaf, Kruger.' He looked around him, as though challenging anyone to test him, or make yet another objection. Nobody moved to speak.

'So, Worboys is still here at his damned great house out in Harrow, but the German's off and running. We know he's in America. New York, we suspect. I'm waiting for one of our lads there to get a fix on him. In the meantime, I think we should make sure of the man Worboys.' He hunched forward to explain exactly what he thought would be the best way.

In New York, Walid, Khami and Hisham ate dinner together in a pleasant little restaurant on West 56th Street.

As they reached the end of the meal, Walid told them that they would be on the road tomorrow. He slid an airline ticket across the table to Hisham, and added that they would have to move very fast. 'We're booked into an exclusive hotel. The Willard,' he dropped his voice. Walid had been searching the restaurant with his eyes since the minute they had sat down. He saw nothing to alarm him and the place was very popular. It was as if, he thought, there was a wall of noise around them.

People talked and gesticulated, laughed and called to one another in a friendly atmosphere.

'We go by different flights, but the reservations are made just as here. The thinking is sound. Certainly the authorities will not be looking for us in such an expensive place.' He leaned close to Hisham. 'I will be paying your account when you check out. The hotel knows this. You take the shuttle, then there is one more thing you must do as soon as you get into the hotel. When we get back to the Parker Meridien tonight, there will be a message for you at the desk. It is a pick-up waybill for a package you must bring to the Willard from National Airport. I will do the other jobs. At least this part of *Intiqam* will work.'

Five minutes after they paid the bill and left, an elderly man wearing a hearing aid picked up his briefcase, fiddled with the lock and left. He walked towards Sixth Avenue and hailed a cab. Fifteen minutes later he was with Big Herbie, Bex Olesker and two FBI men in the service apartment in Trump Tower.

'It's going down,' were his first words, as he opened the briefcase to disclose a maze of electronic equipment. It was one of the latest surveillance tape-machines with a very high-powered directional microphone in the handle. Together they listened to the conversation between Walid, Khami and Hisham. The equipment filtered out all extraneous noise, so they heard the entire conversation clearly.

Later, at one in the morning, Hisham left the Parker Meridien, walked down to Fifth Avenue and found a public telephone. Before leaving Warminster they had given him a number to call. Now, as *Ishmael*, he used it for the third time.

He was telling them what they already knew, but at least he was proving his loyalty.

In London, early the next morning, Tony Worboys' new car blew up in a spectacular sheet of flame. The

Range Rover was there one minute and gone, in a pillar of fire, the next. The people who saw it happen said it was like an illusion, the vanishing of a car blown to fragments.

26

'Just because you think it's all clear, doesn't mean to say that you should take any chances. When your life is under threat by these people, it remains under threat until they've all been either put away, called off, or frightened off.' So the SIS Head of Internal Security to Tony Worboys. 'My advice, sir, is to stay here, with your family, until everything's off the books.'

'I want my bloody car. Damn it all, it should've been delivered here in the first place.'

Worboys had been ecstatic to learn that twenty-four hours after the Range Rover had blown up in front of his house, the Office had okay'd the insurance and ordered a new, identical car to be delivered.

In a snafu which should not have surprised him, Worboys had the keys to the new vehicle. The Range Rover itself had been left at The Hall, Harrow Weald, with a set of spare keys shoved through the letter-box. The people who were checking his house daily had brought in the extra keys, leaving the car sitting idly in the turning circle in front of the house.

'I have an appointment the other side of Heathrow at eleven o'clock. I'd like to drive there myself, in my own damned car.' This was about as angry as Worboys ever got.

The Head of Internal Security sighed. 'Well, I'll get a couple of the lads to pick it up and bring it over here to Vauxhall Cross, sir. They'll sniff it, and check it, and mark it okay. Then they'll bring it here. No sweat. But I have to advise you that, if you go out, I want a chase car with some of my lads in it behind you all the way.'

'Is that really necessary?'

'It's 800 per cent necessary, sir.'

Reluctantly, Young Worboys agreed. He had been getting much flak from his wife who, not unnaturally, was keen to get back to her own hearth and home. Now they had cocked up the delivery of his car. It was nine in the morning. He would have to leave no later than ten.

In New York it was four in the morning, that dreary hour of the night when people finally died in hospital wards, and the morale of men and women under pressure was at its lowest ebb.

In London, Worboys was arguing with the Head of SIS Internal Security. In their service apartment high in Trump Tower, New York, Big Herbie Kruger and DCI Bex Olesker were far from being at their lowest ebb. They had retired at around midnight with the knowledge that they had to be on their way, by car, to Washington DC at six.

The entire team would be on the move, and once in DC the whole operation against the last three members of the *Intiqam* groups would be brought to a quick, sharp conclusion. The FBI and the Secret Service were confident that they had the entire thing buttoned up. Ted Mercer, who led the now more streamlined FBI Counter-Intelligence Department, had given his word that the unholy trio – as they had dubbed them – would be arrested with the explosives, and whatever else they were planning to use, actually on them. After the slip-ups during the World Trade Center bombing, nobody was going to take any chances with this lot. 'Catch them *in flagrante delicto*,' Mercer said. 'We'll have a clear case that way. Nobody's going to wriggle off the hook.'

Herbie had misgivings. After all, they had the surveillance tapes; they knew where the trio was holed up – in one of New York's most expensive hotels – so what were they waiting for? He made it plain that he wanted it on the record that he was against playing the waiting game.

377

In the wee small hours he made it plain again to Bex. 'Don't like it. Don't see it's necessary to wait. We've got 'em cold here, so what's with the screwing around?'

'I didn't know anyone was screwing around, Herb.' Bex looked all innocent and virginal, as she had done when she woke him at just before three.

Herbie had plunged into sleep almost before his head hit the pillow. A deep sleep, with an undercurrent of strange dreams. He was on a tropical beach, ungainly in swimming trunks. Carole was there with him, taunting him and laughing. 'Just ring this number, Herbie,' she shrieked. 'That'll settle it for all time. Dial the number now.' She picked up a conch and it turned into a telephone. He was about to dial when Bex appeared beside him, shouting, 'Herb, don't be a fool. You *know* what she's after. Wake up, Herb. Wake up . . . Wake up . . .'

He felt the hand on his shoulder, gently shaking him, but only half comprehending that he was back in the real world.

'Got to make this telephone call, Bex. Just wait a minute.' His hand was stretched out and he could feel the instrument gripped tightly.

'Please, Herb. Please wake up.'

He was awake. The bedside light was on, and Bex stood, leaning down, her hand on his shoulder. His first thought was that Bex in her night attire was more ravishing than in her usual business suits, or the denim skirts and casual tops she wore.

She seemed to be swathed in silk. A white *peignoir*, trimmed with lace at the neck.

'What the hell's up, Bex?' He was suddenly wide awake, his mind and body alert, butterflies chasing in his stomach. What, he wondered, had gone wrong now?

'Nothing's up. I'm sorry, Herb. I can't sleep. Something's bothering me, but it's just out of reach.' Then she added, in a kind of little girl voice, certainly not what you expected from a DCI attached to the anti-terrorist squad, 'I'm hungry as well.'

Herb's face split open into his broad smile. 'If you're hungry, call room service. If you want to talk, call me. Go, woman. Go call room service and I'll join you.'

'You want anything?' She still sounded a shade modest, as though waking Herbie had been a very daring thing to have done.

'No. Don' think so . . . Wait, yes. Coffee. Real coffee. Black and some tomato sandwiches. Tell them only small amount of butter, white bread, skinned tomatoes, little vinegar on the side – and salt. Tomato sandwiches without vinegar and salt is like kissing your sister.'

'Just one round?'

'Make it two. Who knows what I'll eat?'

'Just your normal, ordinary little midnight dorm feast,' she laughed. Herbie heard the peal of bells in her laughter even when she had left the room. Don' be an old fool, he thought to himself. Don' get stupid. Your day is done. Forget the old snake and keep the one-eyed monk out of this. You are stupid, Eberhardt Lukas Kruger.

He went into the bathroom, straightened his tousled hair, took notice of the thinning which gave him the look of having the start of a tonsure, and sprayed a couple of squirts of cologne around his neck. Then he brushed his teeth and marched into the living-room, where Bex sat on the edge of the sofa, her legs tucked under her.

'Now, mother, what's the matter?'

'Mother?'

'Hamlet.' He grinned again. 'When Hamlet goes into his Ma's boudoir and stabs Polonius in the arse.'

'Arras, Herb.'

'Sure. What's up, Bex?'

'I keep grasping at something someone said at Warminster. Can't quite get a handle on it. Something significant. I keep thinking it's something to do with the telephone logs. I know it's important, but it's just out of sight.'

'Okay. I got the logs in my briefcase.'

As he came back into the room carrying the briefcase, there was a soft knock at the door. He went over and peeped through the security fish-eye lens, then opened up to a crusty-looking waiter who wheeled in a tray containing a huge pot of coffee, the tomato sandwiches, vinegar, salt, pepper and a huge bowl of chef's salad – sliced hard-boiled eggs, lettuce, tomato, cucumber, shredded ham and cheese.

He signed the proffered bill and tipped the waiter who said, 'Have a nice day,' like a programmed robot.

'I see you're only having a small snack also, Bex,' cocking an eyebrow, opening up a couple of the sandwiches and dribbling vinegar onto them, followed by an alarming amount of salt.

'Christ, Herb, that much salt won't do you any good.'

'So, I live dangerously. Let's look at the logs. See if we can tickle your memory a bit.' He dug into the briefcase and produced the thick wedge of print-outs. 'Let's begin at the beginning. Go through it, call by call.'

'Okay. My feeling, Herb, is that we've missed something. Not followed up. That's always something that's haunted me in police work. Things happen so quickly that, somehow, in the hurly-burly . . .'

'Hurly-burly is good.'

'Well, with everything that's been going on, something got missed. That's what's really bugging me.'

Herbie looked her straight in the eyes, gave a quick professional nod and began to go through the logs.

'First we have the night of Gus's death. Call at around two-thirty in the morning. Carole Keene says it was Gus telling her he's on his way home. We know it was from a public telephone in Salisbury, but we have a big query. A missing hour and a half, right?'

'We have evidence that Gus left the magic club at one in the morning. Then he's missing as from then until two-thirty when he calls Carole.'

'Okay. Next call is the first big mystery. Five-thirty

in the morning. Carole says it must have been the cops because they used the telephone. They came and broke the news at four-thirty and had use of the telephone. That's all there in the log. They made three calls out – all to Salisbury. All correct. But this call is at five-thirty and the caller ID print-out shows it came from a public box at a service station on the M4 Motorway, not far from Heathrow.'

'Carole.' Bex sat up very straight. 'The one at five-thirty we know came from the Motorway Service Station. We know it. We have proof. It was answered, but Carole said she had no memory of it. Denied it right down the line. Just as she denied taking the call in the middle of the following night – well, early morning. Twenty-two hours after that proven call from the Motorway Service Station. We *know* that one came from New York. Carole denies answering it. But that's not the real problem. We *did* miss doing a cross-check. On the night of Gus's murder there *was* another call. Five fifty-seven. Twenty-seven minutes after the Motorway call. Carole picked up, said it was the CSIS. The monitors don't tell us a thing . . .'

'Which makes me suspect,' Herbie began. 'Damn. Damn, you're bloody right, Bex. Because we had no Caller ID trace showing on the log, I just believed Carole. The Chief would be calling from a secure phone. Secure phones give no ID signal. I took it on trust. My fault. I accepted that the five fifty-seven call *was* from the Old Man, but I didn't check . . .' His hand lunged for the telephone.

'There was a confirmed call from Heathrow itself at seven seventeen. Carole denied any call for her at that time . . .'

'I can reason that one out. It's the call at five fifty-seven I want to check.' He was already punching numbers.

In the SIS Headquarters at Vauxhall Cross, the switchboard lit up. 'My name's Kruger,' Herbie said quietly. 'I'm not on the books, but I *am* on a special assignment and I have to speak with C, if he's in.'

'One moment, sir.' The line seemed to go dead until a male voice answered, 'Duty Officer.'

Herbie went through the routine again – adding that it was very important – and was again asked to wait. 'Me, they have to check out,' he muttered at Bex. Then:

'Good morning, Mr Kruger. It must be very early in the morning your time.'

'Middle of the night, sir.'

'What can I do for you?'

'I have a question, sir. It should've been asked some time ago. On the night of Gus Keene's death – early morning – his widow took an unidentified call at five fifty-seven. She says it was you calling her, saying you were on your way to Warminster. I have to ask you, sir, did you call the widow Keene just before six that morning?'

There was a long pause, then the CSIS's voice again, terse, with underlying tension. 'Is this a very important point of evidence?'

'Very, sir.'

'Well, neither I nor my PA called Carole Keene that early. By five fifty-seven I was on the way to Warminster by helicopter. We gave no prior indication that I was going there. I went because I thought Carole probably needed to see me. I thought it would help. Worboys knew, but I did not make any call. Understood?'

'Absolutely, sir. Thank you.'

'Good hunting, Kruger.'

Big Herbie sighed, shook his head. 'One more call now. To Warminster, depends who's around.' At the distant end someone picked up and Kruger asked to speak with Martin Brook.

'Hey, Martin,' he greeted the new officer in charge of Warminster. 'Herbie. Look, do you have access to what equipment is in or out? . . . Sure, I know it's a pain, but that what we got computers for . . . Right. I want to know if poor old Gus ever returned his cellular scrambler. If not, I wouldn't mind knowing if it's just

382

knocking around the place . . . I give you this number? Sure.' He trotted out the number, said he would be waiting for the call, then hung up. Turning to Bex, who was gradually making her way through the chef's salad, he gave a little shrug. 'Worth a try.'

'Where are we, Herb? I've only had one side of the conversation.'

'We're in limbo. This much we know, the Chief did not make that call to Carole at five fifty-seven. She was telling us lies. So who made it? Whoever it was called from a secure line, which means the Office or Office property. Let me give you a for instance, Bex. A what if.'

'I know what you're going to say. A what if Gus did not die in that car? Right?'

'Would account for all the calls. Call from Gus, half two in the morning. Again call from Gus from public telephone on the Motorway, then another, on a secure line, twenty-seven minutes after the Motorway. What if, Bex? What if Gus set up his own death? What if Carole knew? What if they had an arrangement about signals? What if he calls from the Motorway? What if he still has a cellular phone with scrambler facilities? This would account for the call she says was from the Chief.'

'Can I play Devil's advocate?'

'Sure, how does it go?'

'It goes, if Gus still had a cellular with a scrambler facility, why does he use an ordinary telephone at the M4 service station? There's also the question of the call at seven seventeen that same morning. The log shows that came from a public telephone at Heathrow. If this is some kind of strange plot, where Gus dies, but is later resurrected, why play ducks and drakes with public telephones and a scrambled cellular? From what I know of Gus, he wouldn't switch from a secure telephone to a very open line. Herbie, Gus knew the routine. He must have known the telephone log was still in operation. That all calls were saved on the computers:

that they would be traced, and that we'd eventually get to them.'

'Sure. Sure, he would. This is pure Gus though, Bex. You didn't know him. I knew him well. He was master of deception. He might just be giving us a bit of misdirection by switching the calls. Damn it, I don't know any more. I didn't know Gus was a great magician until after he was dead . . .'

'If he's dead?'

'Sure, if he's—'

The telephone rang. Herbie spoke in monosyllables for around a minute, then said, 'Thanks, Martin. See you.'

'Well?' Bex nibbled at half a hard-boiled egg.

'Gus didn't turn in his cellular phone. It was a Mark Eight, with all the bells and whistles. Absolutely secure, with a long range. So, Bex Olesker, it could have been done, give me a piece of that egg.'

'Get your own. We have twenty-four hour room service.'

'Rather have a piece of yours, Bex.'

'Really?' She shifted, leaned over and kissed him on the cheek. 'Well, if you're good, who knows what you'll get?' Her eyes twinkled and she blushed like a teenager on her first date. 'Herbie, you must have had some of this in mind, so I have another question. Why'd you let Carole go?'

'I didn't. I let her walk, but she has company. Remember I took two telephone calls in my bedroom last night?'

'Uh-hu.'

'First one was to say that the tail from Heathrow to here, New York, lost her. Second one was to tell me they found her again.'

'So where is she?'

'At this very moment?'

'Now. At this moment, yes.'

'She's in DC. She's staying at the Grand Hyatt Hotel, which, incidentally, we're going to be looking at over next weekend.'

'We are?'

'Sure. We're going to a Magic Convention and guess who's on the bill?'

'Not . . . ?'

'Precisely.'

'Have some of my chef's salad.'

The Head of SIS Internal Security sent two of his best men up to The Hall, Harrow Weald. They were both very well-trained and had a great deal of experience under their belts. They had sought and found bombs from Belfast to London; Beirut to Bahrain. Most explosive devices were meat and drink to them.

Worboys' new Range Rover looked exactly like the one that had blown up in front of his house, and was painted in exactly the same way.

The two explosives experts knew all the wrinkles and they even cut the engine of their own car, so that it coasted to within feet of the brand-new vehicle. In the trade they were known as Mutt and Jeff, because one was called Matthew, and the other Geoffrey. Geoffrey loathed being called by any diminutive.

They worked very much as a team and approached the Range Rover with initial caution, circling it, as animals might circle a prospective victim. Mutt peered through the windows while Jeff got onto his knees, then his back, in order to slide under the vehicle. He knew cars of all types and makes almost down to the last rivet. He detected nothing under the Range Rover.

'Clean as a whistle,' he pronounced.

'Okay. Let's open the bonnet and look at the wires. Will you get the lock inside?'

'With pleasure.'

Jeff put the key into the driver's-side lock and turned. It was the last thing he ever did. The slight nudge of the locks opening tipped the mercury switch which had been balanced precariously directly behind the dashboard. The mercury switch completed the circuit which was run off a 9-volt battery. The bare wires carefully laced into a detonator glowed red hot. The detonator popped off, blowing a one-pound block of Semtex, which, in turn, ignited a long plastic straw which encased yet another set of wires leading to another ball of Semtex lying inside a four-gallon flat metal can of gasoline which, again in turn, sent a charge into the petrol tank of the Range Rover. Matthew, who always prided himself on being a professional, had one last thought which pulsed through his brain before it was swallowed up into darkness. 'That's bloody clever,' he thought. 'Wish I could see this from a distance.'

Indeed, it was spectacular. A rumble, followed by a whoosh and a second rumble and another whoosh. Gallons of gasoline were shot, aflame into the air, so that the whole thing looked like a fountain of fire with the ground shaking underneath it.

Worboys, saddened by the whole thing, was very quiet as he was driven to the Chemical Warfare Centre.

Hisham checked out of the Parker Meridien, just as instructed. Yes, indeed, they told him at the desk, Mr Jaffid was taking care of his account. Mr Jaffid had, in fact, left a note for him.

Hisham went out to the waiting cab. He did not open the envelope and read the note until the cab drew away, starting its journey to La Guardia.

Dear Friend [the note began],
I have made a slight change to the itinerary prepared for you. Instead of staying at The Willard Hotel in DC, we shall all be checking into the Grand Hyatt. All reservations have been made, and they will be expecting you. We shall join you later in the day. Everything else stays as it is. Do not forget the pick-up from Washington National. Please destroy this note.

Hisham burned the note in the Gentlemen's Rest

Room at La Guardia, and flushed the ashes down the bowl.

After doing as he was told, he went to the nearest bank of telephones. He wondered if there were any place to which he could run. Leaning against the side of the telephone booth, he dredged a number from his brain.

Slowly he stripped the credit card and punched the get-out code, followed by the get-in code for a number in Belfast. A man, he thought to himself, has to have all the insurance he can possibly get.

27

Herbie and Bex were picked up on time. Neither looked tired, though they had both remained awake through the rest of the night, talking of possibilities and the likelihood of Herb's what-if theory regarding Gus. In fact, they had become quite comfortable together on the sofa – 'This is just a friendly cuddle, you understand,' Bex had said around five in the morning, giving Herb the hint of a wink as she spoke.

'How could it be anything else?' Herb had growled.

Apart from the driver, they were accompanied by two senior FBI Special Agents from the Counter-Intelligence Unit – Dick Hatch, and a tough attractive female agent – if you liked crew cut blonde hair and a boxy figure – who insisted upon being called simply Christie. 'Same as the crime writer, Dame Agatha,' was her only comment.

They were out of New York and thundering along the I-95 when Hatch mentioned something about *Intiqam*'s sting being pulled.

'Sting?' Herb must have looked bewildered.

'What sting?' asked Bex.

'Oh, you won't have heard.' Hatch smiled, then launched into the story of the aerosol canisters discovered at Heathrow. 'We're waiting for an analysis now,' he concluded. 'The general opinion is that they contain some kind of nerve gas, so to be on the safe side, our people checked out packages waiting for pick-up at Union Station, Dulles, and Washington National. We hit paydirt at National. There was an identical parcel there. It's been moved to one of our own military labs.'

'What if they try to collect?' Bex asked.

Hatch chuckled. 'They'll find one there. Our people

mocked up an identical package – same waybill and everything. It contains a dozen aerosols with exactly the same labels, but with one difference. The ones at Heathrow and National are sealed and have fake spray tops. Your experts pointed out to us that the design of the top of these things includes grooves and a kind of locking channel to which some timing device can be fixed. We've copied this but the sprays are genuine, so we've filled them with water under pressure. If the jokers try to fit any device on top of the spray, it will simply give out a fine mist of water.'

Herbie gave a snort. 'Put fear of God into them if they know it's dangerous.'

'Panic in the streets,' Bex commented. 'We've no idea what's really in the things?'

'None.' Christie was a woman of few words.

The Chemical Warfare Centre is still one of Britain's best-kept secrets. Members of the Cabinet know of it, as do a select number of senior Army, Royal Navy and Royal Air Force officers. Even those in the know only refer to it as Dulas – though it lies nowhere near that Welsh town, the name of which means black stream. Those responsible for coding the place felt that *Black Stream* was an apt name.

Everyone who works at Dulas is an expert in his or her field, and locally it is thought to be a research laboratory for the Department of Agriculture. These days, the biochemists and chemists who live on the site are more concerned with the ways and means of destroying chemical weapons, yet there is still research being done on samples of material brought in from the old Eastern Bloc, the new Russia, and the Middle East.

They had been given due warning concerning the aerosols which were kept in a stable environment within an area where leaks could not spread. Though they had started work on discovering what these canisters contained, the facts of the horrific explosion and deaths at the Swiss laboratory which was supposed to have prepared the samples had not escaped their notice.

Two highly experienced biochemists and one skilled laboratory technician had begun work on extracting the contents under secure conditions.

One of the aerosols was placed in a padded vice so that it could not move during the process of transferring the contents from its pressurized container into a second unpressurized sealed drum. A line, like an IV drip, ran to the drum, affixed to its top by a completely leak-proof rubber cap, while a similar seal was fitted to the side of the aerosol. This latter seal was larger and contained a mechanism which looked like a hypodermic syringe, so that a Y-shaped angle lay inside it. Activating the syringe would, technically, puncture the aerosol, the contents of which, under pressure, would be released and so run from the aerosol into the air and watertight drum.

This was fully explained to Worboys and officers from MI5 who had driven down that morning to be present at the tests. They stood now behind glass, watching the scientists who were dressed in fully protective clothing, including masks and breathing apparatus, similar to that worn by divers. In the cumbersome suits, skin-tight helmets and with air tanks on their backs, they moved as slowly as astronauts in a hostile environment. Every spoken word was heard by those watching from behind the glass, for the three men wore headsets and throat microphones under their helmets, and their words were relayed through amplifiers.

'We're going to penetrate the aerosol at the count of five,' one of the biochemists said calmly. All three men were bent over the apparatus on a steel work-bench in the centre of the room.

They counted down through the five beats, and the watchers saw the slight movement made by the expert as he plunged the needle through the side of the aerosol.

'Fine,' one of the other scientists spoke. 'It's a fine spray that appears to be liquefying as it runs into our container. Moving very fast . . . Done. The aerosol is technically empty, though there are bound to be traces. We're going to seal it off before we remove the tubing. Then we'll do the same to the catchment container.'

It all took a good hour before they could breathe any sighs of relief, though the next step would take longer. The liquid from the spray now had to be analysed and it was not until after seven in the evening that they got the frightening news that the aerosols had been filled with highly toxic Strep A containing the deadly enzymes which would produce the necrotizing fasciitis condition.

'The flesh-eating mystery virus,' Worboys said when he called in to the Office.

The information was flashed to London and Washington where it was immediately understood by the agents in the field. The final intention of the *Intiqam* teams had obviously been to release the deadly bacteria through air-conditioning or heating ducts in the House of Commons and The Capitol, and so paralyse the governments of at least America and Britain. The original plan had almost certainly included the Italian and French governments also. One of the specialists maintained that, had this succeeded, he would have expected to lose 50–60 per cent of the Members of Parliament, and the same number who might be sitting in the House and Chamber in The Capitol.

In Washington it was felt that no further chances should be taken. The three terrorists they knew about should be arrested immediately, but when Herb, Bex and their two companions from the FBI arrived to check in at the exclusive Willard Hotel, they were informed by a waiting Counter-Intelligence officer from Langley that Walid, Hisham and Khami were no-shows.

The suite which had been taken for Herbie and Bex had been organized so that it could double as an operational headquarters. Now all of those who were considered part of what would be known as *Conductor* –

as in Lightning Conductor – sat down to discuss exactly how they should proceed.

They knew the names under which the three Iraqis were travelling – Dr Sa'dun Zaidan, together with Mr and Mrs Jaffid, so they worked the telephones, checking every hotel within a ten-mile radius of Washington.

They worked until late that night, backed up by agents in the Hoover Building, Washington's FBI Headquarters. The no-shows seemed to have disappeared into thin air, so they started again. This time with descriptions.

By early afternoon on the same day, several FBI officers, accompanied by a SWAT team, had gathered in and around a wooded area in the Hudson Valley, some twenty miles from the old and picturesque town of Rhinebeck.

They were concentrating on a lonely cottage, once the retreat of a famous painter, now leased to three men who had been described locally as 'A-rab looking'.

The team watching the house were certain that its occupants were from the Middle East. They had done just what their British counterparts had achieved in Oxfordshire. From the information passed by Hisham, they traced the telephone number and knew the cottage was the site occupied by the American *Yussif* group.

Finally, they went in at four in the afternoon, surprising the trio of *Yussif* as they watched television. Not a shot was fired and the arrests were made with no reference to the media. The trio were driven away to a very secure house not far away, close by Hyde Park, once the seat of the Roosevelt family. They had played it by the book, even bringing in a local resident judge to hear the charges brought against the men, and sign an order allowing them to be held without bail or a court appearance for as long as was necessary.

During the hearing, the three men who had been the *Yussif* team in the United States stood to attention, like well-trained military men, their heads held high. In their eyes you could see that their faith in both country and Allah was so strong that nothing would move them. The trio were ready to die for both their God and country.

In the now empty cottage two FBI agents manned the telephone, connecting it to both a recorder and a fast Caller ID Unit which could trace a number anywhere in the United States within ninety seconds.

The call came in just after five, and one of the agents picked up the telephone but said nothing. From the distant end a voice asked, '*Yussif?*'

Busking it, the Special Agent simply replied, '*Yussif.* Yes?'

'We're in Washington, but we've had to change our location. We have the goods and will begin activation tomorrow.'

'Good. Give me your present position.'

There was a lengthy silence at the other end, then the sound of a quick intake of breath, followed by the dial tone. It was obvious that the Special Agent had not conformed to some prearranged method of contact, but the line had been open for long enough. A Caller ID lit up on the LED. Within minutes they had traced it to a public telephone in Washington's Georgetown. The police were alerted, but when they arrived in the area they found only tourists, students and the usual people you would expect to find in that part of Washington.

Earlier in the day, when Hisham had checked into the Grand Hyatt under the westernized name of James Tait, he was shown to a room on the third floor. He washed, took the elevator downstairs again, and went outside into the sticky heat of late-summer Washington. He took a cab to the National Airport, going straight to the Air Freight collection area. The package was there, as were two FBI Special Agents on surveillance duty to report on the pick-up. They managed to get a whole roll of film showing Hisham arriving at the collection point; Hisham handing over the waybill and retrieving the package; and even a couple of photographs of him getting into a cab.

That was as far as it went. They had no orders to follow him. Their instructions were to get the pictures and then return to the J. Edgar Hoover Building where the film was processed, ready to be checked by the various agents who were dealing with the current situation.

Hisham stood in line for over fifteen minutes in the broiling heat to get a taxi back to the Grand Hyatt, where he paid the cab off and hurried back into the pleasant chill of the air-conditioning. Below the entrance level of the Washington Grand Hyatt there is an ornamental pool which laps around an open-plan restaurant. This can be viewed as you walk from the entrance to the bank of elevators, and Hisham was seriously thinking of dropping off the parcel in his room and returning for an early lunch.

He glanced down at the couples and family parties already eating at the tables below him. Then his heart rate suddenly increased, and he felt his stomach lurch. He stopped dead and looked harder, just to be sure. The longer he looked the more certain he was. There, below him, sipping a drink across the table from an elegant woman was a face from his past. He even recognized the woman, and could not believe what he saw.

Quickly he moved away and walked to the elevators, his mind in turmoil. Once in his room, he placed the package carefully on the table beside the TV, went into the bathroom, sprinkled water over his face and wondered what he should do. What he had seen was unbelievable, and his one thought was to get out of the Hyatt as quickly as possible. It was not feasible, though; he did not even know what time Walid and Khami were due to arrive, nor what name they were to register under.

He called down to room service for food and drink, then waited, not daring to show himself in the main body of the hotel. This place had now become completely unsafe. If he had been on his own, it would have

394

been a different matter, but with the last two members of the *Intiqam* team still to arrive he could do nothing but wait. He considered other possibilities. He could, if the situation were as serious as he thought, throw himself on the mercy of the authorities, citing the British Security Service as his masters. Finally, he decided this was too dangerous.

It was not until almost four in the afternoon that the telephone rang and he heard Walid's voice telling him they were here – Dr and Mrs Hendler – in room 416.

'Get down to my room quickly,' Hisham said, keeping his voice as calm as possible. 'We have a small emergency. I'm in three six four. This is serious.'

Within four minutes Walid and Khami were there.

'We cannot stay here, in this hotel,' he told them. 'There are British Security officers here. I know them. I've seen them with my own eyes.' He went on talking, naturally leaving out sections of his story that he could never share with either of them.

Walid went pale, and Khami turned away and walked to the window, looking down at the traffic. 'Where the hell do we go?' she asked in a small voice.

'To somewhere completely safe.' Walid seemed to have recovered his momentary concern. 'Don't worry, we were only going to stay here for a very short time anyway.' He then explained that, during the planning phase of the operation, *Yussif* had organized two safe houses in Washington. One was in the Georgetown area, a nice apartment not far from the famous Georgetown Inn on Wisconsin Avenue. One telephone call and their local contact would open it up and leave the keys for them. There they would be safe, for this same contact was to deliver the explosives and the necessary timing devices for *Magic Lightning*.

Walid acted swiftly and with great care. The last thing he wanted was to have the people on the reception desk remember them checking in and then leaving after being in the hotel for less than an hour. He made excuses about a death in the family, and had the two rooms charged to a credit card for one night.

Within the hour they were settled into a four-room apartment overlooking the shops and restaurants of Wisconsin Avenue. Hisham was relieved. The people whom he had spotted were nowhere to be seen as they left the hotel. Now, he was alone in this pleasant apartment, waiting while Khami shopped for groceries and Walid went out to use a public telephone to check in with *Yussif*.

Khami returned first, her arms clutching brown bags of what little food they would need, for Walid said he thought it would be quite safe for them to eat in one of the many restaurants along Wisconsin Avenue.

She had only been back for some five minutes when Walid returned, his face grave, and sweat visible on his forehead.

'They've taken out *Yussif*,' he said baldly.

'Taken . . . ?' Khami began.

'I didn't recognize the voice that answered, but I've only spoken to two of that team until now. We talked for a few minutes, and then the code procedure broke down.'

'How?'

'*Yussif* asked "Give me your present position." This is wrong. Very wrong. *Yussif* has one question regarding where we are. He should always say, "Are you at the same place?" They've never made a mistake like this before. We're on our own, which means that we have to begin first thing tomorrow. At least we *can* get on with it. The Semtex is here, in the refrigerator, with timers, detonators, and, of course, the timers for *Magic Lightning*. So everything is possible. We must do all we can.'

'And then?' Khami asked.

'And then we go our separate ways and finally return home.'

At The Willard, Herbie was putting his point of view to the rest of the *Conductor* team. There were five agents present, apart from Kruger and Bex: Hatch and Christie from the FBI; a pair of grey suits from Langley, one introduced as Cork Smith, the other referred to only as Krysak – a cuddly-looking man, built like a fireplug but with clear very light blue eyes which looked as though they had been sculpted from ice. Also in attendance was another woman, Sheila FitzGerald, from the Secret Service – tall, slender and very fit: a woman who moved like a panther and had claimed, at the start of the meeting, that the Secret Service 'owned' the streets around the White House and the Capitol.

'You're all here to round up these pretty dangerous clowns,' Herbie began, looking a little flushed. 'I am only here because these terrorists seem to have wandered into the path of *our* investigation.' He touched Bex's shoulder to link her to himself. 'I'm only interested in the *Intiqam* people if they happen to have murdered my former colleague, Gus Keene. Bex is here for the same reason. We think we now know who blew my old friend into the wide blue yonder, and it isn't your set of Iraqi hoodlums. By rights, we're out of this as from now.'

'You squeamish about terrorists?' Christie looked hard at Herbie and then switched to Bex. The mocking look on her face seemed to be a permanent feature, not a look assumed simply for them.

'Squeamish?' Kruger's voice went up an octave, and his colour changed noticeably. 'Young woman, you call *me* squeamish? I've dealt with bringers of terror for nearly my whole life. Put this lot next to *real* terrorists and they come out like the gang who couldn't shoot straight. Sure, they've killed, they managed to plant bombs, but they've slowly been hived off. They've either got themselves killed or caught.' He paused for a deep breath, as though trying to control his anger. Then:

'I would suggest you get yourselves out on the streets,

search among the crowds, look in every nook and cranny, then put them out of their misery altogether. DCI Olesker and I have a different agenda. What I'm telling you is that there is only a very tenuous link between our job and your terrorists.' He grinned at Bex and quietly said, 'Tenuous is good, yes?'

'Brilliant, Herb.' She winked at him.

Hatch got to his feet, paced the floor for a couple of minutes, then said they could not just walk out on *Conductor*. 'You're under discipline.'

'Been under discipline nearly all my life, Dick.' Herb smiled up at him. 'But this time you're wrong. I'm retired and I'm only being paid out-of-pocket expenses. I'm on this job to find out one thing, and I think it's within reach. Bex is also here for the same reason. Our job is to catch a killer, or killers, who I honestly don't think are connected with *Intiqam*.'

'So the Brits are opting out?' Christie's face showed open disgust.

'You want to put it that way, okay.' Herb turned to Cork Smith from Langley. 'If I were you, I'd get on to your opposite number at Vauxhall Cross. If you still want us on your team, the SIS will have to give it a big thumbs up, but they'll qualify that. In the end, they'll tell you okay, but they'll also tell you that, should we come across a direct link to our real case, it'll have to take precedence. Sure, maybe these Vengeance people *have* got the key to the case we're here to crack,' again he touched Bex's arm to include her. 'But I for one am opting out of your form of discipline.'

'We can always close you down. Take you off to Dulles and put you on a flight to Heathrow, *persona non grata*.' Smith, if that was indeed his real name, appeared to be serious.

'Why not?' Kruger seemed perfectly happy with the idea. 'If that's what you really want. But I think you might get yourself overruled.' As he spoke he noticed Krysak slip quietly from the room.

'Your friend's gone to get a ruling?' Kruger asked brightly. 'We'll abide by whatever answer he gets.' He tilted his head towards the main bedroom, then rose and walked to the door. Bex followed him.

'What the hell's all this about, Herb? We need the co-operation of these guys.'

'Sure we need it, but I want to be 100 per cent certain that we can fold up our tents and leave here on Thursday. Look, Bex, trust me on this. I think we can wrap up our case here in DC, over the coming weekend. But we won't do it if we're tied to the American agencies. Yes, we'll stay with them, trying to flush out this trio of Iraqis, but only until Thursday. On Thursday we have to be able to opt out, with no questions asked.'

'You talking about this magic conference, or whatever it is?'

'Exactly.'

'Herb, why would we want to hang around people doing card tricks?' Her right eyebrow lifted in a sign of doubt which spoke volumes.

'Bex, I know you don't like it. You're one of those people who hate to be fooled by magicians. I think I should call you Witch Finder General. Your whole mindset is one that says, "These guys are frauds. They deceive; they pretend to overcome laws of nature, but I don' go for that. I want to know how they do it and I'm buggered if it's going to impress me." '

'I *am* buggered if it's going to impress me.'

'You mean that last video we saw – Gus doing his lecture about the theory of intelligence-gathering running parallel to the theory of the performing art of magic – you truly can say that didn't impress you?'

'It was very clever in its way, but . . . Oh, Herb, I can't help it. I *know* what they do is impossible – I'm talking about the good ones – but I know it's a cheat, a swindle. For me, magicians are licensed to lie, to defraud in the name of some supposed performing art, and I just don't go for it.'

'Well, you're going to have to go for it at the week-end, sweetie, because that's where I think we'll find the truth about Gus and his death.'

'What did you call me?' There was no hostility in her voice or manner.

'I call you sweetie. Is not good, Bex, then I'm sorry.'

'Don't be sorry. Nobody's called me "sweetie" for a very long time. I'm just not the type to be called "sweetie".'

'To me you're certainly the type.'

'Oh.'

It was over an hour before someone knocked on the door.

'We'd like you to come back into the meeting, if you don't mind.' Cork Smith appeared slightly ruffled.

'I talked with your people in London.' Krysak held the floor, everyone else sat around. Christie was lying down, one elbow on the carpet with the hand supporting her head. 'They'd like a word with you when you have a minute.' Krysak spoke fast, in quick machine-gun-like bursts. 'To put it all in perspective, they're anxious that you assist us with the *Intiqam* business. We would like that. In return, they've asked us to take you at your word. When you tell us you have some direct lead in your own case, they want us to let you go.'

'So, what you tell them, Mr . . . ?'

'Charlie,' Krysak gave Herbie an amiable smile.

'So, what you tell them, Charlie?'

'We've agreed. So will you stay on our op for the time being?'

'Sure,' Herbie looked at DCI Olesker who nodded. 'Sure, but I should warn you that we're pretty close to moving in on the answer to our case.'

'Okay,' Smith took over. 'Charlie, here, says you've been authorized to carry.' He produced two Beretta 9mm automatics and six extra magazines.

Herbie grinned, scooping one of the pistols from the

400

table, checking it before slipping it into his waistband, behind the right hip.

Bex looked dubious. 'I hate guns,' she said.

'Take it, Bex.'

'Where'm I going to carry it? In my knickers?'

'Knickers is Brit for panties,' the Secret Service lady translated.

There were some uneasy laughs.

'Up to you, Bex.' Herbie gave her one of his surprised looks. 'Keep it where you like. Only the Shadow knows.' He looked around the room. 'So, we going to sweep the streets looking for these bozos? They may be stupid, but we're obviously not up to scratch – any of us. We lose Carole. Then we find her again. Everyone now loses the damned Iraqis, and what we get out of it? Damned great wad of Semtex up the arse if you ask me.'

'Herb, I . . . ' Bex began.

'Sorry, but I am righteously mad. Gus gets killed and we end up in the middle of a cockeyed, badly handled, stupid, death-dealing terrorist operation. In one word I'm fucking fed up.'

'That's three words, Herb.'

'Who's fucking counting? I want to get my big hands on these people. See *them* blown away for a change, but my guts tell me something really bad is going down.'

They decided that they should not go out to eat together. 'One at a time,' Walid suggested.

'I bought eggs and things,' Khami offered. 'I can cook for us.'

'I think I'll go out. Need to get off by myself.' Hisham managed to sound composed.

'Okay.' Walid seemed very happy to be left on his own with Khami. 'Don't take more than an hour or so. We have to start making up the bombs tonight if we're really going to see this through.'

Hisham walked down to Au Pied de Cochon, where he ate well, and thought again about making a run for it. Life, at the moment, was like a juggler keeping six chain-saws in the air at once without losing an arm.

He probably would have been more concerned if he had known that he was sitting in a restaurant which, in the mid-1980s, had been the scene of an unfortunate end run by a KGB defector. It was in Au Pied de Cochon that a KGB defector had dined with his CIA minders and then, in the middle of dinner, calmly walked out and back to the Soviet Embassy, returning to his old masters.

Hisham did not know this, so was spared further anguish. After the meal he took a turn around the block, found a telephone and used a credit card to make yet another call. Hisham Silwani had ceased to rationalize regarding which side he was working for. His only thought was to save his own skin. This latest call was to Belfast. He spoke only for a minute, but what he told the people at the other end was flashed to Declan Norton in London. Had Hisham been arrested at this point, he truly would have no good reason or logic to explain any of his recent actions.

The following morning, Declan Norton, accompanied by Sean O'Donnel, left Heathrow on a direct flight to Washington, Dulles. They carried British passports under the names of David Scaif and Frank Meadows. Declan had left Fergus behind in London. He felt the man did not have the stomach for what he was about to do. Later the same day, another familiar figure came into Washington National. He had travelled from London via New York. By the time they all reached DC, the bombs had begun to explode.

28

The first two bombs exploded within minutes of one another around noon the next day. Both were horrific, large and planted to kill, maim and anger. The first detonated in the main concourse of the recently refurbished Union Station at a minute to noon and was heard over ten miles away.

Later, it was established that the Union Station bomb was, in effect, two bombs linked together by an umbilical cord of wire: one in the upper concourse, the other below, in the train-boarding area. Just as it was finally discovered that the four tons of C-4 explosive, two for each bomb, had been brought into DC months before, by articulated truck from Canada. They were even able to pinpoint that the plastique had been brought into Halifax by a container ship from Germany, and from there by truck to DC.

The station was crowded and sections of the building were ripped away as though some magic process had turned the steel, concrete and brick into paper. Some maintained that the fire and blast rolled straight out of the main façade. Part of the roof was thrown clear, fires started, two railway engines were lifted from their tracks and one entire train, loaded and about to leave, was gutted by a fireball.

Most of those who were killed or maimed were either waiting for their trains to leave, or walking around the main concourse. Uncontrolled explosions are not predictable. The Union Station bomb had its fair number of strange incidents. As the smoke, flame and debris cleared from the façade directly behind Columbus Circle, a woman, stripped naked of her clothing, walked out of the wreckage. When the Emergency Squads arrived she was found to be completely unharmed.

In the train which was consumed by a fireball, a man and two women were thrown clear. They were the only people who lived in that part of the incident. All three had their hair and eyebrows singed, and one was deaf for a week.

Of the people caught on the main concourse, only two small children escaped serious injury. Two little boys aged five and seven had been lifted into the air and fell some sixty feet from where they had been standing with their parents. They survived. Their parents, like so many others on that horrific morning, were never found. Whole families were turned into odd bones, pieces of flesh and clothing. It was impossible to put names to the jigsaw of body parts.

At one minute past noon, the second device exploded right behind Daniel Chester French's huge and inspiring white marble statue of Abraham Lincoln set within the temple-like Memorial at the southern end of the Reflecting Pool – the crowning glory of the magnificent parkscape of The Mall.

The noise, to some, seemed like an echo from the explosion at Union Station. The Lincoln statue simply appeared to disintegrate in a ball of flame, sending large rocks of marble arcing in different directions. Smaller pieces flew like shrapnel, cutting people off the steps to the Memorial as though they were mown down by a hail of bullets. The head leaped up from the fire, hit the roof, yet stayed intact as it ricocheted down the steps, smashing into three Japanese tourists who were setting up a complex video camera between the steps and the Reflecting Pool. All three were hurled backwards and pulped by the giant football of a head.

The blast from this bomb also did strange things; it seemed to funnel its way out of the Memorial, sending flame and blast waves forward, as though some invisible force had flashed down the steps, across the grass and onto the Reflecting Pool, where it caused what was almost a tidal wave which ran the length of the Pool, rising into a breaker that broke like surf at the Washington Monument end.

A professional photographer had been taking a panoramic view of the Pool at the moment of detonation. It was a photograph that sold to *Time Magazine* for a large undisclosed sum, for it made the Reflecting Pool look as though some inhuman phenomenon had shattered the water into a million pieces, all blood-red from the flame of the explosion.

In all, the two bombs claimed 400 lives, and injured another 300 persons. On that day alone Washington DC had been turned into a charnel-house.

At ten past noon, *Jasmine* spoke with Claudius.

'I can't stop it,' *Jasmine* said.

'Will there be more?'

'I think many more, and something truly horrible at the end.'

'You've mentioned that. Can I help to stop it?'

'I don't know,' *Jasmine* replied. 'Maybe, but I dare not do anything yet.'

'Jump, then. Jump now. You know how to find me.' By the time Claudius said this, *Jasmine* had already closed the line.

Throughout the country the news first numbed people, then the shock turned to outrage. The two bombs tied up rescue squads, ambulances and police well into the early hours of the evening.

The President went on television and called for calm both in the city and outside. The FBI, together with the police, issued a joint statement which basically said they were of the opinion that the terrorists who had committed this appalling act were probably already out of the country.

As the news spread quickly around the world, messages of condolence, anger and solidarity poured into the city. The British Prime Minister, never one to miss an opportunity, offered specialist aid, saying that the United Kingdom had suffered outrages such as this in the past, and could provide expert technicians to help track down those who had unleashed the dogs of terrorist war upon the United States. His offer was politely declined, and in private many politicians in DC saw a snub behind the PM's offer. 'Quoting Shakespeare doesn't make him into Churchill,' the President said with not a little anger.

Late in the afternoon, Worboys put in a secure telephone call to Herbie Kruger.

'Don't want to get you worried, Herb,' he began, 'but I've just seen an interesting document from the Security Service. Well, not so much a document as a tape.' For some time now, unknown to most people, banks of video-machines which regularly scanned incoming and outgoing passengers had been installed by the Security Service, in conjunction with the airlines who used Heathrow most frequently.

These tapes were checked out in three-hour segments, though there were times when the three hours overran into four or even five. One of the tapes, being viewed by men and women who were current with criminal and terrorist 'faces', had brought in positive ID. Two men, well known to MI5, had boarded the British Airways morning flight to Washington DC.

'People *we* know as well,' Worboys told an anxious Kruger. 'Declan Norton and Sean O'Donnel.'

Herbie scowled, then asked, 'We're talking about the Declan Norton who was shopped by *Ishmael* – the Iraqi Gus ran through "Five"?'

'That's the one. We didn't get the info until well after the flight landed at Dulles, otherwise we'd have had them pulled by the Yanks.'

'What're you suggesting, Young Worboys?'

'Well, we had the word from *Ishmael*. *You* saw the file. Norton was the FFIRA man who asked the *Intiqam* team to do them a favour. The favour was Gus, The Whizz, myself and you, Herb. All of us on a plate, served up

406

with apples in our mouths and garnished just the way they like it.'

Herbie spoke a thought to himself. 'And they got The Whizz, had a couple of goes at you, twice at me, and Gus was dead long before that particular contract went out.'

'You think it's the last few *Intiqam* people responsible for today's carnage?'

'Certain of it. Real panic here, and I don't blame them.'

'You think the FFIRA has got wind that you're there in DC?'

'Could be.'

'Well, watch your back, Herb. Norton might have come over to do the job himself.'

Kruger promised that he would watch not just his back, but every body part.

Meanwhile, in the safe house where the FBI was keeping the three men of the *Yussif* team they had snatched, matters were coming to a head.

These men were unbreakable by normal methods. Six of the FBI's very best inquisitors had worked in shifts on the men. They played it hard and soft; kind and threatening; carrot and stick. None of it worked, so they finally had to resort to other techniques.

A doctor and nurse were helicoptered in from New York, and they began to do the job. In the old days of the Cold War both FBI and CIA had used sodium pentathol, inaccurately dubbed the 'truth drug'. In the jargon, it was called SOAP, but many advances had been made since those times. They could now use a new and improved SOAP, coupled with a measured dose of a new hypnotic. The process was 100 per cent accurate provided that it was administered correctly, hence the doctor.

They did not use the technique often, mainly because information gleaned by this method could be successfully challenged in the courts. Under the incredible system that had no *sub judice* law and regarded this type of interrogation as a breach of the subject's rights, there was little chance of ever getting a judge to allow the results to be brought in as evidence.

The subjects now were a very different matter. By the evening of that day of true shock and abhorrence, the cocktail of drugs brought out facts which were flashed to Washington, and a meeting of *Conductor*'s leading players was called at the sumptuous suite at The Willard.

Hatch began the briefing. 'As you know, we've already issued a statement saying the perpetrators of today's attacks have almost certainly left the area. Normally we would be right, but it is now 99 per cent certain that these people're still here. We've pulled files and you'll be glad to learn that we have at least the identities of the people who have caused such terror.'

He continued by telling them how the information had been garnered, through the *Yussif* trio. Then he held up photographs, one at a time.

'Walid Allush, aged thirty-four. A known former member of Abu Nidal's network who ceased to be one of Nidal's people after the Iraqi leadership banned the organization in 1983. Walid is a trained and ruthless terrorist with all the attributes of leadership. He is almost certainly at the head of this small group.

'Next, Khami Qasim, aged twenty-eight. She has visited the United States on numerous occasions. Was kept under surveillance in 1988 when in New York and Boston. At that time we suspected her of being a courier for a small cell of terrorists who were never actually apprehended. We had no reasons to either arrest or even question her. The photograph is, of course, six years old so her appearance could have been changed. We now believe that she spent some time in one of the Libyan training camps. She is, therefore, regarded as being dangerous.' He looked up at Herbie Kruger. 'Your service has some traces of her being active in London in the early to mid Eighties.'

Kruger nodded, his expression unchanging. *Jasmine*, he thought. If Carole was playing some complicated game set up by Gus, this could be our *Jasmine*. On the other hand, if Carole had told him the truth, and if *Jasmine* were still alive, it could equally be the man Walid.

'Third,' Hatch continued, 'Hisham Silwani, aged thirty-nine. Known terrorist for hire. He has worked in the United States and Europe – he knows London very well. Though he is well trained, there is a suggestion that his loyalties are ill-defined.' He turned to Herbie again. 'I have a note here that it is possible this man was, is, or has been an asset of your Security Service. Can you say anything about this, Herb?'

Big Herbie cleared his throat to give him time to think. 'I can only tell you I know the name, and it is quite possible that he has links with MI5. I cannot tell you more without getting authorization. You would like me to do this, yes?'

'It's an idea. We'd be grateful.' Hatch then held up a grainy photograph of a young man. 'White, male, aged twenty-six. One two-year term in a Federal Prison for criminal damage. Names: Sporty Howard, Sinclair Howth, Stan Husted. Real name: Sidney Allen Hench. This man has been a petty criminal since his teens, and became mixed up with various pseudo-political groups in the late nineteen eighties. He is, in fact, apolitical, and possibly psychopathic. A petty criminal who, it appears, has been paid well for servicing two safe apartments here in DC for the express use of the people who carried out today's attacks. Unhappily, we have no way of getting access to these locations. It is obvious that the men from whom we received this intelligence have no idea where the apartments are located.

'Naturally, we have all this information in the hands of the police and other agencies . . .'

'Which means it'll be in the hands of the media very soon,' Christie sighed.

'True enough, but that might not be a bad thing. For

this country, today's events rank with Pearl Harbor and the assassination of President Kennedy. In twenty years, anyone over seven or eight years old will be able to tell you exactly where they were when they heard the news of the Washington bombings.'

It was also undoubtedly true to say that anyone of an age to understand what had happened now lived in terror of what might come next.

There were four bombs in all on the Wednesday afternoon. In spite of the alerts that had gone out, security was not completely organized. People were frisked, and randomly checked as they entered public buildings; men were asked to open briefcases, women's handbags were examined as they went into the larger department stores. Yet no explosive-sniffing devices were in place by lunchtime that day when Walid, Khami and Hisham went about placing the bombs.

The last members of *Intiqam* were taking no chances. Following the huge bombs, Walid had pointed out that they only needed follow-up devices to cause more panic. At their disposal they had around 200 pounds of explosives. This was moved to the second safe house, prepared for them by the American they called *Henchman*. The toxic-spray cans were left in the Georgetown apartment, together with the timers which they would not fit to the cans until the last possible moment – even though they were exceptionally sophisticated pieces of electronics, capable of a time-lag of up to three months.

The second apartment was in Alexandria, in a street named for a great American general. It was there they prepared the four forty-pound bombs, timed to go off one minute apart, starting at two in the afternoon. All three of them went out and placed the devices without any problems even though, by this time, they were aware that their descriptions were being circulated. There were even photographs on the streets and in buildings.

'Do not fear capture,' Walid told them. 'You know

410

how things go when old pictures are put up for identification. Nobody ever expects to see the living person.
They can look you in the eyes and not even experience
a flicker of recognition. Go where you must go, and do
what you must do.'

The first explosion was inside the Executive Office
Building, close to the White House. It killed fifty people,
injured another forty and caused great alarm. One minute
later, the one they had placed in the National Museum
of American History, on Constitution Avenue, exploded
in the gift shop. Forty men, women and children died,
another thirty were seriously injured.

One minute after that, the bomb in the National
Gallery of Art ripped through a wall, killed eighteen,
injured another fifty and destroyed twelve priceless paintings. The final device, outside the Watergate Building,
killed nobody. It did some damage, but had been placed
out on the Virginia Avenue side. Several cars were
destroyed, a couple of fires were under control quite
quickly and no lives were lost.

Early that evening, the President made a statement
after a meeting with his National Security Adviser,
together with the Joint Chiefs and the Secretary of
State. He was calling a joint meeting of the Senate
and the House of Representatives for the following
evening. He would speak to his administration, he said,
in this grave hour of crisis. In part, the statement was a
message to the terrorists to show that the President was
not going to hide away like a frightened rabbit. Both he
and the governing body would be on show. It also spoke
of a gigantic crackdown, the like of which had never
been seen in the United States of America. Already, the
President emoted, known dissidents, groups of organized troublemakers and similar disenchanted gangs were
being sought out and arrested.

There were rumours that areas in the cold wastes
of Alaska were being readied to take thousands of
disaffected troublemakers and organized anti-American

political groups. They, the rumour mill said, would be made to build their own prisons from which there would be no escape for the rest of their natural lives.

Attached to this rumour was a tale – not altogether untrue – that the President, under emergency powers, would sign a bill allowing the police and security agencies the right to arrest and detain known deviants without the benefit of trial. The detention orders, it was thought, would be for life.

In the Georgetown house, Walid, Khami and Hisham gathered for the final moves. The spray cans were on a table, together with the cylindrical timing mechanisms. They had planned to set these for around an hour after the given time of the President's speech in the Capitol.

They were nervous, as they already knew the place would be hedged off by security and police from now, this Wednesday evening, until after it was over on the Thursday night, but they planned to set the timers in the early hours of the morning and go into the Capitol in the guise of cleaning and maintenance workers. They tried to sleep, but it did not come easily. All three were aware of their proximity to the deadly canisters, and the duty they would have to perform on the next morning.

It was late on the same night that Big Herbie Kruger and DCI Bex Olesker went to the respective FBI and CIA heads of *Conductor* to tell them that they would have to leave the operation by noon on the following day. 'I fear we are now in possession of vital information regarding the case we're here to crack,' Herbie lied.

'We did warn you about the possibility,' Bex added. 'We have to follow up on our leads.'

'That was before these murderers began their attack on DC.' Cork Smith looked pained, as though they were naughty children refusing to do as they were told.

'The case we're following may well converge with *Conductor*.' Herb remained passive and very serious. 'You checked with London. You knew what to expect.'

Smith and Hatch took it very badly, but had no

option other than to agree. Both had the decency to admit they would be weaker without Herbie and Bex.

They were awake by five-thirty. It was not yet light outside. Khami brewed some fresh coffee for them. That was all they wanted. None of the trio could face food. The aerosols were lined up on the kitchen table.

'We're all agreed that, once we've each got our quota of these things into the air-conditioning ducts, we will meet together at the Alexandria house.'

The other two muttered agreement.

'Now,' Walid took the first aerosol spray can and placed it, nozzle away from him. He then took the first timing device and set it to eight-thirty that evening. Once this was done, they all knew, it would be an easy job to slip the collar of the cylindrical timer over the spray unit at the top of the can. They had been told that they would hear a slight click as it closed firmly on the spray section.

Walid slid it into place and pushed down. Instead of a click, the top of the canister hissed out a fine spray of the harmless water substituted by the FBI.

All three gave cries of alarm as they tried to beat each other to the door. Once outside, Khami gasped, 'Do you think we've been . . . ?'

'We won't know until it's too late.' At least Walid remained cool, understanding that they could do little about matters now.

'It's unlikely,' Hisham spoke low. 'None of us was in line with the spray, but we daren't go back in there.'

'Go,' Walid's voice was a mixture of anger and fear. 'Go. Go, both of you. Pass some time and we'll meet in the Alexandria house within an hour to two hours' time.'

'What if we're . . . ?' Khami gasped again, hyperventilating.

'If you start to feel ill, get yourself to an Emergency Room and tell them you think it's a Strep A infection,' Walid snapped at her. 'Now go.'

The city was just coming to life. Hisham wondered what would be the best thing to do. He walked, monitoring his body as he tramped the streets. Was that a twinge of a sore throat? No, just dryness.

Traffic was beginning to move in the streets now, so he made his way over to The Mall. The area around the Reflecting Pool and the Lincoln Memorial had been taped off by the police, but he could see that people had placed candles and flowers all over the decimated area where so many had died.

Hisham had his first twinge of remorse. Just there one minute, then gone like a wraith. He had done what he had to do. He had obeyed orders. No matter that he had betrayed his country in one way, he had no option but to go along with the orders. For the sake of his own life he had obeyed what the Leader had set in motion.

He walked across the grass, up the mound to the base of the Washington Monument, with its flags rippling and cracking around him. Then he trudged down the Mall towards the Smithsonian.

In all he allowed ninety minutes to pass before he hailed a cab and asked to be dropped two blocks from the house in Alexandria.

Few people were about, and he found himself shivering slightly. He only wore jeans and a T-shirt, with a pair of trainers on his naked feet. Was the shivering the first sign of infection? he wondered. No, the sun was shining, but it was relatively cool. What to do? What to do?

Each of them had a key to the place. He climbed the stairs, put his key in the lock and stepped inside.

For a moment his brain could not take in the carnage. Then he reacted with horror. Walid lay, half in and half out of the bedroom, his face almost gone where the bullets had struck him, his quashed and riddled features lolled in a pool of blood.

Hisham called out twice, 'Khami! . . . Khami!'

No reply, just the hint of an echo around the apartment. Hisham moved slowly forward, pressing against the wall to avoid stepping in the dead Walid's blood. Who could have done this? Why?

He remembered that both Walid and Khami had their personal weapons tucked into the waistbands of their jeans before Walid had attempted to set the timer. He now saw that one of the automatic pistols was lying on the kitchen table. Next to it was Walid's briefcase, open, still with hard cash bundled in hundred-dollar bills. Not as much there as he had seen on the previous evening when Walid had been checking on their IDs.

Hisham went from room to room, now holding the pistol from the kitchen table. His heart was beating heavily and he could hear it in his ears as it pumped blood through his body.

'Allah save me,' he thought to himself as he entered each of the rooms, not knowing what to expect on the other side of the door. Maybe some stranger who had been surprised by Walid when he entered the place. He knew that could not be right. Any casual burglar would have taken everything, including the spare weapon.

When he had checked each room and every closet, Hisham sat down at the kitchen table. He felt exhausted; he could not get his brain to work; did not know how to proceed. The smell of Walid's blood was a stench in his nostrils, and the sight of the body lying so near revolted him.

Where should he go? What should he do? Then he remembered who he had seen during the short stay at the Grand Hyatt and a plan slowly started to form in his mind.

He must have sat there in the kitchen for the best part of an hour before all the pieces came into place. Carefully he removed two of the thick rolls of hundred-dollar bills and put them in the pockets of his jeans, together with a completely new set of ID and credit cards in the name of Wilson Sharp. Then he placed the pistol next to the rest of the money in the case and snapped it shut. Within ten minutes he was out on the street, flagging down a cab and asking to be put down at the shopping mall near Pennsylvania Avenue which is called simply The Shops.

It took him around two hours. Shirts, socks, shoes, ties, two suits which luckily fitted him well, straight off the peg. Casual slacks and a light blazer, sports shirts. A name-brand toilet set. Everything the well-groomed man required. In one of the men's shops he changed into a white open-necked shirt and a pair of light blue slacks, finishing it off with the blazer and a pair of brand-new trainers.

He bought a matching suitcase, garment bag and an overnight, and piled all he had purchased into the various cases. After that he went into a barber's shop, was shaved and had his hair cut in a conservative style.

At one of the public telephone booths he called the Grand Hyatt and asked if they had any rooms for the weekend. They told him only suites which had the added bonus of the use of small coffee bars with snacks which were open from seven each morning until ten at night. He said he would be checking in shortly.

The Shops contained several pleasant restaurants, so Hisham lined up at one of these and ate a simple meal of bean soup and a tuna salad. They treated him with respect and even put his cases in a safe place for him.

It was early afternoon when he came out into the sunlight and waited for a cab which took him to the Grand Hyatt. By two-thirty he had unpacked and was ready to go in search of the person who might just give him a way out.

He walked down the passage and realized there were already two men standing in the little lounge area next to the elevators. He did not even look at them until one of them spoke.

'Well that's a surprise, so. Meeting my old friend Hisham Silwani here in Washington. We haven't seen one another since we spent a night at *Les Misérables* in London, so I think we'd better change our plans and go for a nice private talk.' Declan Norton moved in and grasped Hisham's arm, while the other man stepped behind him. Together they made their way back along the passage.

'Just lead us to your room, Hisham old friend. He couldn't have arrived here at a more opportune moment now, could he, Sean?'

29

Big Herbie Kruger and DCI Bex Olesker checked into the Grand Hyatt at five o'clock that afternoon. They had been given a two-bedroomed suite, nicely decorated and furnished.

'I'm enjoying it while I can,' Bex said, doing an almost schoolgirlish twirl in the middle of the living-room. 'I'll miss all this when I'm back in my sordid flat in Dolphin Square.'

'Dolphin Square's not sordid. Dolphin Square's good diggings.' Herbie plumped himself down into a chair.

They had remained with the *Conductor* team for longer than originally planned because of the finding of the body in Alexandria. The door to the apartment had been left open, and a neighbour's dog pushed its way in, then shot out again as though scalded, whimpering and with its hair standing on end. The neighbour had investigated and his 911 call was logged in at two-thirty.

Even with the damage the two bullets had done to the face, the homicide detectives recognized this was no ordinary victim. They called in what they suspected. Dick Hatch, Charlie Kryseck, Herb and Bex had gone straight over.

'Always wanted to drive with the lights flashing and sirens going,' Herb confided to Bex.

'They call it riding the hammer,' Bex sounded almost supercilious.

'You, being a cop, would know that.'

'No, I read it in an Ed McBain book,' she replied with a grin.

There were no grins at the apartment building in Alexandria. The identity would have to be confirmed, but Herbie was 100 per cent certain the body was that of Walid Allush.

'So, we're one down and two left out there,' he murmured as they departed from the crime scene.

They were checking out of The Willard when Sheila, the young woman from the Secret Service, came up to them at the desk.

'Sorry you're leaving.' She had arrived, panther footed, and even Herbie jumped slightly. 'You've heard the latest?' she asked.

'Which latest?'

'They picked up the contact here in DC. The American, Sid Hench. He's singing his heart out. Christie and Dick Hatch've gone over to take a look at the other safe house they were using in Georgetown. The news is that there's very little, if any, explosive left.'

'So, no more bombs?' Bex queried.

'I personally think they'll be on the run. Our Sidney's been able to account for all the dynamite, Semtex and C-4 they had around. Unless they've got some other supply, they've just about done. I think he said around twenty pounds of C-4 still unaccounted for. Even I'm off the case now. They're putting me back on the President's bodyguard team for tonight's meeting at the Capitol.'

'You don't really think . . . ?'

'Don't know, Herb. Stranger things have happened.'

So they said their farewells, and did not give the cab driver any instructions until they were inside the vehicle.

They both felt the atmosphere as soon as they arrived at the Grand Hyatt. Young men and women were gathered in clusters with decks of cards, while older men and women looked as if they were blessed with the secrets of ages. In the suite, Herb suggested they go down and register for the convention, but Bex wanted to hold back. In reality she did not have any desire to be at the Magic Summit at all. 'I'd rather be out there running the last two Vengeance people to earth,' she sighed.

'And my job – yours also – is to find Gus Keene's killers,' Kruger reminded her.

There was a lot of unusual activity in the area of the suites when they left the room. Up the corridor, three uniformed police were stretching crime scene tape around one of the doors. When Bex and Herbie arrived at the elevators they were just in time to meet Hatch and Christie arriving.

'What's up?' Herbie sounded puzzled.

'Want to come and see?' Hatch gestured back along the corridor with his hand.

'We think there's only one of them on the run now.' Christie pulled a face. 'They're dropping like flies.'

In a suite a short way up the passage, Hisham Silwani lay on his back, across the bed. His face was bloated and blue, eyes bulged in a glassy stare of horror, and his tongue lolled out of his mouth. The cord around his neck had bitten deeply into the flesh.

'So, there's only one of them out there now,' Hatch was examining the ligature around the Iraqi's neck.

'And if she did this,' Bex added, 'she has to be damned strong.'

Hatch looked up and shook his head. 'I doubt if this is the work of a woman.'

'If it's not a woman, who the hell's taking these people out?' Bex daintily nibbled on a jumbo shrimp. They had gone straight down to eat, and Herbie had said, 'Leave it to the pros.'

Now, as he sat demolishing a pasta dish, he looked very concerned. 'You realize that was Hisham, aka *Ishmael*? He was supposed to be on the side of the angels, one of "Five's" assets.'

'The one who did the deal with the splinter group from the old IRA.' Bex nodded.

'For me, it's unhealthy here.' He forked another tangle of pasta into his mouth and chewed.

'If you go on eating like that, it'll remain unhealthy.'

'Sure, you want to hear my theory?'

'I know it already, my dear Herbie, and I think we should call in the cavalry.'

'No. We call in nobody. The FFIRA sentenced four of us to death, and the *Intiqam* team in England fouled up. Young Worboys is still in London, so he's easy meat. They can take their time with him. But I think whoever killed Hisham is here to do me. Me, myself and I, plus, maybe, one other. Keep your eyes open, Bex, and don't get distracted. There's a killing team on the loose in this hotel.'

Finally, they went down to the convention area below the hotel, and into a new world. Herbie was in a different kind of heaven, and seemed completely unaware that his life was on the line. They registered, met the pleasant young woman to whom he had talked on the telephone – Jane Ruggiero, who introduced them to her husband, Nick, and her father, Les Smith, whom they quickly gathered was a famous illusion builder.

Bex, who was all nerves, alert, watchful and ready to move at the slightest sign of trouble, wondered at Big Herbie Kruger and his untroubled manner. They attended lectures, watched various performers in a competition of close-up magic, some of which even had Bex mystified.

Herbie, she thought, was like a schoolboy in a toyshop. Many of the rooms in the convention area were given over to magic dealers who demonstrated their wares. Herb began buying on the first day. He approached a tall friendly man who was selling an impressive array of magic books, some of which were old and rare. Bex looked at the prices of the older books and was rocked on her heels. There was more to this magic business than met the eye, she decided.

Herbie, having announced that he was a neophyte to the art, came away happy with four standard works the bookseller recommended. From another dealer he purchased cards and a plastic eyeball with a large bandanna with which Bex became quite irritated, for, in the privacy of the suite, Herb demonstrated the magic properties with monotonous regularity: asking her to keep an eye on the eyeball, resting it on her hand and covering it with a cloth, telling her to say 'Eye Go' and whipping the bandanna away to show that the eyeball had vanished.

'You're not really going to fool many people with that,' she told him after he had performed the bit of business for the thirtieth time.

'Practice', he grinned, 'is the prime rule. Three rules, first two are practice, third is practice again. That is what Nick told me. Bex, I found a new outlet for my spare time.'

She noticed that he was also constantly asking the nice Jane Ruggiero about when Claudius Damautus was going to arrive, only to be told time and again that he was not getting in until just before the big show on Saturday night.

Bex was struck by the friendliness of the people they met, apart from one famous British magician who appeared to mix only with the obviously professional and well known Magi.

On the Friday night, they sat through a banquet which was the usual kind of meal followed by speeches and presentations, then a cabaret which made Herb the happiest man there as he applauded and guffawed at each new miracle.

'You're not actually keeping a low profile, are you?' she said in a finger-wagging voice.

'Why should I? They're here.'

'Who?'

'The FFIRA.'

'You've seen them?'

'I seen one of them. Not at the magic convention but he's in the hotel, and when spring is here summer's not far behind.'

*   *   *

'Why Mr Worboys, Gus, Blount-Wilson and yourself?' she asked, that same evening.

'Why indeed?'

'Come on, Herb, don't be an oaf. Tell me about it.'

He sighed deeply. 'Let's say it's a long story that goes back to the middle Eighties. It has to do with a pretty deep, and very dark, secret connected to four members of an old Provisional IRA Active Service Unit. They got blown away when they weren't carrying anything more lethal than a pencil. The fact that they *were* in the last stages of planning what in those days, they called a "spectacular" had nothing to do with it. The shoot-to-kill policy did. Gus led a pretty amazing cover-up. I helped, so did The Whizz and Worboys. My theory is that this splinter group contains a relative of one of the people who got killed.

'Like the *Intiqam* teams, these guys are out for revenge. Not the same kind of revenge on such a dramatic scale as we've seen from the *Intiqam* folks, but something more personal. Let's leave it there, Bex. It's *very* personal and, to tell the truth, I'm pretty frightened.'

On the Saturday night, all delegates of the Magic Summit were bused to a nearby theatre for the big convention show. Outside, on the steps leading to the glass entrance doors, Herbie's eyes became restless, flicking around like those of a chameleon. As he held a door back to admit Bex, he glimpsed a car pulling up across the road and thought he could make out a familiar face in the driving seat, then wondered again. Was he simply jumping at shadows?

They waited in the foyer, letting everyone else get into the theatre so that they ducked in at the last moment, just as the performance was starting.

Herb waved an usher away, whispering that he did not want to disturb anybody. They would go to their seats in the interval. The usher did not seem to be concerned. 'Over there,' Herb whispered to Bex, nodding towards a familiar figure sitting at the end of the

423

back row. 'If he moves, follow him. I'll be right behind you.'

'That's . . . ?'

'I think so. Shush.'

The first four acts produced both hilarity and mystery, but Herbie was obviously waiting, tense and twitchy. Bex could feel the anxiety building inside the big man. Then, he suddenly stiffened as Nick Ruggiero announced that they had a special treat in store. The first half of the performance would end with a guest who had only just arrived.

'You don't get a chance to see this legend perform every day,' he said with pleasure. 'Ladies and gentlemen, the fabulous Claudius Damautus.'

The curtains parted to show a table set down stage, on which sat a crystal decanter half full of red wine, and three glittering silver cups stacked one on the other. To the right was a small stand on which stood a polished, carved box, and a newspaper was lying on a chair. Manuel de Falla's *Ritual Fire Dance* from *Love the Magician* came thumping out of the sound system and on walked Gus Keene. His dress and make-up were the same as he had worn for the first tape they had seen – the performance at The Magic Circle: Levis, soft moccasins, white silk shirt, his hair grey-streaked and falling to his shoulders, his height an inch or so taller than in real life.

Applause gushed from the audience. This was obviously a great moment for many of them. Bex glanced up at Big Herbie and saw, to her surprise, that tears were forming in his eyes. He put his hand up and wiped them away, then glanced towards the seat he had pointed out earlier. She noticed that, as he returned his gaze to the stage, it was as though he were experiencing great relief.

'Risen from the dead?' Bex whispered.

Herb nodded. 'It was always on the cards. The trick will be keeping him alive.'

Gus walked slowly to the table, acknowledging the

applause, then he moved from the table to centre stage and moved his hands, gesturing silence.

'Reports of my death – which I know has been rumoured – are greatly exaggerated.' Laughter and more applause. Then:

'Most of you are magicians, so I must tell you that I shall be working at speed. I want your attention and concentration, for I am about to give you the history of magic in about twenty minutes – well, maybe thirty, but who's counting? You should all know that this history will not be performed in chronological order.

'First, remember the great illusionists – Philippe producing his giant bowl of water; Robert-Houdin, father of modern magic, with his fishbowl; Ching Ling Foo and Chung Ling Soo and Long Tack Sam; Fu-Manchú; and the Great Lafayette and his huge bowl of water containing enough to be poured into several buckets. Countless magicians down the ages have sought to produce water.'

He flicked a large white silk handkerchief from his breast pocket and draped it over the palm of his right hand, smoothing it across the flat of the hand. Then he lifted it with the finger and thumb of his left hand and dropped it again. A shape had formed under the silk. Gus smiled, and whipped the silk away to show a tumbler full of water.

'I should have done that while executing a somersault.' He took a long sip from the glass.

'There is a famous old trick,' he continued, 'in which a glass and bottle change places when covered by cylindrical tubes. It's old. You all know it backwards. I shall do something more miraculous.' He gestured to the decanter half full of red wine, dropped the silk over the glass again, then once more gestured towards the decanter. In the time it took to make the hand movement, the wine had turned to clear water and, lifting the silk from the glass, he revealed that the wine was now there where the water had been.

He lifted the glass as though to toast the audience, then

threw the silk handkerchief over it, lifted them both into the air, threw them up and clapped his hands over what had been the handkerchief-covered glass. Nothing. Both had vanished.

Once more he gestured towards the decanter. Now, the white silk had appeared within the bowl, and the water had disappeared.

Again, the charm and the smile as he reached for the decanter, grasping it at the neck and mouth. The crystal melted away in his hands with only the bowl of the decanter left on the table, as he appeared to make the glass neck into a malleable substance, rolling it between his hands finally to form a large crystal ball. From this he seemed to tweak off rough pieces of glass, then closing his hands around it he broke the large ball in two, rolling and producing another ball, then another, ending with three clear crystal balls.

He placed two of the balls onto the table, still rolling the third between his hands until the colour changed and he displayed a ruby glass ball. The same actions again with the second clear sphere, changing it into an emerald ball.

With his right hand, he lifted the three stacked and polished cups, saying, 'The oldest trick in our vast lexicon of magic. The cups and balls.'

The house was silent as Gus vanished the coloured crystal balls from under the cups, only to find them again under one of the cups. Once more he separated them to one under each cup, but when the cups were lifted they had gone, finally to reappear together under one cup. Then, again, ruby, emerald and clear balls were placed under each cup, rattled to prove they were there. The cups were lifted and shown empty. A second later the cups were picked up and out of each rolled a large glass ball three times the size of the original – ruby, emerald and clear – each ball so large that it seemed impossible for the cup to have contained it. The applause rose, as he stacked the cups and placed them to one side.

The charismatic, mysterious smile as Gus picked up the clear ball, lifted it over the bowl of the decanter and seemed to melt the crystal back to restore the neck and mouth.

He took up the emerald ball, raised it above the decanter, making it obvious that the mouth of the vessel was impossibly small for the ball to pass through: then with a clunk, the ball flashed green and fell into the bottom of the decanter, leaving him with the ruby ball which he rubbed against the decanter's bowl so that the ball melted away in his hand and a rich red, clear circle appeared on the side of the decanter.

As before the audience reaction was massive applause, even a few people started a standing ovation, but Gus motioned them to sit down. 'You can get more than a drink out of a little glass.' He reached across to the stacked cups, lifted them to reveal another glass ball which he began to roll between his hands. Everyone appeared to be focused on what he was doing, but from the corner of his eye Herb saw the recognizable figure move slowly from the back row and slip out of the door.

'Go,' he whispered to Bex who nodded, gave it a couple of seconds and then exited through the door.

On stage, Gus was rubbing the new glass ball between his palms until it changed, visibly, into an egg. Herbie watched, though part of the poetry of what Gus was doing up on the stage was now lost to him. His concern lay in what was happening outside.

Bex stood for a moment, inside the foyer of the theatre, watching one of the big glass outer doors still swinging from when the man she was following had made his exit. She had just caught sight of him moving to the left. Reaching inside the short jacket she was wearing, she withdrew the Beretta given to her for the *Conductor* operation. Slowly, she went out into the street, moving left but sweeping the scene in front of the theatre.

The buses waited for the audience, the drivers gathered together, talking and smoking. Across the road she saw a small black car, but could not make out if there was anyone in it. Quickly she turned, finding herself at the corner of the building. A narrow passage ran alongside, leading, she presumed, to the stage door.

She stayed close to the wall, and caught sight of the man she was following as he walked into the light from a lamp held in a bracket in front of the stage door. She did not hear the second figure behind her, but her intuition made her turn just as Sean O'Donnel leaped towards her.

Back inside, Gus had a member of the audience up on stage. No coaxing had been necessary, and he was going through a series of quite impossible vanishes and reproductions with the egg and a small black bag – allowing the lady assisting him to put the egg into the bag from whence it disappeared, returned, vanished again, became two eggs, then three, each of which were placed singly into the bag and disappeared. Finally, when the bag was shown utterly empty, Gus produced yet another egg which multiplied to two, between the fingers of his right hand, then three and four. He held up the right hand with the four eggs between the fingers, reached up behind the hand with his left hand, producing yet another egg which, in turn, changed to two, then three, then four, between the fingers of his left hand.

Finally, he asked the spectator to hold the little black silk bag for him, as he slowly deposited all eight eggs into it. Almost immediately he reached in, pulled out one of the eggs, then crushed the bag in his right hand and used his fingers to turn it inside out, proving it was empty. Where there had been eight eggs there was now only one which he rubbed between his hands, then opened them to show that the egg had gone. In its place was a small yellow parakeet which, as he tossed it into the air, vanished, its place taken by a yellow silk.

'Don't worry, he'll be back.' Gus gave them the

old charm and asked the lady helping him if he could borrow a ring. There was some by-play as she worked at getting the ring from her finger and Gus went into the audience to borrow two more rings. Finally, he dropped all three rings into one hand, lifting it slowly to show that the borrowed rings had linked together. He unlinked them, handing one back to its owner in the audience, but inviting the other owner on stage with the first assistant from the audience.

Gus then produced a sheet of newspaper from which he tore a rough quarter of the page, crumpling the remainder and giving this ball of newspaper to the other assistant. He placed the rings onto the quarter sheet, crumpled it into a ball into which he thrust a stick of sealing wax.

On drawing the stick out, he showed that the end had melted, and, on opening the paper, looked amazed, for the crumpled paper had been changed into a nest of three envelopes, each one sealed. In the inner envelope he found, not a ring, but a key.

Gus pulled out his own keycase and there was one of the rings inside. This was handed back.

'The key,' Gus explained, 'goes into this box,' pointing to a beautifully crafted mahogany box on the table. When this was unlocked another box was pulled out, then a third. Gus opened the final box and the parakeet bobbed out onto his hand. Around its neck was a thin ribbon, attached to which was the other ring. As this last happened, Herbie quietly moved, fading through the door into the foyer.

In the alley, Bex had feinted to her right as Sean came hurtling towards her, his right arm swinging a leather briefcase. Then she side-stepped so that his body cannoned against the wall. She vaguely heard the man up near the stage door shout. She thought he was shouting, 'Come on, man. Time's running out,' so, as Sean fell against the wall, all arms and legs, she reached beneath her jacket again and slid out the regulation Metropolitan Police handcuffs she always carried.

Sean looked as though he was recovering, so she brought up her knee, hard between his legs. He gave a yelp of pain and doubled over. She moved in, slipped one cuff around Sean's wrist and the other through the handle of the briefcase. It was all complete intuition and she only knew she had done the right thing when she saw Sean's terrified eyes. 'For God's sake,' he breathed out, winded. 'Sweet Jesus, in the name of God, undo the bloody cuffs. This thing's going to explode any minute. Please.' He was threshing about, trying to hit her, but the pain and the new fear led him into complete panic. He ran back and forth, then towards the other man standing near the stage door.

'Get in there, Sean. Don't waste everything. Go.' The shadowy figure was near to screaming, but Sean, now in terror, just kept running, as though looking for somewhere to hide. Like a child, he put one hand up over his eyes, as though by not seeing anything he would blot out the truth. Through it all he shook his arm violently, as if he could, with some mighty effort, rid himself of the briefcase.

As he came into the street, Big Herbie saw Declan Norton pounding across the road from the black car, his face twisted in anger. He reached the alley with Herbie just behind him.

Declan seemed not to have even noticed Bex, and showed no sign that he knew Herbie was behind him. He simply stood there and yelled, 'Get him inside. Die like a man, Sean, but make sure the bastard Keene goes with you.'

The figure by the stage door tried to block Sean and, like a sheep dog, guide him inside. He was shouting, 'The bomb's for Keene, Sean. Get in there. In . . .'

Sean swerved to the right, avoided the man at the stage door and ran hard, towards the end of the alley.

Herbie stood still, right behind Declan as the case

exploded. For a second, as though in a freeze-frame, he saw Sean engulfed in flame; then, in what seemed like another still picture, he watched as the man disintegrated in the blast that swept down the alleyway.

The figure by the stage door flattened himself against the wall, then turned, as Declan yelled, 'Get in there, man. Do it yourself. Just finish him off. Get in, man, get in.'

The shadow by the stage door turned and disappeared inside, just as Herb chopped the Beretta behind Declan's right ear. Norton made a little grunt and went down, like a beast in an abattoir.

'Watch him, Bex,' Herbie shouted and began to run towards the stage door.

Inside, it was dark; then he caught sight of the stage. In the wings people seemed to have shrunk back in fear. The familiar figure stood alone in the wings, feet planted apart, hands coming up, with a pistol in the double grip.

Gus was completing his act – making thought-of cards rise from a deck placed in a goblet. The final card rose high above the goblet and was caught in Gus's hands.

Herb shouted, 'Stop! Police!' bringing up the Beretta as the figure in front of him brought his pistol to bear on Gus.

Kruger was about to fire when someone detached herself from the crowd cowering back in the wings.

The audience was stamping and applauding, as Gus spread his arms in acknowledgement. Nobody out there heard the shot. The slim girlish figure simply put the pistol to the would-be assassin's head and pulled the trigger. There was a gout of blood from the back of the man's skull as it blew apart and he fell sideways.

'Oh, shit!' Herbie mouthed. 'The fool. He should have known he couldn't get away with it for ever – whatever it is he's trying to get away with.' He began to walk forward as Bex came in through the stage door.

Slowly, with Bex just behind him, he walked towards

the crumpled body. 'Tony,' Herbie choked. 'Tony Worboys, you bloody idiot.' Young Worboys' blood kept pumping.

Carole stepped from the knot of people who seemed to be rooted, unmoving. She looked towards Bex, then saw Kruger's almost wilting smile. He put an arm around her, gave her a squeeze and moved back to stand with Bex, as they watched Gus take his final calls.

'I don't understand.' Bex looked at him and then at the body.

'Gus'll have some of the answers. He'd better have some answers.'

The applause washed up, joined by the stamping of feet as Claudius Damautus took ovation after ovation. At last the curtain came down and Carole ran out to embrace her husband.

Herbie and Bex followed her. 'You'd better have a damned good story, my old friend,' Herb said, then looked to see another figure had joined them out of the darkness. Herbie recognized the girl as Khami Qasim, and saw that her right hand now hung by her side, the pistol pointing at the ground. 'And this, I suppose, is *Jasmine*?' he said, looking over Gus's shoulder. 'She saved your life.'

Gus nodded and pulled Khami into an embrace. 'I think she's saved a lot of lives.'

'And taken some,' Herbie said quietly.

'She finally took out the man Walid. I think the one here – Hisham – is down to Declan Norton. Where is he, by the way?'

'They just took him down town,' Bex told them. 'He'll have a nasty headache when he wakes up.'

'Gus, Young Worboys is dead,' Herbie's face crumpled as he said it.

'I'm sorry,' Gus shook his head. 'I'm sorry, but perhaps it's for the best. I doubt if he could've coped with the rest of his life in jail.'

'As bad as that?'

'Worse.' Gus put an arm around his old friend. 'He was my reason for dying. It's a shock to you, Herb, but he had got himself badly mixed up with the FFIRA, and others. I suspect that bastard Declan Norton had a contract out on him in any case. Tony Worboys just knew too damned much. That's why I had to disappear by dying. It's a long story, Herb. Can I tell it tomorrow?'

'Sure, why not?' Herbie put his arm out to bring Bex into the conversation. 'Gus, a funny thing happened to me on my way to the theatre tonight. It was this nice Detective Chief Inspector from the anti-terrorist squad.'

Gus extended his hand to Bex and told her that when eating with Herbie Kruger you really had to sup with a long spoon.

'I know,' she said. 'I know just how long Herb's spoon is.'

30

'You'll have seen nothing about it in the files,' Gus began 'But I was assigned to interrogate Tony Worboys about eighteen months before I retired. It began as just a routine matter, nothing solid, straws in the wind.'

They sat together in Herbie's suite at the Grand Hyatt. The FBI, CIA and police heads from *Conductor* had agreed to let Kruger and Bex talk to Gus Keene before they carried out their own debriefing. Khami had been taken away to what the FBI termed a place of safety, and Washington breathed a collective sigh of relief when the President made a statement to the effect that the entire team of terrorists connected to the appalling incidents of the past few days was now accounted for. 'This does not mean we can relax our vigilance,' he said in a televised statement from the Oval Office. 'Our beloved country has experienced the cowardly and deadly actions of international terrorism on a scale never before seen here. More could follow.'

'Straws in the wind?' Herb asked. 'What kind of straws?'

'There was a lot on.' Gus gave a weary sigh. 'We had you and that old orchestral conductor filling up the guest facilities. You'll remember that I was hearing everyone's confession at the time – including your former German girlfriend, Herb. Sorry, but I had to mention that. Anyway, out of the blue, the Office called me to London. We were still at Century House then.' Century House had been the Office headquarters for a long time.

'They told me that nobody had done a positive on Deputy CSIS Worboys for years.'

By a 'positive' Gus meant a Positive Vetting. These

were routine examinations of members of the Office or the Security Service. Check-ups to make certain that members of the Office remained clean. The CIA did it with a lie detector and called it fluttering. The Brits preferred to work on people's backgrounds on a face-to-face basis.

'So you gave him a going over?' Herbie leaned back in his chair. He had been upset, even desolate, since the previous night. After all, he had virtually trained Tony Worboys. The man had been his closest associate during the worst times of the Cold War.

'Yes, I gave him a going over. He was tremendous when the Soviets were the main target, but once the evil empire seemed to fall apart, Tony Worboys went through a kind of change. A lot of people did, and you can't blame them. Everyone thought their jobs were on the line. They weren't, of course, because our old profession never dies, and when the Soviets crumbled, things became even worse. The world was more dangerous than it had been for almost fifty years.

'As you know, Herb, only a hundred and twenty people were let go from the Office, and most of them were on the brink of retirement anyway.'

'Sure, I was one myself.'

'That was years ago, Herb. Anyway, they were always hauling on your string to get you back.'

'Worboys was going through a kind of change, Gus?' Herbie pushed on.

'Yes. I had him out at Warminster a couple of times. Talked to him in London, detected something was not right. He'd become more arrogant, but they all do when they climb the ladder and end up close to the Chief's door.' He sipped from the coffee they had brought up for him. 'But Tony's lifestyle seemed to have changed. He'd bought that big place out at Harrow Weald. His kids were at expensive schools. His wife spent money like it grew on trees. He appeared to be living beyond his means – none of us can make a fortune in the espionage

435

business. He told me several stories. His wife had money of her own. He'd had a legacy from some long-forgotten uncle.'

'Long-forgotten uncles can be useful.' Herbie nodded.

'I checked it out, and on the surface it seemed true. His wife *did* have money, and he *did* come into a legacy. There was something more, though. I worked away at it and he became more belligerent. So, I finally got the okay to use the magic machines on his bank accounts – and his wife's, of course. A lot of money had come his way, but not quite the right amount. In fact a good deal more than he'd admit to. Wife was the same.' He gave a deep sigh. 'So, as often happens, I gave him an okay on the vetting, then did something illegal.'

'You, Gus?' It was mock surprise because Herbie knew Gus well enough to be 99 per cent sure that the foxy confessor had often got hold of evidence by illegal wire taps, unauthorized surveillance and quite irregular computer-hacking into financial houses. Often senior officers turned a blind eye, or backdated forms of consent. 'What wicked ways did you go?'

'Put a team on Worboys. Good lads. My people from Warminster up for refresher courses, boys and girls like that. We also tapped his telephone. In the office and at home. I also had some of the computer whiz-kids take a little walk through overseas bank accounts.'

'What do you mean by overseas? Switzerland?'

'Switzerland, Liechtenstein and the like.'

'You can get into the databases of those places nowadays?'

'It's an art, Herb. I had guys that could have found out every investment made by the royal family, with nobody ever the wiser. We came up with some rich results regarding Tony. A numbered account in Switzerland which was topped up at regular intervals. Once we had that, all we had to do was trace back. Find out where the top-ups were coming from.'

'So you did that?'

'Not at first. We got him during the surveillance. It's odd how experienced intelligence officers sometimes make tiny errors when they go off the rails. They usually cover themselves well enough – as he did – but by then I was searching for a chink in his armour.'

'So which rails did he go off?'

'First of all the ones that led to Belfast or Armagh. I couldn't prove it, but I *knew*. If he'd been faced with it, I'm certain that he would have had his own version – written backwards, if you follow me.'

Herbie nodded.

'I logged every meeting he ever had with people acting for terrorist groups, of all shades and conditions in Ireland. I logged every telephone call – even stuff we got with directional mikes aimed at public telephones. Yet I'm certain that if I had laid it all out, Tony would've laid out his cards next to each piece I'd collected. He would have been able to show a good intelligence take; claim that he was working informers. The old trick, Herb. You know how it works. The informer becomes the informed. I *knew* he had answers to each and every piece of evidence. For each meeting he would have chickenfeed claimed to have been passed to him. But I knew he was really doing the passing. Then he widened his field of operations.'

'He moved to the Middle East hoodlums?'

'Middle East; the old Soviet satellites, name it and he had his fingers in the pie. Tony Worboys was passing a great deal of high-octane material to practically everyone.'

Herb nodded again. 'And that led to the usual problems?'

'He should've known better. I don't have to tell you the pattern that develops in cases like this. He got in so deep that people demanded more of him. They demanded more personally.

'They wanted a favour performed here, and another one done there. By the time I decided to retire, Worboys was in hock really badly. Two or three years ago he would never have been led by the nose by the likes of Declan Norton, who's just a hired gun when all's said and done.'

'But people like Declan had him bang to rights. You scratch our backs if we scratch yours.'

'That's it, Herbie. I know of several groups who had him by the short and curlies. Seriously. He'd have committed murder for them . . . Well, he nearly did last night.'

'So what you do with all this information, Gus?'

'Kept it. Just before I retired, I was very foolish. Had Tony down to dinner, then laid the news on him. I told him the lot. Said I had tapes and video and lord knows what else.'

'Reaction?'

'He just laughed at me. Said he would have no difficulty in disputing anything I handed over – I said I'd hand it over unless he promised to come clean, give it all up and take an early retirement.'

'And he just laughed? Well, he would really, Gus. Why the hell you tell him?'

'Because I'd got myself mightily pissed off at everything. Worboys just walked away and told me I should watch my back. I retired and started the book. You know, Herb, I was going to include everything – *Cataract*; the way the Security Service used me to run that idiot asset, *Ishmael* – Hisham; my own folly in running *Jasmine* for my own ends. I was going to air every piece of dirty laundry we had – including friend Worboys. In fact, I had all the Worboys' material put into a safe lock-box at my bank. It's still there, so I guess we'll have to haul it out again.'

'The fact you were using *Cataract* shook me rigid.'

'It was meant to shake you, Herb. I knew you'd be the one doing the donkey work, so I left everything for you to find. Everything except Worboys, because I reckoned that would put you in real danger.'

'How did you know it'd be me?'

438

Gus fiddled with the old pipe he always carried, and did not look Herbie in the eyes. 'Oh, I knew.'

'More, Gus. Come on. How?'

'There were indications. He began to threaten me. Subtle, but enough to scare me off. By that time I had lost all interest. In a way, Herb, I felt I'd wasted my life. You now know what my real passion is. You don't know how many times I wanted to leave and make some kind of life as a professional performer. It's strange, how the two arts run together, the magic and the method. Smoke and mirrors. So, one day I sat down with Carole and we planned how I could do it by killing off the old Gus Keene and resurrecting a full time Damautus.

'You still haven't told me, Gus.'

'Told you what?'

'How you knew I'd be dealing with the case.'

'Ah. Herb, it's quite embarrassing. Tony himself said to me that, should I drop dead, there was one person he could rely on.'

'Me? Why?'

'You were on the booze, old love. You'd lost weight, you were cracking up. He decided you'd be ideal. You'd screw up.'

Herbie nodded sagely. 'He was right. He was quite right.' A pause of around a hundred years seemed to pass. 'You know, Gus, your sudden death saved my life. Thought about it often. You're such an old friend that I became driven. Got back in line, started eating and working – oh, and of course I discovered the wonderful art of magic.'

It was Bex's turn to give a deep sigh. 'He's doing card tricks all the time, Gus.'

'Better than boozing,' Gus nodded at her. 'Much better, I promise you, Bex.'

Herbie's brow wrinkled. 'Gus, if people like Declan Norton had Tony on a string, why'd he put a contract on him with the Vengeance team?'

'The usual. The frighteners. Norton would know

439

that Worboys – once he knew – would move heaven and earth to get back in the FFIRA's good books. Once that contract was out, nobody had any real control over the *Intiqam*. You saw what he did, Herb? Moved himself and his family into safety and stayed there.'

'Letting people get killed in the process.'

'It was his own skin he protected, Herb. He couldn't have cared less about who else got wiped out as long as he was safe. My guess is that he made contact with Norton and offered to do anything to save his own skin. Last night, he paid all debts.'

'And he probably read between the lines of what I was doing. Worked out, like I did, that you were still alive, Gus.'

'I'm sure he was on your back all the way. In the end he would know that you had to go, and that I had to be rendered really dead.'

Herbie nodded, then squinted up at Gus. 'Let's move on. You dramatized your own death, Gus. How'd you do that?'

'Trade secret, Herb. To be truthful with you, Worboys put the frighteners on. Either I had to die or I had to die, if you follow. So, I chose my own time and place.'

'Sorry, Gus. They'll give you hell. How did you manage it?'

'In the magic fraternity there are some big mouths, people who talk, even give away secrets. Luckily I know a few folk who are blind, deaf and dumb when it comes to secrets.'

'Give me a for instance, Gus. That odd business at your grave.'

Gus threw his head back and laughed. 'The Broken Wand Ceremony. Hope you liked that. Yes, a couple of magic friends did that for me. I hear Worboys had an entire watcher team with cameras trained on the grave.'

Kruger nodded. 'That was my first hint that he was concerned. Wouldn't leave it alone. Had the grave watched after the funeral. Silly, I believe he knew you were still alive. Thought you'd come back and see how they'd planted you. But your death, Gus. Give me another for instance.'

'For instance an undertaker who was willing to provide a body. Fellow roughly my age and build. He was cremated on the afternoon of my "death".'

'How the . . . ?'

'Well, he didn't attend his own cremation, if you see what I mean. My undertaker friend and I popped his body in the boot of my car. I'd rigged everything. I got the explosives, set the whole thing up. Did all the wiring, very kosher except that the mercury switch wasn't attached to anything. I put in a remote and switched it on just before we actually blew the thing.'

He and his undertaker friend had driven in separate cars. The undertaker had parked on the far side of where the explosion would take place. 'Found an ideal spot. His car couldn't be seen from the road. Really we didn't expect anyone to pass by us. That road's usually as quiet as the grave at three in the morning.'

'But you were seen.'

'Yes, I gathered that from Carole.'

'Nobody knew what to make of it. So, you pushed the car off the road, then what?'

'Set the remote first, then heaved it off the road. It trundled a few yards and we went on to pick up my friend's car. As you know, I'd salted the body. My old Rolex, the Zippo Carole gave me. My MIMC lapel badge. We got into my mate's car and drove back. I hit the remote just as we went through Wylye. Bloody great bang. Had a car stashed away in Salisbury, several bits of ID and a couple of passports. I was in New York by that night.'

'Carole did a good act. Hell of a good act. Confused me as well.'

'Yes, I coached her a bit, but you have to be an actor to be an interrogator. I also told her to play around with people like *Jasmine* if it ever came up. Make out that

441

Jasmine was a male, that she'd had a run around the park with him. She is *very* good, Herb.'

'Sure as hell she is.'

'I only made one bad mistake . . .'

'The telephones?'

Gus Keene nodded. 'I committed the worst sin, Herb. Didn't check up on the system. I truly thought the Dower House had been disconnected from the Main House. Didn't realize everything was logged. That's how you got on to us?'

'Mainly. It was difficult. In the end it was the telephone calls that did it. If we followed the theory that you were alive, then the calls did the final trick.' Herbie sighed, then: 'Gus, what about *Jasmine*?'

'What about her? I ran her, and I ran that oaf *Ishmael* for the Security Service. Got a terrible shock about *Jasmine*. We had no prior knowledge of the *Intiqam* business, so that just blew up – if you'll forgive the pun – after I had shuffled off this mortal coil.'

'They're going to want a lot more than that when they debrief you.'

'They'll get some nice stories. When it's over, Carole and I are really going to have a go. See if we can make it with the magic. Great retirement scheme really.'

'Wish I had your skill. Just have to pray they don't send you to pokey, Gus. You been a very naughty boy. Wasted police time, nearly got yourself killed.'

'Yes, one of the people that got offed at the time of *Cataract* was Norton's fiancée, Ann Bolan. I thought I'd get away from him as well. In fact, my future wasn't very bright while I was doing the book.'

Herb thanked him, said he would see him around when things began buzzing back in the UK. Then, as though he had just thought of it, 'Hey, Gus. Mary Delacourt?'

'What about her?'

'*What* about her? Well, did you?'

'Did I what?'

442

'In those notes you left. You said you yum-yummed her?'

Bex gave a snort of laughter.

'So?' Gus looked straight-faced, unruffled.

'Well, did you?'

'That's for me to know, and you to find out, Herb. Be well.'

'So what's next for you, Herb?' Bex Olesker asked as they crossed the Atlantic at around 39,000 feet.

'For me? Back in retirement. Got to find somewhere to live.'

'You could always stay with me in Dolphin Square – until you've bought the kind of place you really want, of course.'

'Sure, of course. You want me as a house guest? Really want me to stay for a while, Bex?'

'Why not? It gets pretty lonely at times. Just me and a dozen or so terrorists. Oh, and the daughter of a very famous magician lives almost next door.'

'Okay. Only on a temporary basis though, Rebecca. Yes. Yes, I'd like that.'

'You're on then, Herb.' She looked at his big rugged face and saw the glint in his eye. 'You're definitely on.'

Epilogue

The garden was warm and pleasant, and it was good to be away from the heat and bustle of Baghdad.

There were about twenty of them. All well-trained and well-trusted men and women who had been selected from some 200 possibilities. Now they sat in a wide semi-circle around the *Biwāba* who looked at them with a benevolent smile.

'My children,' he began. 'You are about to leave here on a glorious adventure. You are the vanguard of our Leader's revenge upon the unbelievers who took it upon themselves to deny us our rights.

'You follow in the footsteps of those who have been martyrs. Men and women who will never be forgotten. Your duty will be to avenge their deaths and bring horror from the very hands of our Leader. You, my children, will rain fire, destruction, and sudden death on those nations who, in their pride, barbarity, and gross immorality look down on us and see our Leader and our people as dirt. We shall teach them in many ways. They will learn by sudden death. Death by fire; death by water; death by bullet and by knife. Especially, they will learn by a great new and terrible weapon which we shall call *The Scourge of Allah*. It is neither explosive nor chemical, but we have tested it and found it to be as sharp and deadly as a serpent's tongue.

'This weapon will be feared by you also, my chosen ones, but you shall go forth and use it with courage and in the knowledge that from the end of these nations will come the beginning of a new life. A new time. A new richness and prosperity. These nations will learn when they feel *The Scourge of Allah* rip into their flesh. Go forth, my children. Use your weapons well.

'Through you, we shall triumph.'

Author's Note

This book could not have been written without the assistance of Jeff Busby AIMC, who ironed out many wrinkles in my own magic knowledge, and gave up a great deal of his own exceptionally busy life to make suggestions and offer opinions.

I apologize to my friends Nick and Jane Ruggiero, Rich Bloch and Les Smith – all of Collector's Workshop – for setting their World Magic Summit in Washington DC many months after it actually took place, and for ruining it in this book with madness and mayhem.

Also, for the general reader I must make one important statement. There are a number of magical performances described in this book. Please be assured that every trick, illusion and routine can be, or is, performed by magicians throughout the world. It would have been easy to make up mysteries with no thought of actual performance. I know that some TV viewers watching magicians on television are convinced they use camera tricks. In the main, they do not. By the same token I could have used word tricks with this book, but I did not. What you read is what you can get live, close up, or on stage. Everything within these pages is possible – including the appalling acts of terrorism.

John Gardner
Virginia 1994

MAESTRO
by John Gardner

Louis Passau is America's greatest living orchestral conductor, a legendary, world-acclaimed artist whose ninetieth birthday will be marked by a glittering celebratory concert at New York's Lincoln Centre. But a double shadow hangs over the event: Passsau has recently been accused of spying for Hitler and, worse, the British Secret Intelligence Service have now linked his name to KGB clandestine operations in the USA during the Cold War.

The Maestro agrees to be interrogated, but only after the concert. British Intelligence call in Big Herbie Kruger to question the Maestro, and thanks to the once-famous agent-runner Passau survives an assassination attempt in his moment of glory. Still a target, he now insists on dealing only with Kruger, who desperately seeks a safe-house to conduct the debriefing.

As he grapples with the elusive truth about the conductor – from the man's first memories of his Bavarian village, to his adventures as a young immigrant in New York, his experiences in Capone's Chicago and his ruthless rise to fame and fortune – Herbie Kruger finds himself ensnared in the Maestro's dangerous secrets and deceits.

'Packed with stunning surprises . . . fiction on a soaring scale by a technician of the craft'
  David Hughes *Mail on Sunday*

0 552 13598 4

A SELECTED LIST OF FINE WRITING AVAILABLE FROM CORGI BOOKS

THE PRICES SHOWN BELOW WERE CORRECT AT THE TIME OF GOING TO PRESS. HOWEVER TRANSWORLD PUBLISHERS RESERVE THE RIGHT TO SHOW NEW RETAIL PRICES ON COVERS WHICH MAY DIFFER FROM THOSE PREVIOUSLY ADVERTISED IN THE TEXT OR ELSEWHERE.

14168 2	**JIGSAW**	*Campbell Armstrong*	£4.99
13947 5	**SUNDAY MORNING**	*Ray Connolly*	£4.99
14227 1	**SHADOWS ON A WALL**	*Ray Connolly*	£5.99
13827 5	**SPOILS OF WAR**	*Peter Driscoll*	£4.99
14377 4	**THE HORSE WHISPERER**	*Nicholas Evans*	£5.99
12550 4	**LIE DOWN WITH LIONS**	*Ken Follett*	£4.99
12610 1	**ON WINGS OF EAGLES**	*Ken Follett*	£5.99
12180 0	**THE MAN FROM ST PETERSBURG**	*Ken Follett*	£5.99
11810 9	**THE KEY TO REBECCA**	*Ken Follett*	£4.99
12569 5	**THE FOURTH PROTOCOL**	*Frederick Forsyth*	£5.99
13275 9	**THE NEGOTIATOR**	*Frederick Forsyth*	£5.99
13823 1	**THE DECEIVER**	*Frederick Forsyth*	£5.99
13990 4	**THE FIST OF GOD**	*Frederick Forsyth*	£5.99
14293 X	**RED, RED ROBIN**	*Stephen Gallagher*	£5.99
13598 4	**MAESTRO**	*John Gardner*	£5.99
14223 9	**BORROWED TIME**	*Robert Goddard*	£5.99
13840 1	**CLOSED CIRCLE**	*Robert Goddard*	£4.99
13562 3	**TAKE NO FAREWELL**	*Robert Goddard*	£5.99
13281 0	**IN PALE BATTALIONS**	*Robert Goddard*	£4.99
13697 2	**AIRPORT**	*Arthur Hailey*	£4.99
13678 6	**THE EVENING NEWS**	*Arthur Hailey*	£5.99
13694 8	**THE FINAL DIAGNOSIS**	*Arthur Hailey*	£4.99
12433 8	**A COLD MIND**	*David Lindsey*	£4.99
14389 8	**HAYWIRE**	*James Mills*	£5.99
14392 8	**CASINO**	*Nicholas Pileggi*	£5.99
13918 1	**THE LUCY GHOSTS**	*Eddy Shah*	£4.99
14145 3	**MANCHESTER BLUE**	*Eddy Shah*	£4.99
14290 5	**FALLEN ANGELS**	*Eddy Shah*	£5.99
14143 7	**A SIMPLE PLAN**	*Scott Smith*	£4.99
10565 1	**TRINITY**	*Leon Uris*	£5.99